THERE'S SOMETHING ABOUT YOU, OLIVIA BENNET

VALERIE G. MILLER

Blushing Daisy
BOOKS

Published by Blushing Daisy Books 2024

Brisbane, Qld, Australia

Cover Design by Kylie Sek

ISBN Print: 978-0-6453046-4-0

❀ Created with Vellum

Dedication

This book is dedicated to my husband, Tim. Thank you for all you do to help me find the time to write and create. More importantly, for letting me talk about my writing life on our weekend walks together. You are the hero in my story. Love you, babe.

NOTE TO THE READER

This book contains scenes that depict and reference sexual assault and alcohol abuse.

WRITING STYLE

<u>A note on style, spelling and language</u>

Australian/British spellings have been used throughout this novel.

There are also Australian slang, idioms and use of language that makes us unique.

I have also chosen the single inverted commas to denote dialogue.

PROLOGUE

Her mother had chosen the name.

Olivia.

Her only connection to her ancestral home, where groves of olive trees reached towards the Mediterranean Sea.

Elizabeth.

Symbolic of a life trapped in secrets.

Bennet.

From Benito. 'To be more Australian.'

Olivia Elizabeth Bennet.

A name that held secrets. A reminder of the mysteries her mother had carried close to her heart.

Olivia was determined to make sense of them.

CHAPTER 1

OLIVIA
February 1989

Holding her pants up, Olivia hopped into the living room to catch the ringing phone. In her efforts to sidestep Gin, she lost her balance and landed hard on the floor. Groaning, she stretched up to the antique credenza and flicked the handset off its hook.

'Hello?' a voice called out from the receiver.

Using the cord, Olivia pulled the handset towards her.

'I'm here!' she shouted. She'd been trying to get a hold of Shirley for a few days. There was no way she was going to miss the call. She quickly untangled the cord and placed the receiver next to her ear. 'I'm sorry. I was getting ready for work.' She pulled herself up and sat against the wall.

'Is this Olivia Bennet?'

'Yes, it is.'

'This is Matron Rixon,' said the stern voice. 'Shirley O'Connor was admitted this morning. She's had a stroke. You're listed as her next of kin.'

Olivia's heart slammed against her chest. 'Is she okay? Can I see her?' She glanced at the clock. She was due downstairs at the shop. 'I just need to find someone to take my shift.'

'Miss Bennet, I believe this is a Sydney number?'

Olivia nodded frantically, then realised the woman couldn't see her. 'Yes.'

'It may not be best to come today. Mrs O'Connor is resting, and we have tests scheduled. Tomorrow would be better.'

Olivia fumbled to grab the pad and pencil on the credenza. 'What ward is she in?' The pencil shook as she scratched down the details the matron provided. 'Please tell Shirley I'll be up tomorrow. Thank you, Sister, for calling me.'

Her skin prickled with heat as she hung up. She needed some fresh air. After pulling herself up, she limped to the wooden French doors across the room. She rattled and pushed against the charcoal vintage handles, which already required some force to open. As the warm air blasted her, she sucked it in, working on stilling the panic in her chest.

Shirley had to be okay.

Olivia wouldn't be okay without her.

A car horn on Johnston Street made Olivia jump. She stepped back into the flat and jammed the doors shut with a clank. A heaviness settled in her chest. She glanced at the clock again and grimaced. She needed to compose herself before facing the Saturday morning customers.

Taking slow, deep breaths, Olivia straightened the floral patchwork quilt on the gold two-seater she'd picked up at the retirement village where she volunteered. Tidying up usually had a soothing effect on her. She ran her hands along the length of it, teasing out the crinkles.

After checking that the tap in the old kitchen had been turned tight, she picked up her copy of *Forrest Gump* and tucked it into her handbag.

'Gin,' she called.

Her well-fed marmalade cat sauntered out of the bedroom. As soon as she opened her apartment door, he shot past her and down the wooden stairs. At the door to the street, he meowed, itching to spend the day outside. He rubbed and wrapped himself around her legs as she unlocked the two bolts. The feel of his warm body on her bare ankles calmed her further, but when Olivia pulled open the door and Gin bolted down the street, her heart tightened again.

Today of all days, she wouldn't be able to bear it if anything happened to him. She hoped he'd come and hang out in the bookshop when it got too hot.

Prickles nipped at her chest when she turned and saw the crowd of irritated adults and impatient children outside on the footpath. She checked her watch.

9:45 am.

Why wasn't the shop open, and where was Poppy?

'I'm sorry.' She avoided eye contact with the customers and fumbled for the keys in her backpack. 'I'll get the shop opened up right—'

'I've been here since 9 am,' said a woman wrangling a rambunctious toddler.

Olivia flushed. Saturday morning story time was due to start in fifteen minutes. *Where is Poppy?*

She rushed into the shop to turn off the alarm, and the crowd filtered in after her. An audience of eager kids made themselves comfortable on the scattered cushions in the kids' area while their parents began browsing—most likely the only peace they'd get that weekend.

With trembling hands, Olivia picked up the address book near the cash register and flicked the pages, looking for Poppy's number. When she found it, she tucked herself inside the door frame that led into the staff kitchenette behind the service desk.

Please answer, she prayed.

When someone picked up, she worked hard to keep her voice

steady. 'Good morning, my name's Olivia Bennet, and I work at Bertie's Bookshop. Is Poppy there?'

The woman on the line informed her that Poppy had left for work.

Olivia did some calculations in her head. Poppy should be here by now. She fixated on the door, willing her to walk through. Poppy maintained a laissez-faire attitude to life and Olivia, although only a few years older at twenty-four, looked out for her like a big sister.

A squeal made her jump. The kids were getting bored. She thanked the woman and hung up, then turned to see a mother with her hair pulled back tight in a ponytail tapping the counter with bright red fingernails.

'Excuse me. Isn't story time supposed to start now?'

Olivia gulped. 'I'm sorry. It shouldn't be too long until we get going.'

She loved working at the bookshop, but the Saturday morning shoppers weren't her favourite. They weren't locals but people from the outer suburbs who came into the city for a day out with their children.

Bertie's Bookshop was renowned for its children's books. Short sky-blue and orange shelves arranged asymmetrically stood like a maze around the kids' area. On tiptoes, Olivia could just peer over the top of the highest shelves.

Wanting the shop to be comfortable, Bertie had added three large wing chairs for people to sit and read, each one a different design and colour. Every time Bertie renovated her townhouse in Rose Bay, a new wing chair found its way into the bookstore.

The woman glared at her. 'You know you shouldn't advertise an event if it's non-existent.'

'I'm sorry, but Poppy, the girl who runs story time, is running late. She should be here any minute.' Olivia plastered on a nervous smile, willing the woman to accept this and not stand there giving her annoyed looks. Story time had been Poppy's idea. She had a knack for knowing how to relate to children.

'Well, why can't you do it? I gather you can read. You do work in a bookstore, after all.'

A chill drained the blood out of Olivia. Being the centre of attention, even if her audience was composed of preschoolers, terrified her. Plus, her scar would likely pique their curiosity, cementing the focus on her even more. Avoiding people meant no questions, and no questions meant she could keep her guilt buried. Before she could stammer out a response, a guy who looked to be about her age approached the counter. His bohemian attractiveness—tussled wavy hair and light stubble—forced her to catch her breath. Warmth flooded her body.

'Excuse me,' he said. 'I'm sorry to interrupt, but I'm happy to do story time.'

'You can?' Olivia said, relief joining the warmth.

'Sure. Happy to do it.'

'Are you sure? It's just that—'

'It's what I do nine to five,' he interrupted with a grin. 'Well, nine to three. I teach primary kids.' He glanced over to the kids' area, where several toddlers were pulling books out of coloured crates. 'Though under-fives aren't my speciality. But kids are kids, right?'

Olivia nodded quickly. 'Are you sure? There's craft time afterwards too.'

He leant over, and Olivia caught a whiff of his cologne—cedar and sandalwood.

'Craft is my superpower,' he said with a broad, cheeky smile activating a pair of dimples.

Olivia blushed. Then she quickly reached up and covered her scar with her hair. The redness would make it glow.

'Thank you,' she said, avoiding direct eye contact.

'No worries. What's the story?'

POPPY YAWNED AND STRETCHED. 'I'm beat.'

Olivia nodded. It had been a long day, and worrying about Shirley hadn't helped. People had streamed in nonstop, purchasing books for the new school year. Regardless of the time of year, though, the shop did well.

'You can go home,' Olivia said, continuing to wipe down the picture books with eucalyptus spray. 'There won't be many more people coming in this late in the day.'

'Okey-dokey.' Poppy's blonde pigtails bounced as she hopped up from the stack of books she'd been sitting on near the register. 'I'm going to make a toastie cheese sandwich before I go. Sorry again for being late this morning. I'll make sure I get the earlier bus from now on.'

'That's a good plan.'

It wasn't entirely Poppy's fault she'd been late. Inner-city traffic on Saturday morning in Sydney was awful. Saturday morning equalled sport. For Olivia, lying in bed with a good book and patting Gin on his tummy was enough sport for her.

She took a deep breath, enjoying the smell of the eucalyptus spray. It unlocked cherished memories of her mum. Olivia's childhood had been filled with books. The bookshelf in their lounge had been a timeline of Olivia's growth, marked by her reading ability: picture books followed by early readers, chapter books with pictures, and novels. A voracious reader, her mother, an Italian migrant, had introduced her to the classics. She'd said that reading the classics helped her master English.

'Books and stories make you smart,' she often said. 'A room without books is like a body without a soul' was her favourite Cicero quote.

The memories were bittersweet. The pain stuck to her like a seared cloth under a hot iron.

Finished with her task, Olivia stood, stretched her back and rotated her neck. Tiny clicking sounds escaped. She hoped Poppy would be early from now on. She never wanted to be in that position ever again.

Olivia returned to the register to sort out the sales receipts. Two stragglers were still browsing, but she was never in a hurry to get out on time. It wasn't as if she had any plans.

Poppy sat on the stool in the kitchenette, waiting for the jaffle maker to heat. 'Wasn't he a spunk?'

'Hmmm?' Olivia glanced back at her distractedly.

'The guy doing story time. Come on! You must've noticed how gorgeous he was in a sort of nerdy way. Was he an author? He had that scarf on. One of my professors used to wear a scarf like that. He was nerdy but kinda good-looking too—'

'Who's good-looking?'

Olivia and Poppy both turned to see Demi. Her wild dark curls were caught up in a bright red scarf, and curiosity beamed out of the large brown eyes framed with heavy black eyeliner.

'I found this handsome fella outside—tarting about.' Gin sat, relaxed in her arms. His purr gentle like the soft turning of book pages.

Demi lifted the mood every time she entered a room. Three years ago, Demi had found Olivia sitting at the bus stop a few doors down from Bertie's Bookshop, freaking out about the interview. She'd swooped in and told her straight to take a chance. Olivia knew she'd got the job in part because of Demi's take-the-bull-by-the-horns attitude. They'd been best friends ever since.

'Demi.' Poppy high-fived her as she walked into the kitchenette. 'Olivia's new boyfriend.'

'What? No.' Olivia's chest knotted in embarrassment. 'Poppy was late this morning, and this guy stepped in to do story time. That's all.'

'His name's Sebastian,' Poppy chimed in. 'And he took ages to leave. I think he likes you, Olivia.'

Olivia sniffed the air. 'I think your sandwich is burning.'

'Shit.' Poppy raced to the jaffle maker.

Olivia couldn't stop the small smile that had snuck up on her. *Sebastian.* It suited him.

She'd marvelled at how he'd captivated the kids with his performance of *Hattie and the Fox*. The kids had sat quietly, their mouths gaping like little sparrows waiting to be fed. Even the mother who'd spat out her demands about story time had been taken aback.

'Well. He's certainly got a way with them.' She'd then spun around and disappeared to browse.

The last straggler approached the counter, and Olivia rang up the sale. She tucked the receipt inside the copy of *Silence of the Lambs* and popped the book into a paper bag.

The man ignored Olivia. He was fixated on Demi, who'd plonked down on a beanbag in the kids' area and was singing 'Material Girl'. Her headphones disappeared inside her mass of corkscrew curls, and she waved her hands like a tipsy conductor. Thank goodness she had a decent voice.

'Thank you for shopping at Bertie's Books,' Olivia said, snapping the man out of his reverie. She locked the front door behind him and then moved to the shelves to straighten the books.

Her thoughts drifted to Sebastian again. He'd been good for business, too. All the copies of the picture book he'd read sold out. Olivia had been ordering a copy for one mother when he stepped up to the counter to hand over the box of scissors and glue she'd given him for craft time.

'Thank you,' Olivia had said, busying herself with the order.

'My pleasure. I could tell that looking after a bunch of rug rats wasn't your—'

'Superpower,' Olivia interjected, surprising herself with the quick remark.

He laughed. 'More like being sent to the gallows. The look on your face.'

Olivia passed the order slip to the woman. 'Thank you. We'll call when the book arrives.'

Sebastian stood there looking at her.

She avoided eye contact and began tidying the counter. 'Being in the limelight isn't my superpower.' She willed herself to look at him. He'd really helped her out, and she needed to show some gratitude.

She caught herself in his blue eyes. 'Can I offer you a voucher for your time?'

'Maybe a coffee?'

'Oh.' She felt heat rising under her blouse.

'That's if the boyfriend doesn't mind?'

'Boyfriend?' He might as well have asked if she'd been to Mars.

The invoices she was holding slipped out of her hand, and she dropped to pick them up off the floor. Bugger, she'd have to organise them again. 'No.' She let out a nervous laugh. 'No boyfriend.'

'Great.' Sebastian peered over the desk. 'Think of a place. I'll pop in to find out what day and time.' He glanced at the Dr Seuss clock on the wall. 'I've got to take my nonna to an appointment.'

'Nonna?' The term brought her thoughts back to Shirley, and she felt a pinch in her chest.

'My grandmother. She's Italian.'

Olivia met his gaze. 'I know. My mother was Italian.'

'Small world.'

'Welcome to Little Italy.' She offered a shy smile. 'This part of inner Sydney is full of Italians.'

An attractive woman wearing a navy-and-white netball uniform walked into the store. 'There you are.' She cosied up to Sebastian and wrapped her arm through his. 'Are you ready? I'm starved.'

'Yep.' Sebastian turned to Olivia. 'I'm sorry, I didn't actually get your name.'

'Olivia.' The word seeped out of her mouth. 'I'm the manager.'

'I have said too much unto a heart of stone.' Sebastian tipped an invisible hat and bowed. 'And laid mine honor too unchary on't.'

'What are you blabbering on about?' the woman said. She adjusted the tunic across her breasts.

'*Twelfth Night*,' Olivia said, impressed. How many people, other than her professors at uni, could quote Shakespeare? And at the drop of a hat?

The woman sighed and pouted.

Apparently, taking the hint, Sebastian picked up the Hattie the

Hen craft he'd made with the kids. 'It was nice to meet you, Olivia, manager of Bertie's Bookshop.' He smiled warmly and tipped his invisible hat.

Olivia watched as the woman, most likely his girlfriend, dragged him out. Typical. All the really nice guys were swooped up by girls Olivia could never compete with. The bell above the door tinkled as he left. Her heart made the same sound.

———

'COFFEE, EH?' Demi said as she helped Olivia tidy up the kitchenette. A lemony scent drifted across the room.

'He was only being polite. Thank goodness, too. I don't think I could go on a date. What would I say?'

'Livvie, it's just coffee. You're not picking wedding china. Go. It'll be good for you.' Demi sidled up to Olivia. 'You never know, it might just lead to something more than coffee.' She winked.

'Not helping.' Olivia swiped at Demi's arm.

'I second that,' Poppy said from her perch on the olive-green Formica benchtop. She was flicking through old fashion magazines.

Demi took the mug out of Olivia's hand and started wiping it dry. 'Olivia, what do you want to do with your life?' She waved the tea towel at her. 'All you do is stay at home and work. And home is above the shop.'

'That's not true. I go to movies in the city, and I ride my bike to ... places ... and church.' Olivia sometimes wished she had the courage to be more adventurous, but mostly, she was grateful for her safe world full of movies and books.

'Wow. A whole three blocks away.' Demi hung the dried mug on one of the hooks above the counter.

Olivia wiped her hands on a tea towel and walked out of the kitchenette.

'Don't ignore me, Olivia Bennet!' Demi called after her.

'I'm not,' Olivia said over her shoulder. 'I'm getting the new releases to price.'

She balanced the box of books in front of her and returned with the pricing gun. She held it up to Demi, proof that she hadn't just walked away.

'What are you going to do with that? Price me to death?'

Olivia grinned. 'Not your best comeback, Miss Kokkinos.'

Demi flicked the tea towel at her. 'You need to get out. Do stuff. Let your hair down. Be wild.' Demi's dark eyes widened. 'Kiss someone. Sounds like this Sebastian guy might oblige.'

Olivia knew the lecture by heart. It was one of Demi's favourite topics, especially when an opportunity like this presented itself.

'I'm doing plenty.' Olivia lifted the dirty linen basket towards Demi, who slam-dunked the tea towel into it. 'I'm very content. Exactly how I want to be.' Her skin prickled. She was living exactly the life she deserved.

She began pricing books at the table in the kitchenette. 'And he was just being kind. Sometimes people do kind things without ulterior motives, you know.'

'Demi's right,' Poppy said, wielding her cheese toastie. 'And boy, he was such a spunk, Dems. And he only had eyes for Olivia.'

Olivia got a plate and handed it to Poppy. 'No, his girlfriend came in.'

'Are you sure she was his girlfriend?'

'She was draped all over him!'

'You never know …'

Ignoring Poppy's baiting, Olivia walked back into the shop and placed the books on the specials shelf.

'Wanna hand?' Demi said, coming up behind her.

'Thanks. Just hand them to me. I *need* to get home to my dull life.'

'That's not what I meant. You know I just worry about you.'

'But it's how I like it.' Her heart swelled, knowing she had Demi looking out for her. The truth was, she was lonely. She'd already lost her mum, and now the only person she considered family was in hospital.

'Hey.' Poppy rushed out of the kitchenette. 'Let's go to Bondi tomorrow. It's going to be a stinker.'

'I can't,' Olivia said and swallowed hard. 'I'm taking the train up to Gosford.'

'Oh. Are you going to see Shirley?'

Olivia placed her hand on her mouth, willing the tears not to come.

'What's happened?' Demi grabbed Olivia's shoulders.

Poppy rushed over and put her arms around her. 'I'm sorry! You don't have to come to the beach.'

Olivia offered Poppy a weak smile. 'No, it's not that.'

Unable to hold them in any longer, she let the tears fall as she told her friends about Shirley's stroke. Demi collected her in her arms and let her cry while Poppy rubbed her back.

Olivia bit down on her lip as a barbed black mass strangled her heart. Next would come the memories. Her mind drifted away from the soothing sounds of her friends and snaked towards what was hidden inside her wardrobe—the one thing that could satisfy her demons, if only for a small slice of time.

CHAPTER 2

Olivia finished brushing her wavy auburn hair. It tumbled, shiny and clean, just past her shoulders. She inspected herself in the oval mirror on top of the old dressing table. One door was missing when she found it during the council's kerbside rubbish pickup. Shirley had made a little curtain from some of her leftover quilting material to cover the space.

Working her magic with bobby pins, she arranged her hair so it fell over her temple and hid the scar that ran in an arch from the top of her forehead to just under her cheekbone. After spraying her hair to prevent it from moving, she sat back and sighed. She hated what the scar did to her face.

Demi had shown her how to cover it with make-up, but whenever Olivia tried, she just ended up with a brown smudge on her face. She reached up and fingered the raised skin. It reminded her of a fat earthworm creeping down her soft olive skin. A constant reminder of what she'd done.

Her punishment for not leaving things alone.

Little knots of anxiety quivered inside her. What state would she find Shirley in? Maybe she'd be knitting and watching the television. The other alternative ...

She refused to acknowledge it.

Olivia continued studying herself in the mirror. A tidy but sad, muted woman stared back at her. Today, her eyes were more hazel than olive green—a result of worrying. She rubbed a light film of sunscreen along the smattering of freckles that fell from her small Grecian nose across the tops of her cheeks to cover the rest of her face and slender neck. She smoothed down her long beige paisley skirt and cream blouse and slipped on her tan brogues. She'd never been glamorous, but at least she could ride her bike without worrying about flashing her undies. Sweeping on her favourite and only lipstick, Revlon's Powder Pink, finished the look. Olivia pressed her lips down on a tissue and kissed it—like her mum used to do,

Then she opened her wardrobe. Inside, a small compartment kept her secret. She unlocked the wooden door and reached for the bottle of vodka. Then stopped. Last spring, during a late cold snap, she'd neglected Gin during one of her bad turns. He'd been found wet and hungry, and she'd promised herself she'd give it up.

In the distance, the bells of St Brendan's called. She needed to get a move on, or she'd be late for the train. She closed the sash window against the warming morning. Before pulling the curtains together, she glanced down at the narrow garden, typical of those belonging to terrace houses in the inner city. The summer heat and evening storms nourished the small lawn. It needed mowing. She'd have to call the gardener. Her little herb garden was also thriving, and she made a mental note to give it a good watering when she got back from Gosford.

She moved back to the wardrobe. One little shot wouldn't hurt. She'd make sure she ate when she got to the hospital. She couldn't afford to stop eating. Demi's mum always reminded her of how thin she was, a result of her anxiety. But it was the deep-seated guilt that pulled her towards the bottle.

The vodka's burn warmed and comforted her, settling her mind.

She popped a mint in her mouth.

OLIVIA WHEELED her bike out from under the main stairwell. Opening the heavy street door, she balanced the bike against her hip and manoeuvred it out.

She locked the door and double-checked it. Then she rubbed the material of her skirt together. Her family doctor had given her the idea—a technique to remind her she'd done something: locked the front door, turned off the stove or iron, hadn't locked Gin in the bathroom, et cetera. Whenever she panicked about not having done something, she could think back to the action and make the connection.

The hot and sticky air felt days old. She hoped the train would be one of the new ones with air conditioning. Every time she travelled to Gosford to visit Shirley, she gave herself a mental high-five. She was forcing herself to face her fears. Shirley had been her champion every day since her mother's death, gently encouraging her to move forward.

After Olivia graduated from Sydney University, two choices presented themselves to her: go back to Killcare or find a place in Sydney. She hadn't been keen to live in a share house or share an apartment, which was what you did as a new graduate. Olivia knew all too well what living with others was like. She'd endured it at boarding school and then again at Sancta Sophia College at Sydney University, both times out of necessity.

Shortly before graduation, she'd learnt that her Bachelor of Arts lived up to its nickname: Bugger All. And during the few interviews she secured, she got so nervous she could barely speak, resulting in impersonal thanks-but-no-thanks letters.

Her only income had come from her part-time job at Bertie's Bookshop. A week before she officially graduated, she had no proper job, and soon, she'd have no place to live. After receiving yet another thanks-but-no-thanks letter, she'd accepted defeat and called Shirley from the phone in the common room.

'Olivia, you don't want to come back to Killcare after all these years away,' Shirley had said with firm kindness.

'I'm terrified.'

'Life is scary. The fear is what reminds us we're alive.'

Olivia went silent. The unknown made her heart palpitate, and for the first time in her life, she'd be solely responsible for herself.

'Are you still there?' Shirley asked.

'Yes.'

'Olivia, your mother came to me alone and pregnant. Look at what she did. She raised you, trained as a nurse and made a life for the two of you.'

Olivia glanced around to make sure no one was around, then huddled over the phone. 'I miss her.' Tears threatened to escape.

'I know, sweetie. So do I. But she's with you all the time. She'd be so proud of you. Be strong. Say a little prayer to St Joseph.'

Olivia smiled. Shirley's Irish Catholic ways were strong.

THE DOCTOR'S MOUTH MOVED, but Olivia couldn't make sense of what he was saying. Her brain picked up only a couple of words, and they bounced around in her head. *Died. Peacefully.*

She stood at the nurses' station holding the gardenias she'd purchased at the hospital's flower shop. Shirley loved her gardenias. They were the envy of everyone in Killcare. Olivia had wanted to bring a little of home to Shirley to make her feel better. Now, the sweet scent made her feel sick.

'May I ...' She cleared her throat, which felt like barbed wire. 'May I have some water?'

The sounds around her became magnified, heightened in pitch. A child whingeing on his mother's lap. A nurse typing on her computer. The beeping of hospital machines. Had one of those machines failed at keeping Shirley alive?

A plastic cup filled with chilled water materialised in her spare hand. She took a sip. Her brain managed to find her voice while her heart remained in shock. 'But the nurse yesterday said that she was doing well.'

'Sometimes a minor stroke can bring on a bigger one. We ran tests and were waiting for the results. I'm sorry, Miss Bennet.'

Olivia stared at the doctor, whose soft brown eyes held a sincerity that made her want to sob.

Did he know?

Eleven years ago, she'd been rushed to this very hospital, where her mother had trained and worked as a nurse. While Olivia was in triage, her mother lay lifeless in the mortuary.

The driver of another car had stopped to help and found Olivia screaming at her mother to wake up. Screaming that she was sorry.

'Can I see her?' Olivia managed to say.

'I'll get the nurse to take you in.' The doctor walked up to the nurses' station and whispered something. A nurse looked up and gave Olivia a kind smile.

Olivia sipped her drink. The water made her want to gag. She forced another sip, this time holding the liquid in her mouth before swallowing it with care.

The nurse walked over to Olivia and placed her hand on her arm. 'Are you ready?'

No.

'Yes.'

Shirley lay in bed. Peaceful. Her favourite lemon-yellow knitted bed jacket brought a little brightness to her lifeless body. Her silver hair was unpinned from its usual bun and spilled over her shoulders.

Olivia caught the gasp in her mouth.

'Would you like me to stay with you?' the nurse asked gently.

'No.' Olivia held back the tears with the heel of her hand.

The nurse moved a chair next to the bed and handed Olivia the box of tissues she'd retrieved from the cabinet next to Shirley's bed. 'I'll be at the nurses' station if you need anything.' She went to walk out, then turned. 'She was a lovely lady. So happy. You were lucky to have had her in your life.'

'I was.' Olivia let the tears fall as she sat down and placed her hand on Shirley. It felt cold, but Olivia worked hard to remember its warmth. To remember the gentle way Shirley placed her hand on her cheek when reassuring her or against her forehead when she was unwell.

She sat with Shirley until a nurse came in to tell her that a lady from one of the funeral homes had arrived to see her. After placing the gardenias on the bedside table and arranging the bouquet so it faced Shirley, she placed the back of her hand on Shirley's lined face, leant down and whispered, 'I'm going to miss you so much. What am I going to do? You were always my compass?' She kissed Shirley's cheek. 'Say hi to Mum.'

When Olivia stepped out of the room, a woman in a tailored grey skirt suit approached.

'You must be Olivia.'

Olivia nodded.

'My name's Christine,' she said and extended her hand.

Olivia took it.

'I'm very sorry for your loss.'

The kind words felt like a warm blanket.

'I know this must be such a shock for you.' Christine guided Olivia into a private office just past the lounge area. 'I've just organised some tea.'

The room was sparse and cool. Olivia settled herself on the small grey sofa. Everything in the room was dull and muted. Even the lilies in the plain glass vase on the table in front of her seemed drained of colour.

Christine returned with refreshments on a tray. Olivia watched her pour the tea. The mundane and familiar action settled her.

'Sugar?'

'No, thanks.'

Olivia accepted the cup, and its warmth calmed her a little more.

Christine sat down next to her. 'Olivia, Shirley didn't want you to worry about anything with her passing. Everything is organised.'

'Did she know?'

'In a way. This wasn't Shirley's first stroke. She had one a few months ago.'

'What?' Prickles of shock stabbed up her spine. 'She never told me.'

'She didn't want to upset you. She knew she wasn't well. She also knew that she'd lived a good seventy-eight years. I think she was ready.'

'So she's planned it all? The funeral? All of it?'

Christine nodded. 'She loved you so much. She told me all about how your mum came to live with her and how watching you grow up was the greatest gift from God.' Christine took Olivia's hand and smiled. 'She shared with me that you both filled her lonely heart. She was grateful she got a second chance to care for someone.'

'She did.' Olivia let the tears come again. 'After Mum died, Shirley looked after me. I ended up going to boarding school in Glebe —I didn't want to leave her, but Mum left specific instructions in her will. Shirley was adamant that we follow Mum's wishes.' Olivia caught a sob. 'She was strong like that.' Olivia wiped her nose with her crumpled tissue. 'I always had a home to come back to for the holidays.'

What would the holidays look like now?

With that, her heart exploded with sorrow, and she let herself cry messy tears.

Christine waited patiently, patting her hand.

Shirley had been like a grandmother to her. The best one she could've had. Like her mother, she'd gently encouraged Olivia when-ever she stalled, which seemed to happen more and more often as the years went by. Shirley had always been there for her, stepping in where her mum would've.

Shirley had made everything seem safe and possible. What was Olivia going to do now?

CHAPTER 3

'You're back?'

Olivia glanced up from her book as Demi walked into the shop. 'Yesterday.'

'How was it?' Demi jumped up on the counter and crossed her legs.

'Don't let Bertie see you doing that.'

Demi glanced at her Swatch. 'It's 9.30 am and a Thursday. She won't come in until she's had brunch, played bridge and shopped her immaculate nails off.'

Olivia gave her a gentle shove. 'She can do what she likes.'

'Yeh, I suppose.' Demi picked up two novelty pens—one with Shakespeare's head, the other with Jane Austen's—and made them do a flirty dance. 'I suppose when you're that rich, you can do what you like. I still don't know why she bought a bookshop anyway?'

Olivia grabbed the pens and swatted Demi's arm before putting them back in the sales holder. 'Her accountant wanted her to invest her money in something safe. Apparently, she's invested in everything from wind to ostrich farms.'

Demi shrugged. 'Anyway, how was it? The funeral?'

'Lovely.' On the surface, it had been, but underneath all the prettiness, it was a lie. She didn't want to celebrate a life. She wanted to scream at the universe.

A FEW DAYS LATER, Olivia was deep into a chapter when her apartment buzzer rang.

'Hello?' she answered tentatively.

'Parcel for Olivia Bennet,' said a gruff male voice.

'A parcel? For me?'

'That's what I said, love. Ya need to come down and sign for it.'

Who would be delivering me a parcel? It was her birthday, but she really didn't know anyone who would send a parcel in the post, especially with Shirley gone.

Olivia grabbed her keys off the hook near her front door and placed them between her fingers as she'd seen a female police officer show the audience on *The Midday Show* in a segment about self-defence.

Downstairs, she spied the distorted outline of a man with a bright blue cap through the frosted glass. She opened the door a crack and peeked through.

'Not going to hurt ya, love,' he said, his tone annoyed.

'Sorry,' Olivia bleated.

'Don't be sorry, just sign for the package, okay?' He nodded towards a large pine crate at his feet. Thick plastic bands held it shut, and two large hemp rope handles hung on either side. FRAGILE was stamped in red across the top.

Olivia signed where his nicotine-stained finger pointed. 'You'll need to get some help,' he snapped. 'It's heavy.' With that, he turned and walked off to his van, double parked on the street.

Olivia walked around the crate. Heat flushed through her veins. *How am I going to get it upstairs?*

'Need a hand?'

Olivia whirled around, and her mind spun to match. Sebastian, the teacher who'd saved her in story time a month ago, stood in front of her.

'It looks heavy.'

She averted her eyes and covered her scar with her hand. 'I'm afraid it is. It just got delivered.'

He walked around it. 'We might manage it together.' He smiled at her, his arctic-blue eyes sparkling. Her heart fluttered. She couldn't deny he was attractive, but her reaction discombobulated her.

And once again, he'd saved her from an awkward situation.

He rubbed his hands together. 'Where to?'

'Upstairs. I live above the shop—the bookshop. Bertie's.' As she stumbled over her words, she fumbled with the door and chocked it open with the wooden doorstopper.

'Thank you so much for doing this,' she said as they heaved the crate up the stairs. The rope scratched and prickled against her palm. 'Sebastian, isn't it?'

'Yep. That's me. Mild-mannered teacher of year five and saviour of pretty ladies who have run-ins with cranky couriers.'

What? Had she heard right? Was he calling her pretty? She chewed the inside of her mouth as she considered him. What was his game?

Inside her apartment, Olivia lowered her half down.

Sebastian frowned. 'Don't you want it out of the way?'

'Oh, yes. That would be better. Can we put it in my bedroom?' she blurted. A furious blush punched her face. She'd just invited a strange, good-looking man into her bedroom. Something she had never done before. The only other male who'd entered her apartment was an electrician who'd fixed a rogue power point, and even then, she'd kept her bedroom door firmly closed.

Sebastian nodded, seemingly unfazed.

He's probably used to being invited into women's bedrooms.

Once they got the crate into the bedroom, Sebastian stretched out his arms and stepped into the living room. 'Great place. Art Deco?'

'Yes.' Olivia followed him as he inspected the flat. 'Most of it is still in the original condition.'

'That wallpaper must be the original,' he said as he surveyed the wall in the living room. He glanced up at the wooden fretwork that separated the kitchen from the rest of the apartment. 'That's the original brick recess in the wall, where an old coal stove would've stood.' He inspected the faded blush-pink General Electric stove. 'This place is amazing. It's a museum.' He eyed off the old fridge. 'Another relic. From the 1960s?'

Olivia nodded. 'The stove and the fridge were here when I moved in. The fridge wasn't working, but Bertie—she owns the bookshop—found someone to fix it.' Her nerves bubbling, she babbled on. 'It only needed a new gas cylinder. It was cheaper than getting a new fridge. She rents the flat to me.'

'Not interested in upgrading?'

'Not really. It reminds me of the home I grew up in before I went to boarding school.'

Sebastian raised an eyebrow. 'I went to boarding school, too. Where'd you go to?'

'Our Lady Queen of Peace. In Glebe.'

'Well, we're practically neighbours. I went to Mornington in Stanmore.'

'That's a posh school.' She wrung her hands, and the words fell out before she could stop them. 'Would you like a drink? Tea? Coffee? Juice?'

'You choose.' Sebastian sat himself on a stool at the kitchen bench. He seemed so relaxed. The thought relaxed her a little too.

'I feel like a tea.'

'Tea it is then.' He winked at Olivia. 'Even though you do owe me a coffee.'

'I do?'

'Story time?'

'Oh? Would you like a coffee instead?'

'Tea's fine. I'm more interested in the company.'

She blushed and busied herself with fixing them tea and snacks. 'You seem very interested in the history of this place. Is it a hobby?' She placed a plate of freshly baked chocolate chip cookies in front of him.

'No, I did a BA in history at Macquarie University. Then, I went to teachers' college and trained to be a primary school teacher. They say that a BA is—'

'A bugger all degree.' Olivia laughed. 'I know. I did a BA in literature.'

He grinned. 'Is that why you work in the bookstore?'

'Not exactly. I like it. It suits me for now.' Olivia shrugged. She wasn't keen to share her anxieties along with the tea and cookies.

'Well, what would your dream job be?'

'My dream job?'

'Yeh.'

She hesitated. 'Is teaching your dream job?'

'For now it is.' He paused. 'Yes. It is.'

'For now?'

'You just don't know what the future holds. Life should be filled with new experiences.'

'You sound like my friend Demi.' It seemed everyone except her saw life as this big, exciting bag of adventure. Meanwhile, Olivia was always worried the bag would tear.

'So what's yours?' he pressed.

He held her gaze. There was a kindness in his eyes. And something about him she trusted. Her dream was silly and much too big. Her anxiety would get in the way. But with a silent breath, she took a leap.

'Every few years, the Victoria and Albert Museum offers cadetships in curatorship.'

'In London?'

'I know, crazy, right?'

'Why?'

'Because I'm not that brilliant and'—she poured tea into his cup, avoiding eye contact—'I'm a little afraid of flying.'

'Well, Miss …?'

'Bennet.'

'Well, Miss Bennet, you never know your luck in a big city. Even London.'

Olivia smiled. She didn't believe him, but it was nice to hear.

———

AFTER SEBASTIAN LEFT, Olivia grabbed a pair of scissors. The crate was most likely filled with second-hand books. It wouldn't be the first time the shop had received donations. People assumed that Bertie's sold all kinds of books. From the size of the trunk, someone was a voracious reader.

Olivia pulled off the envelope stapled to one of the wide plastic strips wrapped around the steamer trunk and frowned. It was from Shirley's solicitors. Strange. Shirley's estate was finalised a couple of weeks ago. Curiosity tickled Olivia's mind. Maybe something had been left behind in the cottage. *But why send it? It could've stayed at the cottage.*

The place belonged to her now. Her childhood home. The last thing connecting her to her mum.

'So, are you loaded?' Demi had asked when she told her.

'If owning a three-bedroom timber cottage in a small beachside suburb on the Central Coast makes you rich, then yes.'

'What are you going to do with it?'

'I don't know.'

'Why don't you keep it as a holiday house? You could rent it out.'

'Maybe. I don't know.' She had no desire to deal with strangers in that capacity. 'People get mad when they don't get what they want.'

'Why would they get mad?'

'I'll think about it,' Olivia had said. She could tell Demi was getting impatient with her.

Now Olivia sliced the envelope open and pulled out a letter. A large ornate key dropped to the wooden floor.

The clanging spooked Gin, who'd sauntered over to investigate.

She picked it up and turned her attention to the letter.

DEAR MISS BENNET,

We were contacted by Secure Storage. It appears they were in arrears for a small storage unit that housed this steamer trunk, which we arranged to have delivered to you.

We've determined that Shirley continued to pay the monthly fees on behalf of Rosemary Bennet. As you're her daughter, we have sent the steamer trunk to you. The manager at Secure Storage also forwarded us the chest's key. This is included with this letter.

We have paid the amount owed and have closed the account.

My secretary, Susan, is a history buff, and she advised these trunks were common when migrating from one country to another. There is a stamp on the side. This trunk was made by Imperiale Trunks in Milan. It's most likely from the 1920s. According to Susan, these have been sold at auction for hefty sums. This one is in good condition and should fetch a handsome price. My advice is to get the trunk valued and insured accordingly.

Please note that we have not opened it. This would be deemed a breach of privacy. But because of its weight, we know it isn't empty.

Should you wish to discuss the contents or seek further advice, please contact us.

William Templeton
Solicitor, Partner

EXCITEMENT MIXED with curiosity bubbled in her stomach. No one had ever mentioned a trunk in storage. Her mother hated clutter, so maybe it was just filled with junk or her baby things. Still, she'd take any connection to her mother she could get.

Olivia reread the letter and stopped at the signature. *Templeton.*
The same solicitor who'd looked after Shirley's estate. She ran her
finger along the embossed company name at the top—Morris,
Templeton and Gray. She moved to the credenza, pulled out a file
and removed a wad of papers. Yes. The same solicitors her mum used
for her will. Intrigue buzzed up her spine.

Eagerly, Olivia cut the plastic strips around the crate and lifted
the lid. She tapped the top of the trunk. Metal. The sides had been
nailed. After grabbing a claw hammer, she pried the four sides off,
revealing a navy steamer chest.

She ran her hands along the lid. A pressed-metal design covered
the top. Such a beautiful trunk. How had her mother come into
possession of such a striking piece? This was the type of trunk a
Hollywood actress travelled with. Maybe to London to be in a West
End show.

She picked up the key. It was made of iron and clearly fashioned
by hand. She knelt in front of the large brass lock and took a deep
breath.

CHAPTER 4

March 1989

Olivia sat on the floor with all the items spread out around her. A vintage camera sat next to bundles of photos wrapped in cotton ribbon. She ran her hand along the dresses draped along the edge of her bed. Their luxurious fabric mocking the powder-blue chenille piping on her bedspread. Expensive shoes peeked out of shoe boxes now stained with age. As she touched and studied each item, memories of her mother filled her heart and teased out questions.

Unease flowed through her. Why had her mother hidden all these things? Did Olivia want to know? Shouldn't she respect her mum's privacy? After all, her mum had gone to great lengths to keep the trunk hidden. Did Shirley know about it? The question set off a flare of annoyance within Olivia. Why had she been kept in the dark?

She shuffled through the photos of her mother as a young woman and stopped at the one in which she was dressed in a pale blue uniform with a white smock. Her arms were draped around a woman dressed in a navy nurse's uniform. She picked up a bundle of letters. A gold wedding ring threaded through the ribbon that held the letters together sat on top. She untied the red ribbon and slipped off the ring. Olivia circled the plain gold band between her fingers. A heaviness expanded across her chest. She took in a sharp breath. Her mother never mentioned being married. Olivia believed she'd been conceived out of wedlock. She placed the ring on her finger and twirled it around. Thinking. Mining her memories for anything that she may have forgotten or missed. Nothing. She was certain her mum had never mentioned being married. She leant against the side of her bed and slipped out each letter, unfolding the thin, faded paper, hoping for a clue. They were all written in Italian, in her mother's loping, cursive writing, to a Viviana, but there was no address on the envelopes. Bundled with the letters were faded newspaper and magazine articles.

A loud wolf whistle startled her. Demi. Olivia packed up all the items back into the trunk, closed the bedroom door and raced down to let Demi in.

When she opened the door, Demi unleashed. 'I know you said you wanted to be alone, but as a friend, I reckon not. Besides'—she held up a hessian bag of presents —'I come bearing gifts. From me, Mum and Yiayia. Even Stephanie stopped thinking about her wedding and got you something.' Demi fanned her face. 'Man, it's still hot for March.' She pulled out a bottle of chilled spumante and Greek cake. 'I reckon this will cool us down.'

'You all shouldn't have done this.' Olivia peered inside the bag. It was nice to have people looking out for her. It helped to dull the sharp sadness of her birthday.

'Hello'

Olivia spun around, and her smile quickly vanished from her face.

Sebastian.

Her heart kicked into a gallop. 'Hi.' Heat exploded on her face. Olivia handed the presents back to Demi and grabbed her keys from her pocket, only to drop them.

Sebastian stepped forward and picked them up.

Demi stared at Olivia, then at Sebastian, a Cheshire-cat grin stamped on her face. Olivia groaned internally. She knew her friend was enjoying this.

'So?' She looked Sebastian up and down. 'Who's your friend, Olivia?'

Olivia thought the sides of Demi's mouth might split open. 'Oh. Sorry—'

'Sebastian,' he said, extending his hand. 'I always seem to be around at the right time to give Olivia a hand.'

Demi gave Olivia and then Sebastian a quizzical look. And Olivia watched in horror as realisation flooded Demi's face. She gave her a look, willing her not to go there.

No such luck.

'Oh! You're *that* Sebastian. The story-time prince.'

Olivia's face was now so hot she felt sure its heat could solve the world's energy crisis. She went to put the key in the lock and dropped her keys for a second time.

Sebastian and Olivia both bent to grab them, and an electric shock buzzed up her spine when their fingers touched. Without thinking, she giggled. What a cliché. In a good way. The same tingling feelings swept over her when she read a romantic moment in a novel or watched two people find love after their journey from meet cute to happily ever after.

'Ah, she laughs.' Sebastian smirked at Demi. He then turned around and picked up a bunch of flowers leaning against the wall nearby. 'These are for you.' He handed them to Olivia.

Olivia narrowed her eyes at Demi. She was enjoying this way too much. 'What have you been saying, Demi?'

'Oh, don't blame her. I found out it was your birthday from Fergus.'

'Father O'Casey. At St Brendan's?'

'The very one.'

'Thank you. But? Why would Fergus ... I mean Father—'

'We've been mates for years. We went to school together. He's the one who told me about the teacher opening at St Brendan's.'

Demi jumped in. 'Wow, that's one heck of a superpower you have. One present and poof'—she snapped her fingers—'not only do you know it's her birthday, but when.' She crossed her arms. 'I'm impressed.'

Olivia threw Demi a 'stop it' look.

Sebastian chuckled. 'No superpower, I'm afraid. During question time after Mass, one of the girls in my class came straight out and asked if you were Father O'Casey's girlfriend.'

'What? No. Did you—'

'Fergus explained that priests don't have girlfriends, but he told the entire class about how you run a book club and help at the retirement village. He said you were an angel.' Sebastian winked at Demi. 'He also asked the class to say a little prayer for you.'

'You Catholics are so sweet,' Demi cooed. 'Not as hardcore as us Orthodox.'

Olivia took in the sweet scent of the flowers. 'But there was no need to buy me these.'

'Oh, I don't know. Sometimes even angels need flowers to brighten up their birthdays.'

'Olivia?' Demi sidled up close, mischief in her voice. 'Why don't you invite Sebastian up to help us eat some of this cake?' Demi turned to Sebastian and, in her sweetest voice, said, 'You should taste this cake. *Amazing*. We couldn't eat any of it knowing you were missing out.' She turned to Olivia and, with glee, added, 'Couldn't we, Olivia?'

'I'm sure Sebastian has better things to do.'

'Nope, wide open. Just a lonely Sunday afternoon.'

Olivia's stomach fluttered, and she clutched her presents tight against her chest. There was no way she could manage a whole afternoon making small talk—let alone *interesting* small talk—with Sebastian. She looked over at Demi and, with her eyes, pleaded with her to stay.

Demi smirked.

CAKE AND COFFEE turned into sandwiches and the Sunday afternoon movie on the telly. This week, the movie had been one of Olivia's favourites: *Houseboat*, with Sophia Loren and Cary Grant.

'I love that movie,' Demi said as she stretched. She glanced at the cuckoo clock. 'Shit, gotta go. The weekly Greek invasion is at my house tonight, and I'm not in the mood for Mum's lecture.' She turned to Sebastian. 'We're Greek and wild.'

'I get it.' Sebastian collected the cups and took them into the kitchen. Demi raised an eyebrow at Olivia with a 'and he cleans up' nod of approval.

'My family is Italian,' he said as he came back in to pick up the plates. 'Like Olivia's mum.'

'Well, look at you two. You're practically family.' Demi grinned. 'Where from?'

Sebastian returned from the kitchen and sat on the coffee table. 'Mum and Dad were from near Venice. Just after they got married, they migrated to Australia. In 1958, I think. How about your parents, Olivia?'

Demi gave her a sympathetic look. Olivia hated telling people she didn't know who her dad was.

'Mum's from Italy. That's all she ever said. I don't know who my dad was.' Olivia focused on scratching Gin's tummy. 'Mum kept that pretty secret. She died when I was thirteen and took the secret with her.'

Great. She'd managed to sour the brilliant afternoon with one comment.

She could feel Sebastian's gaze on her. 'My parents died when I was fourteen,' he said. 'They were in Queensland.'

Oh! 'I'm really sorry,' Olivia said. Her heart went out to him. She had lost her mum, but he had lost both his parents—at the same time.

She snuck a quick peek at him. There was no morbid self-pity in his expression. Instead, he appeared to carry his experience with a kind of accepted grace.

'It's okay. It was a long time ago now.' Sebastian gave her a reassuring smile. 'I have Nonna. My grandfather died a couple of years before my parents. We actually saved each other.'

'Well, now I feel like a spoiled brat complaining about having to do stuff with my family.'

Olivia hugged Demi. 'You don't fool me. I know you love your big, wild Greek family.'

Demi kissed her cheek. 'Well, on that note. I'm going. *Yassou.* That's Greek for *ciao.*' As she opened the front door, she turned and twirled her finger. 'Don't you two do anything I wouldn't do.'

Olivia cringed as Demi swept out with a huge wink.

She turned to Sebastian. 'I'm really sorry. Demi's sense of decorum is non-existent.'

He shrugged. 'I like her.'

The revelation wobbled her. Her experience with boys was a stretched-out zero. She had read once in *Dolly* that if a boy liked your friend, he liked you. Unless ...? She sat on the single sofa chair as Sebastian settled back down on the couch, flicking through the TV guide. Unless he only thought of her as a friend, too.

CHAPTER 5

The next day, Olivia fortified herself with a robust glass of vodka before poring over the mysterious items in the trunk again. The burn of the vodka settled the bitterness of her thoughts. Now that the initial excitement had passed, the trunk sat as another reminder of her mother's constant refusal to share anything about her past. She wished she weren't alone.

Demi had just left. She'd stopped by for a sneaky cigarette and coffee.

'So how long did Sebastian stay?' her friend had asked as soon as she arrived.

'Only about an hour.' She didn't want to activate Demi's eye roll by telling her that, at first, they sat in silence, eyes glued to the weekly gardening show, while Olivia tried not to think about how much she enjoyed his company and how uninteresting she was. During a commercial break, Olivia blurted that she had a herb garden downstairs. She'd been both shocked and relieved when Sebastian stood, wanting a tour. Demi would've read more into it, even though it was obvious Sebastian was only interested because he wanted to start one for his class. She wasn't in the mood for a dissection of his motives.

'Well, a lot can happen in an hour.' She handed a mug of coffee to Olivia.

Olivia shrugged. 'It really was boring. We just watched telly, and he wanted to see my garden. Okay?'

'Fair enough. It's dropped.' She flopped onto the sofa and sat cross-legged, jiggling her tea bag. In true Demi Kokkinos style, she moved on to the next thing that popped into her head. 'I'm beat. Boy, I hate Mondays. Bob Geldof got it. I've been flat out delivering food parcels to nearly every elderly Greek person in Sydney.' She sniffed her underarms. 'I smell like one giant lamb souvlaki. Sometimes I wish my mum and dad had office jobs.'

'You love being the daughter of greengrocers. And I bet those elderly folks love you, too.'

'I'm just glad *bum*-day is done and dusted. I put some food left over from lunch in the fridge. We can have it later.'

Olivia loved Mondays. Working on Saturdays meant she got Mondays off, and today had been an especially good day. Poppy had turned up on time and hadn't called her with questions about a book. After nearly nine months at the shop, she was finally getting the hang of it.

Now, alone in her room, Olivia picked up the expensive-looking emerald-green evening dress from the chest and held it against her. It would've looked fabulous on her mum, would've made her light-green eyes pop. Her mum's eyes carried such warmth, but Olivia often sensed a veiled sadness in them as well. Her mother had also had so much determination and drive. She'd been steadfast in her urging Olivia to pursue whatever dreams she wanted to chase.

Olivia couldn't help but wonder whether her mum would be disappointed in her now. Disappointed by the life she was living.

She'd always been shy. Even when she was little, she'd hidden behind her mother's legs and willed herself into the background whenever people talked to them. What perplexed Olivia was her mother's own lack of social life. Her mum had possessed so many incredible qualities—why had she been so closed off? Rosemary hadn't seemed shy. Yet, Olivia's world orbited around the cottage, the village, and the school.

Sighing, she hung up the dress behind her door, away from Gin's inquisitive claws, and focused once again on the letters written to Viviana, penned on thin-lined paper. She'd tried to decipher the Italian but could get no further than a few simple words.

In year eight, when she started studying French, Olivia discovered she had an aptitude for languages. Excited, she'd asked her mother to teach her Italian as well.

'I think it would be good for us to speak Italian together,' Olivia had said. Her mum was always working so hard as a nurse, and Olivia thought this would be a chance for her to do something fun.

'Olivia, no. I am too busy. You are a clever girl—study English. There is no need in Australia to speak another language. We are too far away.' Her mother had kissed the top of her head and gone about her housework.

Her mum was an enigma. She didn't want to speak Italian but still cooked traditional food. She made her own *sugo*—tomato sauce—and filled their fridge with salami, prosciutto and cheese that stank up the train carriage on the way home.

Olivia's chest tightened. Thinking about the food made her miss her mum even more.

She picked up a photo of her mum in a red bathing suit on a yacht, a sunny Sydney Harbour in the background. She was laughing at whoever had taken the picture. Olivia had never seen her mum laugh like this or look so carefree.

What had changed? Was it her fault?

When Olivia was ten, she needed to create a family tree for a school project. Worried that her tree would be bare, she'd asked her mum to tell her about her family and her dad's family. Her mother promptly cut her off.

'Never ask me that again.'

The rejection had seared her heart, and Shirley had found her in the garden under the old frangipani tree, trying to read through her sobs.

'How are ya, pet?' Shirley lowered herself gingerly onto the bench her husband had built when they were young and newly married.

'Mum just closes up. She won't share anything with me. It's bad enough she won't talk about my dad, but she won't tell me anything about *her* life. Nothing.' Olivia sniffed and accepted Shirley's handkerchief. 'Why is she like this?' Olivia whispered, grabbing Shirley's warm hands and studying the freckles and sunspots, a result of years spent working in her garden under the Australian sun. 'What's she so scared of? Do you know? You can tell me. I won't say anything.'

Shirley patted Olivia's hand. 'Even if I knew, do you really think it would be right for me to share information that isn't mine to share?'

Olivia shrugged. She knew Shirley was right, but her heartache and anger kept the words jammed in her throat.

'Look.' Shirley touched Olivia's cheek. 'Whatever happened must've been pretty bad. I reckon she's got a broken heart.'

Olivia nodded through the sobs.

'Your mum came to me to start a new life,' Shirley continued. 'One thing's for sure—someone else would take that pain and sling it around, not caring who they hurt. She doesn't do that. She starts every day looking for the good. Don't be mad at her for trying to make things better for herself.'

Gin jumped down from the bed and startled Olivia out of her memories, sending the photo fluttering to the ground.

She picked up another bundle of photos. All black and white. These were less personal and more artistic, like photos in *National Geographic*. They seemed to tell the story of Sydney in the 1960s. Her mother would've been in her twenties.

Underneath were two much older photos. They appeared out of place with their faded sepia colour. She ran her finger along the photos' scalloped edges. In one, a young girl, about seven or eight, stood next to Rosemary, maybe fourteen. They looked like sisters, but the younger girl's hair was much lighter than Rosemary's raven curls. An ocean was their backdrop.

In the second photo, her mother was with a different girl. They sat at an ornate desk as they smiled at the camera. The girl was dressed in fancy clothes, her mother in a simple floral dress. There was no family resemblance. Her mother's thin frame and dark hair were a stark contrast to the girl's round cheeks and blonde hair. A pile of books sat to the left of her mother.

She put the photos back in the trunk, closed the lid and put the key in her jewellery box. Too many emotions for one day.

She moved to the wardrobe and stopped. One was enough. Besides, Gin needed his dinner. She started moving towards the kitchen but spun around, the guilt, shame and sadness an over-whelming force.

As soon as the vodka hit her chest, the spindly emotions softened. She sat on the bed behind the trunk and cradled the bottle.

Who were these people? Why had her mother kept them from her?

Once again, her mind and her heart spun. More secrets. Wasn't it enough her mother refused to tell her anything about her father? Now, there were more secrets spilling out of the trunk. What had she just set in motion?

THE FOLLOWING NIGHT, Demi jumped at the chance to help Olivia. Together, they placed each item around them on the rug in Olivia's bedroom.

'What are you going to do?' Demi asked.

Olivia shrugged. There didn't seem to be anything to do. The items revealed only superficial things about her mother. None answered any of her questions, only created more.

'You know what I've just realised?' Olivia reached into the trunk to see if she'd missed anything.

'What?'

'Documents. A passport. Migration papers. Mum would've needed these to migrate here. There's nothing. Not even a ticket.' Once again, unease filled Olivia.

'Maybe she got rid of them when she became an Australian citizen.'

'Maybe?' Olivia moved onto her knees and tucked her hands inside the fabric pockets at the side of the trunk.

Demi studied a photo. 'She was a stunner. You said she migrated alone? What would make her come out here without anyone?'

'Maybe she had no family left.' Olivia showed Demi the photo of her mother as a late teen standing next to a younger girl. 'Look, I think she had a sister.' She reached across to the letters. 'These letters to a Viviana are in Italian, but I can only make out some words.' She scanned a page. 'Here. See, *sorella*. Sister. And here. *Mia*. My. My sister.'

The letters were written between June 1960 and September 1964. 'Mum said she arrived in August in 1960. If Viviana is her sister, why didn't she ever talk about her?' She studied the photo.

'Maybe something happened.'

Olivia glanced back at the photo. 'Maybe.' A sadness pushed against her heart.

'Are you okay?'

Olivia nodded. Demi picked up a pair of green satin shoes with beading on a band across the front. 'Roger Vivier. They look expensive.'

'It's all expensive.' Olivia pointed to the butter-yellow crepe wool suit hanging on the door. 'That's Chanel.' She lifted the green gown and showed Demi the label inside. 'Givenchy. And this.' She pulled out a black cocktail dress. 'Dior. Also, the shoes. All designer.'

Olivia took in the out-of-place haute couture in her mismatched bedroom filled with quilted cushions and a red Persian rug. 'Mum worked hard to make ends meet. She didn't have this kind of money when she worked as a nurse, so how would she have had money alone in her twenties as a migrant? All she told me was that a priest at St Mary's Cathedral helped her get a job. I don't know where.' She slumped down on the bed. 'I don't even know where she used to live. I know nothing about Mum's life.'

Demi held up a book of Irish blessings. 'Have you seen this?'

'Yeh, it's from someone called Nora.' Olivia took the small leather-bound book, opened it and pointed to the first page. 'There's a handwritten note.'

Little blessings to take with you.
For you and your little baby.
Love, Nora

AS OLIVIA FLICKED through the pages, a photo fell out.

Demi picked it up. 'Well, hello there.' She held up the photo. 'He's hot.'

Olivia snatched the photo. Dressed in the green Givenchy dress, her mum looked like a movie star. At her side was a handsome man. He gazed at Rosemary, mesmerised, as she stared at the camera.

'She looks really happy.' Demi shuffled closer.

'She does.' Olivia sighed. 'I don't know, Demi. Maybe there's a reason she kept all of this secret.'

Melancholy infused itself into her body as she collected the items, focusing on putting everything back with care. As she went to fold the suit, she felt something hard inside the right front pocket. Olivia laid the suit on the bed and reached in to find an expensive linen handkerchief. In one corner, in gold thread, the letters JS were embroidered inside a wreath of wattle. Olivia unwrapped the napkin and revealed a black velvet box with *Fairfax and Roberts* printed in gold on top.

'Demi?'

Olivia opened the box and lifted out a diamond necklace. The gems sat snug amongst an intricate work of gold.

'Holy moly, Olivia. That looks expensive.'

'It is. Fairfax and Roberts is high end. Bertie owns a few pieces from them.'

Olivia turned the necklace around her fingers, and the diamonds sang as the light captured them.

'How on earth did my mother, my mother who taught me to save, who mended and fixed things to save money, have all of this?' She swept her hand in a large arc as she plonked herself down on the bed again.

'Do you think—' Demi stopped.

'What?'

'Nothing.' She busied herself with picking up the scattered photos, avoiding eye contact with Olivia.

'What, Demi?' Olivia knelt next to Demi and placed a hand on hers to stop her. 'What? Tell me.'

Sighing, Demi sat back on her haunches, holding a pile of photos. 'I dunno, Liv. All this expensive stuff. The fact your mum was alone. I mean, it was the 1960s, you know. Free love and all that. And ...' She held up a photo. 'She was also a stunner. A body like Sophia Loren and—'

'Gina Lollobrigida,' she whispered. She'd watched the movie with Demi a few months ago on the *Bill Collins' Golden Years of Hollywood* TV show. *Trapeze*, with Tony Curtis.

People were telling her mum that all the time. Her mum would laugh it off, embarrassed by the attention. Demi was right. Her mum was beautiful, even though she tried hard to hide it.

'What are you saying?' Olivia swallowed hard. 'That my mum ...' She couldn't get the words out. They tasted bitter and poisonous.

Demi nodded.

Olivia let the comment spill out, feeling sick. 'A hooker?'

'Olivia, I don't think a prostitute makes this kind of money. I'd say ...' Demi paused.

Olivia covered her mouth as a wave of nausea threatened to heave up her lunch.

'More like a high-class call girl,' Demi said in a hushed tone. Her eyes were wide. 'I mean, how else can you explain all of this?' She moved close to Olivia. 'I think you need to find out what all of this means. You might even find out who your dad is. Isn't that what you've always wanted?'

'I don't know.'

'What have you got to lose?'

The all-too-familiar guilt rushed in. Everything. She had every-thing to lose. Wanting to know who her father was had turned her world upside down.

CHAPTER 6

Olivia returned to her mother's items every day for the rest of the week. Each time, both her curiosity and unease increased. She wished Shirley were around to talk to. She might've had at least some of the answers.

By Sunday afternoon, she was no closer to deciding what she wanted to do. She kept reminding herself there was a reason her mother had kept this all hidden. Maybe she should just let sleeping dogs lie.

Or she could talk to Fergus. Things said to a priest were kept in confidence.

Maybe not.

Make up your mind, Olivia.

Gin slinked into the bedroom and nudged her hand.

'Hungry?' He let out a mournful meow. 'I know. I've been neglecting you. This trunk is taking over my life.' She picked him up and kissed his pink button nose. 'Come on, let's see what I've got.'

Olivia opened the pantry. 'You're in luck. One can left.' She scanned the rest of the contents. The shelves were running low on everything. It was time to pull it together and get back to living her sensible, orderly life. She took her magnetised shopping list off the fridge and noted the items she needed. The mundane activity settled her. It was normal. It had a purpose. It made her feel safe and content.

She nodded to herself, her decision made. She'd tuck all the chest items away and let the mystery be. What she didn't know wouldn't hurt her.

The buzzer rang, and she frowned as she answered. 'Hello?'

'Hi. It's Sebastian.'

Her breath caught in her throat. 'Oh.' Her mind went blank.

'Olivia?'

'Yes.' Her heart pounded.

'Are you busy?'

'No, um ... yes. Sort of. No.'

She heard him laugh. 'Listen, I'm getting some strange looks out here.'

She frowned again. 'You are?'

'Can you come down?'

'Sorry. Of course.'

She grabbed her keys off the hook and trotted down the stairs. When she got to the bottom, she stopped and composed herself. Taking a couple of deep breaths, she smoothed down the two pony-tails that fell over her shoulders and rubbed her hands down her jeans.

Sebastian grinned at her as she opened the door, and he held up a picnic basket and bottle of wine chilling in a bright yellow ice bucket. 'I hope you're free. It's such a nice day for a picnic. You don't want all of this to go to waste. Nonna followed my exact instructions on what to make.' A sheepish cringe crinkled his eyes. 'I'm afraid my culinary talents are tapped at toast and tea.'

Olivia's mind tussled with the idea of spending time with Sebastian. A good-looking, confident guy. Willing to share his shortcomings. She chewed the nail on the side of her thumb. What would they talk about?

'We can just lie about and read,' he said as if he'd heard her thoughts. 'I even brought along a book.' He held up *Patriot Games*.

'A thriller' was all she could say.

'No good?'

'All good.'

She smiled. He really was trying. 'I would have been suspicious if you'd shown me an Austen.'

'Well, it's a good idea that I didn't.' He reached into his bag. 'Brontë?'

Olivia laughed and accepted the copy of *Jane Eyre*. 'My favourite. How did you ... Ah. Demi.'

'No. You can't blame Demi for this one.'

Olivia cocked her head.

'Father O'Casey.'

'Fergus?'

'The very one.'

'He's giving all my secrets away. I'm going to have to have a word to him.'

'You can't get angry with him. He's a priest. And you must respect a priest. What did they teach you at the private Catholic school? Geez!' He winked.

A furious blush ran up her chest. 'Okay.' She put her hands on her hips. 'But there's one thing.'

'Tell me.'

———

'SO YOU REALLY PREFER PUBLIC TRANSPORT?' Sebastian raised an eyebrow as he hailed the bus. 'The smell, the sardine feel, the longer-than-usual time to get anywhere?'

'I do. You get to read.' Olivia held up her book, hoping her response was enough to stop Sebastian from probing. Things would snowball if she let on about her fear of cars. She'd have to tell him where it came from. She found it hard enough to bury the feelings as it was.

After getting off at Hyde Park, they took their time strolling to The Domain. Jazz punctuated the busy city street. They followed the music to a free concert in front of the art gallery, where a crowd had gathered. Sebastian noted a free spot under a Moreton Bay and grabbed Olivia's hand as they ran to secure it.

The warmth of Sebastian's hand seared her skin.

He unrolled the picnic rug, and they collapsed under the dappled shade. The autumn day had delivered a bright sky and a soft breeze coming off the harbour. The tree trunk was big enough for both of them to lean on but small enough for Olivia to feel the heat coming off Sebastian's broad chest. He smelt like musk but with a touch of spice, possibly sandalwood. She inhaled and relaxed a little.

'Hungry?'

Olivia jumped. 'Yes,' she squeaked.

She watched, impressed, as he set out a tablecloth and plates with cutlery wrapped in cloth napkins. Once the makeshift table was set, he removed from the picnic basket antipasti with cheeses, cold meats, olives, pickled vegetables, crusty sourdough bread and cold chicken, followed by a bean salad with oregano and feta.

'This is quite a feast. Your nonna's gone to so much trouble.'

Sebastian poured two glasses of white wine and handed one to Olivia. 'She just loves me.' He grinned at her. 'But she was also excited to hear you had some Italian in you.'

'Was she?' Olivia took a sip of the cool wine.

'Yeh. I think she's hoping for an Italian marriage.'

Olivia swallowed too much wine and coughed.

Sebastian reached across and wiped her chin with a napkin. 'Whoa. Averse to marriage, I see.'

'What?' Was this conversation really happening? 'No. It just took me by surprise.'

She looked at him to see he was teasing her. 'Oh, you.' She swiped at his arm.

Sebastian grabbed his heart dramatically.

A lightness rushed up her limbs, and she laughed. His silliness put her more at ease.

'Here.' He passed her a plate. '*Mangia, mangia*. Eat, as my nonna always says.'

Olivia dished up, and as they ate, she enjoyed the company and the music. It was easy to speak with Sebastian. He had a way of keeping the conversation going, and after asking her a question, he'd listen to her response with genuine interest. He talked about being a teacher and about his family. His mum had wanted to be a primary school teacher when she was growing up in Italy, but then she'd met his dad and they got married before migrating to Australia. She was pregnant with Sebastian's older brother when they arrived in Sydney. Three years later, Sebastian came along. When Sebastian started high school, his mum worked part time as a teacher aid. His brother, Marcus, was living in London. He'd met an Irish girl on a Contiki tour a few years ago.

'The kids must love having a male primary school teacher,' Olivia said. 'My teacher in grade six was this huge Scottish man. He had a mane of red hair and a bushy beard. I loved that year.'

He laughed. 'Yeh, we're a pretty rare species.'

'So what made you come to St Brendan's?'

'Nonna. She's getting on and had a fall a year ago. It was time to come back. She wouldn't hear of it, but I'm a rebellious grandson.'

'Oh, I can see you like to get your way.' Olivia gestured at the picnic.

'I didn't hear any complaints as you shoved Nonna's lemon cake in your mouth.'

Olivia picked up a twig and flicked him with it. 'I didn't go for seconds.'

'True.' He reached up, and Olivia recoiled and covered her scar with her hand. As though he hadn't noticed her reaction, Sebastian grabbed a leaf out of her hair and tossed it away. Normally, people asked about the scar. Was it possible he hadn't seen it?

Sebastian poured a cup of espresso and handed it to Olivia. The distraction settled her beating heart.

'Anyway, Fergus told me there was a position available. A maternity leave. I applied and voilà. I also had Clare.'

Olivia's heart stalled. 'Clare?' she said, trying to sound cool and collected.

'You met her that morning in the bookstore. She's a teacher at St Brendan's too. And a friend. From uni.'

Olivia's stomach crunched. *How good a friend?* She sipped the coffee and composed herself, keeping her face neutral while her mind flapped little red flags.

Sebastian had stopped talking and was staring at her.

'Sorry.' A squeaky laugh escaped. 'Great coffee.' She lifted the cup at him.

Sebastian smiled. 'Nonna will be pleased. I was saying it's good knowing someone in the neighbourhood. Now I know two people.' He grinned.

Olivia felt her heart submerge into unease again. Given the way Clare had draped herself over him in the bookstore, it was clear she still liked him. And there was no way she could compete with someone like Clare. Blonde, leggy, blue-eyed Clare.

This was all so foreign to her. This feeling of ... what? Jealousy? Her past experience with romantic relationships amounted to a schoolgirl crush on an actor and to that guy in one of her lectures. She'd never spent any real time with a man before. She swallowed hard in the hope Sebastian wouldn't notice her disappointment.

'I'm stuffed,' Sebastian said. 'Why don't we walk through the art gallery? It closes in a couple of hours.'

Olivia forced a smile. He seemed to know how to defuse her unease without even knowing he was doing it.

Maybe it's because of biorhythms?

Poppy was always going on about them at work. She'd twirl her blonde pigtails and say with a sigh, 'Oh, I think my biorhythms are a bit off today.'

Well, Olivia's biorhythm was doing a weird salsa dance mixed with some Grecian wrestling.

ON THE BUS RIDE HOME, Sebastian napped while Olivia gazed out the window at the high-rise buildings morphing into eclectic terraced houses and tried to find the courage to ask him to stay for dinner. She didn't want the day to end.

They'd spent a couple of hours in the art gallery sharing what they liked and didn't like about some of the paintings. Sebastian's cheekiness shone when he stood in front of a painting and modelled the action of a soldier on a horse, his sword raised. Olivia's laugh echoed across the large hall, causing a bohemian couple to turn towards them and smile.

On their walk back to the city, they stopped for an ice cream and sat on a bench under a Malayan banyan tree. Her heart rippled when Sebastian offered a taste of his mango lime gelato.

For the first time since Shirley's death, Olivia had truly enjoyed herself. Shirley had always been her go-to person when there was a new theatre production or a visiting art exhibition. She'd wondered if she'd ever be able to appreciate art again. Today, with Sebastian, some of the sadness had eased and a little joy had returned.

As the bus approached her stop, Olivia took a deep breath and gently woke Sebastian. 'Can I cook you dinner? If you're not too full. Or too busy. But it's okay. No pressure.' She felt her cheeks burn.

Sebastian gazed at her.

Crap. She'd made a fool of herself.

'On one condition,' he said.

'Okay?'

'If we can watch a movie tonight. What's a Sunday dinner without a movie?'

Olivia's stomach filled with butterflies and a warm glow spread up her chest. She had asked a boy to dinner, and he hadn't laughed at her.

'Deal. Your choice.'

'Even better.' He grinned back.

OLIVIA LOOKED OVER THE TABLE. Her mum would be proud. It wasn't an extravagant meal, but she'd enjoyed cooking for someone. She dished up the spaghetti bolognaise in one of her mum's serving bowls and opened the foil the sourdough was encased in, releasing the mouth-watering scent of garlic butter. She was shaking the dressing for the green salad when Sebastian returned from the video store.

'Something smells good,' Sebastian said as he came into the apartment. He waved the video at Olivia. 'That owner of the video store knows his stuff.'

'Walter? Yeh. He lives and breathes movies.'

'I think he's got a little thing for you.'

Olivia laughed and then slapped Sebastian's hand away as he tried to grab some garlic bread. 'Walter loves all the ladies. There are a few at the retirement village who have their eye on him.' She handed him the garlic bread, now safely hidden under a tea towel, to put on the table.

'He turned seventy last month,' she continued. 'He's seen so much. He used to work at the Century Theatre—you know it's where they showed Audrey Hepburn's *My Fair Lady*? Anyway, they pulled it down in 1983. He started as an usher.'

'I hate when they pull down old buildings.'

'Me too!' Olivia accepted the glass of wine that Sebastian had poured. The merlot went down smoothly. It was a different feeling than the one vodka gave her. Safer. More socially accepted. She could drink one or two glasses, and it would help to relax her rather than numb her.

'Good?'

'Yes. What movie did you get?' She needed to focus on something safer.

'One of your favourites.'

'How do you know what my favourites are? Don't tell me you also read minds.'

Sebastian grinned.

'Walter?'

'Yep.' He held up *Roman Holiday*.

She beamed. 'Yeh, I do love it. My dream is to go to Italy.' She cleared her throat as her chest tightened. She'd wanted to do the trip in hopes of learning more about her mum. Now, thanks to the trunk, she wasn't so sure it was a good idea. 'Come on, let's eat,' she said.

Over dinner, Olivia regaled him with light-hearted stories about customers wanting books and getting the titles wrong, and he returned the favour by sharing the antics and non-filtered comments of his young students.

When they were done eating, Olivia settled on the floor with Gin in preparation for watching the movie.

'I think he missed you,' Sebastian said. He settled down next to her. He reached across the coffee table and picked up the brochure Olivia had grabbed at the gallery. She'd made herself scarce by flicking through flyers while the woman in the cloakroom flirted with him. A strange stinging sensation had pushed against her chest as she watched the woman flick her long brunette hair back and smile while leaning over to display her ample cleavage. Olivia fiddled with the buttons that ran up her dress. Compared to that woman, she felt like a frayed tea towel.

'A photographic exhibition on life in the post-war years.' He passed it back to her. 'Are you interested in photography?'

'In a way.' Olivia's gaze automatically went to her bedroom. Gin stood and rubbed his wet nose against her cheek, just under her scar.

When she looked back at Sebastian, she saw genuine interest in his eyes.

She decided to take a chance and tell him a little. 'My mother lived in Sydney during the sixties and ...' She faltered and took another sip of wine, willing herself to be brave enough to trust Sebastian. 'I don't know much about her life.' She paused. 'She never wanted to speak about who my father was. All my life, I've wanted to know. It's this unrelenting need. It's like a piece of me is missing.' Sweat trickled down her spine. 'I can't really explain it—' She stopped. Tears hammered her eyelid. She swallowed to stop them, but they came. Fat and slow.

'I'm sorry,' she said.

Sebastian jumped up and grabbed the tissue box that Olivia kept on the kitchen bench.

'Why? It's not your fault that you don't know.' He pulled out a bundle of tissues.

Olivia concentrated on fashioning them into a ball.

'I don't want to pry. It's probably none of my business, but from the look on your face, this is important.' Sebastian got up again, went into the kitchen and came back with a glass of water. 'We all have demons in our cupboard.' He sat on the floor opposite her and handed her the glass.

'Thanks.' She took a sip. The cool water calmed her. 'Don't you mean skeletons in the closet?'

'Nope. *Abbiamo tutti demoni nel nostro armadio.* It's what my nonna always says when she's gossiping with her friends. Those widows are first-class gossips.' He smiled. 'Marcus used to say, "Wanna put Telecom out of business, tell an Italian widow".'

Olivia couldn't help but smile. She watched as he poured himself another glass of wine. He held the bottle up. She nodded.

'You're a really nice person.' A mortifying thought bulldozed in. 'Did Fergus tell you to be nice to me?' That had to be it. Why else would he be so sweet to her? Fergus always said she needed to get out more. Meet a nice boy. She pulled her knees up to her chest. How embarrassing to be set up by her priest.

'What?' He frowned. 'No. I didn't even know you knew Fergus when I first met you.'

He looked straight at her. Lines creased his brow. 'I may not know what you've had to go through, but I can probably empathise to a degree. When my parents died, Marcus and I were in Sydney. Nonna was looking after us. I was so angry, fourteen and already confused.' He topped up his wine and then met her gaze again. 'I'm so ashamed about how I carried on. I gave my poor grandmother, saddled with two teenage boys, such a hard time. Marcus was in grade twelve and was too busy to spend time with me. I got involved with some spoiled rich kids at boarding school and lost the plot when I started drinking and smoking pot.' He shook his head. 'Nonna was always called up to school to deal with something I did. I was so close to getting expelled.'

Olivia couldn't hide her shock. 'You seem so together.'

He shook his head again. 'Once, we stole a car and crashed it. It was totally wrecked. I was flung from the car but got lucky. Ended up with only a concussion and a broken arm. Some cuts and bruises. The boy driving shattered his leg. The biggest wake-up call was seeing Nonna crying. That and the look of disappointment in Marcus' eyes.' He swallowed. 'I was such a spoiled brat.'

The air around Olivia thickened as she listened, and time seemed to slow. Visions of mangled metal and smashed glass flicked in and out of her mind. She tried to untangle her empathy from her fear. What had happened to Sebastian was tragic, but it hit too close to home.

'I'm sorry,' she croaked and sipped her wine to swallow the lump in her throat.

'I'm okay. Now. It took some time. Allowing yourself to heal takes courage. For me, it involved what I feared.' He paused. 'Being alone. Then I started to trust life again.' Sebastian picked up the remote. 'Let's enjoy our Sunday night. Nothing like a romantic comedy to heal all wounds.'

But Olivia couldn't concentrate on the movie. Her thoughts kept returning to what Sebastian had said about embracing fear to heal. He'd been open and trusted her, laying out his vulnerability. By the time the final credits rolled, she'd made up her mind. She'd tell him about her mother's trunk. Maybe, as an outsider with no emotional attachment, he could help her make sense of it.

———

THE CASEMENT WINDOWS were open wide, inviting in a sweet, cool breeze along with the sounds of people out and about on a Sunday evening. The hum of the crowd down at the Annandale Hotel drifted in.

Olivia felt suddenly grateful that she always kept her room tidy. Her bed was made with perfect hospital corners, as her mother had taught her. A folded quilt, made with precision by Shirley, was smoothed down and pulled tight, and her clothes were tucked away in her wardrobe with her secret.

Olivia hoped Sebastian wouldn't laugh at the photos of her as a child, tall and gangly and standing shyly between Rosemary and Shirley. The total opposite of how natural and carefree she looked in photos with Demi. It was easy with Demi. Maybe because she had a huge Greek family around her and knew how to love unconditionally. Maybe because she was loud and stubborn and pulled Olivia into her vortex of support, laughter and cheekiness. Demi called it as she saw it, but Olivia also knew that her friend would move the universe for her. She trusted her implicitly.

'You've got a chifforobe.' Sebastian ran his hand over the polished wood.

Olivia's heart caught in her throat when he stepped over to it, but she swatted the fear away. The bottle of vodka was tucked deep into the back. Her rational mind soothed her thoughts. Sebastian was a gentleman—he wouldn't open the chifforobe.

'My nonna's got one in the spare room,' he continued. 'Where'd you get it?'

'It was here when I moved in.' She swallowed hard but kept her voice light. 'Bertie said it was most likely built in the 1930s.'

Sebastian walked over to the trunk and knelt in front of it. 'So this is it.'

'Yep. You can look inside if you like.' She bit her bottom lip as she watched him lift the lid, and her pulse quickened as she waited with bated breath for his reaction.

Sebastian reached inside. 'Your mum liked Neruda?' He held up the book of poems. '*Love poems.*'

Olivia's insides flushed with heat. She averted her eyes as he handed her the book. 'She never mentioned she did.' She held the book tightly and continued to watch Sebastian as he sifted through the items with care.

'These are good,' he said, shuffling through the artistic photos. His eyes flashed with excitement.

'I know.' Olivia knelt next to him. 'I had no idea she took photos, but after Mum died, the counsellor at my boarding school encouraged me to take up a hobby, and I joined the photography club. I liked it because it was just me and the camera.' She swivelled to face Sebastian. 'Don't you think it's strange that I joined a photography club never knowing my mum was also into it?'

'It might be a sign.' He handed the photographs to Olivia and then picked up a bundle of letters. 'They're in Italian. Can you read it?'

Olivia shook her head. 'Only a few words here and there.'

'Do you want to show my nonna? To translate?'

Olivia's mind flew straight to Sebastian's earlier comment. She imagined a group of Italian widows, all in black, gossiping and judging, scorning her mother. What if she'd been a high-class call girl?

'No. I don't think so.' She took the letters back.

'I shouldn't have pried. It's your private stuff. Sorry.'

'It's okay. I have so many questions too.' She paused. 'Mostly about my father.' She swept her hand across the trunk. 'Maybe all of this will hold some clue.'

'That's a start,' he said.

Olivia sunk down and sighed. 'I don't know what to do, though.' Her voice caught. 'I'm scared.'

'Scared of what?'

'That there's a reason she kept this all hidden.' Olivia rubbed her forehead. 'I don't know.'

Sebastian turned to face her, and the scent of his fading cologne settled her. But when she glanced into the trunk, her stomach lurched. There were too many secrets. The prospect of figuring out what it all meant was too big. Finding the *Titanic* would be easier than this. Her head started to throb.

She needed a drink.

CHAPTER 7

April 1989

Olivia buried herself in the back of the store to price books sent from the publishers in time for Mother's Day. Each year, the ache of not having her mum around faded a little more, but this year, with Shirley gone, the melancholy burnt with fresh intensity. She missed choosing a book for her mum as a gift, but it was comparing notes on it while strolling down the beach on their afternoon walks in the days that followed that Olivia had enjoyed the most.

With a wistful heart, she pushed away the memories and focused on reading the blurbs on the romances. How wonderful to have a little romance in her own life.

She laughed at the ridiculousness of it.

Yes, Sebastian seemed to enjoy being with her, but obviously as a friend.

And she hadn't heard from him for just over a week. He'd called a couple of days after she showed him the items in her mother's trunk, wanting to make sure she was okay, and had asked if she wanted to get a meal at the local bowling club. She'd had to decline, though. She was covering a shift for Poppy, who wanted to go on a date with a new guy.

'She collects them like trashy stamps,' Demi had remarked once after Poppy shared with them her weekend plans. A merry-go-round of dates with different boys the entire weekend.

The phone rang, and Olivia cocked an ear towards Poppy's cheerful greeting.

'Livvie!' shouted Poppy. 'There's a bloke on the phone for you.'

Olivia cringed, and as she crept out, two of her regulars smiled broadly at her.

Poppy covered the receiver with her hand and whispered, 'He sounds gorgeous.'

'Thanks, Poppy. Can you tidy up the sale books outside?'

Poppy nodded and grinned, twirling her pigtail. 'I get it. You want privacy.' With that, she skipped out.

Olivia moved into the kitchenette's doorway, her heart playing a drum solo. 'Hello?'

'Hi. It's that gorgeous guy.' Sebastian chuckled.

She tried to cool her hot cheeks with her palm. What must he be thinking? That she spent all day gossiping about him? How embarrassing. She glanced out the window at Poppy, who placed both of her hands on her heart and swooned. Olivia frowned and turned her back.

'I'm so sorry. Poppy's like a seven-year-old in a nineteen year's old body.'

'No worries. I'm an expert on seven-year-olds. I study them in the wild. My classroom.'

Olivia laughed. 'Want another one?' She twirled the phone cord around her fingers, relaxing a little.

'I reckon she'd wear them out. Hmmm.' He paused. 'Send her over.' The line went silent for a moment. 'Sorry, I haven't called. I got roped into the year six trip to Canberra. They needed a strong, commanding bloke.'

'Aren't you the only male teacher?'

'Yep. Slim pickings.' His laughter made her heart tinkle.

'Oh, I bet those kids loved it. Would be hard not to.' A fierce heat hit her face. Why did she say that?

'Listen, I was wondering if you'd like to go see *Back to the Future*. The cinema in Newton always has reruns of popular movies. Then dinner?'

'Oh,' she blurted. Was he asking her on a date? Erratic fluttering filled her belly.

'No pressure.'

'No. I'd like to go. I just have the shop. What time?'

'The movie starts at 6:30 pm. I can swing by and pick you up?'

'Can I meet you there?'

'I'm happy to drive us. I hardly drive now that I live in the inner city. My poor Gemini is always stuck in Nonna's garage.'

Panic gripped the base of her throat. There was no way she was telling Sebastian she wouldn't get in a car. He'd think she was being silly.

'Maybe another time.'

'Really? It'll be fun.'

'Sorry. Actually, I can't. I'm sorry. I need to go.' She hung up before he could say anything else.

'HELLO, DARLINGS.' Bertie placed all her shopping bags on the counter. Colour and vibrancy followed her into the shop.

'Bit of shopping?' Demi raised her eyebrows.

'Aren't you supposed to be helping your parents in their shop?'

'I needed a break. My sister's there. All she does is yack on about her wedding.' Demi pretended to vomit. 'It's turning into one big Greek circus.'

'One day it'll be you.' Bertie twirled her finger at her.

Demi grimaced. 'No way.' She ran her hands down her body. 'I see what marriage ... and kids ... do to your body and style. Just hang out at the Greek Club. Plus, Greek boys are a no-go. Definitely not for me.'

'Don't let your mother hear you say that.' Bertie took off her large dark sunglasses and replaced them with a pair of red-framed cat-rimmed reading glasses.

'Whoa, I love those.' Demi's face lit up, Greek marriage forgotten. 'Where'd you get them?'

'I found them in the back of my wardrobe in a box. Must've been a pair I bought in my youth—1950s or '60s.' She took them off and checked the label. 'Not really sure. The fifties were so long ago and the sixties ... well, the entire decade is a blur.' She winked, then caught Olivia's eye. 'Olivia. Why so glum?'

'She's—'

'Demi.' Olivia threw her friend a don't-you-dare-say-anything look. 'Bertie, did you want to go over the books?'

'What's going on?' Bertie twirled her finger at the two of them. 'You two having a bit of a tiff?'

Demi dragged Olivia in close and smiled. Fake and big. 'All good, Bertie. I better go. Been away from the avocadoes and bananas too long.'

The bell tinkled as she ran out.

As Bertie took off her coat, she turned to Olivia. 'You know, I've known you for a while. When you first turned up at the shop, you looked like a frightened kitten. Skinny, too. But one thing I liked about you, Olivia, was your authenticity.' She studied her with kind eyes. 'It's written all over your face.'

Bertie was always so positive. Effervescent. Then again, how could you not be when you were well regarded in society and lived a charmed life?

'I know it's been tough since Shirley's passing,' she continued, placing a gentle hand on Olivia's forearm. 'But I'm here for you. You don't have to be brave.'

The shop bell rang, and Poppy burst in. 'I brought coffee since you've been so sad.'

Bertie raised an eyebrow at Olivia.

'Oh, hi, Bertie. I didn't get you a coffee. Wanna have mine?' She planted the coffees on the counter, barely taking a breath. 'I can go back and get another one. That new barista at Wild Seed Bakery is gorgeous. Nearly as gorgeous as your Sebastian.' She grinned at Olivia.

Poppy had it all wrong. Sebastian was not *hers*. What if word got out and Sebastian found out? How embarrassing. Her body heat flew up the Richter scale.

Bertie smiled. 'Thanks, Poppy.' She turned back to Olivia. 'But Olivia's offered me a nice cup of tea up at the flat. Right, Olivia?'

Olivia could only nod. There was no saying no to Bertie. She knew Bertie understood her need for privacy, for not making a fuss. Regardless, she wasn't ready to have a chat about a boy who was just being friendly. Keeping her feelings private was safer.

'Why don't you grab the accounts and order books and we'll head upstairs?' She turned to Poppy. 'You'll be okay?'

'Okey-dokey,' Poppy said, already focused on a new shiny thing that had caught her attention. 'Natalie, I love your bracelet. Where'd you get it?'

'She certainly has a way with the customers,' Bertie said. 'Now, how about that cuppa?'

BERTIE WALKED AROUND THE FLAT, leaving a trail of honeysuckle and jasmine in her wake. Olivia concentrated on making the tea the way Shirley had taught her—exactly how Bertie loved it: looseleaf tea in a pot and boiling water warming the teacups.

Olivia opened the antique cabinet with the glass doors and chose two porcelain cups from Shirley's Royal Doulton collection. She'd promised herself she'd use them and not keep them locked away to gather dust.

'You've really made this place lovely, Olivia. The splashes of bold colour mixed with the old furniture works.' Bertie walked past the open French doors to her bedroom.

Realisation hitting her, Olivia raced out of the kitchen. The trunk!

'What's all this?' Bertie asked.

Too late.

Bertie picked up a bundle of photos on the credenza. 'May I?'

'Yes.' Olivia gently closed the door to her room as Bertie flicked through the photos. She wasn't ready to share the trunk with anyone else, not until she could make sense of it. It already felt so big. So unreal.

Bertie made cooing noises as she gazed at the various images. She stopped and held up a photo of Rosemary and a man sitting on a beach towel, both in dark sunglasses and swimwear that screamed the 1960s. The man was whispering something to her mum.

'Your mother?'

Olivia nodded.

'Gorgeous smile.'

'I know.' Olivia sighed and slumped onto the sofa. 'I want to know more about my mum, but ...'

'But what?' Bertie sat next to Olivia and handed the photo back to her.

'I'm afraid all hope vanished when she died.' Her heart turned inside out, and the tears pushed through. She finally let out months of tension while Bertie rubbed her back, just like her mum used to, making shushing sounds.

The affection reminded her of how good it felt to have people care for her.

Sebastian had reached out, and she'd let her fear push him away. She was a mess. She knew she was letting her feelings of loss and abandonment control her, but she didn't know how not to. Demi was right. She needed to be more adventurous.

She thought about the trunk tucked away in her bedroom. Her mum had feared something so strongly she'd kept most of her life secret.

Olivia couldn't let herself make the same mistake.

CHAPTER 8

On Sunday, Olivia decided to do the Bondi to Bronte walk. The fresh air and exercise would clear her head. She got dressed and checked her bag. Her book? She headed back into her bedroom and grabbed her latest read, *The House of the Spirits*. The story had her enthralled, allowing her to escape. Plus, a spot of reading outside would help to settle her too.

Before leaving, she picked up her favourite photo of her mum—the one where she was standing in front of an Art Deco apartment building, leaning forward to blow kisses to the photographer, the hem of her floral-print summer dress fluttering.

'Who were you?'

She popped the photo in her book, patted Gin and headed out.

At Bondi Beach, a cool salty breeze tossed her hair. She crossed the road and gazed towards the waves rolling onto the white sand. Red and yellow flags flapped in the wind. Quite a few people had staked out a spot to sunbake. She didn't blame them. It was a beautiful day. Warm for April. Her favourite time to visit the beach was after the summer months. The crowds were smaller and no sweltering heat. She loved the fresh, briny breeze that filled the air—and even the seagulls who squalled at her for a sneaky scrap. Her stomach rumbled. She'd need some fuel for her walk.

She found a little café and settled at an outdoor table on the main parade. After ordering a coffee and a toasted cheese and ham sandwich, she settled in to read.

'Hello?'

Olivia placed her finger on the page and glanced up. A flush of adrenaline awakened goosebumps on her skin.

Sebastian stood in front of her. Her heart slammed at the sight of him. His chestnut hair was wet, and his black wetsuit was rolled down past his taut bronze stomach. Olivia caught herself staring at his broad chest, noting his defined muscles and chest hair. A warm flush spilled across her chest. She quickly looked away and adjusted the menu in front of her.

'Hello.' Her mind shot to his offer of a movie and how she'd floundered to end the call, refusing him.

Olivia dropped her book onto the pavement. She reached down to grab it, but her chair tilted, and she stumbled off the seat. Sebastian's cool hand wrapped around her arm and steadied her.

'Has that been laced with something harder?' He smiled and nodded at her second cappuccino.

'No.' She flicked away the memory of finishing the bottle of vodka last night to help her sleep. She knew exactly what was causing her current jitters. She avoided making eye contact. Was he also feeling weird about the call? Maybe not. After all, he'd come over to say hello.

'I'm sorry about last time,' she blurted as he released her arm. 'You know, not being able to go to the movies when you asked.'

'I'm going to blame Michael J Fox. Not your type, eh?' His eyes shone with kindness. 'It's all good. It was last minute. Maybe another time.' Sebastian leant the surfboard onto the café's wall and reached down to pick up her book, then chased her bookmark as it fluttered away on the pavement.

Olivia's face heated even more when she caught herself staring at the muscles on his back. Her tummy tingled as she imagined reaching up and brushing away the sand that clung to his shoulders.

'Good?'

'What?' Olivia's heart slammed into the base of her throat. *Busted.*

'The book.' He placed the bookmark inside the front cover and handed her the book. 'I'm afraid your spot's lost.'

Olivia couldn't believe the words that came out of her mouth next. 'Would you like to join me?' She took in a small breath. 'To make up for saying no. To the movie. And the dinner.' Olivia pushed her hands onto her thighs to stop herself from babbling.

'Yeh, I'm starving. Been out surfing since early this morning.' He rubbed his naked stomach. 'Let me put the board back in my car and change out of my wetsuit.' He nodded up the road. 'The car's just up the hill.'

'Would you like me to order for you?'

'Yeh, they do a mean full breakfast.'

Olivia watched as he jogged towards his car, carefree and barefoot, the board tucked under his arm.

Oh my God, she'd made the first move. She grinned. She could almost hear Demi and Poppy screaming.

SEBASTIAN STRETCHED LONG and wide like a bronzed starfish. 'That hit the spot. Thanks for ordering it for me.'

'It was fascinating to watch you wolf it down. I reckon David Attenborough would've loved doing a piece on the eating habits of hungry Aussie men,' she said teasingly, surprising herself. She realised she was relaxed like she was with Demi.

Friends. They were becoming friends. She liked that. It felt safer.

Sebastian bunged on an Attenborough accent. 'The abundance of eggs and bacon attracts surfie dudes to the sidewalk café in the beachside suburb of Bondi. Their ferocious appetites from hours of surfing and dumping make for some uncouth behaviour. They shove food into their mouths, chewing loudly and groaning with delight.'

Olivia laughed. The accent was actually pretty good. 'Very clever. I bet there isn't a dull moment in your class.'

'No, there isn't.' Then a seriousness replaced his smile. 'Are you sure we're okay?'

'Yes.' Olivia flicked the pages of the novel sitting on the table. She focused on the swooshing sound. He was so kind, and she felt silly for reacting the way she had on the phone. 'I'm sorry.'

'Nothing for you to be sorry about. It's just I thought we were getting on well.' His blue eyes probed. 'Then the cold shoulder.' He raised his shoulders momentarily and leant a little closer to her. 'Did I say something? Do something to upset you?'

Before she could reply, he reached over and placed his hand on her arm. His expression was gentle. 'Maybe I'm not someone you're keen on hanging out with, but I thought brunch just now was pretty good. The same goes for our picnic. So I've just been a bit confused about why you hung up so quickly when I rang and asked you to the movies.'

The chatting of neighbouring tables, the clinking of cutlery and the hissing of the coffee machine faded away, and the world stilled.

He moved his hand on top of Olivia's. 'Now, don't get cross at Demi.'

Olivia snapped her head up and looked at Sebastian. 'What did she say?' Her heart pounded. Had she tried to play matchmaker?

Sebastian held up his hands. 'She told me you and your mum were in an accident, and that's when you lost your mum.'

A jolt of unease hit her. She stared out across Campbell Parade and watched the swell of the ocean. Swimmers dotted the waves like Smarties on a blue-frosted cake. A little girl's squeal caught her attention, and she watched the girl's father throw her up onto his oiled shoulders. Her mother laughed.

Sebastian followed Olivia's gaze. 'She also told me she's been encouraging you to find out more about the items. You mentioned you didn't know your dad. She's also concerned that maybe there's stuff about your mum you didn't know. Pretty heavy stuff.'

She nodded. She felt lost, with no sense of where she belonged.

'Of course ...' He stopped and studied her face. 'It's up to you, but maybe the items are the answers to everything you've wanted to know.'

She considered this, then flicked open the book and took out the photo, which she handed to Sebastian. 'She looks so happy. I've never seen her *this* happy. Look at that smile. Should I just remember her like this? Or dig around and uproot something that will change everything?'

Sebastian let out a whistle. 'Man, she's a stunner.' He studied the photo of Olivia's mum standing in front of an Art Deco apartment. 'I can see where you get your looks from.'

Olivia placed her hand over her scar and kneaded her lips together.

'She must've had blokes falling over her.'

She shook her head. 'She wasn't interested. Mum hated the fact that she looked like that. She'd only wear a little mascara and red lipstick and kept her hair in a simple style. When her hair went grey, she never dyed it. It's like she was trying to hide her beauty.'

As Sebastian studied the photo, his eyes widened. 'I know this apartment.' He stood up, and his excitement seemed to spill out of him. He paid for their meal and then grabbed her hand.

'Come on.'

She let him lead her north up Campbell Parade. Trepidation filled her mind as her curiosity raced to keep up.

OLIVIA HELD THE PHOTO TIGHT.

She studied the sky-blue Art Deco apartment and then looked down at the black-and-white photo. The only difference was that instead of her mother in a floral dress blowing a kiss, out front was a white Nissan Navara ute. Two beefy workmen were having a smoke as they sat on the gutter.

'It's the same building. Isn't it?' She held up the photo.

It had a curved front facade with double-hung windows at the side and two single windows that faced out over Campbell Parade towards Bondi Beach and across the Pacific Ocean.

Sebastian took the photo. 'No doubt about it.' He turned it over. 'May 1964.'

'May ...' She quickly calculated. *Nine months before I was born.* Her mind sidestepped the jolt that nipped at her chest. 'It's a beautiful building. What a view, though the windows are so small.'

'They didn't have air conditioning back when it was built, probably in the twenties or thirties. Smaller windows allowed the ocean breeze in but kept most of the heat out.'

Olivia turned to Sebastian, grateful he hadn't made the same connection. 'How do you know that?'

'I did a BA in history, remember?' He grinned. 'I loved it, especially all the research. Always have. I also dabbled in architectural history. Art Deco is my favourite style.'

She looked at him with a raised eyebrow. 'This building, the bookshop and my apartment are Art Deco.'

'I know.' Sebastian winked. 'My secret's out. I'm only interested in being your friend to get close to the apartment.'

Olivia laughed and swiped at his upper arm. 'Very funny.' But a little morsel of disappointment pinged in her chest at the word *friend*. She flicked it away. 'So what would you do if you were me?'

He looked up at the building again. 'We should go to the council or research the building, or the stamp duty office to see who owned the building, or who owns the apartments today. It might still be the original owners. A lot of these apartments stay in the family.'

She chewed her lip. 'I don't know if I could do that. I'd feel like I'm intruding.'

Sebastian placed his hand gently on her forearm. 'It might be public record. And I'll help you.'

If she had someone like Sebastian helping her, then maybe she could grab onto her courage rather than let it quiver in the corner of her mind. Demi had also offered. Well, pleaded. Maybe she could ask Bertie too. She hadn't just lived in the sixties—she'd shaken and assaulted the decade with passion and gusto.

She tucked the photo back into her book. 'I think my planned walk to Bronte might help me untangle my thoughts.' *And emotions,* she thought.

'Would you like me to come with you?' His face beamed with a genuine desire to help.

She shook her head. 'Maybe we could meet at a café in Bronte?' she stammered. 'After my walk. But I'm buying you a coffee.'

'Deal. Besides, you still owe me.'

'Owe you?' Olivia frowned. What was he talking about?

'For my storytelling superpowers.'

Olivia laughed. 'Well, I can't get out of it now, can I?'

'Nope.' He smiled and lifted his face to the breeze. 'Smell that air.'

Olivia inhaled deeply, taking in the woody banksia bushes and the salt off the sea breeze.

Today, life wasn't as sad. Maybe she could just focus on that for now.

CHAPTER 9

Along the four-kilometre walk, Olivia stopped to study the photo of her mother. Who was making her laugh like that? The sound of her mum's laugh floated into her memory. She remembered her happiness as something that was bundled up—soft and understated.

Maybe she wouldn't find all doom and gloom in the trunk.

The questions filtered in. Did any of this have anything to do with her conception? A tight cluster of dread and curiosity pinched at her chest.

The expensive items baffled her most: Why did she keep them hidden? Why keep them at all? And who was Viviana? Was the camera her mother's? Why had she never taken photos of Olivia with the fancy camera in the trunk? And all those photos of Sydney from the 1960s—why keep them hidden? And the biggest question: How would Olivia find the answers?

When she arrived in Bronte, her heart skipped a beat. There he was, sitting at a small table at the café they'd agreed to meet at, relaxed and reading a book.

Sebastian gazed up and shielded his eyes from the afternoon sun. 'How was it?'

'Good. Though my muscles will complain tomorrow.' Olivia sat down in the chair Sebastian pulled out for her. 'Is it good?' She pointed at the book—*The Secret Diary of Adrian Mole*.

'Yeh, funny. Clare told me about it.'

Olivia swallowed. Every time he mentioned Clare, insecurity reached in and shook her confidence. She was no match with her thick, ugly scar.

Let it go, she told herself. She was damaged. There were heaps of prettier girls in Sydney. Sebastian could take his pick.

They were friends. And it was good to have another friend. She didn't have many, though she didn't want many. All she needed was contentment and purpose in an uncomplicated life—one where she could finally escape the shame and guilt. Without the help of vodka.

But she managed her drinking. She often reminded herself it was under control. She couldn't lose her job and didn't want to lose Bertie's respect. Since becoming the manager, she'd worked at not letting herself become catatonic with drink. She limited her consumption to one at a time, or no more than two, and never when she worked. Once again, she promised herself she'd stop completely.

'Olivia?' He was frowning slightly. 'Have you decided what to do?'

'What?' She reached out to grab the glass of water in front of her and knocked it over onto the table. 'Oh, no.' As she reached for a napkin, she bumped the little vase of flowers into the pool of water now dripping over the edge of the table. 'Sorry.' She felt her cheeks burst into flames.

'Only water,' Sebastian said as the server came over to help wipe it up.

'Sorry,' Olivia said to the server, who scowled at her, making her shrink even smaller.

'I wonder who stole her good mood,' Sebastian said as she huffed off.

Olivia could feel tears stinging her eyes and cursed internally. She hated making a scene in public.

Sebastian studied her. 'Are you okay? It was just water.'

Olivia couldn't hold it back any longer. The pressure cooker of anxiety and fear exploded. 'It's all too much,' she said with a quiet sob.

Sebastian leant across to the empty table next to them, pilfered some paper napkins and handed them to her. She blew her nose and became even more embarrassed when a loud snort trumpeted out.

Sebastian moved in close. 'You can trust me, Olivia,' he said, sotto voce.

'Sebastian.' Olivia took a deep breath and focused on the swimmers in the distance. 'I need to tell you something. It isn't fair if I don't.'

'Boyfriend?' His eyebrows knitted together.

She laughed with surprise. 'No.'

'Okay.' He gave her an encouraging look.

'I'm afraid of cars. Being in them.' She avoided eye contact. 'And I don't drive. I'm afraid of driving.' She dared a glance at him, expecting to see him looking at her as if she were from another planet.

Instead, he held her gaze, and gentleness flickered in his eyes. 'Okay.' He nodded. 'It all makes sense. That's why you avoided me when I offered to pick you up to go to the movies. Right?'

Olivia nodded. 'It's pathetic, I know.'

Sebastian grabbed her hand. 'No, it isn't. People have all sorts of phobias. Man, I'm afraid of spiders. I freeze up. You want to see pathetic, put a tiny garden spider in my line of vision and I lose it. Like a baby.' He laughed.

With that, her courage increased. 'That accident you said Demi told you about—it was a car accident. I was thirteen.'

'Is that where you got the scar?'

Olivia reached up and covered it, nodding. Sebastian moved her hand away and then held it.

'Never hide who you are,' he said.

She cleared her throat and stared at her coffee cup, not knowing how to respond to his kindness. 'We were running late. I refused to get in the car. I was angry at her.' The words burst from her, gaining momentum. 'She told me to stop pestering her about who my dad was. I needed to know for a biology assignment on genetics. It was embarrassing only having my mum's name on the chart—we had to present our findings to the class. She refused to understand how I felt. I said some pretty horrible things.' The memory pushed to the forefront of her mind, fuelling her shame. 'Anyway, it was early November, and a storm had brewed over the ocean. The radio said it was going to be a bad one. Flash flooding, lightning strikes, torrential rain.' She swallowed. 'Mum didn't want me to wait at the bus stop because it had no shelter. She planned to drop me off at school and then head up to Gosford Hospital for her shift. She was a nurse.'

Tears threatened again. She took a sip of coffee and swallowed hard, trying to push away the desire for a dash of vodka.

'Mum was furious at me. I've never seen her like that.' She focused on the waves rolling onto the wet sand. 'I caused the car accident,' she whispered, years of pain leaking out with the words. She peeked up at Sebastian. His face held no judgement, only concern. 'I screamed at her. I wanted to know why she wouldn't tell me who my father was. I told her that she was selfish and had no right to keep it from me. It was raining so hard, and then it came out of nowhere.' Olivia wiped away the tear that had escaped onto her cheek.

'What?'

'She ran a stop sign because she was telling me to just leave it. We could hardly see the road. One minute, we were driving straight; the next, there was an ear-piercing shriek. It was demonic.' She shuddered. 'Then an earth-shattering bang before I was thrown against the window. A truck had crashed into our car. It smashed into her side before sending us flying. We flipped over and over until the car slammed into a tree on the side of the road. On Mum's side.'

Olivia realised Sebastian was holding her hand, stroking the top with his thumb. Demi was the only other person she'd shared the full story with. Feeling the tension inside her chest unfurl like a bud releasing its petals, she let the tears fall unchecked. 'I was trapped. Mum lay next to me, barely breathing, telling me she loved me.' A loud sob escaped, and she covered her mouth. 'She whispered that I was the best thing she'd ever done. That she'd done it all for me.'

Sebastian shifted his chair closer, collected her in his arms, and held her tight, making soft shushing sounds in her hair. She felt safe in his protective embrace. Safer than she'd felt in years.

When there were no more tears, Olivia pulled back. 'You're—' She bit her lip.

Sebastian cocked his head, looking at her with curiosity. 'What?'

'Nice. You're so nice.'

'I wasn't so nice when I was a pimply teenager. Remember? I caused a lot of headaches for everyone, especially Nonna. She did it tough. I really put her through the wringer. You know,' he continued, 'blaming yourself isn't going to bring her back. Your mum wouldn't want you to live with this guilt. Shit happens. We're not perfect, and we make mistakes. All we can do is rebuild and heal. Make amends.'

'How did you ...?'

'Get back on the straight and narrow?'

Olivia nodded.

'Marcus and my form master, Mr Russell, helped. He took me under his wing. I had to do community service and got paired up with a senior boy who mentored me. Fergus. That's how I got to know him. He was a senior and a prefect.'

He squeezed her hand. 'Let's get out of here. I think we both need to let our hair down.'

SEBASTIAN PULLED a faded photo of his mum and dad out of his wallet and handed it to her. 'I was twelve, and my brother was sixteen. This was taken in the Barossa Valley in South Australia.' Sebastian sat in a large wine glass—a huge novelty sculpture typical of Australia's love affair with "big things"—a younger version of his broad smile plastered across his face. 'Our last big holiday together. Two years later, Mum and Dad were gone.'

Olivia put down her wine. 'I'm really sorry.'

'They were coming back from a wedding in Toowoomba. Dad worked at an insurance company in the city, and he could only take the Friday off work.' Sebastian finished his beer. 'They reckon he fell asleep at the wheel. There was alcohol in his system. He liked to drink too much.' He pushed the beer glass away. 'I know I drink, but I hate the abuse of it.'

Olivia swallowed hard again and bit her lip. She left the last of the wine in the glass.

'They both died instantly. The coroner said Mum was also asleep when they crashed. The only thing that's given me any peace is they wouldn't have known what happened. Nonna, my dad's mum, was broken.' Sebastian leant forward and rested his chin on his hands. 'I was angry and hurt. That's why I started running around with the wrong crowd. I had these massive punch-ups with Marcus. He'd get so angry that I was making Nonna cry.'

It made sense, but still, Olivia was shocked. Sebastian was so even-keeled. Warm and friendly. 'I just can't imagine you being like that.'

'I was young, stupid and angry.' He put the photo back into his wallet. 'Olivia, we all make mistakes.'

Olivia was silent. Sebastian hadn't caused his parents' accident. That was the difference. What Sebastian had shared only fed the guilt festering inside her. She wanted to disappear, to drink. Would Sebastian continue to be so understanding if he knew that she was drinking to numb her pain? He'd lost his parents because his dad had been drinking. *But my drinking isn't the same*, she thought. *I'm not driving. I'm not hurting anyone.* As soon as the thought formed, a chill shuddered through her body. Then why did no one know about it? Why the secret?

She shoved the questions away. She was doing much better. Doing it less. It wasn't happening every day. Lately, when she needed to, it was only a sneaky little shot, 'a little toddy', as Shirley used to say when she sipped port after dinner. Feeling connected to the people in her life also helped.

But she couldn't deny that the burning desire to belong to a family still pulled her under sometimes. She couldn't keep living like this. For now, she kept herself afloat, but for how long?

Maybe knowing who her mother really was would help. Maybe she needed to uncover what all the items in the trunk meant after all. Maybe that could free her.

'THANKS FOR THE COFFEE.' Outside her door, Sebastian jammed his hands into the pockets of his jeans. He almost looked a bit shy. 'It's great to spend time with an adult. There's only so much talk on *Game Boy* and Polly Pockets a bloke can handle.' He grinned.

Olivia chuckled. 'I don't know, those Polly Pockets are all the rage.' She chewed her bottom lip and met his eye. 'So, if the offer's still there, I'd like it if you'd help me. Only if you have time,' she added quickly. He made everything seem possible. She wanted—needed—this kind of confidence. Plus, she really liked being around him. Her heart quickened.

'Are you sure?'

He stopped and turned towards her. His blue eyes danced. 'When I make an offer, I make it sincerely.'

'Okay. Thank you.' She rubbed her scar. 'It's just ... I don't know how to start. Where do I start?'

'We start with questions. Questions for each item. And we make a list of what we know. It's like research at uni. We look at what we have and ask questions about what we need.'

Olivia hadn't thought of it that way. He was right—it was like doing research for a history assignment. The thought eased her worry a little.

'We can hatch out a plan. The school holidays start in a few weeks, and we can get cracking on it then.'

'That'll be great. I'll call Poppy and see if she wants to work extra hours. Bertie's always trying to get me to take holidays. I've got heaps saved up.'

'How about I come over this week after school? Then we can organise ourselves.'

'I'll tell Demi too.' Olivia suppressed a smile. Demi was going to love this.

CHAPTER 10

It had been a week since Sebastian agreed to help. And Olivia had been waiting a week for Sebastian to contact her and tell her he'd changed his mind. To her relief, and giddiness, he was still coming.

Demi was also coming, of course. She wouldn't miss an opportunity to hang out with a hot guy, especially when she was hoping to set him up with her best friend.

Olivia had set out the photos and letters on the coffee table. She held up the picture of a young Rosemary wearing a shapeless white shift dress, standing next to a woman wearing a dark hairnet. She had solid arms and a scowl on her face. She looked to be in her late fifties. Would she be alive? And if she so, where would she be and what would she remember?

The gowns hung on a clothes rack next to the credenza in her living room. These were what really intrigued her. How could her mother, who'd always been so frugal, have afforded Dior and Givenchy gowns? Her head spun with the possibilities.

Demi's voice drifted up through the open French doors. 'Oh, Olivia, come hither. Come let down your hair.'

Olivia moved to the balcony and leant over. Demi stood on the pavement, her hands filled with Tupperware containers.

Olivia skipped down the stairs and bumped into Sebastian when she stepped onto the path. He caught her and pulled her in close to stop her from falling.

'Whoa, you're not abandoning ship before we've even started, are you?'

'Sorry, did I hurt you?'

'I'll live.' He peeped into the paper bag he was carrying. 'Not sure about these lemon slices.'

'Hello, lovebirds! Some help, please.' Demi handed Olivia more food.

Embarrassment assaulted her, and she turned and glared at Demi, who grinned back.

'What's all this?' Olivia asked.

'Mum made you a bunch of food. You know she has a soft spot for you. You're the perfect daughter. Quiet, smart, and you "dress the way girls should".' She turned to Sebastian. 'Mum loves a shirt and vest number.'

'Hullo, Olivia!' Mrs Kokkinos called from down the road.

Demi rolled her eyes. 'Speak of the devil.'

Mrs Kokkinos waved and walked up, a broom in her hand. 'I gave food.'

Olivia hugged her and took in her apple and rosemary scent. 'Thank you. But it's too much.'

'It is nothing. You are too skinny. I know this will be a big job. Demi has said.' She placed her hand on Olivia's face. 'I know it will be sad, too. The food will make your heart stronger. Yes?'

She smiled. 'Yes. It will help.'

'Hello?' Demi's voice cut into the moment.

'Demi. Be patient.' Mrs Kokkinos squeezed Olivia's hand. 'Go. I am here if you need me.'

Olivia kissed her on the cheek. 'Thank you.'

'Demi. Be a good girl.' Mrs Kokkinos turned and began sweeping the front of the bookshop, making her way past the chemist and video store towards her shop.

'She's so nice,' Olivia said to Demi.

'You can have her. Come on, let's get this started. I need a smoke.'

'I think you're lucky she looks out for you. You'd miss her if she wasn't around.'

———————

SEBASTIAN STUDIED THE ITEMS. 'This is a good start.'

'I numbered them all.' Olivia picked up her notebook. 'See, and I've labelled them.'

'I take it back. This is a great start. You're all over it. My work is done.' He feigned leaving.

She chuckled. She loved how at ease his sense of humour made her feel. She held up the bag of lemon slices and shook them. 'Well, I guess you'll miss out on these.'

'You got me. I'll stay. But only for the slices.' He winked.

'As much as I'm just *so* loving this banter'—Demi rolled her finger in their direction—'I think music is needed. I brought a mixtape.' She put it in the player, and the dulcet tones of Mama Cass floated into the living room. 'I thought it would help put us in the era.'

'That's a great idea,' Olivia said. She scanned the spread around her—photos, unsent letters, designer dresses and shoes, expensive jewellery, a camera, some undeveloped film, tickets to a Dusty Springfield concert at Sydney Stadium, old birthday and Christmas cards, vinyl singles, receipts for school and boarding fees, and torn magazine articles from *Woman's World*, a magazine no longer in circulation.

'Is that all?' asked Demi.

Olivia's mind was drifting off into a fantasy about finding her father and finally having more family. The thought excited her and made her very nervous at the same time. She suddenly wished she were alone so she could take comfort with a few gulps of vodka. The bottle tucked under her arm as she curled up tight, under the covers, waiting to disappear into a numbed blackness.

'Livvie.' Demi snapped her fingers. 'Geez, you've been so distracted lately.'

'What? Yep. All of it.'

'Are you okay?' asked Sebastian.

'I just don't know where to start.' Olivia sighed and sunk into the sofa.

Sebastian sat next to her. 'This is a big job. But we can do it. We just need to break it down. Remember, think of it as a history assignment with intricate research. And mystery. See it with a different mindset.'

Demi plonked herself down on the coffee table in front of them both. 'Sebastian's right. When I did history with Mr Robbins—a hottie, by the way—he used to tell us that history was more about asking questions than knowing facts.'

'Demi's right. I say the same thing to the kids. If it works for grade five students, it'll work for us.'

Olivia shrugged and tugged out a smile. She was grateful she had support. 'Thank you,' she said, pushing aside her uneasiness about what her mother's secret might uncover.

Sebastian gave her a quick bump with his shoulder. Tiny flutters tickled her stomach, and she jumped up to get a notepad and pens. Facing away from Sebastian, she placed her hands on her cheeks to cool them down. *Keep it together.*

'Wait for it.' Demi slotted a new tape into the cassette deck, and Kelly Marie's 'Feels Like I'm in Love' blasted through the small speakers.

'I thought the mixtape was all sixties,' Olivia said.

'We need some fun stuff too. Stuff to dance to. This could become all too serious, and dancing chases the blues away.'

'Demi.' Olivia hugged her. 'You're not just a pretty face.'

'No. I am certainly not.'

DEMI'S PLAN TO stop and dance to a favourite song had been a lifesaver. For Olivia, it kept things fun despite her uncertainty. The very nature of it all, having been kept secret, worried her. Secrets meant bad things. She knew this better than anyone. Her mother was gone. All because of Olivia's relentless need to know who her father was.

Olivia shook away the pain that had crept in and studied the pages of questions she'd written. They all blurred together. Her bum had gone numb, and her brain had gone to mush.

Sebastian stood and stretched. 'Remind me. What've we got so far?'

Olivia cleared her throat. 'We know Mum went to the Cross a fair bit and the botanical gardens and Bondi.' Olivia held up some photos.

Demi shuffled through others. 'There's this apartment. And she's in a lot of them with'—she flicked through a second lot of photos— 'this gorgeous man.'

'And we know where that apartment is,' Sebastian said. 'I mean, you can't miss it with its sky-blue paint.'

'What else?' Demi peeked over Olivia's shoulder.

'Mum is with this nurse in several photos.' Olivia held up a photo, then turned it over. 'Marie Middleton. St Elizabeth's, 1963. Maybe a close friend.'

'They look the same age. How old would your mum be now?'

'Fifty.'

'So this Marie would be about the same age. All we need to do is find her. She never came to visit your mum?'

'Not that I can remember.'

Olivia regarded the items strewn across her living room and

sighed. 'This is really hard.' She held up the notebook. 'All we have is more questions and no answers.'

'That's not true.' Sebastian sat next to her again. 'We have things we can start finding out about, and we have names. May I?' He held out his hand for the notebook and ripped out a blank page, which he handed to Demi. 'Write these names down. Big, bold writing, please. Marie Middleton. Friend.'

'Best friend,' Demi said.

'How can you tell?' Olivia asked

'Because I'm yours and I can tell.'

Olivia nudged Demi and smiled.

Sebastian continued to flick through the notebook. 'There's this Jack Emerson.'

'And a Lacey Hunter,' Demi said. 'They're in all the articles your mum cut out and saved.'

'And we know they got married.' Olivia scooted across the floor to retrieve the yellowing clipping announcing Jack and Lacey's engagement.

'If they got married. I mean, people get engaged and never go through with it.'

Sebastian nodded. 'Demi's right. Okay, there's also Pamela and Eleanor.'

'Any more names?' Demi flicked her lighter. 'I need a ciggie.'

'Just William Templeton, whose name is on your boarding school receipts,' Sebastian said. 'And his firm: Morris, Templeton and Gray. Someone was paying your fees when you went to Our Lady Queen of Peace after your mum passed. You need to call them. Write that down on the to-do list, Demi.'

'His name is also on the letter that came with the trunk.' Olivia shuffled through some of the items. 'See.' She held it up and pointed to the signature. Mr William Templeton.

'There are also these unaddressed letters to a Viviana.' Demi flicked through the bundle. 'Plus this one to a Carmela.'

'Which Mum wrote in an Italian dialect and never sent.' Olivia slumped back again.

Sebastian leant back next to her. 'You're right, it's a big job,' he said, as if reading her thoughts. 'But you need to ask yourself—do you want to know? If you do, like I keep saying, it's no different from a university assignment.'

Sebastian stood and held out his hand to help Olivia get up. 'You know, we all need a break, and I need some food. What you reckon, Demi?'

Demi checked her watch. 'My cousins are coming for dinner, and I need to get home. Can I change here before I go?'

'Sure,' said Olivia, and then gave her a look. 'When are you going to let your aunties know you don't like the good-Greek-girl look?'

'Never.' She winked at Sebastian. 'It's a Greek thing.' She scooted into Olivia's bedroom and, as she was closing the doors, said, 'Now, don't you two get up to anything without me there to chaperone you.'

Heat punched Olivia's cheeks. 'Demi!'

'I'll be the perfect gentleman.' He turned to Olivia. 'Let's put all this away. Have you got something to keep it in order?'

'Order? Like a box?'

Sebastian laughed. 'It's a teacher thing. I gather by the look on your face you have nothing.'

'Not really. Just the trunk it all came in.'

His brow creased as he smiled at her.

Olivia's mind turned over. 'We need to make connections. Like they do on those police shows—but I don't have a whiteboard.'

Sebastian scanned the living room. 'You have the wall over there, and I have tons of butcher's paper, markers and Blu Tack.'

Excitement bubbled inside her. This could work. She could find the answers she'd wanted to know since she was a kid. 'Thank you, Sebastian.'

'For what?'

'For being a good bloke,' Demi said as she stepped into the living room. She was dressed in a pair of shapeless jeans and a tucked-in cream shirt with an olive vest over it. A pair of sensible brown Mary Janes had replaced her Doc Martens.

'Whoa.' Sebastian's stunned face made Olivia giggle.

Demi held up her hand. 'Don't say a word. You're lucky I trust you. No one outside my family, other than Livvie, has ever seen me dressed like this. This is how I have to dress when I visit the rels. Mum gave up years ago. We made a truce: she accepts my style as long as my aunties never see it.' She put her backpack over her shoulders. 'I like you.' She stepped up close to Sebastian and gave him her don't-tempt-me look.

Sebastian put his hand on his heart. 'Your fashion secret is safe with me.'

'Good.' Demi opened the door and turned around. She gave Sebastian a pointed look. 'You look after my bestie over there. Remember, I'm Greek. We get furious when one of ours is hurt.' She grinned.

'Really, Demi.' Olivia pushed her out the door and closed it after her.

'Sorry about that.' She was going to gag Demi the next time she saw her. She'd finally been feeling a little more at ease, but now a fresh wave of embarrassment had been released.

'What? Demi? Never. I love her. She has spirit.'

'That she does.'

Olivia placed the items back in the trunk with care while Sebastian threw a pale-pink striped bedsheet over the clothes on the rack.

'Are you hungry?' he asked. 'I was thinking of a hearty pub dinner.'

At the mention of dinner, Olivia's stomach lurched. 'That would be great. The Annandale? I've never been there.'

'The pub that's just down the road? In fact ...' Sebastian stepped out onto the verandah and leant over the brick balcony. 'You can see it from here—you've never partaken in its fare?'

'Nope.' Olivia stepped onto the balcony. 'I don't even need to see it. I can hear the shouts and singing from inside. Especially when the doors are wide open.'

'Well, let's take you down there, and you can immerse yourself in all the hoo-ha.'

'You're on.' Little bubbles of excitement filled her chest. She stopped and realised her deer-frozen-in-the-headlights worry had leapt away. Tracks of shyness remained, but she felt a little more confident being with Sebastian.

One adventure at a time.

CHAPTER 11

Rosemary

November 1963

Rosemary's feet ached. She'd got off the bus two stops early to get away from the advances of a couple of men travelling home from work. Both wore wedding rings. Their poor wives were probably at home cooking dinner and looking after some little children, and here they were, making sweet talk and standing too close to her.

Seeing her name on her English grammar textbook, one had asked where the name Benito came from. She manoeuvred the book underneath another, wanting to avoid drawing any attention to her status as a migrant. She wished she'd kept the books in her shoulder bag.

'*Obbrobrioso*,' she'd muttered as the bus drove away. Disgraceful.

The men in Sicily were forward, but they kept their distance. They knew fathers and older brothers would visit them. Here, the men were too confident. The other migrant women who worked in the kitchen at the hospital told her it was because they looked down on migrant women. It burnt Rosemary up. Just because their English wasn't good didn't mean they weren't smart. Or that they were easy.

Rosemary passed the main entrance of St Elizabeth's and hurried around the back. She glanced down at her watch as she turned the corner and collided with a doctor.

'*Mi dispiace.* I am sorry,' she said as she bent to pick up the books scattered at her feet. 'I was in a hurry. I am late for work.' She steadied herself and placed the books inside the fabric shoulder bag she'd made from an old dress.

'Do you work here?' the young doctor asked as he handed her one of the fallen books.

'*Si.* I mean, yes. In the kitchen. I take the food to the patients.'

'You work with Gladys?'

'Yes. And I am very late. She will not be happy, but thank you for helping me.'

'Hang on.' He placed his hand on her arm and stopped her. 'If you work for Gladys, you'll need a drink. She's one tough cookie.' He gave her a hopeful smile.

'I am very sorry. I do not go out with people I work with.' Painful memories flooded Rosemary's mind. Memories of her time in Genoa, just before she boarded the ship to come to Australia.

Her friend Marie had warned her about the younger doctors. 'Full of themselves. They think they're God's gift to women.'

'"Full of"?'

'You know?' Marie had kissed her arm, then burst out laughing.

'Come on,' the doctor said, moving in too close and winking at her. 'It'll be our secret.'

It took all of Rosemary's strength to not slap him. 'Secrets are bad. You should be ashamed of yourself.' She spun around and pushed through the old wooden doors into the staff entrance.

'Hi, Hollywood.' Marie ran up as Rosemary punched her time-card. 'Grumpy Gladys is on the warpath looking for you. Here.' She handed her a smock, then grabbed some clean linen napkins from a trolley brought up from the laundry. 'Tell her you were grabbing some cleaner napkins. You know how she is about cleanliness.'

'Yes. If you cannot eat off it, it is not clean enough,' they said in unison, then collapsed on each other and burst out laughing.

Marie checked the watch pinned above her right breast on her nurse's uniform. 'Shit, I'm due back in five. Have you thought about tomorrow night?'

'I do not know. I am tired.' Rosemary patted her bag. 'I have a lot of learning to do.'

Marie snatched the bag from her. 'Not this weekend, Hollywood. You're coming out with us.'

Rosemary reached for it, but Marie held it behind her back. 'Nope. I'm holding this for ransom.'

Rosemary did enjoy going out with the girls. They always had fun. But she also wanted to be good at English. To get into university and become a doctor. Her hard work had helped her achieve excellent results in her leaving certificate last month.

'Maybe one night will be good.'

'There you go. That's what I like to hear.' Marie gave Rosemary a quick hug. 'Toodeloo,' she called out as she ran up the stairs back to the ward. Her footsteps echoed along the old marble staircase.

Rosemary raced into the kitchen, already a few minutes late.

———

THE BUS DROPPED ROSEMARY, Marie, Pamela and Eleanor off at the top of William Street. Rosemary untied the scarf that protected her updo—a broad bun fashioned with intricate rolls that weaved in and out of each other like a silken woven basket. She'd spent all Saturday morning setting it.

The large neon Coca-Cola sign, a beacon enticing people to venture into what locals called Sin City, cast its red glow on the street.

Marie had taken Rosemary to Kings Cross for the first time soon after they became friends. Most of the nurses working at St Elizabeth's Women's Hospital ventured into the Cross on their nights off.

'A cesspool of unsavoury behaviour,' Matron called it. The colourful neon street, with its moving lights, Continental restaurants, and strip joints, was open every night.

Rosemary smoothed the dress that skimmed her hips, adjusted the belt that cinched in her waist and tugged at her gloves. She was a local now. She didn't need to feel nervous, she told herself.

'You look fabulous, as always,' Marie said as she offered Rosemary a cigarette. Rosemary shook her head. 'They're light. Dunhills.'

'Maybe later.' Rosemary had spent some of her savings on a bottle of Dior's Diorissimo at Grace Brothers and hated when cigarette smoke ruined the scent.

Marie shrugged as she lit up. 'Fair enough.'

They strolled down Darlinghurst Street, merging into the crowd that strangled the footpaths. Young women sat at tables on the sidewalks, their stiff beehives and bouffant hairstyles framing hopeful faces, all looking for Mr Right.

Effervescent energy filled the early summer evening. The hum of chatter and laughter punctuated the main drag, along with lurid calls of 'tits and bits' from men with slick hair and cheap suits. Marie always grabbed her tighter, moving them closer to the road to avoid contact with these men. But these comments always made Rosemary laugh. They didn't shock her as they did her Australian friends. In Sicily, old widows used words that were much worse.

When they reached Macleay Street, the enormous new fountain that looked like a big dandelion came into view. Rosemary was looking forward to a proper Italian espresso at Piccolo Bar. In Australia, good Italian coffee was rare. The chance to speak Italian with the owner excited her the most, though. This was the only time she allowed her Italian heritage to bleed into her new life. With each year that she lived in Sydney, she allowed a little more of her Italianness to shed away and to adopt a little more of the vibrant and relaxed attitude of the Australians. Here, she enjoyed the pace, the freedoms and the modern way of life.

'DUSTY SPRINGFIELD IS COMING TO TOWN,' Eleanor said, sipping her coffee. 'One of the solicitors at work is doing the legals for her Australian tour. It's so exciting. Who knows, there might be some tickets floating about.'

'You have the best job,' Marie said with a sigh as she took a bite of her cannoli. 'Gosh, these are good. Did you eat these all the time in Italy?'

Rosemary laughed. 'No, these are delicacies. We were too poor to eat food like this. Maybe at a wedding.'

If she'd stayed in Italy, she would already be married with one, maybe two small children. She would also be working hard in the fields, harvesting olives and lemons. She gazed out at Kings Cross, at all the women who were free to go out with their friends or boyfriends. No one chaperoning them. Australia was better for women, and she was happy. But deep down, she missed her home. She missed the earthy smell of the mountains, the scents of pine and lemon trees mingled with the briny smell of the ocean. She missed speaking her language. Unlike her two older brothers, she missed her younger sister. And she worried about her mother—a sad, broken woman who'd once been the most beautiful woman in the province.

'Earth to Rosemary.' Pamela placed her hand on Rosemary's arm.

Her friends were staring at her.

'Sorry. I was thinking about how clever it would be to be a singer like Dusty Springfield,' she lied.

CHAPTER 12

Olivia
April 1989

The bookshop had been busy, and Olivia finally had some time to sort out the day's orders. A group of schoolkids screamed past the main window, and her heart pounded. School was finished for the day, which meant one thing. Sebastian would be here soon.

For a week, Sebastian and Olivia worked together, sorting out the evidence they had and how to go about finding out more. When he could, Sebastian would pop in after school with a bag of groceries and make dinner before they got to work.

Olivia was glad to have the company—someone to talk to about books and movies and all things happening in the world over a meal. And an extra brain when it came to approaching the items from her mum's trunk was a godsend.

Sometimes their fingers or arms brushed, and a peppering of tingles would run up her body. At the end of each day, when she was alone in bed, she would practise her flirting skills with Gin. She never tried when Sebastian was around. In her mind, she could run technicolour-movie-worthy scenes where everything unfurled perfectly. In reality, her confidence was a steel shutter that slammed down between the words in her mind and her mouth's ability to speak them. He did laugh at her stories about the bookshop, and occasionally she made a funny comment. Though afterwards, she could never remember it. If she could, she would've dissected these comments as if they were Shakespearean sonnets to uncover their complexity and intricacies.

Demi joined them one evening but, after that, made excuses about not being able to make it. Olivia wasn't fooled.

As much as she enjoyed spending time with Sebastian, her nerves were frayed. She constantly worried he'd discover that her mother might not have been as pure as Olivia had believed. Maybe Demi was right. Maybe she was an expensive escort. How embarrassing would that be if Sebastian found out?

Then there was Clare. She sometimes saw them having coffee in the café down the road. Clare seemed so at ease with him, always so familiar—hanging over him, laughing and touching him. She always touched him, and he never flinched. On the contrary, he seemed to enjoy the attention.

Nope. They would only be friends. This was only a silly crush. Olivia wondered if maybe she liked the attention. No man had ever paid any attention to her. She knew the scar on her face made her look ugly, and constantly being reminded of it because of questions from strangers—'What happened to your face?'—discombobulated her. It was safer to hide herself away and avoid social situations as much as possible.

Whenever she started wondering why Sebastian spent so much time with her, Olivia reminded herself that he loved history and mysteries. This whole steamer trunk business was a bit of both.

The bell rang as Sebastian walked into the bookshop. Olivia's heart fluttered, and she checked her watch. Right on time. As usual, he held a bag of groceries. But today, paint covered his chambray shirt.

'What happened to you?'

'We got a little wild in art.' He grinned.

'The mums will not be happy about cleaning paint-splattered uniforms,' Olivia said with a chuckle. 'My mum would've had kittens if I turned up home looking like a Jackson Pollock painting.'

'Brilliant comparison. The kids are fine. I'm the one they picked on.'

Poppy came in from the storeroom with a box of new releases. 'Hi there,' she said, eyeing him. 'Hard day at work?'

'You could say that.' He held up the groceries. 'I thought tonight I'd make ravioli. Nonna made some filled with feta and pumpkin.'

'I hardly ever eat ravioli,' Olivia said with a snort. 'Mum always made store-bought pasta. She never had the time. Shirley usually cooked and was a meat-and-three-veg chef.'

Poppy laughed. 'Sounds like my mum. Meat, peas and mashed potatoes. Potato salad is fancy in our house.' She shrugged and picked up the box again. 'Well, I better leave you lovebirds and do some work.'

Olivia's cheeks flushed red. 'No,' she blurted. 'We're not. I mean. We're just friends.'

Sebastian quickly looked up at the Alice in Wonderland clock above the counter. 'It's changed?'

Relief coursed through her, and she sent him a silent thank you for changing the subject. 'Yeh. Bertie found it at an auction. Would you like the Cat in the Hat one? For your classroom?'

'Sure. The kids'll love it.' He adjusted the parcels of groceries. 'I'll head up and cook some dinner while you finish here.'

'Great,' she said, focusing on putting the bookmarks back in their right compartments.

Sebastian chuckled. 'I'll need your flat keys.'

'Oh yes.' She went out the back and took them out of her backpack. For a moment, she placed her forehead against the cool wall. A giddiness rose and pushed against her heart like an ocean tide. *Come on, Olivia. Get a grip. Just friends,* she chanted to herself before returning to the counter. 'Here you are. If Gin's around, can you let him in?'

'Sure.' He picked up his groceries and headed out, the bell tinkling behind him.

She rushed over to Poppy. 'Listen. I'd hate for you to get the wrong impression, but we're just friends.'

Poppy took her hands in hers. 'I know these things.' Then she smiled and continued pricing books.

Olivia moved in front of her. 'Know what things?'

'Olivia, spending time together. Alone. Before you know it, the love bug will bite. Or you'll decide to drink more wine ...' She stopped pricing and waved the gun around. 'Do you have wine with dinner?'

'Yeh. Sebastian always brings a bottle.'

Poppy winked and clicked her tongue. 'It only takes being tipsy, and before you know it, you're bumping uglies.'

Poppy's words felt like a punch in the chest. Wasn't that what she wanted? She'd never even been kissed, yet she did think about physical intimacy—in a romantic and Hollywood movie kind of way. But the thought of being more than friends with Sebastian freaked her out. Dreaming about him was harmless, but following through on it ...

A ribbon of heat ran up her spine and she felt her lips go numb. She swallowed hard to stop the anxiety attack. This was starting to feel too familiar. The last time she'd been on the verge of one was when she presented a literary report to her tutor group at university. The first one had occurred on a school camp trip while she was on the high ropes course—ten metres up.

'I'm just going to finish the accounts in the kitchenette. You can go home once the books are priced.'

Breathe, breathe, breathe! Olivia raced to the phone and called Demi's shop.

'Kokkinos Fresh Fruit and Vegetables.'

'Demi, please, please, please come tonight and help.'

'What's going on?'

She could hear the words in her head, and they sounded pathetic. What was she going to say? I'm scared of being with Sebastian because Poppy said we might have sex?

'Livvie?'

She needed a shot of vodka. Just a nip. She could go into her bedroom and close the door to freshen up. Yep. That would help.

Her heart tore. She hadn't had vodka for a few weeks. The need had vanished. Spending time with Sebastian had allowed contentment to tiptoe into her heart, and examining the trunk's connection to her mum was filling her with joyful energy.

'I just miss you,' she croaked.

'That's so sweet. Me too. But I can't. I have to go to dinner with Stephanie's future family-in-law. Maybe tomorrow night?'

'Okay.'

Olivia placed the phone down. This was officially getting too big. The reality was, right now, at this very moment, she knew she was falling for Sebastian.

And it freaked her out.

She wished she'd never got the trunk and could go about living her safe, insignificant life, tucked away with Gin and her books and movies. She had Demi and the shop. She didn't need more. The last time she'd pushed to know more, she'd lost her mum. Maybe this time, she'd lose herself.

WHITNEY HOUSTON BLARED out of her apartment, and the front door was ajar. She'd never leave it open, even though you had to ring the buzzer downstairs to be let into the building.

Gin squeezed out and rubbed his body against her legs. 'Hello, young man. Whitney not your taste?' She picked up the cat, and he relaxed into her chest.

With tentative steps, she walked into her flat. Something on the stove held Sebastian's attention. She couldn't help but smile as he wiggled his bottom to the music and used the wooden spoon as a microphone. She revelled in how much unadulterated fun he was having, totally unaware of her presence.

When the song finished, she clapped.

Sebastian spun around. 'How long have you been standing there?'

'Long enough to know that the pasta sauce speckled over my fridge was caused by your microphone.'

'It could've been worse. I could've been listening to Phil Collins's "In the Air Tonight".'

She frowned in confusion.

'You know.' He air drummed with a spoon and spatula.

Olivia laughed. 'I think you've missed your calling.'

Positive energy oozed out of him, and just like that, her anxiety about being around Sebastian disappeared.

He turned and beamed a gorgeous smile at her, then wiped his hands and poured her a glass of white wine. 'Tell me what you think.' He pulled out a stool for her. 'Sit. Relax. I've got this great idea for our trunk project. It's superb.'

'Superb.' She giggled. 'Who says that?'

'This daggy bloke in front of you. It's one of my words of the week.'

'Dinner smells good. Your nonna would be proud of you.'

'You can tell her that yourself. She wants to meet you.'

'Me? Why?'

'I hope you don't mind. I told her about your mum's trunk and your quest. You know she really could help you with the translations.'

'Oh? And that's your idea?' Shards of anxiety returned to pierce her skin. What if the letters contained unsavoury content and tarnished her mum's reputation? She didn't want anyone to think she was a tart. The word made her insides shudder. The image didn't fit her mum.

Once again, Olivia doubted whether digging into her mother's past was the right thing to do. This wasn't respecting her and letting her rest in peace. Why did Olivia think she could disturb her secrets?

'You don't look pleased about that.'

She felt bad. He'd been so keen.

'Can I think about it?' She gave him a forced smile.

'Sure.' He put down the wooden spoon and walked over to her. 'Hey, I didn't mean to bamboozle you with it. It was just a thought.'

'I know. I'm just hungry. And tired.'

'You sure?'

'Yep.'

Sebastian settled his gentle blue eyes on her. Inside, she melted, but embarrassed by the attention, she picked up Gin and cuddled him so tight he meowed in protest. 'How long will dinner be? I was hoping to have a shower.'

'It depends. Are you a get-in-get-out kind of gal or an I'm-going-to-sing-a-whole-opera girl?'

'I'm a how-long-have-I-got-and-will-make-it-work kind of person.'

'Fifteen.'

'That'll work.'

When Olivia stepped back into her living room, she found the table set and a steaming bowl of ravioli in the middle with two fresh glasses of red wine placed beside their plates. Music drifted out of the tape deck.

'I see you found Demi's mixtapes.'

'Yeh, I've never seen so many. She's quite prolific.'

'Yes, she is. Which one did you choose?'

'The one labelled *When I feel like some pop in my life.*' Sebastian grinned and pulled out her chair.

As she sat down, Sebastian placed a present on her plate.

She picked it up. 'What's this for?'

'Open it.'

She eagerly unwrapped the paper to find a journal with a frame embedded in the cover. Inside sat a photo from a birthday lunch a few years back: one of Demi, Poppy, Bertie, and her. She laid her hand on her heart as it drummed with delight. The gift surprised her yet deeply moved her.

'Where did you get this photo?'

A broad grin crept across his face.

'Demi!' they said together.

'Whatever happens'—Sebastian tapped the photo—'this is your family. I can tell how much they all love you.'

Her heart lurched. Nobody other than Shirley and her mum—and Demi—had ever been this kind or attentive to her. She swallowed hard to stop herself from tearing up.

Sebastian sat down opposite her. 'Olivia, I want you to know that whatever happens, you call the shots. And whether you find all the answers, you hit a dead-end, or you don't find any answers, whatever happens, you have a family. This doesn't define you, okay?'

His thoughtfulness left her speechless. She touched the journal gently and opened the cover. There was a handwritten quote on the first page.

'Love is a great master. It teaches us to be what we never were.'
Molière

'DID YOU WRITE THIS?'

Sebastian laughed. 'Does my scrawl give it away?'

'Thank you.' She placed her fingers on her lips, trying to contain her emotions. A swirl of tenderness flowed through her.

Sebastian grabbed her hand from across the table. 'Listen. Some people might not think what you're doing is a big deal, but they're not you. They haven't lived your life. I get it. If I got a box of stuff from my parents, stuff I never knew about, I'd be as curious as hell. Especially if it contained stuff that didn't seem part of their lives.' Sebastian's face blazed with warmth.

And the way he gazed at her unleashed a new kind of shyness within her.

She nodded and cleared her throat. 'We better eat. I don't think your nonna intended for her ravioli to be eaten stone cold.'

Sebastian held her in his gaze for a little longer. 'No. No, she wouldn't.' A subtle look of humour flitted across his face.

The buzzer shrilled, slicing through the sudden thickness in the air.

Olivia launched towards the intercom. 'Hello?'

'It's Demi. I got away.'

Olivia pushed the button. A sliver of disappointment invaded her thoughts. The evening was going so well. She liked having Sebastian all to herself.

'Whoa!' Demi said when she walked in. She immediately stepped up to the wall covered in butcher's paper, which was plastered with notes and questions. 'You two have been busy. It's a quest wall.'

'I like that. The Quest Wall.'

Sebastian came out of the kitchen. 'Where can I put the wet tea towels?'

'The laundry in the cupboard in the main bathroom.'

Demi's eyes followed Sebastian as he walked away. 'I love watching that tush.'

'Demi!'

'So?' She sat on the couch. 'What have you two been up to?'

'Working out a plan of attack.'

'No—' Demi stopped when Sebastian headed back into the kitchen.

'Wine?' he called out.

'Love some.' Demi looked at Olivia and traced a heart with her fingers, then placed the back of her hand on her forehead and pretended to swoon.

'Stop it,' Olivia hissed. She sat next to Demi. 'He's just kind. Besides, I've told you he's quite cosy with that other teacher, Clare.'

'Is there a ring?'

'No. I don't know.'

'Then he's fair game, I say.'

'Who's fair game?' Sebastian handed a glass of wine to Demi, then Olivia.

'All those people on that wall. It looks impressive.' Demi snuck a wink at Olivia.

Olivia focused on the wall, trying to stop the blush from getting any more scarlet. Demi was right. It was impressive. They'd broken it all down into steps. People to look up, places that could reveal information and questions that could lead to answers.

'When do we get started?' Demi took a sip of wine. 'Mmm. This is excellent. You've got all the moves, don't you?' She winked at Sebastian.

'Demi!' She shoved her. 'I apologise for my friend's bad manners. She's Greek.'

'Spoken like a true smart arse, Miss Bennet,' said Demi. 'I'm impressed.'

'I am, too.' Sebastian chuckled. 'Maybe you're not the sweet young lady I assumed you were.'

Demi high-fived Sebastian.

Normally, a comment like this would've sent Olivia running for cover. But Sebastian's face was lit up. He wasn't being mean. He felt comfortable at home with Demi and her.

Clare was lucky to have him.

CHAPTER 13

Rosemary
February 1964

Four martinis appeared at their table.

'From the gentlemen at the bar,' the waitress said. 'A Valentine's cocktail.'

Marie, Pamela and Eleanor eyed Rosemary.

'You're good for free drinks,' Marie giggled, she sipped and lifted her glass at the men.

'Si,' Pamela and Eleanor chanted while raising their glasses to the men at the bar. Rosemary looked down at the drink and cursed. She didn't like this attention.

'Yeh. Listen.' Marie leant in close. 'I know you hate the attention, but you're gorgeous. Just like you've stepped out of the big screen, Hollywood.'

Marie was right—the attention unsettled her. People focused only on her appearance, never on who she was on the inside. This is what had got her into trouble in Genoa and she resented it. Under her thick dark hair and behind her green eyes was a love of learning and a desire to be more than a man's kewpie doll on a stick. She took comfort in knowing that she was with her friends tonight. Especially Marie. Marie had always been genuine, honest and kind. Their friendship had blossomed over the past four years, and they spent almost all their free time together, going to the beach, the movies, and shopping. For the first time in her life, Rosemary had a close friend. The only thing that saddened her about the friendship was that it reminded her of her sister, whom she missed every day.

Despite their closeness, Rosemary had shared little about her time in Italy or her journey to Australia with Marie. She wanted to forget. Not speaking of it helped to lock away her feelings of shame and guilt. There was nothing Marie could do about the past anyway. It was done.

Before meeting Marie, Rosemary had seen little of the city. She spent most of her time working at the hospital, taking English classes and studying at the house they all shared with its owner, Nora. She liked Nora, who had become like a mother to her. An Irish immigrant, she also knew about loss. She'd lost her husband in World War I and her oldest boy in the second war.

––––––––

THE WALLS, now faded to a dull cream, were scuffed from the trolleys that moved up and down the corridor. The floors squeaked under Rosemary's feet. On the afternoon shift, only the soft patter of nurses' footsteps echoed in the hallway. A trail of florescent tubes ran along the roof and competed for space with the exposed pipes painted to match the ceiling.

The wards, on the other hand, buzzed with chatting mothers. The cacophony of their laughter and solemn wisdom fuelled by old wives' tales or scientific titbits from women's magazines filled the rooms. In the small moments of silence, a baby cried or gurgled in the nursery.

With military precision, the nurses maintained a schedule of feeding and cuddle time. The wards were beehives, both in colour and in busyness. Faded, pasty-yellow paint clung to the walls. Neutrality dominated and frowned upon the bursts of colour from flowers in vases.

Crisp blue curtains were closed with a sharp whack to hide the practised hands of large-bosomed, stoic matrons ready to check nipples and torn and stitched vaginas. Behind billowing curtains, large, gentle yet impersonal hands, holding reams of bandages, bound engorged breasts of mothers, refusing to or unable to feed. Some lifted milk-filled breasts to little budding lips of hungry babies.

Rosemary took extra care with the single mothers. Their titles—'miss'—branded them as naughty girls who'd been unfortunate. These young women were placed in a separate part of the hospital. A different tone filled these rooms. When delivering meals and afternoon tea to them, Rosemary always offered a warm smile and a kind comment.

She preferred the single mothers' ward. There were no husbands who appalled her with their deceitful advances. In the other wards, some were so bold as to ask her out while their wives slept after a long and tiring birth. Others brazenly followed her down the hall, asking to go for a quick drink.

A few weeks after she'd started at the hospital, a husband waited outside the staff entrance. He'd tried to kiss her, and she'd gifted him with a hard slap before running down the road to catch her bus.

On that walk home, she'd decided she'd do two things: learn English very well so she wouldn't be treated like a second-class person with no intellect, and work extra hard to become a doctor. It had been her dream since she was young. Becoming a doctor would allow her to be independent, financially and emotionally.

What Rosemary saw were *egoista e arrogante*—selfish and arrogant—men. Every experience she observed further confirmed that being independent was what she desired. The men who gave her unwanted attention didn't see her as someone to love and be companions with but as a possession.

Outside, Rosemary held herself proud and strong. But inside the wards, she softened. Inside the wards was true beauty. Rosemary felt at ease with the mothers who offered heartfelt conversations. Her English improved, though her accent remained.

Eleanor always told her how romantic her accent was. 'When you talk, you sound like you're purring,' she said.

Her accent defined her, and this unnerved her.

People usually said, 'Love your accent. Where're you from?' Her favourite was 'You're not from around here, are you?'

To this, she'd often respond with a blank expression and a 'No, I am from Surry Hills.'

Marie laughed when she first heard this response. 'You're turning into a right smart arse.'

But most of all, she loved the babies. Their innocence and their sweetness.

When Matron wasn't looking, there was always a quick cuddle.

Today, during her break, as the sun dipped, she sat with Marie in their usual spot out in the courtyard, where medical and food deliveries came in. The heat of the day wafted off the cracked concrete path, burning any plants that dared to survive.

'Close your eyes,' Marie said as she stood and turned away towards her bag.

'Why?'

'You just have to trust me.'

Rosemary did as she was told, straining to hear what Marie was up to.

'Are they shut?'

'Yes.' A shadow fell over her closed eyes.

'Okay.'

She opened them to find Marie in front of her with a large gift box tied with a shimmering bow made from silver fabric. 'Happy birthday. I know it's late, but it took ages to come in. I ordered it in especially for your birthday.'

Rosemary opened the box, and her heart filled with love as she lifted out a Nikon camera. 'This is too much.'

'Nonsense. Plus, I wanted to give you a gift for getting outstanding results in your leaving certificate last year. Better late than never.' Marie shrugged, then nudged Rosemary. 'My best friend with the smartest brain.'

Rosemary arched her eyebrows at Marie.

'Don't look at me like that. Who else could work full time *and* go to night school?'

Rosemary touched the camera reverently. 'How did you know?'

'Lucky guess.'

Rosemary squinted at her.

'Okay. I saw how you looked at the cameras in the shop on George Street after our picnic in the Royal Botanic Garden.'

Rosemary remembered. The cameras on display had caught her attention. She'd been fascinated by them, but they'd also ignited the memory of Genoa.

Her throat constricted, and she pushed the fingers of shame away.

The owner of the camera shop, an elderly man, had waved to her and ambled out before Rosemary could grab Marie and walk away.

'You like taking the pictures?' he asked. His words sat in a thick accent. A migrant like her. The revelation dissolved her cool reserve. 'I am George. This is my shop. See.' He pointed to the lettering on the window, then offered his hand.

Rosemary shook it. 'I have never taken photographs.'

'I see.' He took off his glasses and polished them with a handkerchief. 'You are not from here.'

'No, I live in Surry Hills.'

'I mean you are not from Australia.'

Rosemary laughed. '*Mi dispiace*. Sorry. I am from Italy.'

'Italy. My neighbour is from Italy too. Bruno. Bruno Martini.'

'Martini is a name from the north. I am from the south. Sicilia.'

'*Vlakas*,' he chastised himself. 'I am an old Greek fool.'

Rosemary liked him. He was funny and warm. She pointed at the cameras in the window. 'Is it hard to take photos?'

'No, very easy. You just point and shoot. Want to have a look? We have a good special this month.'

Rosemary looked at Marie. 'Why not,' she said.

She soon found she loved holding the camera, looking through the viewfinder and taking photos.

George showed her an album with the types of photographs the camera could take. Rosemary traced each one with her fingers. Their corners sat tight inside little black triangles, four for each photo.

'We have lessons on Saturday afternoon and Monday at night. To get the night pictures. And we develop the film here too.'

Rosemary left the camera shop with a price and planned to save for a camera of her own.

Now, she held it. 'This is too much,' she said again.

'Nonsense,' said Marie. 'And don't you dare tell me to take it back either. It took two cigarette packets and a box of chocolate to bribe Matron so I could go and pick it up from George's.'

'But I was saving for the camera.'

'I know, and now you can use the money to pay for classes. George has booked you into your first one.'

Rosemary threw her arms around Marie. 'You are a good friend.'

She placed the camera back in the box with the silver bow. Building new memories was what Rosemary needed to focus on. Happier memories. And taking pictures would be a way to collect all new experiences. She knew that one day, it would be these photos that defined her.

CHAPTER 14

Olivia
May 1989

'Olivia!' Demi called as she entered the bookstore. 'I've got news. Wonderful news.'

She shook a piece of paper as she bounced into the back room, ceremoniously placed the note she was carrying on the table in front of her and then lit a cigarette.

Olivia yanked it from her mouth and stubbed it out in the sink. 'You know you can't smoke it in here. Paper—'

'I know, paper and fire don't mix. You sound like Bertie.'

'What do I sound like?'

Olivia and Demi spun around. Bertie was standing in the doorway dressed in a loud top with three bold stripes. Her hair was pulled up in a messy beehive, channelling a sultry Brigitte Bardot. Hot-pink glasses set off the look and magnified her bright blue eyes and fake eyelashes.

'Oh, hello Bertie, you look amazing,' Demi cooed.

'You know flattery will get you everywhere.' She glanced at the cigarette in Olivia's hand. 'But rules are rules.'

Demi grabbed the cigarette and threw it in the bin. 'What cigarette?' She grinned.

'That's my girl.'

Demi grabbed the piece of paper and shook it again. 'Look what I found.'

Bertie placed her shopping bags down on the table. 'Anyone want a cuppa?'

'I'll do that for you,' Olivia offered.

'Thank you. You're a sweetie.' She fluttered her bright-orange fingertips. 'Just had my manicure.' She sat down, kicked off her shoes and wiggled her stocking feet. 'What have you got there?' She cocked her head at Demi and looked at the crinkled paper.

Demi scooped it up and thrust it into Olivia's hand. 'Great news. A breakthrough.'

Olivia took the note. *Nora Kavanagh, 22 Vernon Street, Surry Hills.* Anxiety fizzed in her chest. 'Demi, this might be *the* Nora. How?'

'I was at the clinic with Yiayia for her doctor's appointment. As usual, they were running late, and Yiayia was getting anxious because she didn't want to miss her crochet club.'

'What's a crochet club?' Bertie asked, touching up her hot-pink lipstick.

'Oh, they don't just crochet. They knit and embroider. For the church.'

'Demi,' Olivia said, getting antsier by the second. 'About Nora?'

'What's going on?' Bertie sat up and accepted the cup of tea from Olivia.

'Go on, tell her. Bertie might help. She's old—' Demi stopped.

Olivia gave Demi her second warning glance of the day. Bertie was obsessed about her age and made sure she never appeared like an 'old decrepit thing', as she was fond of saying. She had nothing to worry about. She looked fabulous.

Bertie laughed, snuffing out any tension. 'You mean old enough? For what?'

'I found a book from a Nora to my mum,' Olivia explained. 'Tucked inside was a photo of my mum with an older woman. They were standing in front of a terrace house. I decided to try to piece together Mum's life when she lived in Sydney during the sixties.' Olivia turned to Demi. 'Do you think?'

'Why not?'

'This sounds intriguing. Why didn't you mention this before?'

Olivia looked at Demi, who shrugged. 'Tell her,' Demi said.

'Because ...' Olivia sat down next to Bertie.

'Tell me, dear.' Bertie patted Olivia's hands.

'A trunk was delivered to me after Shirley died. Inside were a whole lot of things, including those photos you saw. There were also expensive gowns—'

'Dior,' Demi blurted.

'Yes. Haute couture. And designer shoes—'

'Also Dior. Matching too.'

Bertie whipped around to look at Demi, who had perched herself on the back of the chair, her boots on the seat. 'Maybe let Olivia finish.' She turned back to Olivia. 'And?'

'There was expensive jewellery.'

Demi squeaked out a noise.

'Go on,' Olivia said to Demi, shaking her head in resignation.

Demi slid down on the chair. 'It's all diamonds and gold. A necklace from Fairfax and Roberts—they're really expensive, you know.'

'I do.' Bertie turned back to Olivia. 'But why the secrecy?'

Olivia shrugged. She felt her cheeks burn when she thought about what her mum might have done. 'Maybe she was some high-class call girl.'

'That's what I said.' Demi slapped the laminated table, causing all the cups to rattle.

'It's possible. Mum said she had no family and came to Australia alone. And whenever I asked about her past, she clammed up. Sometimes she got upset.' The image of her mum trapped in the car next to her flickered in and out. Olivia tensed and shoved the memory away.

'Do you think your mum could've done this kind of work?' Bertie said. 'No judgement.'

Olivia shrugged.

Bertie took Olivia's hand. 'Sometimes women make choices to survive. If she was alone, she might not have had any choice.'

'I don't know. But—' Olivia's chest tightened.

———

BERTIE STOOD in front of the butcher-papered wall. 'This is impressive. You did this with that new teacher over at St Brendan's?'

She nodded. 'I couldn't have done it without Sebastian. There's more. In the bedroom.'

Bertie followed her in, and Olivia removed the bedsheet protecting the two dresses hanging off her wardrobe.

'I know this dress,' Bertie said, gently stroking the green one.

'You do?' Olivia asked.

'It's a classic Givenchy.'

'How can you tell? You didn't even look at the label.'

'Darling, I know these things.'

Demi checked the label. 'Man, she's good.'

Olivia placed the green dress on the bed as Bertie inspected the black cocktail dress.

'Dior?'

'Yes. Really, how can you tell?'

'Olivia, one thing I know is haute couture. This is one of Dior's famous styles. Only a handful were ever made. Usually on order. This isn't something you pick up in a charity shop. These dresses belong in a museum.'

Olivia opened her wardrobe door and took out the yellow woollen suit.

'Oh my goodness. Another Givenchy.' Bertie took it from Olivia.

'This is like the one Audrey Hepburn wore in *Paris When It Sizzles*.' She glanced back at the evening dresses.

Bertie leant in and picked up a green satin shoe with a crystal buckle. 'I have a friend who used to work at *Woman's World*. She went to all the society parties, events and balls. These dresses would've been worn to one of these. From the style, I'd say it's circa mid-1960s. How old was your mum?'

'Mum was thirty-nine when she died. In 1978.'

'She would've been in her twenties,' said Bertie. 'You have more photos?'

Olivia lifted a small album. 'I put them in this to protect them.'

'Just a moment.' Bertie reached into the trunk again and took out a bundle of magazine clippings. 'Jack Emerson,' she said, reading the caption. Olivia noted the curious look on Bertie's face. 'There was another photo. The one on the credenza I picked up last time.'

'Yes!' Olivia grabbed it and handed it to Bertie, who held both up to compare.

'Well, I never. How did I miss this?' she muttered to herself.

'Do you know him?' Olivia sat on her bed next to Bertie.

'Not personally. I was acquainted with his father, Richard Emerson.' Bertie studied the clipping. 'Richard was a dish.'

Olivia gaped. A possible connection? 'How did you know him?'

Bertie laughed and waved the question away. 'We moved in the same circles. Old money sticks together.' She stood and took the gown from Demi. 'It's all intriguing.' She turned to Olivia. 'I can ask my friend who used to work at *Woman's World* what she might know.'

'I don't know.' Olivia's chest tightened again. 'I didn't want this to get out.'

Bertie pursed her lips. 'I know the Emersons. I also knew, well, heard that Jack was popular with the ladies. I just can't imagine him using an escort. But I do have a theory.' She held up a finger.

'What?' Olivia held her breath.

'These may have been gifts. Possibly from Jack. They were a very wealthy family.'

'Great,' Demi interjected. 'Let's go and see him. Have you got an address, Bertie?'

'I'm afraid I don't. Again, when I said I knew Richard, it was only socially. He wasn't the kind of man who ... how can I put this? Rocked my boat.' She glanced at her watch. 'I better go. Martin will be getting antsy about sitting in a no-standing zone. I was only supposed to be here for a few minutes.'

'I love that you have a chauffeur,' cooed Demi.

Bertie nodded graciously. This would be the only acknowledgment she'd offer. Although she was as rich as Roosevelt, she never discussed her wealth or the perks that came with it.

'Why did you come to the shop?' Olivia asked. Bertie never just popped in. She was confident Olivia had everything under control.

'Oh, I got so sidetracked I nearly forgot. I'm closing the shop for a month or so to remodel.' She held up a hand as Olivia's mouth flew open. 'Don't worry, you and Poppy will still get paid. I just feel that it looks a little tired. With the nineties just around the corner, I thought, new decade, new look.' She handed the dress back to Olivia and kissed her on the cheek.

'Try to be positive. Secrets don't like being kept hidden for long.' She turned and examined the items laid out on the bed. 'I think you're doing the right thing. There was a reason the trunk came to you.'

'Did you hear that?' Demi said once Bertie had sashayed out. She stepped onto the balcony and lit a cigarette.

'I know. What will I do for a month?' Olivia collapsed on the marble step at the foot of the French doors. Working in the bookshop kept her mind busy.

'Not that. Bertie knows the father of the man in all those pictures. Now we know for sure it's Jack Emerson.'

Olivia dared to let hope bloom inside her. *Finding the answers might just be a real possibility.*

OLIVIA PACKED the items back into the trunk. She loved touching each one. Every time she did, she felt closer to her mother. She just wished they didn't hold so many secrets.

She needed a few shots of vodka to wash away this tiresome sense of doubt that pulled her down. But with Demi still in the apartment, she decided a calming cup of tea would help settle her instead.

While making the drink, she realised she felt freer.

She returned to the verandah, where Demi had perched herself on the ledge, and handed her friend a cup of tea. 'I get so nervous when you sit up there.'

'I promise I'll hand the cup back before I fall onto the pavement.'

'Yep, that's what I'm worried about.'

Olivia focused on the cars moving down Booth Street as she sipped her tea. There was so much to process.

'Are you still worried about what you'll find out?'

She nodded. 'And I mean, the fact the shop will be closed for four weeks has thrown me off-kilter.'

Demi took a drag. 'I think it's perfect.'

'You always see the positive in everything.'

'No, seriously. Already we have so much to go on. With four weeks off work, you might just have the time to solve the mystery. And oh my God!' Demi jumped back to the verandah and grabbed Olivia by the shoulder. 'Sebastian can help. He'll be on school holidays soon.'

'Not sure his girlfriend will be pleased about it.'

Demi rolled her eyes. 'You're like a broken record. You still don't know they're a couple. Have you even bothered to ask him?'

'No. I don't plan to either.'

A barrage of Greek exploded across the street.

'Shit. I've been away too long. That'—she nodded towards her mother, who was outside the shop shouting for her—'is what one needs to be scared about.' Demi leant over the balcony and returned her own barrage of Greek. She stubbed out her cigarette, popped in some gum, and gave Olivia a hug. 'You know I'm here for you.'

'I know.'

She walked Demi to the front door. As Demi opened it, she turned. 'And it's going to be okay.'

A WEEK LATER, Olivia woke to hammering and men shouting orders. She rolled over and checked the clock to see it was 7:05 am.

So much for sleeping in.

She slipped out of bed to make herself a coffee. While the kettle boiled, she gazed at The Quest Wall. Questions and evidence stared back at her.

After Bertie's announcement about renovating the shop, Olivia had kept herself busy packing up all the books to put away in storage. She and Poppy had worked so fast that they finished two days early. Poppy was excited that she was getting four weeks off with pay. Olivia wished she could've been as excited. She knew that this was the perfect opportunity to do some detective work, but fear still loomed over her like a winter storm. Soon, it wouldn't just be about her and her mum. She'd be intruding into other people's lives—people she didn't know, who didn't know her.

She placed a door sausage under the door to her apartment to keep the cool May air out and then moved to the sofa with her coffee and wrapped herself in a woollen throw. The hot drink warmed her palms. She stretched out her legs and continued staring at The Quest Wall. Olivia reached towards the coffee table and picked up the card Bertie had sent with a care package filled with books, chocolates, a voucher for a treatment at her salon, and four bottles of wine. Then she retrieved a black marker out of a bicentenary cup and walked to the wall. In capital letters, she wrote the quote from Bertie's card:

The only real voyage of discovery consists not in seeking new landscapes but in having new eyes.
– Marcel Proust

. . .

GIN RUBBED HER LEGS, and she picked him up.

'If I don't do this, I'm going to spend the rest of my life wondering,' she said to the cat, who promptly meowed for more attention when she stopped scratching under his chin. Sebastian was right. She could use her skills to search for answers. She mentally ticked them off: good at analysing, planning and scheduling. Able to think critically. Good at interviewing? Her chest constricted but relaxed when she thought of Sebastian. He would step in for that.

Her heart quivered at the thought of him, the sensation fuelling her feelings of uncertainty. To make things worse, she hadn't heard from him since they finished sorting out a plan of attack a few weeks ago. Class assessments and reporting were keeping him busy, and though she understood, she missed him.

Olivia suddenly needed some cold air to settle her burning cheeks. She opened the French doors before settling back on the couch.

The school holidays started next week. He and Clare were probably going on some fabulous holiday. There it was again, that prickly jealousy. *Stop it*, Olivia scolded herself. *Just because he's kind doesn't mean he likes you.* There was no way she could compete with Clare.

Clare with her curves and her long, shiny, non-flyaway hair. Her perfect white teeth and button nose. Her polished and sophisticated voice like a TV presenter. Clare reminded her of the girls at boarding school who'd come from wealthy families. The ones who travelled the world and went to the theatre and ballet. Whose parents picked them up on Friday afternoons in expensive cars.

Gin settled into her lap.

'You always know when I need a little affection.'

He rubbed his cool nose against her hand, and she obliged with a rub between his ears before picking up her copy of Capote's novella *Breakfast at Tiffany's*. The photo of her mother in her red swimsuit kept her spot. Olivia loved this one.

'What happened?' Olivia sighed, tracing her mother's face. 'Why did you hide your beauty and choose to live a quiet, unassuming life?'

I miss you.

It was too much. She headed to her bedroom to dull the ache. She took a shot. Took another. Guilt seared through her, and she heard her mother's voice.

'Take chances. Be strong.'

Olivia collapsed on the bed. She'd always lacked courage. The vodka gave her a small sense of fearlessness, but as if it were air in a punctured tyre, it always seeped out slowly.

She turned to a framed photo of the two of them. 'Have I disappointed you, Mum?'

Her mother's face smiled back at her. Olivia's heart pounded. She had to find out what had stolen that joy. Her mother deserved to have someone know who she really was. After all, didn't people live on in the memories of those left behind?

CHAPTER 15

Rosemary

March 1964

A month after Valentine's Day, Rosemary sat outside the hospital on her break, enjoying the warm morning. Closing her eyes, she lifted her face to catch the sunrays.

Marie burst out and startled her.

'Hey. I don't have to work tonight, and I checked with Cranky Gladys. You're not on either.'

'Yes, I am going to have a hot bath and read my new book. The lady at the library—'

'Librarian.'

'Yes, librarian.' She held up *Mrs Dalloway*. 'She told me she was a clever writer.'

'Virginia Woolf. I know her. She was a troubled writer, topped herself. I don't know this one, though.' Marie gave Rosemary a thoughtful look. 'You know, Hollywood, any medical school would be honoured to have you. You're such a bright spark.'

'Spark?'

'You know, smart.'

'It is a metaphor?'

'Yep.' Marie laughed. 'But you won't be reading Ms Woolf tonight. Let's enjoy the last few weeks of these warm nights. I want to celebrate. Plus, I've bribed Matron with cigarettes and booze to get out of here. We're going to a swish restaurant in Bondi.'

Rosemary waved the idea away, but Marie bulldozed over it.

'Nope. No excuses. My treat.'

CLASSIC LUXURY SURROUNDED ROSEMARY: rosewood trim and plush carpet. A large light with cascading glass pendants fell towards a decadent arrangement of tall white hyacinths and roses. Soft, romantic music from a three-piece band in the corner.

A sister of one of the nurses worked as a waitress and had pulled some strings for them.

Rosemary and Marie were met by a hostess with an elaborate hairstyle. The hair that wasn't in the twisted knot on top of her head fell over her shoulder in a thick ponytail.

'Most likely an expensive hairpiece,' Marie whispered as a waiter took them to their table. He pulled out Rosemary's chair and flapped her napkin before draping it across her lap.

The table was set with glasses, cutlery, and plates in all shapes and sizes.

'I love the bar,' Marie said with awe from behind her menu.

Rosemary turned to see a neon-blue bar running along the wall of the restaurant. The bottles of liquor sparkled like jewels.

'Too bad Lorna's not working tonight. We could've had a couple of free drinks. But she spoke to the manager, and they're giving us a little discount. So, order up big.'

Rosemary did just that, though she found the big plates with bite-sized food amusing. No wonder rich people were thin. As they ate, she and Marie bantered about work and the latest Bond film, *From Russia with Love.*

When the waiter cleared their plates away, Rosemary felt him catching glimpses of her, and he loitered a little longer than needed. She peered over her wineglass at Marie, who raised an eyebrow before turning to him.

'Thank you.' She smiled sweetly at him. 'I think you'll get waiter of the year for your admirable attention tonight.' Rosemary swirled her wine and pushed down the urge to giggle at the man's shocked expression. Marie always looked out for her. 'I know my friend's husband would be so pleased to know that you were extremely attentive.'

Rosemary glanced up and smiled at the waiter, who finished clearing the dishes and scampered off, leaving a fog of blush behind him.

Both women laughed quietly into the crisp linen napkins.

'It's like they've all been on a deserted island and have never seen a woman before.' Marie lit a cigarette and blew the smoke up towards the ceiling. 'I think I get it now. How do you stand it?'

'I have to be careful—what I wear, what I say, what I do. I must be strong. But I have a weapon.'

Marie tilted her head. Rosemary opened her purse, pulled out a book and handed it to her.

'*Mrs Dalloway* is your weapon?'

'Yes. When you read, people leave you alone.'

'Maybe 'cause they're dumb bastards.'

They laughed again and glanced around to see if they'd made a scene. An elderly couple shook their heads at having their quiet dinner disturbed.

'You are a good friend. You always look after me.'

'Always.' Marie held out her hand, and Rosemary took it.

'*Anche io.* Also me.'

'I have a wild idea. Are you up for an adventure?' Marie gave Rosemary a lopsided grin.

––––––––

THE SAND WAS STILL WARM. A gentle breeze blew off the Pacific Ocean and carried a bright trail of moonbeams across the rippling waves towards them.

'*Un bellissima luna*,' Rosemary whispered.

'I know this one. A beautiful moon.' Marie gazed up and took Rosemary's hand.

'Yes. Very good.'

'Right. It's time for the leap year skinny-dip.' Marie unzipped her dress and stepped out of it.

'What are you doing?'

'What's it look like? I'm taking my clothes off. Can't go skinny-dipping with your clothes on. Come on.'

Rosemary glanced around. 'This is bad. No?'

'Na, naughty but never bad.' Marie giggled as she ran naked down to the water and dived in.

Rosemary took another look around, but the beach was deserted. Marie waved to her from the water.

She took a deep breath and stepped out of her dress and then her slip. When she got to the water's edge, she unclipped her bra and stepped out of her silk pants, which she flung into the sand before rushing into the water. Rosemary squealed as the cold water assaulted her naked body.

They swam, flicked water at each other and floated under the stars. Finally, when their teeth started to chatter, they raced out of the water and back up the beach, collecting their discarded clothes along the way.

Wrapped together in Marie's cashmere shawl, they sat on the beach with only their slips on, borrowing each other's body heat. Their undergarments sat in their dresses at their feet. They said nothing as they gazed at the pregnant moon suspended in the starry sky.

Contentment washed over Rosemary. This was all she needed. Only good friends. She didn't need to be married or have children. Instead, she would train to be a doctor and help children. This would be her marriage. Her life.

Signora Castello believed she could do it. She'd always told her she was smart, a magnificent gift from God. Rosemary yearned to be known for more than her beauty. It was a curse. Being free was what she craved. She *was* smart, and living in Australia offered her more choices. Women in Australia were free. She'd be her own boss. Control her own life. Make her own decisions. No man was going to make her change her mind about this.

Nessuno. Nobody.

ROSEMARY WOKE FEELING CHILLED.

She shook Marie, who slept soundly next to her. The moon had moved higher in the sky and behind some clouds, and the beach was swathed in darkness. The only light came from the streetlights on Campbell Parade behind her. She stood, stretched and jabbed Marie with her sandy feet. 'Marie?'

'What?' She stirred and rolled over, missed the shawl and face-planted in the sand. She brushed the sand off her face. 'We fell asleep.'

'Yes. I think it is time we go home. But all the buses have stopped.'

'We'll find a phone box and call a cab.' Marie stood and peeked around.

Rosemary handed over her bra and undies. 'Maybe it was not good we did not wear these when we were asleep?' A smile slipped from her mouth. The naughtiness of it made her feel excited and alive. This was what freedom felt like.

'Nah, we're pretty safe. This is Sydney. Bondi. The only things to fear at Bondi are sharks and greedy seagulls.'

They shook the sand off their clothes, dressed and trudged up the beach.

Once on the road, they brushed off as much of the sand as they could. Then Marie reached into her purse and squinted at her watch. 'Nearly one.' She brushed more sand off. 'Come on, there's bound to be a public phone box at the Surf Life Saving Club.'

They'd walked only a few steps when a man stumbled out of the shadows of the Surf Club building. 'Well, hello there, ladies,' he said, slurring his words.

Marie grabbed Rosemary's hand. 'Keep walking,' she whispered into her tangled hair.

'On a lover's rendezvous, eh? Out catcalling, have yaaa?'

Marie stopped, turned around and faced the drunk man straight on. He grabbed at his crotch, jiggled it and snarled, his face contorted and puffy.

'You're disgusting.'

The man lunged at Marie. Rosemary squealed and pulled her back before he could grab her.

'Oi!' a voice bellowed out of the darkness.

Rosemary turned to see a tall man crossing the road. He smacked a golf club across his palm.

The drunk scampered down the road, stumbling and swaying. A few metres down, he turned, spread his legs to help him balance and gave the three of them an up-yours gesture before falling onto his backside.

Rosemary tucked in her lips, trying not to laugh. Marie wasn't as polite. She let out a laugh that cut through the still night.

'What's going on out there?' a cranky voice called from an open window across the road.

'Sorry, Mrs Abernathy,' the man with the golf club called back.

'Well, keep it down, will ya?' The window slammed shut.

He stepped into the light.

Rosemary's heart skipped a beat.

He was handsome. Very handsome. She glanced at Marie, who stared at him too. He was the type of man everyone would stop to look at. Even the breeze seemed to stop in his presence.

'Are you okay?' He gazed at Rosemary, holding her with his eyes, before turning to Marie.

Marie looked at the man, then back at Rosemary with a small smirk. She stepped forward. 'Hi, I'm Marie. This is my friend.' She gave him a broad smile. 'My single friend, Rosemary.'

'Marie!' Rosemary gave her a pointed look and ignored her cat-that-swallowed-the-canary look. 'I am sorry about my friend. She is not always on her best behaviour.'

'Jack.' He smiled at Rosemary and extended his hand. She took it, and he held it a little longer than necessary.

'Jack Emerson. I live in the top apartment across the road.' He nodded at an Art Deco apartment block. Both Marie and Rosemary turned.

She knew the building—she'd taken a photo of it when she visited Bondi a few weeks ago. Everyone remarked on its design. Painted sky blue with a concave front wall, she was a gracious old lady from a decadent era.

She also knew the name Jack Emerson. She peered at him. 'You are a writer with the newspaper.'

'That's right.'

'You are a talented writer.'

'That's very kind of you.'

'I am sorry. I am Rosemary. This is my friend Marie.' She heard herself bumbling away.

He laughed. 'Yes, I know, your friend here shared that information.'

Rosemary swallowed the lump in her throat and sidled up to Marie for support. Instead, all she got was a grin. She was having a good time at her expense.

Jack eyed them. 'Looks like you've been swimming.'

Rosemary felt heat chase away the chill. The hairs on her arms prickled. Had he seen them swimming naked?

'Yep,' Marie piped up as she lit a cigarette. 'Skinny-dipping, in fact.'

Rosemary rolled her eyes. Her friend was always stirring up trouble.

'I see.' Jack nodded.

'Did you?' Rosemary asked, embarrassment taking hold of her.

'No, but I heard you both. The squeals and laughter echoed up from the beach. On a still night like this, the sound carries.'

Rosemary covered her mouth, horrified. Marie beamed.

Jack gave her an amiable smile. 'We're used to it around here. Comes with the territory. Have done it myself frequently.'

Before Rosemary could stop it, her imagination drifted to what his body might look like under the linen shorts and short-sleeved shirt he was wearing. With his broad shoulders and defined arms, he looked like a swimmer. The streetlight illuminated his skin. He was what Australians liked to call this country's men: a bronzed Aussie.

'Rosemary, it's getting late.' Marie tapped at her watch. She turned to Jack and extinguished her cigarette on the stone wall. 'Sorry, we have to find a cab to get home. I'm a nurse at St Elizabeth's, and I've already breached my unofficial curfew. Matron is going to have me for breakfast.'

'Not sure you'll have much luck getting a cab now.'

'Bugger.' She shrugged at Rosemary. 'How's those shoes for a walk? It's only what? Fifty or so minutes to Bourke Street? There'll be a cab round there for sure, thanks to the Cross.'

Rosemary glanced at her shoes. They were her favourite, and the walk would ruin them.

'Would you like a lift?'

They both looked at Jack. Then each other. Marie shrugged again, and an unspoken *He looks safe* passed between them.

'If it is not too *unconvenient* for you?' Rosemary said, turning to Jack.

'Inconvenient? No. Can't have two young ladies wandering the streets of Sydney. We have to keep them safe.' He grinned.

Rosemary liked him. He'd corrected her without making her feel *stupida*. There was also something about him that intrigued her. She sensed Marie reading her thoughts and glanced at her. Her suspicions were validated by a wink and a grin.

CHAPTER 16

Olivia
May 1989

Olivia stood and rolled her neck, releasing the tightness, then lifted onto tiptoes to elongate her spine. She'd spent the past three days at the library, getting there as soon as the doors opened and leaving just before they shut. Small pieces of the puzzle were coming together. What she'd found so far was fuelling her curiosity and teasing out more questions.

The library held an abundance of information on St Elizabeth's Women's Hospital. It had closed in 1979, the year after her mother died, after having operated for 110 years. It had been the centre of midwifery and obstetrics in Sydney.

Olivia tucked her journal in her backpack, stacked the books on the table and glanced at the clock above the circulation desk. Just after 1:00 pm. Four hours had whooshed passed, leaving hunger in their wake. She picked up her things and looked at the flyer someone had pressed into her hands when she got off the train at Wynyard

Station that morning. A special on laksa. Poppy had raved about how delicious it was. *Why not?*

She walked up to the circulation desk.

'How can I help you? My name's Nerida.'

'Olivia.'

'I know.'

'You do?'

'Your library card.' She handed it back to Olivia. 'Besides, I get to know people when they come in regularly.' She leant forward and said quietly, 'Actually, did you go to Our Lady of Peace?'

'I did.'

'I knew it. I never forget a face.'

Olivia held her arms tight against her body and winced. Had she been one of the girls who always whispered behind her back? Painful memories of hiding away in the library or some other quiet part of the school, alone, surfaced. 'I'm sorry, I'm afraid I kept to myself. I usually spent all my time in the library.' She gave a small smile. 'Not much has changed.'

'I only remembered because my little sister was a year ahead of you. Ruby. She was friends with Everly. Everly Hunter.'

Olivia felt her heart jump. Everly had been her floor captain. She'd always admired her, with her long, straight blonde hair and soft blue eyes. To Olivia, she looked like a princess. She was thin, always wore the latest fashion and rode horses.

When Olivia arrived at Our Lady of Peace, Everly had happily taken her under her wing. She always seemed interested in her day and what she'd been up to. It was what Olivia imagined having an older sister might be like. Everly had this uncanny way of materialising when Olivia was being teased. She'd place her arm protectively around her shoulders and flick the tormentors away with a dark look. She carried a sophistication, even when warning people off. Everyone loved and respected Everly. She was the *it* girl. After Everly graduated, a year before her, Olivia missed her. She often wondered what wonderful achievements she'd accomplished by now.

'Does Ruby still keep in touch with Everly?'

'Not since Everly moved to London.'

She felt a swell of disappointment. Then her stomach gurgled, and she remembered the laksa. 'Do you mind if I leave all the books on the table while I get some lunch?'

'Sure. When will you be back?'

'In about forty minutes.' She held up the flyer. 'Do you know if this is far?'

'Longtime Laksa. Unfortunate name but great laksa. It's just down Bent Street. It's a little restaurant on the corner of Bond and George.'

'What's unfortunate about the name?'

Nerida laughed. 'If you don't know, I'd leave it. I wouldn't want to be the one who corrupts you.'

The downtown crowd bustled with people on their lunch break. Ferries blew their horns up from Circular Quay, and their mournful bellowing cut across the buzz of traffic and drifted through the high-rise corridors.

Unfamiliar with this part of George Street, Olivia stood on the corner of Bond and George and scanned the buildings, looking for the restaurant. Olivia's mouth flew open with surprise when she saw it across the street—not the laksa place but a photography shop with the same name as the one on the back of her mother's prints. George on George Cameras and Film. It was still here. Twenty-five years later.

Olivia tucked the leaflet in her back pocket and crossed the road. Lunch could wait.

She stood in front of the shop, which appeared to have been frozen in time. Its name was displayed in old-fashioned lettering on the front window, along with advertisements from the 1950s, '60s and '70s. She pushed open the door and stepped back into the past. A little bell tinkled, and the bitter scent of coffee mixed with dust welcomed her. An old grey cash register stood on a glass cabinet. The olive-and-cream-chequered linoleum, clean yet worn, clashed with the veneered cabinetry.

'Can I help you?' said an elderly woman. She looked at Olivia as she continued her crocheting.

'I'm just browsing.' She walked to a cabinet filled with cameras covered with a film of dust. The same model as the one inside her mother's chest sat at the centre.

'Are these cameras still for sale?'

'I not know.' She turned towards an opening at the back of the shop and shouted, 'George!'

A man around the same age as the woman came out from behind a curtain. 'Why you shout so much?' Then he stopped and stared at Olivia. '*Theé mou. Den borei na einai.*'

Olivia squinted at him. 'I'm sorry, my best friend is Greek, but I don't speak it.'

'What cannot be?' the woman said to Olivia. 'This is what George said.' She turned to the man again. 'What is the matter with you, George?'

'Who is your friend?' he asked, still staring at Olivia.

'Demi Kokkinos. Her parents own a fruit and vegetable shop in Annandale.'

'Yes. I know her yiayia.' The woman held up her crocheting. 'We make together. George?' The woman placed her crocheting down and shuffled to him. 'You look like you have seen a ghost.'

'I am sorry.' George approached Olivia. 'You remind me of a young lady. She was Italian. New to Australia. Very beautiful but sad. In her eyes.'

'My husband here used to talk about her all the time. If he did not look like a shepherd, I would worry she would run away with him.' The woman laughed.

Olivia took off her locket and opened it. 'Is this the woman?' Her heart raced with excitement, and she pressed a hand against her mouth, hope flickering like a newly lit fire inside her.

George took the necklace and squinted at the image. 'Despina, get my glasses.'

Despina grabbed them from under the counter and handed them to him.

'Yes.' He held up the locket. 'Look, Despina. It is Rosemary, yes?'

Despina looked at the photo and then at Olivia. 'You are alike.'

'How is Rosemary?' George asked, his face lighting up. 'Did she become a doctor? She wanted to be a doctor for children. She was very smart.'

'I'm sorry.' Olivia heard her voice crack. 'My mother died eleven years ago. When I was thirteen.'

Despina gasped and made the sign of the cross, kissed her bunched-up fingers, and then pulled Olivia into a warm hug. 'I am so sorry.'

Sadness clouded George's eyes.

'I'm sorry.' Olivia's chest constricted as the guilt pounded inside her head.

'What happened?' George pulled out a handkerchief and wiped his eyes.

Shame joined the guilt. How could she stand here and tell them that her mother had turned to her, to tell her to 'leave it', and that's why she'd crossed into the path of an oncoming truck?

'A car accident.' The words ripped her heart open.

It was too much. Prickly heat exploded across her body, pushing the air out of her lungs. 'I'm sorry. I have to go.'

She rushed out of the shop.

Tears blinded her as she crossed the road, and she jumped when a car's horn screamed at her. She mouthed a sorry and raced down Bond Street before she stopped. Bent over, she tried to take in gulps of air.

It's your fault. It's your fault.

The words whispered themselves in her brain, torturing her.

Olivia dropped onto a nearby step. She'd caused so much pain, continued to cause pain. Her mum had wanted to be a doctor, and Olivia had taken that away from her. Had taken everything away from her.

———

Olivia stirred. Her head pounded, adding to the noise from the bookshop renovations. She lay coiled up tight, fully clothed, on her bed. Gin had found the curve in her body and was curled up inside it. As she rolled over, Gin shot off across the bedside table, knocking the empty bottle of vodka onto the floor.

'Sorry, buddy.' Her throat was dry and itchy. She reached to the table for a glass of water, but there was none. Reaching down, she picked up the bottle. Guilt for breaking her dry spell gripped her heart.

She heaved herself up, shuffled to the kitchen, placed the bottle near the sink and filled a glass with tap water. She searched for a Panadol to ease her searing headache.

The scene in George's shop burst into her head again, and she cringed.

She'd eventually returned to the library in a daze, no longer hungry or having any desire to continue her research.

On the train home, she huddled in the back and stared out of the window, watching the terrace homes shuffle past like playing cards. Was she going to react like this every time she found out something new about her mum?

This is my punishment. The thought circled around and around in her mind.

Resting her head on the window, the vibration of the train drumming against her forehead, Olivia reached deep inside her memories, where there were scattered comments—her mother telling her about applying to Newcastle University to study medicine, how she would work as a relief nurse to pay the bills while she studied. Olivia banged her head on the glass. Why didn't she just leave it all alone?

Her mother would've turned fifty in November.

When she'd skulked into her apartment, The Quest Wall had laughed at her. The emergency money jar sat on the top shelf above the fridge. There had been enough in it to buy a bottle of vodka.

Gin's cry for food snapped her back to the kitchen.

How could she have allowed herself to slip up?

Come on. Move forward.

She picked up the bottle, wrapped it in newspaper and put it in the bin. There was no more in the apartment. Done.

Coffee. That's what she needed.

She put the kettle on. The noise from downstairs grew louder, and the drilling and hammering shredded her patience. She needed to disappear. Maybe up to Killcare. Forget all about this whole stupid quest.

The buzzer shrilled, and she jumped. Maybe whoever it was would think she was out. The buzzer called out a second time, followed by banging on the front door.

'Olivia?' Demi's voice called up from the street. 'Let me in.'

Without thinking further, she pressed the button and opened her apartment door. Demi's thick boots pounded up the stairs. Leaving the door ajar, Olivia moved to the sofa and curled up under a quilt.

Demi burst in. 'I've been trying to call since last night.' She stopped. 'Are you sick?' She approached and sat next to her, putting her hand on Olivia's forehead. The maternal gesture was too much.

Olivia burst into tears and let Demi's arms wrap around her.

Demi let her cry it out and then, without saying a word, got up and busied herself with making her a coffee.

'What happened?' Demi placed a mug in front of Olivia and sat on the coffee table facing her.

Olivia told her about George and the camera shop, about how he'd known her mother when she was younger.

'That's good, isn't it? To find someone who knew your mother.'

Olivia shrugged. 'That's not it. He really liked her. You should've seen his face when I told him Mum had died.' Fresh tears bubbled up. 'I took everything away from her.'

'That's silly talk. Do you have a crystal ball? No!' Demi took hold of Olivia's hands. 'Look at me. From what you've told me, it was an accident. This'—she swept her arm, gesturing to the wall filled with photos and questions—'was not your fault. Shit happens.'

Olivia looked up. 'I don't know if I can do this. I know everyone's already put in so much time, but I can't. There's this ugly black monster inside me.' She sniffed. 'It's just too painful.'

'*Aftò pou den se skotònei se kànei poi dynatò*. What doesn't kill you makes you stronger. That's what my yiayia says all the time.'

'My mum used to say that too.'

'There you go. My grandmother is wise, and from what you've told me about your mum, I know she was smart too. Look at what she did. On her own. Migrated here. Survived and had you. And I think you turned out pretty okay.'

Olivia let a smile sneak out. 'Thank you. What would I do without you?'

'Now *there's* a reason to cry.' Demi grinned, then looked at The Quest Wall. 'I think you've got to keep going. You also need to go back and speak to George. It's a start.'

Olivia's skin prickled. 'I can't. I just ran out. It's embarrassing.'

'I'll come with you. Back to the camera shop. You know, as your wingman ... well, woman.'

'How about the shop? Don't you have to work?'

'Leave it to me.' She winked. 'My parents love you.'

'Are you sure?'

'Yep. I'll even say I'll go to the Greek Club with them.'

'You'd do that for me?' Demi spent much of her energy trying to stay away from the Greek Club, what she referred to as the 'marriage factory'.

'That's what friends are for. Which is why I'm here, by the way. My cousin's wife, Helena, said she's happy to translate the letters. I mentioned them to her. She warned it may take a bit of time. You know, with all those kids. Man, that woman is a baby-making factory.'

'Do I know Helena?'

'She's the one with the four kids under five—one of those mums who's always volunteering at their kids' school and at the church. My mum loves her. She's always telling me to be like her. If she wasn't so nice, I'd hate her.'

'Are you absolutely sure she's happy to do it?'

'Yep, and the good thing is, whatever is in those letters, she's promised it'll be kept private.'

Despite Demi's words, Olivia felt terror grip her. She thought of her mum being an escort. 'I don't know ...'

'I know Helena. She never judges. She's a living saint. "The Madonna", my mum says.'

Olivia took in a deep breath. She needed to let go a little. This was a start. 'Okay.'

CHAPTER 17

Rosemary

March 1964

The week after the encounter with Jack, Rosemary was run off her feet at the hospital. A bad stomach bug had gone through the kitchen staff, and only Gladys, Rosemary, and two other women were spared.

'Peasant stock,' Marie had said to Rosemary with a laugh when they were on one of their rare breaks together. The bug hadn't invaded the wards, so the mothers, babies, and ward staff, including Marie, had also been spared.

They sat under the only tree in the back lot, where someone had tried to create a garden. Some of the autumn perennials survived, and spots of pink and purple peeked through the over-grown weeds.

Rosemary took off her shoes and rubbed her feet. 'The extra work is good. I am saving. But I am tired.'

'You better be careful, or you'll get a face like Gladys. Cranky lines. Like a shrivelled-up apple.' Marie screwed up her face.

Rosemary let a small smile leak out.

'Have you heard from Mr Heartthrob?' Marie flicked her lighter on and off.

Rosemary shook her head.

'Ah well, come and go.'

Rosemary didn't know why, but Marie's comment unnerved her. After all, she didn't want to be in a relationship. She wanted to be married to herself. To her freedom.

Marie lit her cigarette and pulled out a romance novel. She waved the paperback at Rosemary. 'Do you mind? I've only got a couple of chapters to go.'

'No.' She closed her eyes, happy for the quiet.

JACK HAD DROPPED Marie off first that night. When he pulled up outside Rosemary's place, she quickly collected her purse and wrap. On the drive, his body language had been relaxed, especially compared to hers. She knew her coolness came across as rude. *Stuck-up* was the term Marie used. Sometimes it worked and the men gave up. Others were too confident or ignorant.

That night, though, her rigidity had come from nervousness. Her heart had fluttered as though she were a love-struck schoolgirl. She'd never felt this way before. The feeling, though foreign, was delicious.

Jack turned to her. 'Let me walk you to your door.'

'No. It is alright.' She was glad her gloves covered her sweaty palms. 'Thank you for driving my friend and me home. It was very kind.' She held out her hand for a shake.

His grip was firm. 'My pleasure. Saving young ladies after midnight is my second job.' He grinned.

That smile. It switched on the light in his soft blue eyes—the colour of the sea near her village.

She walked up the path to the front door, and as she put her key in, she turned around. His gaze was locked on her. Her heart shuddered.

He was incredibly handsome and confident.

He gave her a quick wave, and she stepped inside and leant her back on the closed door. Placing her hands on her chest, she breathed, '*Mamma mia*.'

She took off her shoes and, watching the spots in the hallway that creaked, crept to her room. The wooden stairs moaned under her bare feet. There was still sand between her toes. She made a note to vacuum the hallway runner in the morning. Nora kept a clean house.

She needed a warm bath. Her lips tasted like salt, and she reached up and pressed her fingers on them. What did Jack's lips taste like? She shook her head and threw out the image.

This was silly. No relationships. She'd made that promise to herself.

But as Rosemary soaked in the bath, her mind kept filling with thoughts of Jack. They both excited and worried her. He appeared to be a man who got what he wanted, yet she was drawn to him. She wouldn't be surprised if other people felt the same way. His smile was so *ipnotizzante*. Mesmerising.

Although Rosemary had switched on her wariness in the car, there'd been an ease between them. Jack's confidence filled the space. What had they talked about? She racked her brain. She couldn't remember. Only the deep, even tone of his voice filtered back into her thoughts. Then a proverb her grandmother used to quote popped in. *Quando il diavolo ti accarezza, vuole l'anima*: When the devil caresses you, he wants your soul. Jack was tempting, but what price would she have to pay? Men were all the same. They all wanted the same thing. Every antagonistic encounter she'd had, as a daughter and a woman, bitterly proved this. Jack seemed to be a man who enjoyed owning beautiful, luxurious things. The Mercedes Benz, the Rolex watch, the apartment—he was wealthy, well-spoken and educated. The city was full of men like him.

Rosemary sighed. It could never be. An impossible dream. All migrant women knew what Australian mothers wanted for their sons, and a migrant from Sicily wasn't one of them.

A magpie warbled on the ornate iron gates of the hospital's entrance, pulling Rosemary back to the present. To her, the sound was a warning to let it be.

She looked over at Marie, who had dozed off.

St Elizabeth's constantly revealed the fallout of unwanted attention from men.

She gently woke her friend.

ROSEMARY WALKED HOME SINGING an old Italian tune she'd learnt as a child. The afternoon sun's warmth wrapped her in happiness. It was another autumn day like the ones she'd enjoyed back home. She loved being able to wear a light cotton dress and a little cardigan instead of her starched hospital uniform and apron. Only the breeze coming from the south carried a chilly edge to it. *Winter is coming.* She also loved winter days in Sydney. The sky stretched crisp and blue, as if Mother Nature had tipped the world upside down and allowed the ocean to remain suspended above.

On her days off, she enjoyed the freedom to go where she pleased. Every spare moment, she combed Sydney with her camera. Her photographs nearly covered her bedroom wall. She'd gifted Nora and the girls black-and-white photos of their favourite places in frames she'd found in a second-hand store in Newtown.

She visited the Central Business District, Kings Cross, Potts Point, Paddington and Rose Bay and took photos of the terrace homes, interesting objects, and people going about their business. Most people loved having their photo taken. One lady sweeping her path outside her crumbling terrace in Woolloomooloo asked if she was a famous person.

'No,' Rosemary had said with a laugh. 'I am from Italy.'

'Well, that's pretty fancy to me.'

As summer came to a close, she'd captured the brightness of the season at Bondi and had taken ferry rides across the harbour. One afternoon, she discovered the Bondi to Coogee walk. The path hugged the coast, and the salty breeze brought with it a longing for her coastal hometown. The natural baths at Coogee were a delightful find.

After chatting with the lady in Woolloomooloo, Rosemary had headed down to the dock where her ship had pulled in four years ago. Today, it lay bare. Only a few workmen walked in and out of the metal hangers that lined the wharf. She bought a pie with mushy peas at Harry's Café de Wheels, taking photos of the café as she waited. Two sailors from the naval base joined her at the counter and tipped their caps. She offered a polite smile and, without delay, grabbed her pie and camera and pushed on. Today was about her. A date with herself and this fresh, energetic city.

She walked through the Royal Botanic Garden and sat in her favourite spot at Mrs Macquarie's Chair. She loved the view of the harbour and the Harbour Bridge. The construction of a new opera house had begun. Tall cranes, like large metal fingers, worked at building the roof. The newspaper had run a story about the controversial building and people were saying the roof looked like sails on a boat. The city's harbour was new, shiny and modern—starkly different from the ancient stone and marble of Patti and Genoa.

Genoa. She swallowed and pushed down the invasive memory and the guilt it stirred. It was done. *Finita*. For a fleeting moment, she thought about going to confession, but this would make it real. She didn't want to share what had happened with anyone. Not even a priest.

Instead, she thought again about her nursing application. Marie was confident she'd be accepted. The hospital was crying out for student nurses, and Eleanor had written her an admirable reference letter. Yes. It was all good. This is what she would focus on.

When she returned to Darlinghurst Road, she bought the daily paper. The one Jack wrote for.

Jack.

It had been a week since he drove her home. Why did she even care that she hadn't heard from him? She was adamant she didn't want a relationship with any man. She kept telling herself that she was simply grateful for the lift home.

But she couldn't stop thinking about him. A few times, she even caught herself fantasising.

'He's a rare specimen,' Marie had said. 'A gorgeous man with a kind heart who had nothing better to do late on a weeknight. Untouchable, in my books.' She shrugged, then swooned. 'But boy, what a catch.'

When Rosemary thought about him, her heart snagged like a favourite jumper on a wire and threatened to unravel fast. They'd spent only a moment together, but he'd left her feeling admired *and* respected.

The previous day, Marie had marched into the kitchens and shoved a newspaper at Rosemary. 'It's him. Jack Emerson.'

Rosemary looked at the article and continued to fold the napkins. 'Yes?' She wasn't going to let herself get carried away over Jack's kindness in driving her home. He was attractive, and yes, her heart had skittered when he looked at her with his captivating pale blue eyes, but she was determined to not be infatuated like a lovesick romance heroine.

'So?' She rose an eyebrow. 'Still no word from him?'

'*Niente.* Nothing. He dropped me home. That is all.'

'I don't believe you, Hollywood. Look at you. Look at him. Two of the most beautiful people in the world. Sydney's own Elizabeth Taylor and Richard Burton. Oh, the babies you both would make.' Clearly, she'd abandoned her 'untouchable' theory.

'Shhh.' She hip-bumped Marie and hung up her apron. '*Buonasera*, everyone,' she called out to the other ladies.

A chorus of goodnights and a nasally *ciao* from Gladys followed.

'Did Gladys just say *ciao*?' Marie whispered.

Rosemary giggled. 'Yes.'

In the corridor, Marie waved the newspaper at Rosemary again. 'Well, you do have a way with people.' Her face took on a conspiratorial look, and she stabbed at the photo as she followed Rosemary into the staff room. 'Maybe even Jack. He's a reporter for the *Sydney Morning Herald*.'

'Yes. I know he is a reporter. Very clever too.' Rosemary walked to her locker and reached for her day clothes on the hook.

'Yeh, but now we know who he is for sure.'

'Why is this important?'

'Oh, come on.' Marie stepped in front of Rosemary. 'I saw how he looked at you and how *you* looked at him.'

'You are right. He is very handsome. You look at him like you would look at a Botticelli.' Rosemary removed her apron, unbuttoned her uniform and stepped out of it. Then she placed the dirty clothes in her laundry bag and threw it in the basket. 'You can look but not touch.' She paused and met Marie's gaze. 'I know men. Look at me. They just see a pretty—'

'Beautiful.' Marie grinned.

'Pretty face.' Rosemary tried to keep her frustration at bay. 'I am more than a pretty face. You know this.'

Marie sidestepped the comment. 'I made some enquiries.'

'You mean snooping.'

'Whatever. Potato, tomato.'

Rosemary smiled at the error. So much of the English language was fresh in her mind, and she was starting to know more than some of the native speakers.

'You're my friend, Hollywood. It's my job to make sure you're protected.'

'He was a kind man who helped us. That is all. *Finita*.'

'But there's more.' Marie did an excited dance, the sound of her shoes on the floor echoing across the staff room.

'Okay. Tell me. Before you have cats.'

'Kittens,' Marie said, beaming. 'He's rich. Really, really rich.' She clapped, and little noises came out of her mouth. 'His family owns this huge cattle farm up north. Look.' She shoved a magazine, opened to an article, in front of Rosemary's face. 'One of the nurses found it in the magazine pile for patients.'

'How does this nurse know about this?' Rosemary said with a frown. She didn't like people knowing her business.

'Oh, I kept you out of the conversation. I just mentioned him, that's all. Now iron out that frown. No one ever remembers anything.'

Rosemary took the magazine from Marie. There was Jack, dressed in black tie. A blonde woman in an exquisite rose-pink gown stood close to him. He was looking at the camera, smiling. She was laughing and looking at him. Rosemary flipped to the front cover. *Australian Woman's World*. January 1964. Nearly two months ago. Her heart quivered, and she scolded.

'See, he has a girlfriend. Maybe a wife.'

'Nope.' Marie took the magazine back and flicked to the article. 'Read this.' She pointed to a paragraph.

'*Jack Emerson opened the* European Masters Exhibition *at the Art Gallery of New South Wales. The collection, sponsored by the Emerson Family, is the biggest the gallery has ever curated.*'

Rosemary stopped reading and looked up. 'We already know his full name and that he is rich.'

'Keep reading.' Marie jiggled on the spot.

Rosemary took a deep breath and continued. '*Lacey Hunter, a childhood friend of Emerson, was the creative brains behind the exhibition, one of the best Australia has ever seen.*'

'Friend,' Marie sang out.

Rosemary worked at keeping her face calm while flicking away the bubbles of excitement inside her chest. For a moment, she latched on to the possibility of Jack being single.

No. 'I am not interested. My dream is to be a doctor. I do not want a man. I will only be a possession. I know this. *You* know this.'

Marie took Rosemary's hand and pulled her down to the wooden bench. 'Not all men are like the men in Sicily you told me about.

Some are happy for their wives to do things for themselves. You just have to find them.'

Rosemary squeezed Marie's hands. 'You think because I look like this, because God made me beautiful, it is good? I know the ugliness of looking like this.' She stood. 'I know because of this face and body that the secrets of men come out.' Her voice cracked as her mind returned to Genoa. 'I know how cruel men can be. They want to control—always.'

Marie stood too. 'You're crying?'

Rosemary had waved away the comment and wiped the tears with the back of her hand. She continued in a hushed voice. 'If you let them, they will always use their strength and the law of society to have power over you.'

ROSEMARY SAT at the back of the bus. In front of her, a group of teenage girls was squawking like a pack of parrots. She couldn't stand it any longer. She reached up and pulled the cord.

Walking the rest of the way home would settle the buzzing in her head.

It had been a hard day.

One of the unmarried mothers had threatened to harm herself if they didn't give her baby back. Her screams had echoed throughout the ward, setting off the babies.

Rosemary had heard snatches of words slingshot at the nurses who'd tried to calm her down.

'She tricked me! You stole my baby!'

Matron had told Rosemary in a brusque voice to deliver the meals quickly and make sure all the other mothers got their cups of tea to help calm them down. 'We don't want their milk to stop flowing.'

Rosemary, like Marie, hated seeing these mothers distressed.

Marie had told her about a new pill that could stop you from getting pregnant, but it was only available to married women.

'It's ridiculous,' Marie had said. 'Married mothers don't have their babies taken from them to be adopted. You know the Catholic Church is against this pill, too.'

Falling pregnant without being married was a taboo Rosemary was very familiar with. Once, an unmarried girl in her village had disappeared and when she returned, a new baby boy was being raised by her mother. There were many whisperings. Everyone knew Signora Arena hadn't looked pregnant. Plus, she was in her late forties.

She turned the corner and headed down Vernon Street. She would be her own person. *Il suo capo*—her own boss.

Nora was sweeping the front path when she arrived home.

'There's an enormous bunch of roses. Red as a bishop's cloak.' Nora cocked her head over her shoulder. 'They're in the kitchen.'

'For me?'

'Yep, some bloke brought them round. Nice man. Handsome.' She winked.

Jack?

Rosemary couldn't help but smile.

'You better go in. Eleanor's biting at the bit to see which of your many admirers has the dosh to spend on that kind of bouquet.'

Rosemary had barely stepped inside when Eleanor grabbed her hand and dragged her down the hallway. 'Oh, my goodness, Rosemary. They're huge. He must be *so* rich.'

When she walked into the kitchen, she took in the enormous arrangement of red roses. The sweet scent filled the room.

'I was here when they arrived. He had strict instructions.' Pamela pointed to the cut crystal vase the roses sat in. 'He did it all, asked Nora if he could fill the vase with water, and then arranged the flowers himself. What guy does that?'

'A gentleman,' Nora said as she stepped into the room. 'You must've made an impression.'

'There's this too.' Pamela handed over an expensive-looking envelope.

Rosemary looked at her name, which was printed professionally. A thick embossed symbol was stamped in the middle—a wattle wreath with *Jubilee Station* in the centre. The letter had been sealed with wax.

'Thank you.' Rosemary opened the note. As she read it, a knot twisted in her heart. He was inviting her to the Premier's Ball. Was he delirious? They'd barely met. Everyone knew the ball was the social event of the year. She couldn't think about it. It was all too much. She feigned a smile, tucked the note in her handbag and picked up a single rose. 'I will leave the flowers here,' she said, taking in the flower's scent. 'They are too special to be left in my room. Yes?'

'They certainly give the house a la-di-da look,' Nora said as she moved the vase to the centre of the table. 'Are you sure you don't want them in your room?'

'No. Flowers make the world sing. *I fiori fanno cantare il mondo.*'

'That's beautiful.' Pamela sighed. 'Is it an Italian proverb?'

'No, an important lady I once worked for had the most beautiful flowers in her garden. Her maid filled every room in her villa with flowers. Even the ones not used.' She took three more roses from the bunch and gave one to Nora and one each to Pamela and Eleanor. 'For you. Everyone must have flowers in their life.'

Rosemary thought of Signora Castello. What would she think of this enormous bunch of flowers?

CHAPTER 18

Olivia

May 1989

The next day, Olivia waited for Demi outside the bookshop. Although a bright blue sky stretched out above her, the cold winter breeze made her shiver. Her heart was lodged at the base of her throat. How could Demi have talked her into going back?

She watched the workers trying to distract herself. The shop had been stripped of its old wooden shelves. Painters standing on a makeshift scaffold chatted as they patched and sanded the sixty-year-old walls. Olivia was a little sad that it would all be changed. But she knew more than anyone that life was about change. You couldn't stop it. She wished someone could patch her cracked heart and smooth away the guilty stain.

A horn startled her. Demi sat on her battered cream Vespa. She got off and handed Olivia a helmet. 'Ready?'

Olivia held it as if it were a bomb about to go off. Motorcycles were even more off-limits than cars. And this one looked like a toy.

Fear took her breath away. 'I can't,' she whispered.

'You need to get this fear of cars and stuff stamped out. You can't cycle and take public transport everywhere. I promise I'll drive carefully.'

Olivia chewed her lips, pinched the fabric on her sleeve and rubbed it to calm herself. She felt as if her feet had been cemented to the pavement.

Demi reached over and squeezed her arm. 'Trust me.' When she received no response, Demi sighed and took the keys out of the ignition. 'Okay, if you want, we can catch the bus. It would've been fun. Like Audrey Hepburn in *Roman Holiday*. I'd even be Gregory Peck.' She gave Olivia a cheeky grin.

Olivia closed her eyes and put on the helmet, ignoring the sinking feeling in her chest. Her mum's voice floated in. *Vivere con coraggio.* She needed to start living with courage. Getting on the scooter was a start.

Demi clapped. 'Yeh!'

'Please,' she whispered. 'Don't drive like a maniac.'

True to her word, Demi drove like a nanna and stayed under the speed limit. With peak hour behind them, there were fewer cars to contend with as they chugged towards the Central Business District.

When they got to George's camera shop, Demi parked on the path outside the front door. Olivia peeled herself off the Vespa. Her legs shook, but she couldn't stop herself from grinning. It had been scary yet thrilling all at once.

'Won't you get in trouble parking it there?'

'Nah. It looks like it's part of the shop's cosmopolitan appeal.'

Demi was right. The shop had a European feel to it. Small white-and-blue square tiles covered the outside, and a bright blue awning jutted out above the window. The Vespa added to the charm.

Demi barrelled into the shop, and Olivia followed, wringing her hands.

'Hello.' Demi patted the counter.

A good-looking guy in his twenties looked up from a book, and his gaze locked on Demi.

Demi motioned her over.

Olivia bit her lip. 'My name is Olivia. Is George here?'

'He stepped out to go to the bank. Can I help you with anything?'

Olivia turned to Demi, who nodded and mouthed 'Go on.'

'Do you know when he'll be back?'

'I can't say for sure. I'm Theo. His grandson.'

He shifted his gaze back to Demi, and the two of them stood there, staring at each other.

'This is my friend Demi,' Olivia added, grateful for the distraction.

She watched as the usually cool Demi blushed and fumbled to take the hand Theo offered her. Olivia itched to grab one of the many cameras around her and take a priceless photo—Demi all coy and lost for words. In the three years she'd known Demi, she'd never seen her blush.

She cleared her throat, and Demi jumped.

'Is there anything I can help you with?' Theo said again, not taking his eyes off Demi.

Olivia spoke up, feeling a little braver now. The amusing interaction had eased some of her tension. 'I came in here yesterday and spoke to George, and I was hoping I could speak to him again.' She pushed the next words out. 'It's about my mum. He knew her. In the sixties.'

Theo looked at her, and a smile spread across his face. 'You're *the* daughter. My grandfather came home so happy yesterday. He couldn't stop talking about her.'

'He wasn't upset with me?'

'No. He worried he upset you. You made his day.'

The shop door opened, and Despina stepped in. 'Oh, the girl has returned. We were sad about you. Why you rush out?'

'I'm sorry. That's why I'm here. I wanted to apologise.' Olivia stopped and took a deep breath. 'And to find out more about my mum.' Olivia took a step forward. 'Mrs—'

'Despina. Despina Diakos.' She looked at Demi. 'You are Anna's granddaughter. You have her eyes.'

'Yes? How do you know Yiayia?'

'We are Greek.' Despina turned to Olivia and rolled her eyes.'

Despina took Olivia's hand. 'Come, I will make coffee. George will be back soon, and we can talk. Theo, you look after the shop. Maybe Demi can help.' She looked at Olivia and winked. 'Come.'

Olivia followed Despina into a cosy kitchen area at the back of the shop.

'Coffee? Sit.'

'Thank you.' She took a seat at the old Formica table.

Despina snuck a glance into the shop. 'Theo is a good boy. But shy. Like you. Demi is a strong girl.'

Olivia looked at her with a curious expression, wondering how she knew that.

'Anna tells me she is a rebel.' Despina put a mug of coffee and some shortbread biscuits in front of her.

Olivia jumped in to defend her friend. 'She's her own person. She loves her family, but she wants to express her own style. Be independent.'

She sat down and patted Olivia's arm. 'I know she is a good girl. Anna tells me. It is okay to be who you want to be. Your mother was the same. Strong, but something sad underneath. For a while she was happy. In love, I think.'

Olivia reached into her bag and pulled out a copy of *The Queen's Gambit*. She removed a photo from it. 'Was it this man?'

Despina's glasses hung around her neck on a gold chain. She slid them on and studied the photo. 'He is very handsome, but I am sorry. I did not meet him.' She looked at the photo again, then at Olivia. 'You look like your mother. Only your hair is lighter. She had beautiful hair. Like the raven. An exquisite woman.'

'Theo! Who is this beautiful girl?' George's voice filtered in from the shop. Demi giggled. 'Hello, I'm Demi. Demi Kokkinos.'

'Good boy, Theo. A good Greek girl.'

Despina scuttled to the doorway. 'George!'

Olivia listened to the string of Greek reprimands. Based on Theo's and Demi's chuckles, she assumed they were light-hearted.

George stepped into the kitchen area and extended his arms. 'Olivia. I was worried I upset you the other day.'

Olivia stood and clenched her hands tightly. 'It was silly of me. I'm sorry. I didn't want to worry you.' Feeling the emotions percolating, she took deep breaths to steady herself.

'Sit. Sit.' George flapped his hands and sat at the table.

Olivia did as requested. Despina put a coffee in front of George and joined them.

'Now, what can I do for you?' George smiled. His wrinkled face held a kindness that made Olivia feel safe. She wondered if her mother had felt the same in his presence. The thought gave her some comfort.

'My mother died when I was thirteen.' She moved her hair away from the side of her face. 'This is how I got this scar. We were driving, and it was raining very hard. I missed my bus, and she was driving me.' Olivia looked down. Shame gripped her heart. She looked at their kind faces and blurted, 'I was shouting at her.' Olivia felt the tears coming and stopped to hold them back. Despina reached over and held her hand. The compassion pried open the floodgates, and the tears tumbled out.

'We had a terrible accident,' she said through messy sobs. 'When I came to, I was being cut out of the car. Mum was barely breathing. I kept saying I was sorry, telling her not to leave me. To hang on ... She didn't make it.'

Despina collected Olivia and held her.

Olivia took comfort in the motherly embrace. She pulled back and wiped her tears.

George and Despina looked at her gently, and she continued.

'We had been living with a lady called Shirley, who'd been in my life since I was born. Mum said Shirley saved her. Gave her a home. Shirley was all I had after Mum died.' Olivia took a sip of the coffee.

'Shirley passed away a few months ago. After her funeral, a steamer trunk arrived at my place in Annandale. It had all these items I'd never seen, including photos with your shop's details at the back.'

'Yes.' George wiped his eyes. 'Rosemary found the photography. This is how I knew her. Her friend bought the camera for her. She also developed the film here.'

'The camera was in the trunk, too. I still have it.'

Demi laughed loudly, and Despina looked out and smiled.

Olivia grinned. Her friend deserved to be happy. She turned to face George. 'Can you tell me anything about my mother?'

'She was very private. But I do have a copy of the receipt from when she developed the film.' George stood and walked to a dented grey filing cabinet in the corner.

Despina clicked her tongue. 'George throws nothing out.'

'See, and now I have reason,' he lobbed back at his wife, who swatted the comment away.

He opened the top drawer of the cabinet, pulled out a file and returned to the table, shuffling through the receipts. 'Benito. Rosemary Benito.'

'Benito?' Olivia frowned. 'My surname, my mother's surname, is Bennet.'

'Here. This is your mother's signature?'

Olivia took the receipt. She recognised the *R* and *B* in the large looping signature. 'This is like her signature, but the name is different.'

'Sometimes when we come here to Australia, it is hard as migrants.' Despina looked at the receipt. 'How do you spell your name?'

Olivia took out a pencil and notebook from her backpack and wrote *Bennet*. Despina studied it. 'It is similar. What do you think, George?'

He nodded. 'The woman I knew is the one in this photo.' He walked over to the wall and retrieved a picture, which he then handed to Olivia.

Someone had taken a photo of Rosemary as she was framing a photo herself. In the background was Luna Park's iconic happy face. Sparks of excitement ignited inside of her. She couldn't believe the coincidence. Olivia had many fond memories of the park. On her tenth birthday, she'd travelled down with her mum and Shirley. The day had been filled with thrilling rides, cotton candy and games—she'd won a kewpie doll playing the laughing clowns on sideshow alley.

'I will give you a copy? Yes?'

'Thank you.' Joy and sadness wove themselves together inside Olivia.

'Despina is right.' George took the photo back. 'Migrants often change their names to make them more Australian. My cousin changed his from Adamos to Adams.'

Olivia looked at the name on the receipt again. It was possible. The two signatures were very similar. Why not? She glanced at the address: 22 Vernon Street, Surry Hills. The same one Demi had found.

Olivia wrote it down, and a lightness descended on her. 'Thank you. The address is a start.' She couldn't believe her luck. Sebastian would be pleased. She'd let him know when she got back home. 'Can you tell me anything else about Mum? I know nothing about her life when she lived in Sydney.'

'Not a lot.' George placed the receipt back in the folder. 'Like I said, she was tight-lipped about her life.' He sat down and picked up the photo Olivia had brought. 'I did not know about this man.' Then his face lit up. 'But she had a friend. Mary? Maria?'

'Marie?' Olivia offered. 'Inside the trunk, I found a card from a Marie. And a picture of my mum with a nurse.'

'Of course. Rosemary worked at the big hospital where they have babies. Near Kings Cross.'

Through her research at the library, Olivia had matched the nurse's uniform Marie wore in the photo to some records of nurses working in the wards at St. Elizabeth's. 'I think she worked at St Elizabeth's Women's Hospital. But not as a nurse.'

'No,' George said. 'She was not a nurse. She worked in the kitchen. She delivered food to the patients.'

It wasn't a huge amount of information, but it was more than she'd ever had. Her mother had changed her name. She'd lived in Surry Hills and worked at St Elizabeth's Hospital.

'Would you like another coffee?' Despina smiled at Olivia.

Demi's laugh floated into the back room. Olivia nodded. 'Yes, please.' She'd give Demi more time.

'Good.' George clapped. 'Tell me all about Rosemary's life after she left Sydney. She was a good mother. Yes?'

Olivia smiled. 'She was.' And as she shared stories, a new light glowed inside her, bringing a comfort that had been missing for years. Her mother existed not just in her memories but in the memories of others. Listening to how George spoke of her mother, realising how much he'd cared for her, Olivia began to understand that some of the belonging she was searching for was woven into these memories. Connections existed all around her and in the most unexpected places. She just needed to open up more and give the universe a chance to surprise her.

The wooden cuckoo trilled and bowed. The sound always reminded her of her mum, who cherished the antique clock.

Olivia placed her mug of tea on the little side table next to the large wicker chair on the verandah. She'd found the chair in a second-hand shop last week and fallen in love with it. Now freshly painted a glossy canary yellow, it brightened the verandah, and the large peacock back allowed her to rest in comfort. The padded seat was large enough to cross her legs, and there was even room for Gin to cuddle in with her.

Peace drifted up from the bookshop. Right at midday, the workman took their lunch.

She settled back in to finish the last few chapters of *The Queen's Gambit*. The intricate chess moves detailed in the story were lost on her, but she felt a connection with the protagonist, an orphan. Olivia had read her fair share of stories featuring orphans.

Today, the story made her feel a little sadder and lonelier, though. Since meeting Theo a week ago, Demi had been spending most of her time with him. Her mother had cried with joy when she brought Theo home. After working so hard to avoid her Greekness, Demi had fallen hard for what her mother had always wanted for her.

'A nice Greek boy.'

Olivia was happy for Demi, but she missed her company. It didn't help that she wasn't working. It only stretched out her loneliness and made her think about Sebastian more. Sebastian always came when he could, but school had been busy, and she respected this. The school holidays had started on Monday, though, a couple of days ago, and she hadn't heard from him or seen him around. A niggly feeling of something she couldn't make sense of sat lodged in her chest. Did she miss his company? Did she ... She stopped herself. She wasn't going there. He was probably on some amazing trip with Clare.

Stop it.

He had every right to go where he wanted with whom he wanted. She needed to be grateful that he'd been around to help her uncover her courage to find out about the items. He'd been the nudge that got her started.

Olivia finally found her reading groove and escaped from her reality until the buzzer downstairs blared intrusively. Probably a workman looking for sugar again.

She tucked a bookmark into the novel and headed downstairs.

When she swung open the door, her heart leapt. Sebastian stood in front of her. Grinning.

'You!'

Sebastian cocked an eyebrow. 'Yep. Have I come at a bad time?'

'Yes. No. I mean. I didn't expect you.' Heat coated her cheeks. 'I thought you were on holidays.'

'I am. Can I come in?'

Olivia stepped to the side, and Sebastian came in and hugged her. 'I've missed you.'

All coherent words escaped her. She could manage only a nod. He pulled away and bounded up the stairs. 'Coming?'

'Yes,' she squeaked.

In her apartment, he plonked down on the sofa and pushed a lock of hair out of his eyes. 'I've come bearing gifts.' He patted the seat next to him and pulled out some books from the canvas bag he was carrying. It had Cookie Monster on the front. He handed the books to Olivia as she sat. 'I pilfered them from the book pile destined for next month's church fete. I've spent the last few days helping Nonna sort out titles into genre piles.'

So that's where he'd been. Helping his grandmother. She grinned to herself.

He leant in close, and she could smell his fresh, citrusy cologne. Her heart kicked up again.

'You'll love these. *Rebecca* and *My Cousin Rachel*.' He tapped the covers. 'People say Daphne du Maurier was a romantic novelist, but she wrote in the gothic style. Spooky stuff.'

This is what I love about Sebastian, she thought. *He's as passionate about literature as I am.*

She checked herself. Love? No. A teeny-weeny crush, maybe. Who wouldn't? He ticked all the boxes: kind, funny, supportive, accepting. The list went on. Geez. Love? No. This was *not* possible. She never gushed. Admired. Yes. Adored. Yes. She felt her cheeks burn at the very thought of feeling this way.

'Thank you.' She turned the books over in her hands and then gave him a feigned look of disapproval. 'Should you be stealing books meant for the church fete? It's not very Christian to steal.'

'Trust me, if they'd been Mills and Boon books, I wouldn't have survived the retreat. Oh, I also have some cake. Nonna made it for you.' He pulled out a Tupperware container.

'For me? But she doesn't even know me.'

'Well, not yet.' He winked. 'She's still waiting for you to come to dinner.'

'Would you like a coffee with it?' she blurted to deflect the wink.

'Sure.'

Olivia busied herself with making the coffee as Sebastian reacquainted himself with The Quest Wall. Olivia filled him in on everything they'd discovered so far. Finally, she took a bite of cake. It melted in her mouth, and she groaned. 'This is so good.'

'I'll let Nonna know.' He wiped a crumb from the side of her mouth, and she tried to hide the shiver that ran through her. 'So George didn't know anything about a bloke?' Sebastian asked, then shovelled another bite of cake in his mouth.

'He knew she was spending time with someone but said she was tight-lipped about it. The biggest breakthrough was getting the address of where she used to live. In Surry Hills. It's the same one Demi found.'

Sebastian turned to her. 'I think we should go and see Nora.'

Olivia almost choked on her cake. 'What? Now?'

'Why put it off?' A hint of cheekiness danced in his eyes. 'I promise to drive like a nanna.'

She felt her insides tangle and offered him a thin smile. 'What if no one's there?'

'We'll go back. Or leave a note.'

'What if they've moved?'

'We won't know until we find out.'

'Don't you want to finish your coffee and cake?'

Sebastian set his plate on the coffee table. 'The cake can wait. We can eat cake anytime. It'll be okay. We can just go and see. No pressure.'

The old heaviness returned. She didn't want to get her hopes up only to be disappointed. 'I've had this tiny fantasy playing in a loop inside my head for so long ...'

'How's that been going for you?' Sebastian gave her a broad grin.

She looked at him. 'Not great.'

'Come on. I'll be there with you.'

His hand was there, waiting for her to take it. She took a deep breath in and accepted it.

Outside, he unlocked the passenger door and opened it. Olivia stared, her heart beating fast.

'It's okay. You'll be safe.' Sebastian stepped up close. His voice was gentle. Reassuring.

He leant in, hung his arm across her shoulders and pulled her into him. For a moment, she felt nothing but the heaviness of his muscular arms.

Then an image of Clare popped into her mind. She pulled away.

'Let's go before I chicken out.' She avoided eye contact and slid into the front passenger seat. Swallowing hard, she gripped the seat belt. For the first time in a long time, she didn't know if her anxiety was related to being in the car. She couldn't deny it. She was falling hard.

CHAPTER 19

Rosemary

March 1964

'Show me.' Marie stubbed out her cigarette under the heel of her shoe.

They were sitting under an ancient Moreton Bay with Rosemary's picnic lunch spread out in front of them—ham and salami sandwiches, cheese, and pea arancini with a bean salad.

The sun beamed through the canopy, creating a dappled effect, and the skies were dotted with long clouds. A perfect autumn morning in the Royal Botanic Garden. Dusky moorhens with ruby-red beaks pecked at bugs around the edges of the pond in front of the two women. The harbour shimmered, and ferries crossed the sparkling blue water. Rosemary would never tire of this view.

She reached into her skirt pocket and pulled out the envelope.

'Fancy,' said Marie, taking it from her.

'Open it.' Rosemary popped a green olive in her mouth.

Marie's eyes widened. 'The Premier's Ball. Bloody hell, Rosemary, most first dates are dinner or a movie—maybe both if he really likes you. But the Premier's Ball? Geez. Anybody who's anybody will be there.'

Rosemary took the note back and slid it inside the envelope. 'This is too much. I do not know him.' She ran her fingers over the embossed emblem, then flapped the invitation at Marie. 'I only spent a little time with him. This ball is important, yes?' Her surprise at receiving the invitation had been followed by a sliver of excitement, but apprehension and unease soon lathered it away. She wasn't sophisticated enough to attend such a prestigious event.

'Pretty swish.'

Rosemary took a deep breath and let it out. 'No. It is nice to be invited, but I would not fit in.'

'Hollywood, have you looked at yourself in the mirror? You're a knockout. You will definitely fit in. In fact, you'll be the belle of the ball.'

———

JUST AFTER 2:00 PM, they packed up the picnic, and Marie left for the late shift at the hospital. Rosemary stayed in the garden to take photos. Her lessons were proving to be a worthwhile investment. In George's four-week course, she'd learnt how to use the camera to take artistic pictures and how to frame the shot for the best angle and focus.

She decided to head to George's to buy more film and pick up the photos she'd dropped off to be developed after the last lesson. As she made her way out of the garden, she stopped periodically to take photos. She loved capturing people just being themselves. The older man sleeping on the park bench with his hands on his cane and resting his chin on top. The two young mothers with their children, already tired as they sat and smoked on a park bench while the children chased pigeons. *Una vita semplice*. A simple life. Rosemary smiled.

She headed down Macquarie Street to Martin Place. Sydney wasn't as old as Sicily or Genoa, with their ancient villas and basilicas, but it had a fresh old-world charm to it.

Martin Place buzzed with activity.

Her creative radar pinged when she reached the grand post office. The imposing golden sandstone archways loomed ahead. In front of the majestic building, the granite cenotaph, with its bronze statues of soldiers on each end, intrigued her. 'To our glorious dead,' she said quietly. She lifted the camera to frame the shot and clicked away.

'Rosemary?'

She spun around and came face to face with Jack and another man. She startled, and her heart pounded. 'Hello.'

Jack returned a broad grin. The other man scowled—cool, handsome and broody, he stood straight and silent. Watching her. Had Jack told him about her? That she was an Italian migrant? There were many people in Sydney who were friendly, but some looked at her as if she'd come from the moon. Maybe he didn't approve.

She took a small step back.

'I hope we haven't disturbed you?' Jack asked.

'No. I was taking pictures. I have discovered photography since coming to Australia.' She held the camera up as evidence. The other man continued to stare at her. She swallowed.

'Do you take photos?' she asked Jack.

'Me? Only the obligatory ones at weddings and birthdays.'

He grinned, making her feel at ease. It surprised her that he was friends with someone as unfriendly as this other man. They appeared to be complete opposites.

'Sorry. This is Frank,' he said, gesturing to him. 'My best mate.'

'Have you known each other long?' Rosemary asked, attempting to be polite and deflect how uncomfortable Frank was making her feel.

'Since school,' Frank responded sharply.

He didn't like her. Rosemary fiddled with her camera strap.

'Excuse us, Frank.' Jack led Rosemary away. 'Did you receive my invitation?'

'Yes. Thank you also for the roses. They were very beautiful, but too much.'

A silence fell between them. Rosemary continued to play with the strap. The clock on the post office boomed out. Four o'clock. She needed to get to the shop before it closed.

'I have to go, sorry.'

'You haven't replied to my invitation.'

'Yes. I am sorry.' Rosemary packed her camera in its case. Looking at him would make her change her mind. His warmth and magnetic kindness would pull her in. He was easy to be around, but she didn't fit in his world. Frank had made that clear. A migrant woman wasn't the best choice for someone like Jack. It was the same in Italy. Those from a nobler class never married peasants. Even northern Italians looked down at the southerners, who were thought of as second-class people, as 'gypsies' and 'thieves'.

'Are you okay?' he asked quietly.

She could feel the heat coming off his body.

'I didn't mean to force you?' He stepped closer and touched her arm gently.

Her body vibrated. But she had already decided. 'I am sorry, but I cannot go.' She looked straight at him and ignored the burning desire in her heart. 'I will not fit in. This ball is very important, yes?'

'Well, yes, you could say that. But there will be all kinds of people. Even artists.' He nodded at her camera case.

She sighed. He wasn't going to let her off the hook. She needed to stand her ground. She wished she could lie, but for some reason, she felt as if lying to Jack would be like dishonouring the Church.

'I am sorry. I cannot go. I have nothing to wear. And my wages do not allow me to buy the kind of dress you must wear to a ball.'

'We've got to go, Jack.' Frank approached and tapped his watch.

Jack also checked his watch. 'Bugger. Thanks, mate.' Then he looked at Rosemary and whispered, 'I really hope you will say yes.'

He stepped back, held her gaze for a moment, then tipped his hat and rushed off. While the men waited at the lights to cross George Street, Jack turned and smiled at her. Frank, noticing where Jack's attention landed, turned to Rosemary and threw her a dark look.

Rosemary stood there, a searing heat sweeping down her body.

A combination of heartbreak and fear.

ROSEMARY MADE herself a cup of tea and took it onto the back verandah. She loved watching the sky dress for dusk. The verandah faced north and held the day's heat, staying warm until the sun dipped past the terrace rooftops. Rosemary lit the candles, a sweet defence against the insects that loved to share the house with them. The freshness of lemon myrtle and eucalyptus drifted around her.

The house stood quiet. Everyone was out.

Her thoughts continued to meander back to her home in Italy, and a wave of sadness filled her. She missed her little sister. Her mother too. Nearly four years had passed since she arrived in Australia, and it had been even longer since she'd seen any of her family. Her father would've disowned her as soon as he found out she'd shamed them—for running away days before she was to marry Emilio. She shuddered at the memory of her last meeting with him. Fifteen years older, he smelt of wet wool and bad breath, which seeped through his unkempt yellow teeth. When she noticed his calloused hands, she recoiled at the thought of them groping at her body.

Jack smells good. The thought burst in uninvited. She guessed he was in his late twenties. He had a youthful cheekiness in his eyes. His hands were broad with tidy nails, and when he touched her, they felt soft. She imagined he would be gentle.

'Am I too stubborn?' she murmured aloud. The words drifted away into the breeze as she sipped her tea.

Shaking her head in resignation, she picked up her worn copy of

Pride and Prejudice. A Christmas gift from Marie. Rosemary loved the story of the stubborn Elizabeth and the proud Mr Darcy. This was her third time reading it, and she was still discovering new things about the characters. She also loved *Emma* and *Sense and Sensibility.* The librarian had recommended other classics as well. Yesterday, Rosemary finished *Jane Eyre* and was keen to read other novels by Charlotte Brontë, as well as some by Charles Dickens, EM Forster and James Joyce. The classic novels helped her with her English vocabulary.

'Your English is so good,' the young librarian had remarked.

'Why, you think because I am from Italy, I cannot learn to speak English well or quickly?'

'No, no. Of course not. I'm terribly sorry.' The librarian blushed. 'It's just ... well ... we don't get a lot of migrants in the library. Borrowing classics,' she blurted, then offered a kind smile. 'Not many Australians borrow them either. They like their James Bonds, Mills and Boons, and Agatha Christies, but not the literature you're interested in.' She passed Rosemary's books to her. 'It makes me a little sad.'

'I am sorry.' Being an 'Iti', as she was often referred to, and often ignored or spoken to as if she were unintelligent, made it difficult to trust. But the librarian was only being kind. 'My friend says I must tame my fiery Sicilian temper. But it is no excuse. I do not like people to think I am not intelligent because I do not speak English well.' She smiled. 'I am Rosemary.'

'I understand. It mustn't be easy.' The young librarian held out her hand. 'My name's Pearl. Pearl Fitzwilliam.'

Rosemary accepted her hand. 'Rosemary Benito. You have the same name as—'

'Darcy, yes.' She laughed loudly, then covered her mouth. 'You know, Benito sounds like an Italian version of Bennet.'

Rosemary took in this little gem with a smile. 'Yes, it does.' *A good omen,* she thought.

Just as she began reading Elizabeth's reaction to Mr Darcy's proposal, the brass bell at the front door clanged. Rosemary checked the time. *Someone has forgotten their key.* She stood and stretched, long and languid like a cat. The bell sounded again with an air of impatience.

'*Pronto,*' she called out, slipping on her shoes. 'Coming.'

She opened the door to find a woman dressed in a severe navy suit. Her hair was swept back in a tight bun, and she peered over a tower of white boxes. 'Miss Benito?'

'Yes.'

'My name is Audrey. Audrey Parker. Mr Emerson asked me to deliver these to you.' She held out the boxes.

'Mr Emerson?'

'Jack. Jack Emerson.' She tapped her foot. 'He asked me to deliver these to you with strict instructions that I was not to leave until you accepted them. Which I hope you do because my duties do not usually involve delivering parcels to women.'

'Of course.' Rosemary took them, and the weight surprised her. 'What is it?'

'I don't know, and I'm not at liberty to open other people's parcels.'

She turned and clicked her fingers at a taxi idling in front of the terrace. She started walking towards it, then turned back. 'This is none of my business, but I've worked with Mr Emerson for a while now, and I've seen young women come and go. Not once has he asked me to run an errand like this.' She looked at Rosemary, and a smile like a thin crack in a china plate appeared on her face. 'You certainly have made an impression on him.'

Rosemary could only gape as Audrey clipped down the path.

'CAN YOU TALK?' Rosemary asked.

'Hang on.'

Rosemary heard movement on the other end of the phone, followed by Marie's muffled voice.

'Are you okay?' Marie asked.

'Did I disturb you?' Rosemary wrapped the cord around her fingers.

'Nah, I just asked Sal to play my hand. I was losing anyway. What's up?'

'Jack sent me something today.'

'How many flowers this time? Still trying to get you to go to that ball?'

'Yes.' Rosemary paused. She still couldn't believe it. 'But he did not send flowers.' There was a silent pause. 'Marie,' she said in almost a whisper. 'He sent me a dress. A gown. A Givenchy gown.'

'What? Are you sure?'

'If there is one thing I know, it is *alta moda*. You know, high fashion. An old friend used to have many magazines, and ...' She stopped, not wanting to reveal any more about the Contessa.

For a moment, there was silence down the line. 'Gosh. Geez, Rosemary, the bloke's smitten.'

'I am not sure. There is this saying in Italian: *Le cose luciccantisi appannano sempre con la vita*—Shiny things always tarnish with life.'

'There's also this saying in Australia—you only live once. What are you scared of?'

'Everything.' Rosemary placed her forehead on the floral wallpaper. Maybe it was time to share her past. She was starting to feel as if keeping it inside would tarnish the best parts of her. Living with the girls in the terrace house and becoming close with Marie, she marvelled at their unhindered talk about their families, their exploits as children, and their real experiences that formed authentic lives. Rosemary now felt that keeping quiet about her past had resulted in a broken identity. Lies and secrets corroded the very essence of who she was. She existed like an outline of a drawing—the shape was recognisable, but inside lay a blank reality void of tangibility. Like an infected wound, she needed to endure the emotional pain and lance her secrets.

'Marie, I think I need to tell you why I came here. I must also tell you that my real name is Rosamaria. Rosamaria Fazo.'

CHAPTER 20

Olivia
May 1989

As soon as Sebastian pulled his car away from the curb, Olivia's body heated and her heart raced. Embarrassed, she swallowed hard and took gentle breaths to calm herself.

'I'm going on holiday and I packed an accordion.' Sebastian smiled as he turned off her street, but his eyes stayed glued to the road.

She glanced at him. 'Sorry?'

'Your turn. Say, "I'm going on holiday and I packed a ..."' He shot a quick look at her. 'Finish the sentence with any item that begins with the letter *B*.'

'Banana,' Olivia said.

'I'm going on holiday and I packed a cactus,' he lobbed back.

'I get it!' Olivia laughed. She continued with the letter *D*.

By the time Sebastian pulled up in front of the house, they were halfway through the alphabet. Olivia let go of the seat belt sash she'd been gripping since leaving home. Her hands were cramped, but the game had been a welcomed distraction. Her heart swelled with appreciation for the easy way Sebastian had handled her fear.

'It looks neat,' Sebastian offered, looking out of the windshield. 'Ready?'

Olivia peered at the home. The home her mum had lived in. Excitement and uncertainty pushed the anxiety of the drive over to the side. She imagined her mum leaning over the wrought-iron balcony on a balmy summer evening or rushing down the path on her way to work. Had the man in the photo come here too? Knocked on the door with a bunch of flowers before taking her to dinner and a movie?

'I'm nervous.'

'I'm here.' Sebastian placed his hand over hers.

She warmed briefly and nodded.

Her legs felt as if they were filled with sloshy cement as she made her way to the gate. She let Sebastian take the lead and followed him up the path. The garden was quaint and gorgeous. Whoever lived here loved gardening. Her mum had loved keeping the garden in Killcare too. People were always amazed that she got plants to thrive so close to the ocean. Shirley had always said she had a way with nature. Had her mum also tended to the flowers here? The questions tumbled inside her mind.

Sebastian took her hand again before he rang the brass bell. The house sat still. Then she heard faint footsteps. Her heart fluttered.

A plump woman wearing a crisp white apron opened the door. She looked up at Sebastian. 'Hello?' she said in a lilting Irish accent.

Then she looked at Olivia and her hands went to her lips. 'It's you? Wee Olivia, is it?'

Olivia looked at Sebastian, then at the woman. 'Yes.' Confusion swirled inside her head. This woman knew her.

'My word and willywags.' She collected Olivia in a big, warm hug. 'I've always wondered if you'd come. Ever since your poor mother passed away, I wondered and hoped you'd find your way to me.' She held Olivia out at arm's length. 'Now look at me nattering on.' She laughed. 'I'm Nora.'

Olivia grinned. She already loved this woman. 'Hello. This is Sebastian. A friend.' She didn't look at him.

'Come in. I've just pulled a pie out of the oven. Do you like pie? I even have some clotted cream.'

'Sounds great.'

They followed Nora into the terrace home and up a dark, cool hallway into a tidy and bright kitchen where time appeared to have stood still since the 1950s. The only modern appliance was the microwave on the bench.

'Sit. A cuppa?'

'Please don't go to any trouble,' Olivia said.

'Never. I don't get a lot of visitors. The girls come as often as they can.'

'Your daughters?'

Nora smiled. 'No, the girls who used to live here. With your mother. My son passed away.' A shadow crossed her face. 'Vietnam. I live here now with my daughter-in-law and the grandchildren. They're on holiday on the Gold Coast having a ball of a time.'

Nora chatted away about her grandchildren and how she missed having them around as she prepared the tea. She placed warm pieces of apple pie and a large dish filled with cream in front of them. The pie looked exactly like the one her mum used to make. The sight and smell instantly transported Olivia back to her childhood. After school, before her mum started a shift at the hospital, she'd tell her about her day while they ate pie. Ache drummed across her chest, and she forced herself to focus on the present. She took a bite.

'This is delicious. Mum used to make the same pie.'

'Your mum loved cooking. She always cooked. Her Italian food was amazing. We used to swap recipes. She taught me to make pasta, and I taught her how to make cakes. *Anglo dolce*, she called them.' Nora pulled off her apron and sat down. She looked at Olivia. 'You're the spitting image of your mum. Except I see you were blessed with auburn hair.'

'You're the second person who's told me that this week.' Olivia teared up. 'I'm sorry. It's just ... all of this, it's bringing up a lot of stuff I'd chosen to ignore.'

'I'm so sorry about your mum's passing. It just broke my wee heart.'

'How did you know?'

'Marie. Your mum's best friend.'

Olivia brightened and reached into her backpack, thankful she still had the photos from her visit with George. She shuffled through them.

'Is this Marie?' She handed a photo to Nora and pointed. Her mum was sitting around a small table with three other women. They were all dressed up. All happy.

'Yes, that's Marie. The others lived here. The tall, elegant woman is Eleanor. She married a wealthy businessman and lives in Spain now. No children. By choice.'

'How about her?' Olivia pointed to the woman who reminded her of Brigitte Bardot. Her breasts were much more exposed than the others, and she was smoking a long white cigarette.

'That's Pamela. She was a hostess for Qantas. Funny. She was the wild one. There's always one.' Nora laughed. 'But she surprised us all and married a dairy farmer. They have a brood of little ones, and she helps run the farm, which is near Ballina. As soon as she met him, she changed. I've never seen her happier.'

Olivia took the photo back. 'I feel like I'm getting to know Mum all over again.'

'She never told you any of this?'

'None of it.' Olivia glanced at Sebastian, and he nodded. Olivia slid another photo over to Nora. 'Do you know who this man is?'

'Yes,' she said immediately. 'Jack. He was besotted with your mother. In the beginning, she was giddy with love, but something happened a couple of months before she moved away.' Nora squinted. 'Something happened that changed her. She never talked about it.' Nora sighed. 'Refused to. We all knew that if Rosemary didn't want to do something, you could never force her. She had a fiery temper.'

A shiver shot up Olivia's spine, and she felt a sudden urge to feel her mother's arms around her. 'I do remember her temper,' she said, nodding her head slightly. 'She was so stubborn.' A chill ran up her arms. Olivia gazed at the photo of Jack and her mum. 'You really don't know what happened?'

'Like I said, I knew not to pry. Your mum was lovely and polite, and the other girls loved her, but I always sensed there was something beneath the surface with her. Just a feeling. Call it mother's intuition.' Nora collected the empty cups. 'More tea?'

'Are you sure? I'd love to hear more about Mum.'

Nora looked up at the kitchen clock, also a throwback. 'I have a bit more time. I'm off to play bingo later. I do like my bingo.' She winked at Sebastian.

For the next hour, Olivia listened attentively as Nora told stories about the girls. When it was time to leave, she offered to help collect the dishes.

'No need.' Nora picked up her cup and then stopped. 'Oh, there is something. Goodness, I don't know why I didn't remember before.' She sat back down. 'A few weeks before Rosemary packed up and left, I came home as this elegant woman was leaving. I remember her because I had all this shopping, and she just pushed past me. Very rude. She had this hoity-toity way about her. You know, a decent person would've offered to carry some of my parcels up to the front door. She had airs about her, that one.'

Olivia's curiosity lit up. 'What did she look like?'

'Gosh. It was so long ago. My memory's not what it used to be. Funny, her actions have stuck with me, but not her face. Tall. Yes, she was tall, like one of those models in *Woman's World*. She reminded me of Princess Grace.'

'Grace Kelly?' Sebastian asked.

'Yes. Whatever happened while she was visiting Rosemary, what-ever she said, it upset your mother very much. Afterwards, your mum carried an air of fear, as if it had been chained to her.'

Olivia stilled as a dark cloud descended inside her mind.

What might she uncover?

CHAPTER 21

Rosemary
May 1960

A week before her wedding to Emilio, Rosamaria Fazo woke before dawn. Dressing quietly in the bedroom she shared with her little sister, she wished she could bundle up the girl and smother her with kisses. A deep sadness wrapped itself around her heart as she held back her tears and placed her only doll on the pillow next to her.

She could never tell her sister where she was going and why.

At eight, Viviana was still too young to fully understand, and it was too dangerous to leave such a big secret with her. She was a chatty little sparrow. Viviana knew how much the doll meant to her sister, so Rosamaria hoped it would be a little consolation for leaving and a sign that she loved her with all her heart. Maybe one day she could return and explain why she left.

'*Ti amo,*' she whispered and blew a kiss to where Viviana slept.

Rosamaria opened the heavy wooden door and looked out. The sun was rising, and she prayed the chickens were still asleep. They associated her with food and would cackle and sing when they saw her coming. She held her breath as she ran past the hen hut. There was no movement, and she sent a thank you to the heavens. She scurried down part of the rocky drive before turning sharply to run to the olive grove where she'd hid her belongings.

Then Rosamaria travelled across the fields towards Contessa Castello's grand villa to avoid being seen. The villagers knew that if they trespassed on the contessa's lands and were shot by her farmhands, it would be their fault. No one crossed Carmela Castello, especially if they leased their farm from her. She had the power to remove farmers from their homes and take away their lands. The woman was feared, and Rosamaria was grateful that over the past three years of tutoring the contessa's daughter, she had gained her respect, admiration and friendship.

Rosamaria arrived at the villa just as pink seeped into the faded blue of the late spring sky. Even though a chill lay in the air, sweat ran down Rosemary's spine, making her petticoat stick to her body.

She entered the villa by the servants' entrance and found Lucia waiting for her. Rosamaria's heart sparked with fear. Carmela had promised it would be their secret.

'Don't be angry,' Lucia said in Italian. 'I heard you talking to Mama. I promise I'll keep your secret for life. Even if I'm captured and tortured. I'll never breathe a word.'

'Lucia, I think I let you read too many stories.' She hugged her. 'But it's nice to have your support.'

Lucia pulled away and held both of Rosamaria's hands. At twelve, she was already as tall as Rosamaria. 'I was bursting with fear that you'd be caught. Mama is upstairs. We've run you a bath. She has a new plan.'

'Lucia,' Carmela said as she entered the kitchen. 'Have you offered Rosamaria a coffee or'—she took in Rosamaria's flushed cheeks and wet underarms—'a cold glass of lemonade?'

'No, Mama.' She turned to Rosamaria with bright eyes. 'Would you like a drink?'

'A cold glass of lemonade would be nice, thank you, Lucia.'

The women stood in silence until Lucia brought Rosamaria her drink and set a pitcher of lemonade on the wooden table.

'Lucia, go and check all is well upstairs while I talk to Rosamaria.'

They waited until the sound of footsteps on the stone stairs faded.

'She knows.'

'Yes,' said Carmela. 'I'm sorry. She heard us talking. My daughter has a vivid imagination. I think she'll be a great writer because of all your work with her.'

A flush of pride filled Rosamaria's chest. She loved tutoring Lucia. She was bright and shared Rosamaria's thirst for knowledge.

Carmela carried the pitcher of lemonade and led Rosamaria into her sitting room, shutting the door behind them. Rosamaria sat on the Venetian sofa and sipped her drink. The gold brocade seat sat firm against her thin cotton dress. The room was cool and filled with beautiful furniture and ornaments from the travels Carmela had taken with her late husband.

'I've arranged for you to be a proxy bride,' Carmela said as she placed the pitcher on a small marble table and sat opposite in a matching high-back walnut armchair. 'This is better. It is the same as migrating for a new life but with a purpose. Many single women travelling on the boat will be such brides. You will blend in. It's better that you don't know the details. We'll travel with you to Messina, then to Naples. This way, no one will be suspicious. I always have business in Naples. I've also organised some new clothes for you—you'll need them for your new life in Australia. They're more modern. In Naples, no one will ask questions about my purchases. I'll also pick up your proxy papers in the city. You'll take a new name as if you are married.'

Rosamaria took a deep breath as the reality of what she was about to do hit her. *Am I brave enough?*

'Are you okay?' Carmela poured some more lemonade into her glass.

'Yes.' She sat a little further forward in her chair. 'Carmela, am I a bad person for doing this?'

'Rosamaria, we women have a right to be free. To love freely and use our minds. You are strong and intelligent. Go make the world a better place. Be free. As God intended.'

'But would God want this? For me to dishonour my family?'

Carmela took her hand. 'You forget that God bestowed the greatest gift to Mary, who was a virgin. Though afraid, she took on the challenge and gave birth to our saviour.' Carmela made the sign of the cross and offered a kiss to Heaven. 'When you are successful and being free is part of your soul, you can come back. You can ask for forgiveness then.'

It made some sense to Rosamaria, but Mary had wanted Joseph. Rosamaria, on the other hand, had rejected her father's choice of a husband. And there wasn't a saviour in her womb, only heaviness and uncertainty.

FOR THREE DAYS, she stayed hidden in Carmela's villa, out of sight of even the servants.

The day after Rosamaria had run away, Lucia had said that she'd heard the help talking about it. Her older brothers had been in the piazza, stopping people to see if they'd seen her. They knew that some of her belongings were missing too. Some speculated that a famous Hollywood director had enticed her to America to be a great actress. Others were saying she had run away with a secret lover.

A heavy silence draped the parlour. Carmela leant forward on her chair and placed her embroidery in her lap. She looked over at Rosamaria, who looked up from her novel and offered her a reassuring smile.

'Lucia,' Carmela said, turning to her daughter, 'you must never breathe a word of this to anyone.' Her tone was calm but urgent. 'Promise on the Virgin Mary that this will be a secret.'

'But secrets are sins,' Lucia said, her brown eyes blazing bright.

'Sometimes, we have to bend the rules to make a better life. Rosamaria will make a good life. She'll become a doctor and give back for all of this.'

Nausea pushed itself up Rosamaria's throat. What was she thinking? She could feel the shame filling her veins. She'd carry this guilt for the rest of her life. 'Carmela, this is not fair to Lucia. It is too much for her—'

'No.' Lucia grabbed Rosamaria's hand. Her sweet, freckled face was set in a stern pucker. 'I will keep your secret. I promise I will never speak a word. I will say nothing. As God is my witness.'

'So much drama, Lucia.' Carmela smiled at Rosamaria.

Rosamaria felt some of the weight lift at the sternness of this twelve-year-old girl who was the sole heiress to the Castello estates. She admired her desire and determination to do the right thing, and with passion. Rosamaria placed her palm on Lucia's olive skin and looked into her dark, almond-shaped eyes. 'Thank you, Lucia. You'll be a wonderful noblewoman one day.'

Lucia lifted her shoulders and blushed. Then she threw her arms around Rosamaria. 'You will always be my big sister.'

When Sunday arrived, they prepared to leave for Naples. It was the perfect day to go, as Carmela gave the servants Sundays off to go to church and spend the day with their families. And because she'd be gone for a few days, Carmela had gifted the servants with a few extra days off. This would keep them away from the estate for longer.

Once all the servants had departed, Carmela drove the car out of the garage and parked it in front of the servants' quarters to allow Rosamaria to move into the back of it in secret. Lucia sat in the front.

As she walked out the door of the house, Rosamaria felt a burning desire to be on the boat to Australia before she changed her mind or worse—was discovered.

ROSAMARIA GAZED out of the hotel room window that overlooked Naples's narrow streets. Washing flapped in the wind like coloured flags at a festival. She hadn't left the room since arriving. For the past two days, Carmela had returned to the hotel room each evening, tired and hungry. Running errands wasn't something Carmela was used to; her servants usually attended to these types of tasks. With Rosamaria needing to stay hidden, the responsibility of getting everything organised for Rosamaria fell on the contessa and her daughter.

They had just returned to the hotel.

'Lucia, can you go downstairs and ask for coffee and antipasti to be delivered to the room?'

Rosamaria and Carmela watched as Lucia left and closed the door behind her.

'I don't want Lucia to know any more than she does,' Carmela said. She moved towards the small wooden table with a lopsided leg. A large wooden crucifix, the only ornament on the wall, sat above. Her purse sat on top. She reached inside and pulled out a bundle of papers tied with a red ribbon. 'It's better this way. Better for you.' She handed them to Rosamaria and rubbed her temples.

'Carmela, how can I thank you for all of this? I can see how tired you are.'

Carmela strode over to Rosamaria. 'I'm happy to do it. You have been so good to Lucia and a good friend to me. You never asked for anything.'

She kissed Rosamaria on each cheek, then handed her the bundle. 'You're now free to travel. You're married. By proxy. Tell people that your husband lives in a town in New South Wales called Griffith. Many Italians live there, and proxy brides too.'

She continued. 'Now listen carefully. You'll get off the boat in Sydney. Then, after a few days, you must buy a train ticket to Griffith.' She handed her another bundle. 'Here's the money. But you won't get on the train. You can decide where you want to go. If you want, you can stay in Sydney. It's full of Italians, and there's a priest at St Mary's Cathedral who will help you. His name is Father Silvio Paoletti. Or you can go to Melbourne. Any other place, really. Your new name, your married name is—'

'Benito.' Rosamaria sunk onto the edge of the bed as she read her marriage certificate. 'And this is the man I have pretended to marry—Arturo.'

'Yes.' Carmela sat down next to Rosamaria on the bed and took her hand again. 'When you get to Australia, find a new Christian name. Don't tell me what it is, and don't write to me or Lucia. We won't know who you are, and you'll disappear. It's better this way,' she said again.

Rosamaria hugged Carmela, no longer able to hold back her tears. 'I'm scared,' she whispered.

Carmela pulled away and looked her in the eye. 'You are clever. You are strong. People will see your kindness.'

Rosamaria nodded, weeping.

'Learn the language fast,' Carmela continued. 'Get an education and be free.' She reached up and held Rosamaria's face with both hands. Then she retrieved something from her pocket. 'Here.' She placed a gold ring in Rosamaria's palm. 'Your wedding ring.'

'No, Carmela, I cannot accept this. You've done too much for me already.'

'You're married. You must have a ring. Otherwise, people will be suspicious of your story. Saying you're a proxy bride in a city like Genoa is an easy deception, and the ring will keep you safe. Keep your reputation safe, Rosamaria,' she said, her voice becoming stern. 'You were born exquisite. I see how men watch you. It can be dangerous. Be careful.'

Rosamaria understood. She'd endured the catcalls and whistles whenever she went to the piazza to run errands for her mother. Her father was the only reason no one touched her. His reputation was one to be feared.

She'd grown to view her beauty as a curse. Her school friends had tried to convince her to enter the Miss Messina pageant, but she'd refused. Many young women entered, hoping to be discovered by talent scouts. A friend's second cousin had been, and she was now making movies—there was talk that she was shooting one with Marcello Mastroianni. But this had never interested Rosamaria. She wasn't just a pretty face or an object to be owned or admired. God had blessed her with looks, but he'd also given her a thirst for knowledge and the ability to learn.

She'd already paid the price for her beauty. Her own father had sold her to the highest bidder.

'Tomorrow morning,' Carmela said, 'I'll take Lucia to buy new clothes and shoes. When we're gone, you'll go to the train station and make your way to Genoa.'

Carmela had already explained that Rosamaria would wait for the ship to Australia there. She handed her a piece of paper. 'This is a restaurant. The owner will let you work there until your ship leaves, and there's a little room to rent too. Work hard and save money. And again, be careful. It's not always safe to be a woman alone in a big city.'

The next morning, Rosamaria watched with silent resolve as Carmela and Lucia walked down the cobbled streets. Then she picked up her suitcase and her handbag with her documents.

Finally, she took a deep breath, slipped on her wedding ring and disappeared from everyone and everything she knew.

CHAPTER 22

Olivia

May 1989

Olivia was silent on the drive home. Sebastian left her to her thoughts after a few rounds of car games, and she was grateful for that.

After parking near her place, he turned to her. 'I'm going to shout you dinner.' He held up his hand as Olivia was about to protest. 'No. I insist.' He looked at his watch. 'I'll pick you up at six.'

She offered Sebastian a weak smile. 'I don't think I'll be great company.' Olivia opened the car door and got out, then stood on the footpath, waiting for him to drive off.

Instead, Sebastian leant across the seat and rolled down the passenger window. 'I don't mind. By the way, it's a date.' He flashed a cheeky grin and drove off before Olivia could protest.

A date?

What about Clare?

After leaving Nora's, he'd mentioned something about Clare needing his support on something. Some big decision that involved seeing her parents in Canberra. Only snippets of information had filtered into her brain, given how hazy with fear her mind had been.

Once inside her building, she kicked the door closed and ran up the stairs, then fumbled with the key to the flat's door. *What am I doing?*

She paced the living room until Gin, wanting a scratch, got under her feet. She picked him up and held him close. Maybe Sebastian had meant a friend date, like something she and Demi would do. She shook her head to try to clear it of the chaos.

She headed to her room and pulled open the chifforobe door. Then closed it and stared at it. Her chest rose with anticipation. She sat on the bed and popped Gin down beside her.

No.

Walk away.

Just walk away.

Gin's big olive-green eyes followed her as she moved to stand. He meowed, and her heart crumbled. He loved her unconditionally and depended on her. What would happen to Gin if something happened to her? He would be alone. Wondering where she'd gone. The thought punched her in the chest. She picked him up again and walked out of the room to stand in front of The Quest Wall. She took deep breaths.

In for five, hold for seven, out for nine.

She slid down the sofa to the carpet and kept her gaze on the wall. Olivia felt her heart settle, and with the sensation came some peace.

There were still so many questions, but a clearer picture was beginning to emerge. She looked at the photo of Jack leaning against a brick wall. He was wearing swimming trunks, and his hair was wet and tangled. His smile accentuated the freckles sprayed across the bridge of his nose and his cheeks.

Her mother had been seeing this man. Dating? In love with?

She looked at the magazine article next to the photo and focused on the woman beside him. Tall and elegant. Her hair in a stylish chignon. Nora had said the rude woman looked like Grace Kelly. The name on the article was Lacey Hunter. Was this the woman Nora mentioned? What had she said to her mum that had upset her?

LEANING AGAINST THE KITCHEN SINK, Olivia glanced at her watch. It was already 5:30 pm. The panic of having nothing to wear was outweighing her nerves. Everything she owned was too casual. She was boring, and her clothes said as much.

She took small sips of her water. Maybe she could tell Sebastian she wasn't feeling well. Demi's voice punched into her thoughts: *Don't be silly!*

She finished her water and leant on the servery, her head in her hands. When she looked up, the rack of clothes tucked in the corner next to the sofa caught her attention. Her mother's outfits.

Olivia rushed over, pulled off the sheet and lifted out the black cocktail dress. Made of a heavy brocade, it had three-quarter sleeves and black sheer chiffon on top. Vintage and elegant. Olivia slipped it on. It was a little tight around her hips, and her breasts didn't quite fill the top, but it was comfortable.

She studied herself in the mirror. Her simple black kitten heels would suit the dress, but she needed an updo. She brushed her thick hair straight and fashioned it into an ample bun on top of her hair. Better, but the outfit still needed something.

She rubbed her fingers together and glanced over at the chifforobe. An idea formed. She rummaged inside her sewing kit until she found the black velvet ribbon Demi had given her. Weeks ago, she'd tried to convince Olivia to wear it around her neck like a rocker chick. Now, she sent a mental kiss to Demi. Somehow, she always delivered. She placed the ribbon around the base of the bun and tied it in a small bow. She smiled. It was elegant.

Next, she gently teased out some of her hair with a rat comb and fashioned it so that it sat over most of her scar. She dulled the pink raised skin that was still visible with some foundation and then concealer. Demi had told her to emphasise her eyes to draw attention away from her scar, but she didn't know how. Remembering the photos of her mum, she found a closeup of her face and copied the eyeline, sweeping the black kohl up at the end for a cat's eye look. She darkened her eyebrows and tidied them into a smoother shape before sweeping on copious amounts of mascara, forcing her thick eyelashes to curl up and open her eyes.

Olivia stepped back. Not bad, though she felt a little exposed. What would Sebastian think of her Dior dress?

She picked up her purse. As she popped her keys inside, she caught sight of her novel on the coffee table and hesitated. She picked it up and shoved it in her purse, forcing the clasp to close, but it looked too bulky. Sighing, she took it out and wished books could be carried around in little electronic devices that were the same size as a wallet.

Olivia took one more look in the mirror, smoothed the dress down and took a deep breath before opening the door to head downstairs for her very first date.

She stopped.

Should she wait until Sebastian rang the buzzer? Was she being too eager?

Olivia closed the door and sat on the sofa.

Within minutes, the buzzer trilled, causing her to jump. She stared at the door as her nerves danced a jig inside her belly. It rang again. She stood and glanced around the apartment, stepped onto the landing, closed the door and locked it. Sebastian's shape was visible in the frosted glass downstairs.

She took a deep breath. 'Okay,' she whispered, then walked down the stairs and opened the door.

'Wow.' His mouth hung open. 'You look—'

'Too much? I didn't know what to wear. It's my mum's.'

'I know. It looks amazing on you.' Sebastian moved his hand from behind his back and held out a bunch of roses.

Olivia didn't know what to do or say, so she just stood there, looking at the roses. Roses were romantic, right? All the books and movies said as much. Oh my God, this was a date. An actual date.

'In case you're wondering, these are for you.' He smiled. That beautiful smile. Then he leant forward and placed them in her hands.

'Thank you,' said Olivia.

'You're welcome.' He leant down and gave her a kiss on her scarred cheek.

Embarrassment gripped her. 'Water. They should be in water.'

She turned away and shut the door on Sebastian. After fumbling for her keys, she let herself back into her apartment and placed her hand on her cheek. He'd kissed her. Roses and a kiss. What did it all mean? He had Clare. She didn't want to be part of some sordid love affair. Her hands shook as she filled her water jug and placed the roses inside.

She'd be careful. They were just roses, and friends kissed each other hello.

When she opened the door, she found Sebastian standing where she left him. She gulped. 'Sorry. I didn't want them to wilt.'

'Okay.' Sebastian looked at her with amusement stamped on his face.

'Are you making fun of me?'

'No.' He smiled again. 'Are you nervous?'

'No. Yes.' She chewed her bottom lip. 'A little.'

'I promise I'll be on my best behaviour.'

She relaxed a little. 'Does that include not telling corny primary school jokes?'

Sebastian grabbed his shirt above his heart. 'Ouch.' He laughed and grabbed her hand. 'Come on. I got us a table at the Abbey.'

Now Olivia was even more nervous. 'That's expensive.'

'A mate from school is the sous-chef there. He pulled some strings to get us in tonight.'

She felt both relieved and a little disappointed. They were going there because he knew one of the chefs.

During the five-minute drive, Sebastian kept the atmosphere light, offering morsels of information about his mate. He'd always come first in his home economics class—the other boys had thought the subject was a big joke. Olivia became so enthralled by his stories, she forgot about her anxiety. The fact that it was only a short trip helped too.

After parking, Sebastian got out first and raced around to open Olivia's door. She giggled as he held out his hand. She'd only experienced this through the heroines in her books. A warmth filled her body, and she felt a little giddy.

After Sebastian locked the car, he turned to her, his blue eyes shining in the early evening light. 'You do look beautiful.'

Olivia didn't have time to blush because he grabbed her hand. 'Come on, I'm starving.' He escorted her to the large wooden cathedral-style doors.

The food looked like art on a plate and tasted just as good. As they dined, Sebastian entertained her with stories about the antics his class had got up to in the last week of the school term. Olivia watched his eyes dance with passion. It was obvious he loved teaching. *Those kids are lucky to have him*, she thought, not for the first time. Listening to him eased her nerves.

Halfway through their first course, Sebastian fell silent and gazed at her. Calmness bathed his face. 'So, do you know what you're going to do with everything you've uncovered so far?' He placed his hand on the table close to her. 'You were quiet after we left Nora's. Are you okay?'

Nora had given her an address. Marie lived in northern New South Wales. She wanted to speak to her, but what if the feeling wasn't reciprocated? She stirred her soup. Took a sip and stirred some more.

'Is something wrong with your bisque?'

She realised she hadn't responded to his question. 'No. It's great.' She took a mouthful. 'I was thinking.'

'Ah, the reason for that little crease above your nose.' Sebastian pointed to the spot on himself. She was taken aback by his intimate observations. A veil of tenderness woven with tiny knots of bemusement wrapped itself around her.

'I want to see Marie Middleton.'

Sebastian nodded and waited for her to continue.

'What happens if she doesn't want to talk to me, though? Or worse still, slams the door in my face? What if my mother did ... was doing something ... well ... you know ... unsavoury? Or they had a fight, and that's why Mum went away?'

'Whoa, that's a lot of questions.'

'I know. That's why my head hurts.' She took a sip of wine and looked at Sebastian. 'I don't think I can do this alone.'

'I'll come with you.'

Olivia sat back. She'd hoped he'd say this but hadn't actually expected it. Teachers worked so hard, and their holidays were precious. It was the only time they could travel and catch up with friends. Plus, all that planning they had to do. Besides, he'd already given up so much of his time.

'Why? I mean—' Olivia stopped. Excitement and fear jostled inside her chest. She'd be alone with Sebastian. On a road trip. In a car. She rubbed her forehead.

She shrugged, trying to not let him see the emotional war waging inside of her. 'Why would you give up your holidays to go on what might be a wild goose chase?'

'Lots of reasons. We'd be getting out of the city. We could make it into a fun road trip. You know, sing songs, eat red frogs, drink buckets of Coke.' He wiggled his eyebrows.

'What about your nonna?' *And what about Clare?* 'And don't you want to spend time with your other friends?'

'Olivia, if you don't feel comfortable travelling with me alone, I understand.'

He was right. She was also nervous about spending time with him. Alone in the car. In a motel ...

'It's not that. Well, it is. I know you're not some kind of serial killer. But ...' Unable to stop the blush, she took another sip of wine.

Sebastian touched the top of her hand. 'Of course, we'll get separate rooms. Or I'll happily sleep on the couch.'

Olivia gave him a small smile. That solved at least one problem. 'You must think that I'm such a prude.'

'Olivia, my nonna raised me to be a gentleman, and I'll always respect a lady. Especially one I like.'

Olivia's mind tripped over itself. She moved her hand from under Sebastian's and put it on top. 'Thank you. I like you too.' She cleared her throat. 'You're a good friend. You've been so kind and helpful.'

'Like I said. Nonna wouldn't expect anything less.'

'There's one more thing. I know Demi wants to be involved. She's just as intrigued as I am about Marie Middleton.'

'Tell her to come too.'

'Are you sure?'

'The more the merrier. See, nothing to worry about.'

Yes, just friends. Why else would you be so keen for Demi to come too?

CHAPTER 23

'No way.' Demi lit a smoke and jumped onto the verandah ledge. Olivia squeezed her eyes shut. One day, her friend was going to topple over.

Ever since her dinner with Sebastian two days ago, she'd been rehearsing her speech to convince Demi to come along on the road trip.

'You have to come. I don't want to be on my own with Sebastian. Please.'

'How's he going to make a move on you if I'm hanging around like an annoying mozzie?'

'Demi. He's a friend. Period.' She didn't want to tell her about Sebastian's gentle kiss on her lips after he walked her to her front door. Feeling even more unsure about moving forward with any relationship with him, she'd simply said thank you and rushed inside. *Thank you!* Those two unromantic words bounced around her head. Reliving it again sent a racing heat to her checks. What a ninny.

'You keep telling yourself that, Livvie.'

'Please, Demi. You said you wanted to come.'

Demi took a long drag. 'Fine, but if I get a sniff of romance, I'm catching the first train home.'

'Deal.' Olivia was confident that romance would not be on the cards.

THE NEXT MORNING, the phone jolted Olivia from her sleep. She rubbed her eyes and turned towards the clock on her bedside table. It was after nine. She peeled herself from the warm bed and wrapped herself in her dressing gown. The cold floorboards shocked her awake. She really needed to get some slippers.

'Hello.'

'Olivia? Olivia Bennet?'

'Yes. May I ask who's calling?'

'My name is Susan Collins. I'm from Morris, Templeton and Gray.'

'Sorry?'

'Solicitors. We received a letter from you enquiring about receipts for Our Lady Queen of Peace.'

Oh. She perked up. 'Yes.'

'Mr Templeton wants to know how you came upon these receipts.'

'They were with some items my mother had. She passed away.'

'Yes. In 1978.'

'How do you know?'

There was a moment of silence. 'Mr Templeton was wondering if you could come in and see him.'

After hanging up, Olivia walked over to the butcher's paper on the wall. Next to *William Templeton—solicitor* (*school receipts?*), she wrote, *Contact made—appointment next week.*

She glanced at the web of intrigue and thought about the headway that had been made. She'd found out about George and his camera shop. Met Nora, who'd given her Marie's address. And now she could find out why her school and boarding fee receipts had come from the law firm.

Her mind constantly spun back to the question of who her father was. Was it this Jack person? Was her mum having an affair with him, or was he a ... client? This question was the one that scared Olivia the most. Her mother had lived in Surry Hills, which was only a thirty-minute walk to the Cross or a quick taxi trip. And from the photos, it seemed she'd spent a lot of time there. Was this why her mother had been so secretive about who her father was? Did she even know who the father was?

She forced up the images of the woman she'd known—a kind, caring person who worked as a nurse and went to church when she wasn't on a Sunday shift. Olivia couldn't imagine her mother working in a profession in which she'd be required to give up her body in the most intimate way. She let out a long sigh and hoped Marie would have some answers.

The phone rang again, startling her. 'It's like Central Station this morning,' she said to Gin, who jumped onto the sofa with a contented look now his tummy was full.

'Livvie, don't hate me.'

Olivia hated it when Demi started a conversation this way. 'What have you done?'

'Not me. My sister. And my mum. I have to go out to Woop Woop to get fitted for a bridesmaid dress. Apparently, they're having a special. This wedding of my sister is getting bigger than Ben Hur.'

Olivia's stomach twisted into a tight ball. 'Oh' was all she could squeak out. She looked out at the bright blue sky and focused on the chatter of the morning out on the street. A cool breeze blew in, and she shivered.

'I'm really sorry. Are you okay? If you're worried about being alone with Sebastian, don't be. I could give him, you know, "the talk".' Demi said the last words like a Mafia boss.

Olivia couldn't help laughing. 'I guess I need to pull up my big-girl pants and trust him. Demi, do you trust him?'

'Yep. Besides, would it be so bad if he makes his move?'

'What are you saying—'

'I'm coming,' Demi shouted, away from the phone. 'Hang on.' The phone clunked about. 'I'm on the phone to Olivia. She's very upset, Stephanie.'

Olivia tried to talk over Demi. 'It's okay. Demi?'

'Shit, I've stirred up the moussaka here. Gotta go. Mum sends her love.'

And in Demi's whirlwind style, she was gone.

Olivia sat down on the couch and placed her hand on her chest to still it. Alone with Sebastian.

Gin looked at her and let out a low meow.

'I know how you feel.'

CHAPTER 24

Rosemary

June 1960

A small lunch crowd sat under the red awning in front of Trattoria Chiara. A cool breeze always found its way up the narrow laneway from the Gulf of Genoa, but the summer sun was already warming things up. The café kept her busy and occupied her mind. The next ship to Australia was due to depart in six weeks. She'd purchased her ticket, which had substantially depleted the chunk of money Carmela had tucked away in her papers. It was strange to see her new surname written across the top. She kept the ticket with her savings underneath her mattress.

A few days earlier, a young married couple from Australia had stopped at the trattoria for lunch.

'*Buongiorno.*' Rosamaria had smiled at them. They were clearly in love, whispering in each other's ears and grinning. '*Cosa vorresti?*'

'Good morning,' the woman said to Rosamaria, then turned to the man. 'She asked what we would like.'

She looked back to Rosamaria. 'I'm sorry, I don't speak a lot of Italian. Only what I studied at school. This is William, my husband, and I'm Tillie. We're on our honeymoon.' Tillie stopped, and her brows knitted together. '*Questo William, io e mio marito siamo, Tillie. Siamo in luna di miele.*'

'That is very good,' Rosamaria said in English. 'As you can see, I am not good at English. Maybe together we will be able to talk. *Si?* Yes?'

Tillie clapped and smiled. Her blonde curls bounced, catching the sun. Rosamaria warmed to her straight away.

William extended his hand and smiled warmly. 'Nice to meet you ... I didn't catch your name.'

'Rosamaria. It is nice to meet you.' She returned the handshake.

She served them lunch, and afterwards, William invited her to join them for a glass of wine. The café owner didn't mind, being friendly to the customers meant return business or referrals.

Tillie and William told her all about their honeymoon and the places they had been. They laughed and held hands, clearly in love.

Rosamaria's heart swelled. This was what love and marriage should look like.

Tillie and William ate lunch at the trattoria every day they were in Genoa, and Rosamaria enjoyed serving them. She wanted to tell them she was moving to Australia, but they already knew she was Rosamaria, and Carmela had told her to find a different name. Besides, the chances of her ever seeing them again were as slim as catching a falling star. Australia was a big country.

When business was slow, Rosamaria would teach them some Italian so they could impress their friends back in Sydney. In return, they'd help her with some English phrases. It was a wonderful three weeks. Having people to talk to made her feel less lonely and eased the shame of dishonouring her family, which usually sat heavy in the pit of her stomach.

Before they were due to head to London to catch their flight back to Australia, Tillie and William stopped in to see her, and Tillie flung her arms around her. 'You've been awfully delightful.'

'*Grazie.* Thank you. It has been nice for me too.' Rosamaria returned the hug and swallowed her tears.

'Oh, I nearly forgot.' Tillie handed Rosamaria two books. 'To help you with your English.'

'No, *mi dispiace*, I cannot accept this.' Rosamaria handed the books back.

'Of course you can. I've already read them both. You'll be doing me a favour and lightening my luggage. William would appreciate it. Wouldn't you?' She smiled at her husband.

'Tillie's right. As she always is.' He brushed a kiss onto the top of Tillie's head.

Rosamaria looked at the books. '*A Room with a—*'

'*View.* And *Tess of the d'Urbervilles.* My mother is a teacher and says that to master English, one must read and read widely,' Tillie said in an exaggerated British accent.

'Thank you.' Rosamaria opened *A Room with a View.* A note sat inside.

'It's our address in Sydney. If you ever come to Australia, please look us up.' Tillie had also signed it:

Love Mrs Matilda (Tillie) Templeton

'This is my card,' William said, handing one to her. 'I'm joining my father's law firm when we return. If you ever need any advice. I'm not sure what the law's like here in Italy, but I could be of some help.'

'Thank you. Here, it is every man for himself.' Rosamaria laughed. Inside, she wasn't laughing. In Sicily, the law was primitive and patriarchal. Her heart tightened at the thought of what her father would do to her if he ever found her.

———

AFTER TILLIE AND WILLIAM LEFT, Rosamaria kept to herself, feeling a little sadder than she had before their arrival. She bought food at the market near the Piazza De Ferrari, close to her home, and every Sunday, she went to Mass. She enjoyed the five-minute walk from her little flat to the Church of the Holy Name of Mary. Afterwards, she stopped at a little café tucked away in an alley to enjoy an espresso and read the books Tillie had gifted her.

One week before her departure date, the boat taking her to Australia arrived. Curious, she went to look at the ship that would be her home for nearly two months. Standing on the dock, she felt both excitement and anxiety. This was it. She was really going to leave Italy forever. She was going to abandon her identity and throw away her true self and her culture.

A salty breeze blew off the sea. Gulls circled and screeched above the fishing boats that chugged out. Rosamaria took a stroll and stopped to buy gelato from a café that had only just opened after the *riposo pomeridiano*, the city's afternoon sleep.

'*Buonasera*,' Rosamaria greeted the young girl at the counter. Exercise books lay sprawled across it. She noted a page filled with numbers and mathematical symbols. 'For school?' she asked in Italian.

The girl nodded. '*Ma non mi piace matematica.*' Her Italian was softer than the usual verbal gusto that filled the Genovese streets.

'I don't like mathematics either, but it will help you be clever.'

'Silvia, why have you not served this beautiful lady?' scolded an older woman.

'It's my fault,' Rosamaria said to the woman. 'I was asking about her homework. May I have a pistachio gelato, please?'

The woman grabbed a cone. '*Grande o piccolo?*'

'Small, please.'

'You know, everyone here talks about you. The beautiful woman with the body of Sophia Loren and the face of the Madonna who arrived one day from nowhere. "Is she married?" they all ask.' She glanced at Rosamaria's gold ring. 'Ah, you are. But we never see your husband. Are you a widow?'

'My husband is in Australia. Melbourne.' The lie came easily. It was the first time she'd spoken it. The knowledge that the ship had docked had kindled a fragment of courage in her.

'*Sei una sposa per procura?*'

'Yes, I'm a proxy bride, Signora.'

'I see. I hope he is a good man. My sister's cousin went to Australia as a proxy bride in 1955. He sent a photo. A very handsome man. When she got there, it was not the same man. He sent his cousin's photo. Disgraceful. But there were no more men in their village. She is happy. She has children. They have learnt to love each other.'

Rosamaria paid for the ice cream and turned back to the girl. 'Be good and work hard at school. It is important for girls to use their brains.'

'Says the woman who is married and will spend her life birthing children. By the look of you, you will be very busy. Your husband has got himself a prize.'

Rosamaria seethed inside and plastered on a smile. 'Goodnight, Signora.'

She walked off. The ice cream tasted like sour milk, and she threw it in a nearby bin. The seagulls immediately swooped down to peck at it. To Rosamaria, it felt as if they were pecking at her heart. She was so tired of the comments about her looks. Maybe Tillie was right. Maybe she should go to Hollywood. Then she'd make a lot of money and shut everyone up.

The woman's comments continued to fester in her mind as Rosamaria walked back to her flat. She thanked God she wasn't actually a proxy bride. She'd heard the stories too—about men who lied about their age or who said they had good jobs and owned grand houses. Sometimes it worked in the bride's favour, though. Without this arrangement, some women would never find a husband because of a disability or because they were plain-looking. The grass was always greener. Rosamaria shook her head at the absurdness of it all. For her, beauty didn't bring great romance or great love. If anything, it shackled her to people's perceptions of her.

She climbed the rickety stairs to the third floor. As she reached her flat, a chill shook her. The door was ajar.

Her money. Her ticket.

She rushed in.

'Buonasera, Rosamaria.'

Lying on her bed was Lorenzo, a waiter from the trattoria where she worked. Her heart dipped when she saw he was holding her ticket. She glanced at the bottom of her mattress.

'You don't need to worry. Your money is safe. But there's a lot of it.' He removed a cigarette packet from his shirt pocket and offered her one.

Rosamaria shook her head, clocking him. He lit a cigarette and took a long, slow drag. Then he picked out a piece of tobacco and flicked it to the floor.

She continued watching him carefully as he turned the ticket in his hand.

'Going somewhere?'

'Yes.' Through the open doors, the sea was visible. Down on the dock was the ship. It would be months before another could take her. By then, her father and older brothers might have found her.

She looked directly at Lorenzo. 'My husband is in Australia.' She held up her left hand.

'*Bella donna.* I do not believe you.' Lorenzo got off the bed, leaving the ticket on it, and strutted towards her.

Rosamaria stiffened. He moved around her and picked up the bra she'd left on a chair. He held it to his nose. She lunged towards the bed, but Lorenzo moved faster and grabbed her arm.

'No, no, no.' He tsked, then reached across her and grabbed the ticket. 'It seems this is very important to you.'

'What do you want?'

Lorenzo pushed her towards the bed. 'Sit.' He pulled up the old chair she kept near the French doors and sat directly in front of her. He pushed her skirt up so it was high on her thighs and ran his fingers up and down her legs. 'You know, I have a friend who likes women like you. I help him find beautiful women.'

Rosamaria grabbed her skirt and pulled it down. 'I told you I'm married.'

'Listen.' He grabbed her wrist, and she winced as he squeezed. 'If you want to see your ticket again, you have to do this.' He studied it. 'I see the boat leaves in seven days. I think you don't have a choice.'

Rosamaria looked up at him. She wanted to rip out his eyes, the colour of bile. 'What does he want? Your friend.'

'Good. It's good you understand.' He released her wrist and reached inside his jacket. 'You see, I know what you are. You are a whore. And he likes whores. He will pay me handsomely for finding you, and then I can give you your ticket back.'

He picked at his teeth.

Something gripped her lungs and squeezed the air out of them. Nausea rose from the bottom of her stomach. 'No! I cannot. It's disgusting. A sin. I will be shamed forever.' Hot tears threatened to erupt, and her temples pounded with anger. 'No. I won't do it.'

She watched in horror as he put the ticket in his jacket. 'If you want your ticket, come the day after tomorrow. To this address.' He held out a card. Rosamaria refused to take it. 'It's your choice.' He flicked it on the bed. 'You come, I'll give you the ticket back.'

Once he left, she flew to the door and locked it, and the tears she'd been holding back escaped down her chin. She shivered and wrapped herself in the shawl Carmela had bought her in Naples. She walked to the balcony and tightened the wrap around her shaking body. The sky, now filled with stars, mocked her stupidity.

She heard a woman's laughter. A young couple walked by. A man pulled her in tight as he protected her with an arm across her shoulders. Tourists. Free to live the way they wanted.

'Gracious Mary,' she whispered to the heavens. 'Forgive me.'

ROSAMARIA STEPPED into the foyer as the maid closed the panelled walnut front door. The echo ricocheted off the white marbled floor. A heaviness pushed down against her chest as she allowed small amounts of breath to stealthily enter her lungs.

'*Per favore vieni con me.*' The maid clipped up the winding staircase.

Rosamaria stiffened and followed. When they reached a set of closed doors, the maid stopped.

'Paolo Orsini will be with you in a moment.' Opening the door, she locked her gaze onto Rosamaria and pressed her lips tight.

Rosamaria lifted her shoulders and pushed the pounding fear deep into the darkest pit of her mind. Left alone, she took in the opulent four-poster bed. She reached up and fingered the gold cross. Taking off her gloves, she steadied her hands, unclasped the necklace and placed it in her handbag.

'You are more beautiful than Lorenzo has said.'

Rosamaria spun around. A striking man in his early thirties stepped into the bedroom. Her stomach clenched as she took in the black silk rope he wore. The reality of what was to come strangled her vocal cords.

'You speak English.'

'Yes, when I was at university, I made friends from America, Britain, even Australia.' He rotated her papers in his hands. 'A place I see you are going to.' He grinned at her. 'Maybe?' He held the documents up.

An anger rose within her. All semblance of fear dissipated. 'How dare you? I have come. Now you dare play with me. *Disgustoso.*' Rosamaria untied her headscarf and flung it onto the bed. She wanted to spit in his face. Instead, she reached around to unzip her dress. She wanted this sordid event to be done.

Paolo moved swiftly and held her hands as he 'tsked' in her ear. 'No, no, no.' He placed her arms by her side. 'You belong to me for the entire afternoon.' He stroked her cheek, and Rosamaria used every strength within her to not bite him like a rabid dog. Instead, she focused on the bundle of papers on the red velvet chair.

Paolo hooked his finger under her chin and brought his lips to her as he pressed his manhood against her. Rosamaria stilled her mind and focused on one thing—the only thing. Her freedom and new life in Australia.

CHAPTER 25

April 1964

Marie's eyes were full of compassion as she sat on the bed listening to Rosemary's story. 'I'm sorry this happened to you,' she said when Rosemary had finished. 'No wonder you shy away from the way you look. But ...' She took her hand. 'You're safe now.' She nudged Rosemary. 'This is Australia. And the 1960s. People are changing their stuffy ways. Besides, you live on the edge of the Cross. Believe me, I reckon there are plenty of girls who've done the deed—by choice ... or not.' She offered a lopsided grin.

Rosemary shrugged.

'Rosamaria Benito. I get Rosemary. But why Benito?'

'It was the name Carmela chose. At first, I did not like it because it was Mussolini's first name. But here in Australia, it is just another Italian surname. I am filled with such shame. After the incident, I was so desperate to leave Italy. *Per fortuna,* thankfully, it was only a few days before I left Genoa. I did not leave my room. I could not face the outside world for fear that people would know. Or that he would come for me again.'

Rosemary's throat constricted. 'I was a *puttana*, a whore; it made me sick. I went to confession, but it did not still my shame.'

Rosemary stared out of the open sash window. A kookaburra chuckled. Nora told her they sang when a storm was coming. She looked across the terrace houses framed by a sky washed in purples and pinks as the sun set behind their metal roofs and brick chimney stumps.

'Rosemary,' Marie said with care.

Rosemary turned and locked eyes with her friend.

'You can trust me. Promise.'

She knew she could. Marie always listened to her without judgement, always with kindness. More than anything, she wanted someone to listen. Someone she could rely on. Someone who cared about her.

'You were forced into it, Rosemary. You had no choice,' she consoled and put her hand on Rosemary's back. 'What was the word you used?'

'Puttana.'

'You know it's just a word. Kind of like "harlot". It doesn't define you.'

'You are right. It is just a word. Sticks and stones. Yes?'

'Yep. Pootarna,' Marie said with a cheeky grin.

'Puttana.' Rosemary tittered at Marie's accent.

'Poo-tar-na!' Marie giggled. Rosemary shrugged and then joined in. They fell upon each other, shrieking with laughter.

'What's so funny up there?'

They both stopped and peeked through the fretwork. Nora stood on the pavement, looking up at them.

They scrambled to their feet and leant over the balcony. 'Oh, nothing.' Marie giggled again. 'We're just talking about how women are defined by our actions, not by labels.'

'I could've told you that,' Nora said as she trundled up the path towards the front door.

Marie turned to Rosemary. 'Wanna go to the pub for a drink? I think we both need one.'

'That is a good idea.'

Sharing what had happened during those last days in Genoa had made her feel lighter. Somehow less shameful and lonely. It was a big risk telling Marie about it, but she was so glad she had.

'Marie?'

Her friend met her gaze.

'Promise this will be our secret. That you will tell no one about what I did. Ever. I am serious.' Rosemary's heart thumped. 'Please promise me.'

'I give you my solemn word.' Marie wrapped Rosemary in a hug. 'Pinky.' She wiggled her little finger.

'Okay.' Relief settled in the pit of her stomach. She ran her hand along the cool fabric of the Givenchy gown hanging on the open wardrobe door. She adored the texture. Jack had spared no expense. She turned to face Marie. 'I have also decided I will go to the ball.'

Marie clapped. 'Finally.' She reached out and took Rosemary's hand. 'You won't be disappointed. Jack is such a catch.'

Rosemary hoped she wouldn't regret her decision. She'd been so careful to remain free. Regardless, she knew Marie would always be there for her.

This she was certain of.

CHAPTER 26

Olivia

May 1989

They left Annandale early and Sebastian had driven with care, keeping the car snuggled in the left lane. A few times, cars had blasted their horns and Olivia had jumped, but once they were off the motorway, she was able to focus on the rural landscape and rippling hills, which helped ease her anxiety.

Sebastian also kept her occupied. He told stories about teaching in the Northern Territory as a novice, and they sang to songs on the radio and played I Spy.

Olivia chewed on mints throughout the trip to settle the queasiness in her stomach. The first one was to mask the vodka. She'd snuck in a couple of shots before Sebastian picked her up. The alcohol's heat collected some of her anxiety as it moved down her throat.

During her first year of university, she'd discovered vodka's ability to help ease her crippling anxiety—its ability to numb the guilt and shame when the monster within broke through and forced her to remember the accident.

Now, thinking about the shots she'd taken that morning, Olivia chewed her fingers. They'd got her in the car, and she wasn't hurting anyone, so no harm done. What she did was her business.

'You're quiet.' Sebastian turned down the radio.

'Just thinking about your stories,' Olivia said quickly. 'They're hilarious.'

'I'm glad you enjoy them. They're getting old for Clare.'

Clare.

She'd forgotten about her for a moment. Olivia wondered what Clare thought about Sebastian helping her on this trip. She'd probably encouraged him to go, to do a good deed for the disfigured orphan girl. Her cheeks warmed with embarrassment.

'What's Clare doing while you're away?'

'She's gone to Melbourne with friends. They go every year to buy clothes. Not my scene. But I always get a new shirt. Can't complain.' He winked at her.

Of course. He'd offered to help her because Clare was away for the holidays. And why not? They were friends. Her secret fantasy— where Sebastian pulled her into his arms and kissed her, soft and sweet—would remain just that. Another dark secret pushed into the depths of her heart.

She did her best to shake off the disappointment, and soon enough, they'd arrived.

SEBASTIAN PARKED out the front of the 1920s bungalow. A neat row of roses, pruned for winter, bordered a mowed patch of lawn. In bloom, they would be a spectacular show of colour and fragrance.

'Are you ready?' Sebastian switched off the engine and turned to face her.

Olivia nodded and offered a grateful smile. 'I appreciate you doing this for me,' she blurted. 'I do. I mean, you're using your precious holidays.'

Sebastian took her hand gently, and her skin erupted in goose-bumps. 'I wouldn't want to be anywhere else.'

Olivia pulled her hand away as she stepped out of the car. She couldn't get attached, especially as she was now certain Clare was a significant woman in his life.

She took in the timber cottage. The neat garden continued all the way to the verandah. Several hanging pots with autumn annuals spilled over the edge. On either side of a buttery-yellow front door was a ficus tree in a stark white planter. An enormous set of wind chimes tinkled.

Sebastian came up next to her, draped his arm around her shoulder and pulled her in tight. He smelt fresh. Her heart skipped a beat.

'Ready?'

Olivia took a deep breath. 'Okay.'

She took the brass knocker and rapped only once. The door flew open. A woman with grey streaks through her chestnut hair looked out at them.

'Hello, my name is—'

'Olivia!' Marie stood motionless.

The world stilled for a moment. 'Do you know me?'

'In a way.'

Olivia opened her mouth, but no words came out. This scenario hadn't been one of the many she'd played in her mind over the past few days. Quite frankly, she'd expected Marie to say 'I don't know you' and close the door in her face.

Marie gave Olivia a once-over. 'You certainly have grown into a beautiful woman.'

The comment ignited her curiosity. There was no denying it—Marie knew her. But why hadn't Olivia seen her before? There was something familiar about her, though.

Sebastian held out his hand. 'Sebastian. The chauffeur.'

Olivia relaxed, grateful for his humour. He always knew how to make things feel comfortable.

'Please. Come in.'

Olivia nodded and followed Marie up the hallway. She turned to Sebastian and tilted her head. He shrugged and motioned her to keep following Marie.

Marie led them to a room with large windows. Beyond was a backyard with an enormous expanse of green turf. Dense camellia bushes framed the lawn. Marie clearly liked order. Olivia wondered if her beds were made with traditional hospital corners.

A cast-iron wood burner kept the room cosy.

'So, how is your mum?'

Olivia glanced at Sebastian and then back at Marie. 'Um ... I ... Mum passed away.'

Marie's hand shot to her mouth, and she gasped. 'When?' she asked, tiny tears springing from her eyes.

'Eleven years ago.'

Marie's eyes widened. Clearly in shock. It took a few moments to regain her composure.

'I'm so sorry I'm the one telling this,' Olivia said, tears pooling in her eyes. She paused and swallowed. 'Marie, I came here to ask you a few questions about my mum.'

Marie nodded and got up to put the kettle on.

MARIE RETURNED with the tea and lemons, and teacups which bore a vibrant mosaic pattern. 'I bought these on a holiday in Spain,' she said, lightening the mood.

Olivia took a sip, and the hot liquid soothed the untidy knots in her chest. 'This is nice.'

'You really are your mother's daughter. She's the one who taught me to drink tea with lemon.'

Olivia adored being compared to her mum. The comments were like sweet little pouches filled with all the beloved parts of Rosemary. But today, sadness tugged at her throat, and she took another sip.

Marie pulled up a wicker chair and sat next to Olivia.

'Help yourself to some biscuits.' She offered the plate to Sebastian, who took two and smiled. Olivia picked one up, and as she bit into the buttery shortbread that tasted subtly of rosemary and lemon, her heart wrenched.

'My mother used to make biscuits like this.'

Marie lifted a biscuit and turned it over. 'I'm grateful every day to have met her. Your mum taught me more than I ever could've learnt on my own about courage, determination, independence and strength. And how to make these amazing biscuits. They were a family recipe from Sicily.'

'My mum was from Sicily?' Not from Genoa, as she'd suspected.

'Yes.' A shadow drifted across Marie's face. 'Did she never tell you?'

'She never spoke about what her life was like before I was born. She just said she was "once Italian". It's like she was ashamed of her heritage.'

'Or it hurt for her to remember it,' Marie said with a kind smile.

'I never thought of it like that. That's sad.'

'It is.'

Olivia saw Marie's eyes glisten.

That was it.

She sniffed and caught the tears with her fingers. 'I'm sorry.' She picked up a linen serviette and wiped her eyes. 'I loved Mum so much. But I know nothing about her. I don't understand why she kept so much from me. Did I do something wrong?'

Marie grabbed Olivia's hand and held it. 'Your mother loved you so much. You were her world. Everything she did, she did to protect you.'

Olivia smiled. 'I'm sorry, but I don't remember you, Marie.'

'It appears Rosemary was very good at keeping her life private.'

'Secret.'

Marie let out a sympathetic sigh. 'I used to come up from Sydney when you were little. Before I moved to England.'

'Were you good friends?'

'The best. I loved her dearly. Would do anything for her.'

'Then why did you go to England?'

'She encouraged me to apply. It was a great opportunity to head a new maternity ward. She said women needed to take all opportunities—to grab chances tightly and never let go. *Una vita non vissuta è uno spreco.*'

'A life not lived is wasted.'

'Yes. Can you speak Italian?'

'Not really. Mum said this to me all the time. I was very shy. Still am. But Mum always encouraged me to try new things, meet new people and go to parties. Which I avoided at all costs.'

Marie laughed, sweeping away the sadness hanging in the air. 'You sound like a mum's dream teenager, not wanting to go to parties.'

Olivia chuckled. 'She wanted me to live. Truly live and experience life. She was persistent. But I was content to read in my room or on the verandah so I could look out at the beach.'

'Once Rosemary believed in something, she kept at it. She was stubborn—and had a fiery temper.' Marie shook her head at the memory, and the room fell silent for a moment. 'We had a huge fight just before I left to go to England.'

Olivia placed her cup down. Something in the way Marie shifted in her seat stilled her breath. A quiet 'Oh' snuck out. She bit her lip and glanced at Sebastian. He sat still. Sensing the change in the room, too.

A thought nipped inside her head. 'Was it about me?'

Marie reached her hand towards Olivia's, then stopped, not quite touching her. 'In a way ... yes.' She cradled her cup. 'When your mum found out she was pregnant. The bottom fell out of her world. She had been accepted into the nursing program at St Elizabeth's. It was to be her stepping stone into medicine.'

'Did she regret having me?' Fear gripped the back of Olivia's neck.

Marie's hand found Olivia's and squeezed. 'Never. The complete opposite. You were her world. Your mum never once complained. It was admirable.'

'Admirable?'

Marie took a sip of tea. The cup rattled onto the saucer as she placed it back. 'I found myself in the same ...' Marie paused '... predicament. I didn't tell Rosemary until I ... decided not to go through with it.'

Sebastian shifted. Olivia avoided looking at him.

'You had a—'

'Abortion. Yes.'

Sadness flooded Marie's eyes.

'That must've been so sad. You don't have to tell me.'

Marie shook her head, lifted the corner of her apron and wiped under her eyes. 'No. I want to—need to.' She rubbed the tablecloth next to her teacup. 'When I told Rosemary, she was livid. Telling me I had committed a mortal sin. I was so fragile, and her comments pried open the shameful anger I already had for myself. For being so stupid in getting pregnant at all. I was a nurse—I had access to the pill.'

Marie bit her bottom lip. 'We had never fought. But boy, did I make up for lost time. My words flew out! Once unleashed, I could never take them back.'

Olivia swallowed the lump lodged in her throat. 'What did you say?'

'I shouted at her. Telling her what would she know? That she'd stupidly given up everything she'd sacrificed for. Throwing everything she ever wanted away. Of all people, she should've understood about choices—especially as a woman.' Marie stopped and wiped the tears with the back of her hand. 'Rosemary sat there. Quiet. After what felt like an eternity, she stood, picked you up and walked out. She didn't utter a single word to me. But her eyes said it all.'

'I'm sorry.'

Marie stood up and picked up the empty plate of biscuits. 'We never spoke again.'

'When did you come back?'

'A few years ago. It was time for me to come home. I grew up around here.'

She stopped. Olivia caught a sadness in her pale hazel eyes. It was clear that Marie regretted the fight with Rosemary and missed her badly.

Marie returned with a fresh pot. 'More tea?'

Olivia held up her cup for a refill. 'You never wanted to return to Sydney? Didn't you work in that big hospital?'

'St Elizabeth's. Yes, but I needed to be where my roots were. I was always happy growing up here. Your mother also understood the importance of place—a sense of home. She was no stranger to heartache and the feeling of not belonging. Moving in with Shirley was one of the best decisions Rosemary ever made. It gave her a chance to build a new sense of place.'

Olivia's head spun. 'There's so much I don't know. How she came to Australia, why she came here, who her family was.' Olivia fiddled with the tablecloth. *Who my father was?*

'I can tell you about some of those things. Some things I don't know. And some things ...' Olivia saw a flicker of sadness cross her eyes. 'And some things we'll never know.' Marie leant forward. 'I can tell you this. Rosemary migrated in 1960. She never spoke of her life in Italy.' Her face took on a dreamy expression. 'Your mum was the total package. Beautiful and intelligent. I used to call her Hollywood.'

Olivia smiled. 'I like that. It suits her. Mum was smart too. She'd been accepted to study medicine in Newcastle when—' Olivia stopped, shrugged and quickly changed the subject again. 'How did you two meet?'

As Marie shared how she met Rosemary, her face lit up with joy. Listening to Marie reminisce about her mum warmed her heart.

'I'm sorry to pry, but I went to see Nora.'

'Oh, Nora. How is she? She was like a mum to Rosemary.'

'She was so kind. She lives with her daughter-in-law and her grandchildren. Her son died in Vietnam.'

'What an insidious and fruitless war.' Marie shook her head. 'Too many good men and nurses, all gone.'

'There's one more thing.' Marie drew a deep breath and gripped Olivia's hand. 'I should've told you this sooner. That last time. The fight. It changed so much between us.' Marie leant forward and looked straight at Olivia, holding her in her gaze. 'I'm your godmother.'

The words bubbled out slowly as if spoken underwater.

'What?' Olivia whispered. An immediate sense of betrayal roused a sedated anger inside her and she stood. Her teacup rocked on its saucer, spilling some of its contents. She steadied it. 'I've been so alone. Especially after Shirley died. And all this time, I've had a godmother.' The fury grew ferocious. 'Who cares about a stupid fight? People fight all the time.' Flashes of her fight with her mother in the car intruded, but she swatted them away. The anger erupted, and she unleashed it. 'Isn't a godmother supposed to step in when your parents can no longer look after you? Like when they die?'

'But I didn't know.' Marie reached out to comfort her.

Olivia pushed her hands away. All sensibility vapourised. Tears exploded from her, and she raced out of the house.

'Olivia!' Sebastian called after her.

She ignored him, running as fast as she could.

———

OLIVIA SAT on the grassy bank, watching a couple of ducks dive and glide. The river was at high tide. Occasionally, a flying fish would disturb the tranquillity.

'Olivia?'

She turned and saw Sebastian walking down the embankment.

'Are you okay?'

She shrugged. 'How did you find me?'

'This is a one-horse town, partner.' The cowboy accent teased a little smile out of Olivia. 'There's only one road from Marie's house. I just followed it.'

'Is Marie upset?'

'A little.' He held out his hands in a gesture of surrender. 'Not at you. About the whole situation.' Sebastian sat beside her, picked up a stick and threw it into the water. Brown ducks swam over to see what had disturbed their moment.

'I knew there'd be stuff that would upset me. It just feels like I'm being sucked inside out and losing more of who I am.'

'I know.' Sebastian took her hand. 'And it's not over. I think this is just the tip of the iceberg. We're the *Titanic*. We can see the iceberg, but it's too late to get out of the way now. We have to hit it.'

'The *Titanic* sank.'

'Bad analogy. Sorry.'

Olivia smiled and shook her head. 'You always make me feel better. How do you do it?'

'It's just my lovable charm.'

Olivia pulled up her knees and tucked them under her chin. She wrapped her arms around her legs. 'I'm ruining your school holidays.' Her voice wobbled.

'I want to be here.' He wiped her tears away. Then his fingers swept across her scar, down her cheek and over her lips.

'Come here.' Sebastian pulled her closer, took out a cotton hand-kerchief and dabbed away the rest of her tears. He looked deep into her eyes and, with care, lifted her chin.

'I want to kiss you, Olivia Bennet.'

Olivia's heart raced. Was he joking? It didn't seem like it.

So she nodded.

More than anything, at this very moment, she wanted to be loved. She didn't care about anything else. She just wanted the loneliness to go away.

Sebastian leant in and pressed his lips softly against hers.

A pitter-patter of pulses ran through her as tiny bubbles of joy popped inside her chest. She fluttered her eyes open when he pulled away, and a smile tugged at her lips. She liked being kissed.

He sat back, and their eyes met. His burnt with passion. For the first time, she could believe he wanted this as much as she did. She moved in to kiss him back. His mouth was warm and soft. Needing more, she leant in and let herself go. Her body tingled. If only she could disappear into him.

Clare.

The moment evaporated.

Olivia pulled away. 'We can't do this.'

'What? Why?' Sebastian ran a hand through his hair. 'That was amazing. I've wanted to kiss you ever since that first morning I walked into the bookshop.'

She jumped up and scrambled away from him, extending her arms out. 'I shouldn't have. I'm sorry. I'm not that kind of girl.'

'What kind of girl?' Sebastian remained on the ground, a look of surprise etched into his face.

'Clare.' The name exploded out of her, and she clamped her mouth shut. Except it was too late. It was now out there.

His confusion deepened. 'What about Clare?'

'Everything. You two. Together.'

He frowned and then smiled broadly. 'You think Clare and I ... that we're—'

'An item. Yes.'

'God no.' He stood and took a step towards Olivia. She moved away.

'No. No more kissing.'

Sebastian caught her by the shoulder. 'We're just friends.' Olivia ducked away from him. 'Olivia.' He moved closer again, his hands held up. 'There's nothing going on between Clare and me.'

Olivia wrapped her arms around her like a shield.

'Please.' He beckoned her to him. 'I'm telling you the truth.'

The wind flicked her hair into her face and she reached up and brushed it away, standing her ground.

Sebastian closed the distance between them, placed his hands on her shoulders and looked deep into her eyes. In that moment, she saw he was serious.

'Clare is gay.'

'Oh!' Humiliation thumped up her spine. 'I thought ... because ... she's so comfortable around you ... Oh, God! I'm so embarrassed.' Olivia cowered behind her hands.

Sebastian reached out and gently lowered her arms. 'Yes, we're close—we've been friends for years. But that's it.'

His soft smile opened a little box of confidence inside her. Olivia placed her hands on his chest to help steady herself. Was this happening? Were the distinct, safe lines of their friendship really collapsing?

She reached up to touch his cheek, then paused midair. Sebastian caught her hand in his broad one and smiled. Butterflies danced inside her belly, and she gave him a trusting smile.

He wrapped her in a hug, and she nestled into his body, taking in his cedar scent. She loved the feeling of being contained in his arms. When he kissed the top of her head, an electric charge moved through every nerve in her body.

And then, out of the blue, the revelation slammed into her mind. 'Oh my God!'

'Was it that good?' Sebastian laughed.

'What? No! I mean, yes. The kiss was nice.' The words scrambled out. 'But the woman!' She looked at Sebastian. 'At Shirley's funeral. The woman who came up to me was Marie. I didn't make the connection. The whole day was a daze. It was her.'

Sebastian took her hands. 'I think you need to give Marie a second chance,' he whispered.

'I know,' she said quietly. She turned in his arms to face the river.

He rested his chin on the top of her head. 'Life is filled with happiness, but sometimes we can only see it if it's framed with darker moments.'

'Wow, a good kisser and a poet laureate!'

He chuckled. 'My nonna always says this. I know pain, Olivia. I understand what you're going through.'

'But you had your nonna.'

'And you had Shirley.'

Olivia swallowed. Sebastian was right.

Because of the sacrifices and decisions her mother had made, Olivia had grown up with Shirley in her life—the most loving person she'd ever known. The person she'd depended on after her mum died. She might not have been Olivia's real grandmother, but she was as good as the real deal. Ten times over.

Shame seeped in. She'd shouted at Marie, then run away like a petulant child. The poor woman didn't deserve that. 'I want to go back and apologise.'

She felt Sebastian's nod. 'Even though she wasn't around, she cares about you.'

Tears welled up again. 'It just makes me sad that Mum never had the life she dreamt of. Really sad.' Olivia sniffed. 'Could I have your hanky again?'

'Sure.' Sebastian pulled it out of his pocket and dabbed her eyes again. 'I don't think your mum was lonely, though. She found love elsewhere.'

Maybe Sebastian was right. There were all kinds of love, and her mum had lived in a house filled with women who cared for her. She'd also had George and Shirley. Her heart ballooned with affection for them all.

'Let's go back,' she said.

Sebastian brushed his hand over hers and interlaced their fingers.

They walked back up the hill in silence. When they got to the front gate, Sebastian stopped. 'You think I'm a good kisser, eh?'

'Yes, but don't let it go to your head.' She nudged him playfully.

The door flew open as Olivia and Sebastian were walking up the path, and Olivia's heart sunk at the sight of the worry on Marie's face.

'I'm so sorry.' Olivia looked down at her feet.

Marie rushed forward and hugged her. 'Don't be,' she said, pulling her closer.

'I do have more questions.' Especially the one burning question. It sat primed, ready to be asked.

'I wouldn't expect anything less. Come on. I've got a casserole on. Stay for lunch.'

MARIE DISHED out chocolate pudding into bowls. Sebastian added two large scoops of vanilla ice cream. 'Smells great.' He winked as he shoved a spoonful in his mouth.

'An old family recipe.' Marie sat down.

'You know, Rosemary loved photography.' She added.

'I did find these amazing photos of people and places during the sixties.' Olivia giggled. 'The hair and clothes gave it away. The camera was also in the trunk. I'd never seen it before.'

'It was a gift. From me. I can't believe you have it. Taking photos ignited this passion and life in her.'

'The photos are so beautiful. Emotional and artistic. I wondered why she stopped?'

'She did?' Marie tsked. 'That is a shame. She was very good at it. Maybe working and being a mum kept her busy.' She patted Olivia's hand. 'And fulfilled.'

Olivia's heart lurched. For a short time, her mother had seemingly had the world at her feet. And for some reason, it had all just vanished. *Maybe that's why Mum was always so insistent that I experience life to its fullest.*

Why had she chosen to abandon her passions?

'I have this photo.' Olivia picked up her backpack from the floor and took out the photo of her mother and Jack—her favourite one of the two of them. They were laughing and sitting on a wall in front of the bright blue block of flats in Bondi. Both were in swimwear.

Marie looked at the photo. Olivia watched her carefully and saw sadness float across her face again.

'You know him?' Olivia asked gently.

Marie nodded. 'Jack. Jack Emerson. They were in love. He told your mum he wanted to marry her. But his family weren't too keen on Rosemary as a potential daughter-in-law.'

'Why?'

'She was an immigrant. They didn't like the idea of their youngest son marrying beneath him.'

Marie studied the photo a moment longer, then looked at Olivia. 'When your mother found out she was pregnant, they were no longer together.'

'What happened?' Anticipation bubbled up her arms.

'After Rosemary told me she was pregnant. She answered an ad to rent a room. She'd made up her mind to leave Sydney and start again.'

'Shirley!' Olivia blurted out.

'Yep. We visited Shirley.' Marie nodded and sighed. 'I don't know how, maybe it was the fear in Rosemary's eyes, but Shirley knew something was up. When Rosemary confessed, Shirley offered a plan. Rosemary would live with her. Shirley promised to go along with the story that your father died in Vietnam. No one would press a grieving widow—she knew that from her own experiences. At that point, Shirley still had connections at Gosford Hospital, and she also pulled some strings to help Rosemary start her nurse's training there. Being a mum whose husband had supposedly died in Vietnam, she didn't have to live in the nurses' quarters like the other student nurses. It was the perfect plan. Until ...' Marie stopped.

'... Mum died.' Olivia hung her head. Sebastian leant over and pulled her into his chest. The security of being held close made her heart ache.

'Do you need a break?' he asked gently.

Olivia shook her head. She'd come this far, had opened the trunk, her very own Pandora's box, and she needed to see it through. Otherwise, the questions would eat away at her. Slowly. With relentless cruelty. Until she was an empty shell.

She picked up the photo again, and her stomach filled with butterflies. She knew that Marie didn't know the answer, but she had to ask the burning question anyway. 'Could he be my father?'

Marie shrugged. 'What I do know is that your mum went with Jack to his father's sixtieth birthday, and something happened at the party because your mother came back alone. From there, everything unravelled. Rosemary refused to see him.'

'Do you remember when?'

'Not the exact date. In late May. It was definitely after the Dusty Springfield concert in May '64.'

Olivia did the maths again. It was possible. 'I was born in February 1965.'

'Yes, I did the same calculations.'

'Did you ever ask Mum who my father was?'

'Yes, but she told me to never ask her again. She said you'd been conceived and that was all that mattered, that she needed to move forward and focus on being your mum so she could give you the love she'd missed out on in her own life.'

'Yeh, that sounds like Mum. She always focused on moving forward. But I sensed she was also running away from something.'

'Or someone.' Marie sighed.

Olivia looked at Sebastian. He gave her an encouraging nod.

Marie picked up the exchange. 'What is it?'

'Marie ...' Olivia closed her eyes and swallowed. 'Was Mum working as an escort?' She avoided making eye contact with Sebastian and crossed her arms tight against her chest. What must he think of her? Of her mum.

'What? No! Why would you think that?'

She felt like throwing up. 'You must think I'm a horrible daughter.'

'No. Olivia, my God! But why would you think this?' she asked again.

'There were designer dresses and shoes in the trunk—Dior, Givenchy, Roger Vivier. My mother wasn't rich. Money was always tight, and she was a migrant. You even said that Mum held secrets tight inside her. Maybe she kept this from you too?'

'Olivia, your mother had strict morals for herself. She was—' Marie glanced at Sebastian.

'You know, I need another tea. Can I make you all a fresh cuppa?' Sebastian stood and stretched.

Olivia smiled gratefully at Sebastian.

'I think a cup of tea would be great,' said Marie, looking up at Sebastian. 'There are also some biscuits on the shelf. Homemade. Will you be okay?'

'I'm a teacher. We live on tea and coffee.'

'He's a lovely young man,' Marie said after he'd left.

Olivia shook her head sadly. 'Sebastian has been so kind. I don't know why. We've only known each other for about six months.' Olivia turned towards the kitchen and fingered the scar on her face. 'I think he feels sorry for me. I mean, look at me. He could have anyone he wants ...'

'Listen to me, Olivia,' Marie said sternly. 'You're beautiful. That scar doesn't change that. Your mother was also beautiful, and I knew she'd make gorgeous babies. She reminded me of a dark-haired Marilyn Monroe.' Marie smiled at the memory.

'And they both had tragic endings.'

'Maybe Marilyn, but not Rosemary.' Marie's eyes glistened. 'She had you.'

Reaching forward, she tucked a strand of hair behind Olivia's ear. 'Let me tell you this. And I'll be straight with you. I worked in a hospital next to Kings Cross. I saw my fair share of escorts and prostitutes. Your mother was not an escort or a call girl or whatever you want to call it. Ever.'

'But the clothes? The jewellery.'

'Jack,' Marie said firmly. 'All Jack. He was a talented journalist and came from a very wealthy family. Old money, I believe. That was one reason his family felt Rosemary was beneath him and not a good match for the Emerson dynasty. One thing I knew. Well, two things. Jack showered your mum with gifts, and he loved her. What happened to that love? I don't know because Rosemary refused to talk about it.'

Hoped stirred inside her as an idea formed. 'Do you know where I can find him?'

Marie shook her head. 'I know his family had property and that he worked for the *Sydney Morning Herald*.'

It was better than nothing. When she got back to Sydney, she'd make another trip to the state library and find out everything she could about Jack Emerson.

Sebastian came in with tea. 'All good?'

'Are we?' Marie asked Olivia.

Olivia hugged her. 'Yes. More than good.'

Marie's arms made her feel safe. Regardless of the years of separation and secrecy, Olivia's heart swelled. She'd connected with her godmother—someone who'd loved her mum and with whom Olivia could share memories.

She might not have all the answers yet, but she was beginning to understand her mum a little more.

CHAPTER 27

Rosemary
April 1964

Rosemary stepped into the Christian Dior shoes. The crystal beads on top of them seemed to float, and they shimmered under the light in her room. The cream-coloured satin contrasted the dress perfectly. Jack knew his fashion. She sprayed her signature Dior fragrance in the air and walked through the mist. She marvelled at the coincidence of his buying her Dior. Maybe this was a good omen. She'd also worn the fragrance the night she met Jack.

She walked into the kitchen. Petula Clark's voice drifted from the radio on top of the fridge.

'Oh, Rosemary, you look like a Hollywood starlet.' Nora placed her hand on her chest.

Eleanor looked up from the torn pages of *Vogue* spread out on the kitchen table . 'Wow!'

Pamela joined them, dressed in her pyjamas, her hair wrapped in a towel. 'Not sure if the camera goes with the outfit, though.' She grinned.

Rosemary grinned back. 'I promised I would take a photo for Marie.'

'Your hair looks fabulous.' Pamela twirled her finger, and Rosemary walked around in a circle. 'It's the perfect style for that dress.'

'Thank you for paying for my hair to be done. It was so kind.'

'Don't be daft,' Nora said, wiping her hands on the tea towel. 'You can't go to a fancy ball and not get your hair done.'

'Yes, there'll be photographers,' Pamela said, taking the camera from Rosemary. 'Okay, where should we take the photo?'

'The living room.'

Eleanor stood and placed her mug on the papers. 'I'd love a photo with you. You're the first person I know who's worn haute couture. Holy moly, look at those shoes. They're spectacular.' She bent down. 'Those crystals look like diamonds. Gosh, Rosemary, it's like Cinderella—except your sisters love you.'

Pamela clicked some action shots before swapping with Eleanor so she could be in some photos too.

Rosemary glanced past the kitchen table towards the red-faced clock on the sky-blue wall. 'Jack will be here soon.' She took a deep breath. 'I am nervous.'

'You just be you, and everyone will love you.' Eleanor squeezed her hands.

'And they're all going to love your accent. I've always said you sound so exotic.' Eleanor beamed at her.

'Wait!' They all turned as Nora came into the living room. 'I want you to wear my pearls.'

'No, they are too precious,' Rosemary said.

'Don't be silly. They deserve to be shown off. Owen would be pleased to know they're going to a fancy ball. Pamela? Can you do the honours?'

'Love to.'

Pamela fastened the pearls around Rosemary's neck.

'Thank you.' She reached for Nora's hand and squeezed it.

'Okay, photo time.' Eleanor held up the camera. 'Before your gentlemen caller arrives,' she said in an exaggerated Southern accent.

Rosemary laughed as she posed for the photo with Nora. 'You Australian girls watch too many American movies.'

Jack turned up right on time and charmed them all. Rosemary had to admit to herself that his warmth and interest seemed genuine. Even the usually cynical Pamela looked impressed.

Eleanor insisted on taking a photo of Rosemary and Jack before they headed off. Rosemary's body ignited when he stepped in close. She took in the fresh scent of his aftershave, the weight of his arm around her waist.

When they got to Sydney Town Hall, Jack handed the keys to his Mercedes convertible to a valet in a red jacket.

'You are not scared he will take your car?' She watched as the valet drove the car away.

Jack chuckled. 'No.'

'You laugh at me.' Rosemary crossed her arms. 'You will not be laughing if he takes your fancy car.'

He smiled at her. 'I'm not laughing at you. I find it refreshing to be with a woman who cares about me and not what I have.' He placed his hand on the small of her back. 'I promise if the car is gone, I will pay for a taxi home.' He winked.

Rosemary couldn't help but smile.

As they walked up the sandstone stairs, she held Jack's arm, working at quietening her nerves.

'Are you okay?' Jack asked as they checked their coats.

She dropped her voice. 'I have never been to a ball before.'

'Just think of it as a big party. I won't leave you. I promise.' He looked around and stepped closer to her. 'But from the way everyone is looking at you, I don't think you'll be alone for very long.'

'Jack, no, please. I am not used to being in ... what do you say? Light spot.'

'Spotlight?'

'Yes.'

They moved into the ballroom, and for a moment, Rosemary forgot her fears. Fairy lights hung from the ceiling and met in the centre, where a large chandelier emerged like a rose in full bloom. Large standing candelabras stood at attention around the room, the candles lit and dancing. At the end of the hall was an organ as large as the piazza in her village. Jack escorted her to their table, at the centre of which was an enormous bouquet of red roses and white freesias surrounded by waxy greenery.

Rosemary's chest tightened again. She'd never seen so many knives, forks, spoons, and glasses in one place setting. So this was how wealthy people lived.

'Well, hello there, handsome.' A woman dressed in a periwinkle-blue gown swept in and took his arm. The dress's high collar caught the fabric and gathered it above her breasts. The lack of sleeves emphasised her bronze shoulders and shapely arms. She was elegant. Like Grace Kelly.

'Hello, Lacey.' Jack accepted her kiss on his cheek. 'Mother told me you were coming tonight.'

'Well, I am on the board. St Elizabeth's is my favourite charity.'

Rosemary's ears pricked at the name of the hospital.

Lacey accepted a glass of champagne from a passing tray. 'What they're doing for obstetrics is just wonderful.' She turned towards Rosemary. A small glint of judgement flashed across her eyes.

'Hello. You are?' Lacey offered a cream-gloved hand to Rosemary.

'Rosemary. Rosemary Benito.' She shook Lacey's hand, noting the hard squeeze in return.

'By the sound of your accent, you haven't been in Australia for long.'

'I came in 1960, from *Italia*,' Rosemary replied, in the strongest accent she could. She didn't like this woman, and she got the sense the feeling was mutual.

Lacey offered a tight smile. Rosemary glanced at Jack, who was staring at Lacey. Something hung between them. *Be careful,* she warned herself. Old lovers?

'That is interesting.' Lacey spun towards Jack and flicked some imaginary lint off the lapel of his black tuxedo. 'Say hello to your mother, Jack.'

'Why don't you say hello yourself? You speak to her more than I do.'

Rosemary heard strained amusement in Jack's voice, but Lacey gave a light laugh. She kissed him on his cheek again before moving in closer and whispering something in his ear.

Rosemary stepped to the side to give them a moment, but out of the corner of her eye, she saw Jack blush and look down.

A tight feeling kneaded at her heart, and she flicked the silliness of her jealousy away.

Her unease increased when she noticed that Jack's friend Frank had been seated at their table. His date was a chatty woman who was besotted with him. Throughout the meal, Rosemary watched her try to charm him, expanding her chest so that her breasts spilled out from her strapless dress like clotted cream, but nothing worked. He spoke with a coolness that made Rosemary quiver. It was nothing like the coolness she'd seen in Jack's interaction with Lacey.

She caught the looks of disdain he threw her way. His cobalt-blue eyes darkened with contempt. Yet when talking to Jack, he was relaxed and often smiled.

Once she was finished eating, Rosemary looked around the ballroom. These people were all very proper, and there were no Europeans other than the waiters. Rosemary surprised their table when she spoke to their waiter, Vincenzo, in her dialect.

Jack and several others looked impressed, and Frank's date, Sylvie, applauded. 'That was so clever,' she cooed.

Frank stilled her clapping and glared at Rosemary.

Her rebellious nature now fired up, Rosemary picked up her champagne flute. '*Salute*,' she said as she lifted her chin at him.

Everyone lifted their glasses and followed suit. A nasally chorus of 'sal-loo-tay' followed, and then everyone erupted in laughter.

Frank stood, and his dark, brooding eyes bore into her. Rosemary braced herself for his abrupt departure. Instead, he walked towards her.

'Would you care to dance?' He stood next to her, his hand out, waiting for her to take it.

Rosemary froze. Confusion raced through her mind. She looked at Jack for reassurance.

'I dunno, Frank. We all know you're a better dancer than me.' He laughed with the others. 'Do I want Rosemary to realise she's with the wrong bloke?'

He took a sip of his champagne and winked at Rosemary.

She stared at Frank's broad hand with its well-manicured nails. Then she stilled her breath and stood, not wanting to cause a scene. 'Thank you.' She ignored his hand.

Frank led her to the dance floor with his hand on her back. She could feel its heat searing the silk taffeta.

Jack was right. Frank was a fabulous dancer, taking control. All Rosemary had to do was let him lead her. He spun her around the floor, the brass band egging him on. His herbal, woody cologne clung to his neck. He held her close as if she were a captured animal. She worked to keep her breath even while waiting for the song to end.

When the number finished, she broke away, but he grabbed her wrist and pulled her back as a waltz began.

'One more,' he whispered in her hair.

'I am here with Jack.'

'Don't worry about him. He knows where his bread is buttered.'

These were the only words he spoke to her. Which suited her. She did not understand some of these Australian sayings. She did not want to ask. *Sono cavoli miei* . What concern was it of hers. Instead, she smiled and endured the dance.

After the waltz, Frank let go of her and led her back to the table, which was buzzing with a heated discussion about Australia's involvement in the Vietnam War. Rosemary sat in silence and avoided making eye contact with Frank.

'When's it my turn?' Sylvie finally said, pouting and batting her false eyelashes.

Rosemary watched Frank salaciously study Sylvie's heaving breasts.

'I've had enough.' Frank picked up Sylvie's mink shawl and flicked his head in a 'get up' gesture. The look on his face told Rosemary that dancing wasn't the preferred physical activity he had in mind for Sylvie.

'Okay.' She giggled. 'Can I go to the ladies'?'

Frank leant in close to her but stared at Rosemary. 'You can use the bathroom at my place.' He reached around and slapped her bottom, making Sylvie squeal. A few people stopped their conversations and turned their attention to Frank and his date. Rosemary studied their looks. Frank's behaviour didn't appear to surprise them.

'See you at the cricket,' Jack said, saluting. 'Try not to be too hungover.' He smiled.

'I play better that way.' Then he grabbed Sylvie's hand and dragged her away.

This was what men were like. What they did. Anger burnt down the length of her spine. She picked up her purse. She needed some time to herself to wash Frank away.

She touched Jack's arm. 'I will be back in a minute.'

ROSEMARY WAS outside talking to one of the waiters when Jack approached.

'I wondered where you got to.' He walked down the steps and stood in front of her. 'We're the last ones.' He turned towards the waiter sitting next to Rosemary on the step and held out his hand. 'Jack.'

'Good evening. Gino.' He shook Jack's hand. 'I was just talking—'

Rosemary interrupted. 'Gino and I were having a pleasant conversation and remembering life in Italy. It is good to speak to a fellow *paesano*, countryman.' Rosemary tightened her jaw, waiting for the challenge.

Jack didn't bite. Instead, he gave Gino a warm, friendly smile. 'It must be hard to be away from home. I'm from the country, and I sometimes miss home. But I'm only six or so hours away.'

'Yes, it is hard,' Gino said. 'But it is better here. We must make the sacrifices for a better place.' Gino reached into his pocket, took out a photo, and handed it to Jack. '*Mia moglie*, my wife, will like it here when she comes.'

'She's very beautiful.' He looked at Rosemary. 'Like all Italian women.'

Rosemary's jaw tightened as she felt tension build in her body. He'd hit a nerve, referencing both her migrant status and her beauty. 'Gino is working two jobs to save enough money for her ticket.'

'Two jobs? What else do you do?'

'I work making bread.' He looked at his watch. 'It is late; I must go finish, then get some sleep before I need to be at the bakery.'

Jack glanced back at the venue. 'It's all winding up inside. I'm happy to take you home.' He handed Gino his photo.

'Thank you, but I must help clean up in the kitchen. It will give me extra wages. When my wife comes, we plan to open a restaurant.'

'That's fantastic. That's what Sydney needs: more authentic Italian food. Maybe Rosemary here will cook me something authentic sometime.' He smiled at her.

'Yes, all Italian women are wonderful cooks. Good lovers, too.' Gino winked at Jack.

Rosemary let out a jovial tirade in Italian.

Gino laughed. '*Buonasera*. Goodnight.' He tipped his head at

Jack. 'Be careful.' He pointed at Rosemary. 'This one has a Sicilian temper.'

'Well, I think I've been warned.' He handed her coat to her. 'Ready to go home?'

They were silent on the drive home. Rosemary focused on the headlights that threw a pair of triangular beams in front of them.

She snuck glances as Jack drove and smoked his cigarette. His profile was strong and handsome. All evening, he'd been the perfect gentleman. And charismatic. People gravitated to him like a bee to a flower. He was knowledgeable and spoke eloquently, presenting his opinion in a way that made others consider it, even if they vehemently disagreed. It was his friendship with Frank that didn't sit right with her. What was the saying Marie always used? *Gesso e formaggio*: chalk and cheese. Jack's face was full of light. His eyes danced when he smiled. Frank held a darkness that dressed his whole body, and his black eyes ran deep.

'You're quiet.'

She cleared her throat. 'I was thinking about the ball. It was wonderful. Are all parties like this?'

'No.' Jack laughed. 'Only the ones that Lacey's involved in.'

Pinpricks jabbed at Rosemary's heart. 'Lacey is your friend? Or maybe an old girlfriend?'

She watched him. He took a long drag on his cigarette and rubbed his forehead before answering. 'A very old friend. Our families have known each other for centuries.' He smiled at Rosemary. 'It's complicated.'

She rolled down the window, and the rush of air cooled her heated cheeks. She was grateful when they turned onto her street. She gripped her purse. Cinderella had lost her slipper, but Rosemary wanted to take off her shoe and fling it at Jack.

Jack parked the car and Rosemary moved to get out, but he gently grabbed her arm. Rosemary turned and glared at him.

'Rosemary,' he said in a hushed voice.

'Thank you for the evening. You are very kind. I must go now. It is very late.'

'Whoa. It's not just chilly outside.' He adjusted himself so he was facing her. 'You asked me a question. Let me explain.'

'It is none of my business. I do not expect anything. And I do not owe you anything. *Niente*. You came to me. I did not want to go. But my friends said to go. It would be an experience.'

'Was it?' He smiled again.

'Yes. It showed me how different I am because I am from Italy. A migrant. And I see how Lacey looks at you. How friendly you are with her.' Jealousy twisted in with her anger.

'Fair enough. Yes, I'm friendly with Lacey. We've known each other since we were kids, babies, and yes, Lacey would like more. But I'm not interested.'

'Why? Why are you not interested? She is beautiful.'

'Yes, she is, and smart, and exactly who my parents hope I marry.'

'Goodnight, Jack.' Rosemary slid out of the car.

Jack jumped out and blocked her path. His eyes danced with affection. 'Let me finish.' He grabbed her hand. 'I'm not interested in Lacey,' he repeated and stepped up close. His breath was hot against her ear. 'I'm interested in you.' He brushed his lips against her cheek. Rosemary's heart raced, and she worked to still it. 'Rosemary, I know what I want. And what I don't want.'

A flying fox screeched as it flew out of a nearby tree on the pavement, breaking the silence of the street momentarily.

Rosemary looked down.

Jack lifted her chin. 'Thank you for saying yes.' His blue eyes locked onto her, holding her in the evening's stillness. She could hear her heart beating and lifted her purse to muffle the sound.

'You are welcome. I had a pleasant time.' She broke away from his stare and looked at her shoes. 'I will get the shoes and dress cleaned and return them to you.'

'They were a gift. I want you to have them. Besides, green isn't my colour. Clashes with my eyes.'

Rosemary let out a loud chuckle, then clamped her hand over her mouth and looked up to see if she'd woken any of the girls.

'You are very funny,' she whispered. 'Thank you. I will cherish it.'

'Good. But I do want something.'

Rosemary's heart plummeted. *Stupida.* All men were the same. She stepped back and hissed, 'I am not that kind of girl. What? You buy a dress and shoes for a girl, and then you expect payment? I am not a mule to be bought and ridden.'

'Whoa! Who said anything about physical payment?' The corners of his mouth lifted slowly. 'Gino was right. You're one fiery Italian.'

'Sicilian,' Rosemary said, glaring.

'Ah. Sorry.' He took her hands in his and smiled. 'What I was going to ask, if you'd given me the chance, was if you'd like to go sailing with me next Sunday.'

Rosemary rolled her eyes and pouted sheepishly. 'Yes. That would be nice. I will ask if I can swap my shift.'

Jack rubbed the tops of her hands with his thumbs. The motion made her feel warm and secure. 'Rosemary ... may I kiss you good night?'

One kiss does not mean anything, she thought, and nodded. Jack kissed her, soft and chaste, on her lips, and she let herself enjoy the moment. She had never been kissed like this before.

After the kiss, Jack bounded down to his car. As the red taillights of Jack's Mercedes disappeared around the corner, Lacey's pinched smile slinked back into Rosemary's mind.

CHAPTER 28

'Ready for some sun and sailing?'

'Almost. Excuse me, I nearly forgot.' Rosemary disappeared down the hallway. Jack's whistling echoed down to the kitchen, where Nora stood in her bathrobe and her hair tightly bound in rollers. She held up the picnic basket Rosemary had prepared.

'Sailing must be heavy work. What have you got in here?' She handed it to Rosemary.

'A feast. And I do not know how hungry you get sailing. I have never been.' She opened the basket to check everything. 'Oh—'

Nora held up the bottle opener. 'The one item always forgotten.'

'Thank you.' She gave Nora a hug. 'You look after me.'

'All my girls. Now, scoot. There's a dashing dish waiting for you, and by the sound of his whistling, a cheerful one.'

'WHY DID you call the boat *Zale?*' she asked, watching Jack work. The muscles in his arms flexed as he pulled the sails into place. The boat cut through the water, leaving the harbour behind them.

'It's Greek for "strength of the sea".'

'Do you speak Greek?'

'A little. I studied it at school. We also studied mythology. I loved the stories of adventure. A lot of tragedies, though.'

'Yes, but they also had their comedies. There was always a balance.'

'Your favourite?'

'*Lysistrata,*' she said.

'About the women who go on strike.' He grinned. 'I'm not surprised.'

'Why? Because it is easier to understand the comedies? Or because you are told I have a Sicilian temper.' Rosemary sat straighter and placed a hand on her hip.

'Whoa.' He pulled tight on a rope and tied it into place. 'No.' He sat down next to her on the edge of the boat.

She held her chin up in defiance. 'Because I read. I understand. The tragedies too. In English *and* Italian.'

Jack held up his hands in surrender. 'It's a compliment. I can tell that you've got a mind of your own. You're independent.' He tapped the side of his temple. 'Intelligent. I've met no one like you. It's captivating.'

'I am sorry.' She poured some wine and offered a glass to Jack as a further apology. 'I dislike people thinking I am not capable or smart. I get attention that is not always good. I am more than this.' She waved her hand down the length of her body.

'Forgiven.' Jack smiled at her and took a sip. 'This is great. I must have more Italian wine.'

'Wine is the drink of love and truth. *In vino veritas.*' She offered up her glass for a toast. 'Where are you taking me?'

'I'm going to show you the best harbour in the world. Then we'll stop at a little cove and have lunch.' He tapped the picnic basket. 'I'm looking forward to seeing what's in here.'

They dropped anchor off Milk Beach, a quiet little cove in the north of Sydney Harbour. The water was paler in the cove, as if the sun had stonewashed it.

Jack disappeared into the galley and returned with a picnic rug, plates and cutlery. He disappeared once more and came back with a bottle of champagne chilling in a silver ice bucket.

'Do you do this for all your lady friends?'

'Only the ones who bring a feast.'

They sat close together on the narrow deck, and Rosemary made up a plate of antipasti to start them off. Jack's only experience with olives was in martinis, and the rest of the food was all new to him: prosciutto, various cheeses, marinated artichokes, and eggplant. She broke apart the traditional bread she'd picked up at the Italian delicatessen in Leichhardt and taught him to dip it in the oil and balsamic vinegar. Jack beamed with each new food he tried, and it made her laugh. She loved how his face lit up every time he tasted something unfamiliar.

When Jack dripped oil onto his chin, Rosemary reached up to wipe it off with a napkin. Their gazes met for a moment, and her heart purred. Then the boat rocked as a wave hit them, and she fell against his chest. He reached up and steadied her. Their mouths were inches apart. Embarrassed, she dished out the lasagne she'd made. She also piled onto his plate the bean and caprese salad she'd made following an old family recipe.

They ate in silence, enjoying the warm sun as it beat down on the gently rocking boat. A comfortable ease settled over Rosemary. She enjoyed being with him, the relaxed way he carried himself. His warm attention towards her awakened her attraction further.

'That was fantastic,' Jack said, putting his plate down, 'but I'm full as a boot.' He rubbed his stomach. 'You're a wonderful cook. You should start a restaurant. Food like this would be a hit.'

'I am sorry you are full.' She removed a container of cakes and biscuits from the basket. 'It is a shame these will go to waste,' she said teasingly and lifted the lid. The aromas of almond and honey wafted out. 'These smell very good.'

'I'll make a deal with you,' said Jack.

'What deal?'

'For now, we lie here and soak up some sun and then go for a swim. Do you swim?'

'Of course I swim. I lived in a village on the sea.'

'And did you bring your cosies?'

'Cosies?'

'A suit to swim in. What do you call it in Italian?'

'*Costume da bagno.* Bathing suit.' Rosemary reached into her basket and pulled out the red bathing suit Pamela had lent her.

'I'm impressed.'

'We were going on a boat. Of course, one must come prepared. You?'

'I'm wearing them. I also came prepared.' He grinned.

Rosemary got up and shook the picnic blanket over the edge of the boat. 'And the rest of this deal?' she said, concentrating on folding the blanket. She wanted to give off a nonchalant air, but her curiosity churned.

'You let me cook dinner tonight, and we can have those sweets for dessert.'

'Alone in your home?' Rosemary's heart dropped. Of course. This was all a ploy to get her into bed. So typical. Jack was a man. This was what men wanted. 'I do not think this is a good idea. Alone in your place.'

'Rosemary, I promise it's just dinner. I'll even leave the front door open so you can get away.'

His boyish charm made her heart hum. Rosemary laughed. 'Okay. Deal.' She offered her hand to shake, and his touch warmed her insides. She'd never felt like this about anyone. But could she trust him? Should she?

ROSEMARY STOOD in front of the mirror. The shower had cooled her down a little. Her skin had turned a deep golden brown, and her green eyes sparkled against her sun-kissed face. She towel-dried her hair and combed it straight, only to have it curl up again. If she didn't set it, her hair fell in unruly curls, making her look wild and carefree. As she put her checked yellow top and white shorts back on, she heard Jack whistling in the kitchen. The sound filled her with contentment.

The aromas coming from the kitchen were mouth-watering. She walked past Jack's bedroom and peeked in. It sat sparse and tidy. The afternoon sun sliced across the made bed, and a cool breeze floated in from the ocean. She tiptoed inside, intrigued. A large black leather chair sat near the window next to a round table with a pile of books on it. John le Carré sat on top. She lifted it and unearthed Ernest Hemingway. *Well read.* She moved Hemingway and picked up Pablo Neruda's *Love Poems* and Charles Webb's *The Graduate.* A journalist and a romantic.

The photo on his bedside table caught her attention. She picked it up.

'That's my family.'

Rosemary spun around and nearly dropped the photo. She could feel her face burning. 'I am so sorry. I saw ...' She pointed to the books. 'I was ... curious. I am so sorry.'

Jack smiled broadly and wiped his hands on the tea towel draped over his shoulder. 'Maybe I should open my front door for me.'

'You are a funny man.'

'Did you like what you found?'

'Oh no, I do not come inside to—' Rosemary glanced towards the chair.

'The books,' he said. 'Find anything that interested you?'

'Yes. I am impressed. To see Neruda.'

Jack walked over and picked it up. 'Here, you can borrow it.'

'Oh, no.' Rosemary waved it away. 'I could not.'

'Of course you can.' He placed the book in her hands. 'But it's a loan.' His eyes sparkled. He was enjoying this. His playfulness put her at ease.

'I will look after it. Thank you.' Rosemary looked towards the kitchen. 'Something smells good.'

'A roast. My nan's recipe. I'm the favourite grandson and the only one she shared her recipe with.'

'I am not sure putting a piece of meat on a tray in the oven requires something special,' she teased.

'You'll be surprised. Now I think maybe we should go into the living area. I'm liking the look of you in my bedroom too much.'

A smile tugged at her lips, and she quickly pressed them together.

While the dinner roasted, Rosemary settled in a burnt-orange cushioned chair with the book. The salty breeze floated in through the open window.

Jack handed her a martini.

'Grazie.' She held up the toothpick with two olives threaded onto it and smiled.

Jacked laughed. 'A little of Italy in there.'

All her remaining tension and wariness flowed out of her.

She looked out the window and saw the beach where she and Marie had swum naked. It offered an uninterrupted view of the sand and water. Had he stood watching as they frolicked in the water naked? A streak of bashfulness ran through her veins while little bubbles of excitement burst inside her chest.

'You have a good view.'

'Yeh, it's a great place.' Jack set the roast on the table. 'Dinner is served.'

AFTER DINNER, they took a stroll along the beach. The soft swishing of the waves and gentle breeze lulled Rosemary into a peaceful reverie. The flats facing the beach, with their pockets of lights, reminded Rosemary of amber eyes. They seemed to chaperone her as she walked with this wonderful man—a man she was fighting to not be attracted to.

As if sensing her uncertainty, Jack took her hand. A warm, electric feeling filled her body. Her heart swelled, growing large and stopping her breath. But her mind quickly intervened. Being with a man meant being controlled and possessed. Keeping a house and having children. She loved working and earning money. Even here in Australia, many women didn't work once they got married. People looked down on mothers who worked. The nurses all left once they got married. In her heart, she didn't want a domestic life.

She glanced at Jack. She couldn't tell him of her plans. Most men didn't like women with careers. Was Jack one of these men? Would he feel threatened?

She shivered, and Jack wrapped his arm around her. 'Do you want to go back?' he asked.

'No. This is nice. My family always walked after a big meal. *Una passeggiata.* My mother said it was good for the indigestion.' Her voice caught at the mention of her mother, and sorrow filtered up from her heart in small pieces. She'd been working hard to not think about the family she'd abandoned in Sicily.

'Do you keep in contact with your family in Italy?'

'No. They are all dead.' Rosemary stiffened under his arm as she heard the lie come out of her mouth.

They stopped walking. Jack looked down at her. Compassion filled his eyes. 'I'm sorry.'

Rosemary just shrugged. She didn't want to expand the lie further.

'We don't have to talk about it if you don't want to.' He rubbed his thumb against her hand.

'Thank you. It is not good to go back and think about the past. Today is important.' This was not a lie. Carmela had told her the same thing before she left her in Naples. '*Look ahead. Never look back.*' Rosemary didn't want to think about the past. It was done.

Today, right now, was important. The choices she made today would affect her tomorrow. Always.

Rosemary pushed the focus off her. 'What about your family? What are they like?'

'My family are cattle farmers. They have been for generations.'

'But you are not working on the farm?'

'No, I'm afraid I'm the black sheep. You know, the son who didn't want to follow in the family's footsteps and work the land.'

'I know what that is. *Pecora nera.* We say the same thing. I was a black sheep too. For a girl. My father expected me to be married, have children and live on the farm. I did not want this. I loved school and wanted to learn.' Rosemary stopped. *Stupida.* She had said too much. 'But now they are gone,' she quickly added. 'Nothing is left for me in Italy.' She shrugged and manoeuvred the conversation back to Jack. 'You wanted to be a journalist instead?'

'I got a cadetship in my final year, and when I told my parents, they weren't happy. But I was already in Sydney and refused to come home. In the end, they relented. My mother, she always worried about her boys. She convinced my father to get the flat for me. She didn't want me living in one of those drug-den share houses in the Cross.'

'People say your family's wealthy?'

Jack stopped. He gazed down at her and studied her with care. 'You're not going to judge me?'

Rosemary's heart softened when she saw the concern flood his face. She placed her hand on his cheek. 'No. I know about being judged. I do not judge you.'

Jack took her hand and kissed her palm. A searing heat ignited her whole body, and once again, she felt a sweet heaviness in the deepest parts of her.

She shivered.

'You're still cold.' He took her into a tight embrace, and she felt his heart beating. She breathed in his warm, manly scent—citrus and cinnamon.

They strolled back in silence, holding hands the entire way. Back at the flat, Jack helped her out of her coat. As she turned to take it from him, she looked into his eyes, now darker with desire. Her breath stilled.

He reached up and traced her cheek and chin with his finger.

Rosemary stepped back. His hand hung in the air for a moment.

She placed her hands on her hips. 'How do I know you are not like the others? You are rich.' She flung her hand, gesturing to the flat. 'And handsome—' She stopped, horrified that she'd admitted that to him.

Jack laughed, and her hackles rose. Was he laughing at her? Had she made a fool of herself, letting him see her vulnerability? She flung her coat over her shoulders and moved to retrieve her purse from the hall table. 'I must go.' As she walked past Jack, he grabbed her, turned her towards him and kissed her. She pulled away. 'See?'

Jack smiled. 'Handsome, eh?'

She couldn't help it—a grin snuck up from inside her. She worked hard to offer him only a subtle movement of her lips. 'Maybe?'

'Rosemary. You are not my conquest. Yes, you are extraordinary. But not just your beauty. You. All of you. Your mind, your conversation, your passion. Even that temper of yours is extraordinary.'

Rosemary wanted to let herself go. But she'd heard pretty words before. 'I—'

Jack moved in and kissed her again. This time with passion. Her coat slipped off her shoulders and onto the floor, but she didn't care. His broad hands cradled her head with reverence, their firmness evidence that he was her protector. She would let her mind duel with her heart and sort out their differences themselves.

She let go.

CHAPTER 29

Olivia

May 1989

Olivia took a deep breath, focusing on her breathing. The midmorning sun streamed into the car, warming her face. Sebastian was driving through a picturesque part of the Pacific Highway on the way back towards Sydney. Olivia's fear of being in the car had diminished a little. She was beginning to trust Sebastian's driving, and this helped to ease her anxiety. Although she still held on to the seat belt, she wasn't quite strangling it. Writing in her journal about what she'd discovered at Marie's helped to settle her as well.

'How are you feeling?'

His question pulled her away from her journal. Olivia tucked her pen inside the front cover and closed it. Sebastian glanced at her, then back at the road.

'Okay,' she said. 'It's funny. I never knew I had a godmother. And she's so nice.'

'She isn't hard to like. And I could tell she adored you.' He reached over and squeezed her hand. 'I know it's been hard since

Shirley passed, but it must feel good knowing there's someone out there who knew your mum and cares for you.'

She looked out the window. 'I don't feel as alone now.'

'You're not alone. Look at all the people around you who love you.'

She nodded. She did have people who cared about her—Demi, Bertie, and Poppy, in her scatty way. Now she had Marie, who'd promised she would write so they could get to know each other better. She'd also invited Olivia to stay anytime. Olivia wanted Marie to visit her, too.

Then there was Sebastian. He'd been wonderful. For the millionth time, her mind wandered to their kiss in Woolbrook, and her chest tightened. He hadn't kissed her again. Had he changed his mind? Did he regret it? Olivia placed her head on the window and let the world flash past.

She woke with a jolt. 'Where are we?'

'Just passed Morisset.'

She glanced at the clock on the dashboard. They'd been driving for nearly three hours. 'We're only about an hour from Killcare,' Olivia said, looking out her window. Her breath fogged the glass.

'I know.' Sebastian took hold of her hand. 'I'd like to see where you grew up.'

Olivia looked at him, and her heart tumbled. He threw her a quick smile.

'Really?' she said.

'Yeh. I get the impression you loved growing up there.' Sebastian tapped the steering wheel. 'Actually, I thought—' He stopped.

'Tell me?'

'I thought we could spend a bit of time there. For a few days.'

Olivia fell silent. Had she heard him right? 'Sorry?'

'I'd love to spend some time with you. Just the two of us.'

Olivia's heart pounded. She took a deep, silent breath. 'I'd like that.' With those three words, her face ignited. She quickly looked out the window again.

They travelled the rest of the way, listening to the radio. The silence between them was comfortable as Olivia drifted into her thoughts—she was thrilled yet nervous about the prospect of sharing her childhood home with Sebastian.

Her heart both ached and soared as Sebastian drove through the village and she uttered directions. She hadn't been to the house since Shirley's funeral.

Sebastian pulled the car into the driveway and turned off the engine.

Olivia looked at the cottage standing quietly in front of her. 'I loved it here.'

Sebastian got out of the car and stretched. 'You're right on the beach.'

Olivia joined him. 'This cottage was one of the first built at the turn of the century. This whole coastal strip had once been farmlands before being subdivided. That's how the village got its name. As the locals say—killing one's cares.'

'Clever, yet so obvious.' Sebastian laughed. 'Smell that air. I wish I'd brought my board.'

'Shirley's son's surfboards are in the back shed.'

'Ripper.'

'Come on.' She grabbed his hand, and they walked down to the beach.

'Let's have a splash.' Sebastian kicked off his shoes.

Olivia pulled hers off. 'Race you!' she called as she ran down to the water. Only a few people were on the beach.

Sebastian quickly caught up to her and pulled Olivia into the wash. The water was warmer than Olivia had expected. She'd forgotten how wonderful it felt to have the waves tickle her toes. 'I've missed being here so much.'

'Have you missed this?' Sebastian lifted his long leg and kicked water at her.

She squealed. 'You didn't!' She returned the gesture, then ran through the wash away from him.

She was no match for his long legs. He came up behind her, grabbed her about the waist, picked her up and flung her over his shoulder. Olivia shrieked.

'That's it,' he said. 'A dunking you shall receive.'

She pummelled her fist against his broad back. 'No! My clothes.'

Sebastian shifted her off his shoulder and cradled her in his arms. 'No can do.' He began to swing her, counting.

On three, Olivia closed her eyes, ready to plunge into the crashing waves. Instead, she felt Sebastian's lips on hers. She smiled. The stubble on his chin tickled her face. She looped her arms around his neck, and he pulled her closer, gently pushing at her lips with his tongue. She invited him in, the waves the soundtrack to the moment.

Sebastian pulled away and kissed her forehead, and Olivia buried her head contentedly in his chest as he carried her out of the water. Then she caught sight of the people on the beach and a flush of embarrassment swept through her.

Back on dry sand, she moved away from him as her old shyness engulfed her. She focused on the cottage ahead. 'I'd like to show you my home.'

They started walking up the beach towards the little white cottage with the sky-blue trim, but after a few steps, Olivia stopped and looked at it. A warmth filled her. She did love it here.

'Are you okay?' Sebastian stood next to her. An adorable wrinkle sat above his nose.

'I've been wondering what to do about the cottage, thinking I might sell it. Looking at it now, after all these months, I remember how much I love this place.' She turned to Sebastian and smiled. 'Thanks for bringing me here.'

Inside, it was cool and musty. Covered in coloured fabric, the furniture sat like ghosts. Feeling exposed after their moment on the beach, and being alone with Sebastian in her childhood home, Olivia quickly moved to the windows and started opening them. 'We have candles to make it smell nice. A lady here makes them and sells them at the markets.' She opened a cabinet in the living room and took out two.

Out of the corner of her eye, she saw Sebastian wandering around, looking at the photos on the walls. Her hand shook as she tried to light the candles.

Sebastian moved to her. 'Let me try.' He lit them and held them up. 'Where would you like them?'

'One in here and one in the hallway. That way, the bedrooms get some of the scents too.'

Her chest tightened. Where would they sleep? Did Sebastian want her to sleep with him? Although her body wondered how his touch would feel, her mind panicked. She was the oldest virgin she knew. Demi always banged on about just getting it over and done with, warning her that the longer she left it, the harder it would be to lose it.

'You lose your virginity when you're young and stupid. Once it's gone, it's done.' Demi had lost her virginity at the ripe old age of eighteen.

'I'll get the stuff out of the car.' Sebastian bounded out, a spring in his step.

He certainly seemed happy. *Oh my God.* Did he think this would happen? Did she want it to?

He was always positive, though. The total opposite of her, who saw the glass as half empty. He came in and held up her duffel bag.

'Which bedroom's yours?'

'The second one on the left.'

Sebastian placed his luggage down and headed towards her bedroom.

Olivia pulled in some courage. She wasn't ready. 'Sebastian.'

'Yep.'

'Your bedroom is this one.' She pointed to the first bedroom on the left.

'Great.'

OLIVIA WOKE on the sofa with a rug covering her. She sat up and rubbed her eyes. Pots clanged in the kitchen. She yawned. Her head felt groggy. The empty bottle of wine on the coffee table told her why.

After picking up Chinese food, she and Sebastian had strolled to the bottle shop and then popped into Relaxed Video and decided on *The Princess Bride* since Olivia had never seen it.

'You're in for a treat. I can't believe there's a female out there who hasn't seen it.'

A tingle swept up her cheeks at the suggestion of her cloistered life, but Olivia just shrugged. 'I like to read.'

Back at the cottage, they'd chatted over steaming bowls of crispy sesame chicken and sweet and sour pork. She shared stories about her childhood and school days, and Sebastian told her he wanted to buy a hobby farm on the outskirts of Sydney and have chooks and horses. He wanted to find Mrs Right, get married and have kids. Lots of them. 'A football team,' he said, spooning up a second helping of sweet and sour pork.

Olivia had never allowed herself to think about having kids. Her focus on building a life on her own mostly overshadowed any thoughts of falling in love, let alone starting a family. In her narrative, she was alone. But hearing Sebastian speak about wanting a family ignited her curiosity. What might it be like to have her own family? A glimmer of happiness danced up her spine.

'You better tell your prospective wife,' Olivia joked.

'Maybe I just did.' He nudged her and smirked.

Olivia almost choked on her wine.

Sebastian patted her back. 'Easy on the booze.'

'It went down the wrong way.'

'I can see that.' He passed her a paper napkin. 'So what do you want in life, Miss Bennet? Other than discovering the secrets in your mother's trunk.'

'I don't know.' She sipped some water and tried to recover from his comment. An electrifying buzz pushed against her chest. Was he playing with her, or was he serious?

She nudged her feelings away. It was safer this way. No expectations, no disappointment, no hurt.

'Before the trunk arrived, I was content with my quiet life, managing the bookshop, hanging out with Demi, volunteering at the retirement village, and reading.'

'You don't have any other dreams? Things you long to do?'

She did. But she would *never* be able to get on a plane to do it. Getting somewhat comfortable in a car again had been hard enough. 'Nothing big. Not that important.'

'Nothing is ever nothing. Especially when it comes to your dreams.'

She nodded and focused her gaze on her food. 'Okay. I really want to travel around England and Paris and go to where all the great writers lived and wrote. Sit in the cafés Hemingway sat in. Go to the Shakespeare and Company bookshop in Paris. See Charing Cross Road in London. I read this wonderful book about an American writer living in New York who started ordering books from a shop called Marks and Co.'

'Why don't you?'

Olivia touched the scar on her face. 'I don't like being in a car; the thought of being in a plane for so long terrifies me.'

'Olivia, you're stronger than you think you are.' He took the cutlery out of her hand and took both of her hands in his. 'You need to follow your dreams.' He leant forward, lifted her chin and kissed her.

Her heart fluttered, and she smiled when he pulled away. 'So you think a kiss will'—she clicked her fingers—'give me the courage to travel in a big silver flying machine?'

'Yep.' He grinned. 'Come on, let's finish this food off and watch *The Princess Bride*. That will show you how to face your fears and follow your dreams.'

After tidying up, opening a fresh bottle of wine and filling two bowls with ice cream they'd picked up at the servo in town, they hit play on the video player. Olivia snuggled in under Sebastian's proffered arm. He smelt nice, like fresh pine soap and some woody cologne, but she didn't get to enjoy the moment or the movie. Feeling safe and happy, she'd drifted off.

Now, as the morning sun seeped into the living room, the memory of sitting close to Sebastian made her heart sing.

She folded the quilt, picked up the empty bottle of wine and strolled into the kitchen. Sebastian looked so at ease at the stove. The smell of bacon made her mouth water.

'Something smells good.'

Sebastian turned around. 'Good morning, Miss Lightweight. You owe me ten dollars for the video hire. Actually, I'll deduct two dollars for the thirty or so minutes you watched.'

'Sorry about that. I was so tired. Did you watch it all?'

'Hell yeh. There's no way I was going to miss out on the ending again.'

She frowned. 'But you said you saw it at the movies.'

Sebastian turned to deal with the bacon. 'I didn't get to see all of it.'

Olivia poured herself a coffee from the percolator. 'Why not?'

Sebastian gave her a sheepish smile.

'Oh!' She felt her cheeks go hot, and that awkward lump rammed back into her throat. What was wrong with her? *Of course he goes on dates. Look at him.* And such a nice guy too. Maybe he was trying on women for size in his search for Mrs Right. That was it. Sebastian was just trying her on for size. She was a pleasant distraction. She felt light-headed. This dating thing, if that's what this was, was all too new for her.

She decided that there would be no more kissing. They were heading home tomorrow. Today, she'd visit some neighbours and her mum's grave while Sebastian went out surfing. A day apart would be good for them.

The board games on the bookshelf caught her eye. An idea bounced inside her mind. That evening, she'd cook him a meal to thank him for everything, and then they could play Scrabble. This would help them pass the time in a fun way so neither of them would feel awkward—she might even let him win. Maybe?

And when they got back to Sydney, she had work to do. She needed to find Jack Emerson.

CHAPTER 30

Rosemary
April 1964

Three days had passed since their date, and Rosemary found she was missing Jack, who was away on an assignment. She kept busy with work, and thankfully, Gladys had been in a good mood all week. Rosemary chatted with the mothers when she delivered their meals or picked up their trays. During the afternoon tea round, it was easier to stop and have longer chats, and whenever Matron wasn't looking, Rosemary got to have a cuddle when a new mum insisted on sharing her precious baby.

She wondered what it would be like to have a baby of her own. With Jack. She sighed internally. She wanted to be a doctor. But deep down, she also wanted to be a mother. To love and be loved back.

When Rosemary returned to the kitchen, Gladys growled. 'You know, this ain't a delivery station.' She stepped to the side to reveal an enormous bunch of flowers on the workbench.

'For me?'

'Well, they're not for me. My Bill wouldn't even know what flowers are. Unless there's a horse running at Randwick named after one.'

Rosemary gazed at the grand bouquet of red and fuchsia roses, orange tulips and yellow daisies. Not even at Carmela's villa had she seen anything like it. A small envelope peeked through the petals.

She lifted it out.

Dear Rosemary, I cannot stop thinking about you. Your green eyes burn into my thoughts. Remembering your laugh, your smile, heats my heart. Even your fiery temper brings on a cheeky smile. My photographer thinks I've lost my mind. Dinner and a surprise on Saturday? I'll pick you up at 7 pm. Love, Jack.

'It better be a respectable man that's sent flowers like that.' Gladys's voice pulled Rosemary back into the kitchen.

Giddy, she reached in, took out one of each flower and handed them to Gladys. 'For you. Everyone should get flowers. Maybe show Bill what they look like.' Rosemary watched joy seep across Gladys's lined face.

'Well, the work's not going to get done on its own, is it?' she said, turning her back.

Rosemary grinned. She'd made another woman feel special today.

ROSEMARY GOT off the bus on William Street and strolled down towards Stanley Street. For a Thursday night, Darlinghurst buzzed with energy. Her heart fluttered with excitement—she'd been looking forward to meeting up with the girls. Lately, their days were pulling them into busy routines, and they only passed each other in the kitchen or at the front door as they came and went. On this rare night, they were all available. Even Pamela was in Sydney.

Rosemary loved Stanley Street. It carried a small essence of Italy, and locals called it Little Italy—a pocket of great restaurants and coffee shops and a refreshing alternative to the business and glitz of the Cross.

Pamela clicked her fingers at the waiter. 'I think we all need another drink while you tell us what you've been up to, young lady.'

The waiter, only about nineteen, bumbled over nervously.

Pamela took charge. 'We'd like four more glasses of that delectable wine.' She placed her hand on his wrist and leant in closer. 'Maybe a bottle, darling,' she said, walking her fingers up his bare arm.

He blushed the colour of the wine they were drinking and glanced around for help. 'I ... am a sorries ... I cannot speak the English very well.'

Rosemary jumped in and ordered in Italian.

'I love it when you do that,' Eleanor gushed. 'Italian sounds so romantic.'

'Unfortunately, not everyone thinks the same. I was at the bakery yesterday, and an Italian woman was speaking to her daughter. A lady in the queue told her she should speak English now that she was in Australia.' Rosemary paused. 'How did she put it? "That *gobble gook* is not our language." I was very angry.'

'What did you do?' Marie asked, eying her.

'This'll be good.' Pamela sat up straight, her eyes wide.

'I said to the woman that she was not speaking this *gobble gook* but Italian and that we have a right to speak in our language and that she was not hurting anyone. I said that Australia was a fair country and that what she said was not good.'

'That was quite a decent thing to say,' Eleanor said.

Marie grinned. 'Oh, I know there's more.'

'There is?' Pamela raised a perfectly pencilled eyebrow.

'Rosemary?' Marie beamed.

Rosemary grinned. 'Okay.' She picked up the water jug and poured herself a glass. 'I called her a disgraceful cow and said she was as ignorant as a slug.' She paused and took in the shocked looks of her friends, relishing every moment. 'In Italian, of course.' She giggled.

'An Italian woman behind me laughed, and the rude woman became upset and huffed out of the shop.' Rosemary sighed. 'I am afraid not everyone is happy with the migrants here. I am lucky because I have good friends. But sometimes, too many times, I see and experience things that are not good.'

Marie lit a cigarette. 'Well, I'm sure that Jack doesn't feel the same way. The girls have been telling me that there's a new bunch of flowers delivered every day.'

'Not *every* day.' Rosemary grinned. Jack had been sending flowers to the terrace most days since their date on the boat.

'So?' Pamela said. 'Is it serious? When Nathan first gave me flowers, he told me he loved me.'

'No, no, no, there is no love but—' Rosemary blushed.

Marie and Pamela chimed in unison, 'Did you—'

'No!' Rosemary fired back. She leant forward and whispered, 'But we kissed. For a long time. A very long time.'

All the girls squealed, drawing the attention of the other patrons.

'Shhh.' Rosemary laughed and blushed again, thinking that they must look like a bunch of giddy schoolgirls. But ever since that night, she'd been wanting to squeal too.

Over the past two weeks, Jack had taken her out for several romantic dinners, and they'd even gone to a movie, where they'd kissed and cuddled like love-struck teenagers. After Rosemary caught her friends up on the activities that had been keeping her away from them, she insisted on hearing their news. During their meal—a collection of pasta and salad with bitter lettuce, bocconcini cheese and tomato—they caught up on work, bosses, boyfriends and dates.

The women lingered until the waitstaff began cleaning the restaurant, blowing out the candles in the chianti bottles and replacing the checked tablecloths with fresh ones.

Eleanor rubbed her stomach. 'I'm full and a little tipsy.' She counted the bottles of wine on the table. 'I think we've all got vino running in our veins instead of blood.'

'Yes, we better go.' Rosemary stood. 'Some waiters have day jobs too.' They put on their coats, and as they walked out, Rosemary sang, '*Buonasera.*' A chorus of good evenings followed, and she smiled when two waiters whistled. Just like in Sicily. It was good there was a bit of Italy in Sydney. It didn't make her feel quite as homesick.

It was only a fifteen-minute stroll back to the nurses' quarters. As they walked up Crown Street, Rosemary and Marie hung back as Pamela and Eleanor linked arms and powered ahead. They were dropping off Marie before heading home.

'Jack invited me to go to his father's sixtieth birthday party,' Rosemary said to Marie as they walked. 'I do not think I will go. This is a big event. I have only spent a few weeks with Jack. It has been good. He is a kind man, and we have many laughs, but this is too serious ... and important. Time with family must always be.' The comment caught like a fishhook in her mouth. Thoughts of her own family washed into her mind.

'Do you like him?' Marie asked.

Rosemary didn't answer straight away. She did like him, but it felt complicated.

She knew he was interested physically. Very interested. She could feel it in his kisses—his long, warm kisses that transported her into a starry void. The passion was intense, yet he was also a gentleman and kind. But lurking in Rosemary's mind was the persistent worry that he wanted to possess her. Getting what he wanted had to come with his privilege.

She wanted to trust Jack. He was loving and intelligent, and he made her laugh. They talked about the news, the Vietnam War, books and art. He also took an interest in her photography and always begged to see her photos. She was still taking her camera with her everywhere. She loved the thrill of framing a shot and seeing the result when the film was developed. She kept her photos in a neat bundle, aside from her best ones, which she framed and hung on her bedroom wall.

Marie lit a cigarette, then took Rosemary's hand. 'Well?'

'I do. Very much,' Rosemary said. As she spoke the words, the truth cemented itself in her heart.

'I sense that there's a *but*.' Marie let out a long stream of smoke as she searched Rosemary's face.

'I am scared. For me.' She squeezed Marie's hand. 'My experience with men has not been kind to me. They like what they see. They want a trophy. I do not want to be owned. To serve them.'

'You can have love and not be possessed.'

'Maybe.'

'Well, he must be pretty special,' Marie said with a small smile. 'You're spending a lot of time with him.'

'I am sorry. I have neglected our friendship.'

'Don't sweat it. I've been busy at work.' Sadness crossed her face. 'Actually, I'm glad we got to catch up tonight. I'm going home for a few weeks. Mum's not well. I've booked a little beachside cottage on the south coast. I'm hoping the sea air will help a little. Matron's given me the time off.'

'Oh, Marie.' Rosemary folded her into a hug. 'I am sorry.' She knew her friend was close to her mother. They'd grown closer after Marie's dad died of cancer shortly after she finished high school. His death was why she'd wanted to become a nurse. Rosemary thought of her mother, and a sharpness stabbed at her heart.

CHAPTER 31

Olivia

May 1989

Olivia opened the trunk and located the receipts. The top receipt was for the enrolment deposit. She looked at the date. 7 December 1978. She flipped through some more. Fees paid for term one, dated 18 December 1978, and one for her uniform dated 9 January 1979. Her mother had died in November 1978. Why hadn't she noticed this before? Everyone had missed it. Even Demi, who missed nothing—one reason why she got away with so much when it came to her family. Someone had put these receipts in the steamer trunk after her mother passed. Most likely Shirley. But if it was Shirley, why did she keep this secret?

It had to be Shirley.

Then it hit her.

The scholarship she'd been awarded. Was it all tied together? The same benefactor? The scholarship to Sydney University had been a huge surprise, even for Shirley. If she'd known, she'd been an excellent actor.

Olivia remembered the day Mrs Crawford called her into her office to tell her the news.

'Why me?'

'Olivia, you will finish here in the top five. Second. You deserve it. Now, please keep this to yourself. It will be officially announced on your graduation night.'

Olivia could only nod. For years, she'd dreamt of going to Sydney University. She'd known her marks wouldn't be an issue, but finances were a different story. Shirley had planned to help as much as she could, and Olivia would have to work while she studied.

The only scholarships the school offered were one for the student who came first in the year, one for a student planning to study overseas, and one for a student pursuing a lucrative degree in medicine or law at Sydney University. Olivia wanted to study literature and get a Bachelor of Arts degree—it didn't attract a scholarship.

Mrs Crawford invited Olivia to sit on the Chesterfield. Olivia did so, twisting her hands in her lap, while Mrs Crawford sat straight and tall in her large scarlet wing chair.

'Sometimes a benefactor comes along with an offer of a new scholarship. This one comes with the stipulation that it goes to a student who might not have the financial means because of family hardship or loss.'

Olivia blinked.

'The benefactor wants to remain anonymous, as is usually the case, and this person has decided, with board approval, that you should receive this inaugural scholarship. The Artemis Scholarship. Like the Greek Goddess, this scholarship is to help one student here at the college succeed into adulthood.' Mrs Crawford smiled.

For a moment, Olivia was lost for words. 'Because I'm an orphan?' She could already hear the girls' catty remarks. The scholarship would be fodder for the veiled bullying the popular girls dished out, not just to Olivia but anyone who was marginalised in some way —because of their cultural background, their looks, or their socioeconomic status. 'I'm not comfortable with a scholarship based on pity.'

Mrs Crawford came over and sat next to her. 'We all need a little boost in life sometimes. As a mother myself, I want my daughter to take every opportunity.' She held Olivia's hand. 'There's something about you, Olivia Bennet. Take it. Take all that life gives you that is good. You deserve it as much as the rest of the girls here do.'

After accepting the scholarship, Olivia asked Mrs Crawford if she could write a thank-you note to the benefactor, but Mrs Crawford reminded her that the benefactor had requested anonymity. Respecting this, Olivia left it.

Until now.

On The Quest Wall, she wrote: *scholarship???* Was there a connection somehow?

She needed to go back to the library.

THE OFFICES OF MORRIS, Templeton and Gray were plush and accented with rosewood and red velvet. Olivia half expected a butler to arrive with cognac on a silver tray while she waited for Mr Templeton to finish with another client.

'Miss Bennet.' A well-dressed man in his late fifties entered the waiting area and extended his hand to Olivia. 'I'm sorry I've kept you waiting. Please, come into my office.'

He offered Olivia a chair before taking a seat behind his polished desk. The office was tastefully decorated. A vintage globe stood on a stand to his left, underneath the large window. High-rise buildings filled the view. A bookshelf filled with leather-bound books covered an entire wall, and the crimson leather furniture matched the polished rosewood.

'I was surprised to get your letter,' he said. 'Most young people don't care how their school fees were paid for.'

'Well, I suppose I'm trying to solve a mystery of sorts. My mother died in a car accident.'

The solicitor nodded. She steadied her breath and explained what had led her to his office.

Mr Templeton listened. He had a kind face. When she finished, he opened a file and studied it. 'It's serendipitous that you contacted us. We had been planning to get in touch regarding Shirley's estate. As you know, in her will, your mother gave Mrs O'Connor, Shirley, the authority to look after all her affairs, which is how Shirley came to us and employed this office to look after her own affairs. Since Shirley had no living relatives, you inherited her estate.' He took off his glasses and wiped them with a crisp white handkerchief. 'But in your recent letter, you enquired about the payment of your school fees, not the estate.'

Olivia nodded. 'I saw this office's name stamped on some receipts.'

She reached into her backpack and pulled out the bundle. 'They're all dated after our accident. When I first started at Our Lady of Peace, I asked Shirley who was paying for my schooling. She told me not to worry about it and to focus on my studies—that it was all taken care of. I was a kid, so I didn't really think about it much after that. For a fleeting moment, I wondered if maybe someone my mum had looked after as a nurse had heard about her death and felt sorry for me, knowing how much Mum believed in the importance of education. Or if maybe Shirley was paying for it with money she'd squirrelled away and was being humble about it. I don't know, maybe I should've taken more notice.' She slumped back into the chair.

William seemed to sense she wasn't done and waited patiently.

She leant forward again. 'Mr Templeton, I'm ...' She paused and swallowed the boulder in her throat. 'I'm also hoping that the receipts might hold the answer as to who my father might be. With my mother gone, I may never know. She refused to tell me.'

'I'm sorry for your loss.' Mr Templeton looked at her with warmth. 'This must be very hard on you, but I hope you can appreciate that we cannot give out confidential information.' He tapped a folder on the side of his desk and slid it a little further from her.

Olivia stared at the folder. Did it contain the answers she was looking for? She forced herself to look away.

'Yes, we arranged for your school and boarding fees to be paid,' Mr Templeton continued, 'but our client requested that their identity not be disclosed.'

'Even though I'm twenty-four.' Olivia heard the whine in her voice but ignored it. 'Don't they want to know how their money was spent? How I did at school? That I got a scholarship to university?'

'I'm sorry, Olivia. I cannot help you other than to confirm that this firm arranged for the school fees to be paid. But there's another reason we've asked you to come in.'

She braced herself for another piece of information that would keep her whirlwind universe spinning wildly.

'Shirley's documents held information that she had a safe-deposit box. There were documents belonging to your mother inside.'

'What? But Shirley's estate was settled months ago?'

Mr Templeton flushed and coughed. 'I'm sorry. Somehow, some of Mrs O'Connor's file became separated and found its way into another client's folder. We are truly sorry for this. This sort of thing can happen, though rarely.'

'It's okay. I'm sure it wasn't intentional.' Olivia offered a weak smile.

'It was registered under her real name, Rosamaria Benito.'

'How do you know her real name?' she whispered. 'I only just found out recently.'

'My wife, Tillie, and I met your mother when she lived in Genoa. We were on our honeymoon, and she was waiting for a boat to take her to Australia, though we didn't know that at the time. We met at the trattoria where Rosemary worked. Tillie and your mother became quite close in the weeks we stayed in Genoa. Your mum helped Tillie with her Italian, and Tillie introduced Rosamaria—Rosemary—to the

English classics. She gave your mum a couple of books she read during our honeymoon.'

'*A Room with a View* and *Tess of the d'Urbervilles*,' Olivia said. 'Your wife is the Tillie who wrote the note inside?'

'Yes.'

Olivia now knew of two Italian cities connected to her mum: Sicily and Genoa.

William's voice interrupted her thoughts. 'Rosemary made a huge impression on us. I was surprised when she called me just after you were born. She wanted to make a will.'

'Mr Templeton—'

'Please call me William.'

Olivia pressed her lips together. 'Do you know anything about my mum's life before I was born?'

'I'm afraid not. Though when Rosemary came to see me, she always told me how you were going and about her work as a nurse. She did call when she got accepted to Newcastle University to study medicine.' He stopped and shook his head. Sadness flicked across his face. 'Rosemary would've made a wonderful doctor.'

All Olivia could do was nod. Every time she was reminded of her mum's missed opportunity, the sticky black mass inside her squeezed all her organs. A little voice chanted inside her mind. *Your fault. Your fault. Your fault.* She looked down at her hands clenched in her lap.

'Are you okay, Olivia?'

She nodded. 'Can I look at the documents?'

'There yours.' He handed her an envelope.

Olivia felt the room spin as she took out all the missing documents. Her mother's passport, and there it was, another secret. A marriage certificate written in Italian—Olivia recognised '*Matrimonio*'. She placed her hand on her heart to stop it from beating out of her chest. 'My mother *was* married. To someone called Arturo Benito.' *The gold ring!*

'It appeared so.'

'And she never said anything to you when you spent time with her in Genoa.'

'No, it didn't come up, and Rosemary certainly didn't share that information with us.'

Olivia shook the envelope. 'Nothing else?' Her chest throbbed as pieces slammed together. 'No divorce papers. Which means ...'

'She may have been married—'

'When I was conceived.' The second realisation slapped her. 'Which means my mother was having an affair and found herself pregnant.' *No wonder she never wanted to talk about it. The shame she must've had to live with.* But who ... where was her father? What happened to their marriage? The room began to close in. She needed to get out. Walk and think. There were still the details she needed to know about her education. William looked at his watch. 'I'm afraid I have another appointment.'

'Can I ask one more question?'

'Yes.'

'I was awarded a scholarship to the university. It was the first of its kind at Our Lady of Peace. Do you know anything about it?'

'I'm afraid I don't.'

A caring, warm smile caressed his face. She understood why her mum liked him. Her spirits lifted a little, along with her confidence.

'Can you give me any information about my school fees?'

He shook his head. 'Those are client details I'm not able to divulge.'

Olivia nodded and sighed internally.

The phone rang, and William picked it up. 'Yes, Susan, put her through.' He turned to Olivia. 'Please excuse me; my youngest daughter is getting married, and it's my duty to calm Tillie down once a day.'

William turned away from Olivia. She looked at the back of his leather chair and then at the file on his desk. Her heart thumped. This was so not like her, but she was sick and tired of being in the dark. She glanced at William's back once more, then, without another thought, reached out and slid the file towards her. With care, she lifted the cover. On top was a letter with a Jubilee Station logo on the top. At the bottom was a name.

Jack!

Olivia slid the folder back just as William turned around. She felt guilty about the deceit—he'd been so kind—but didn't regret the action. Maybe she wasn't as sweet as everyone thought.

Jack. She repeated the name in her mind, her hope inflating once more, her heart pounding. Could he be her father? Why else would he pay for her school fees? She worked at keeping calm and containing the buzzing within her. She needed to find out more.

'I apologise for the intrusion. Weddings. Bigger than Ben Hur, this one.'

Olivia smiled. 'My friend said the same thing about her sister's wedding.' She stood and shook his hand. 'Thank you for your time.'

'Any time. I'll get Susan to call you as soon as we get any information on the box.' He stepped around the desk. 'I'm sorry I can't give you all the other information.'

'I understand.' Olivia was about to leave, then stopped. 'Can I give you a hug?'

William responded by stepping forward and giving her a big hug —one that Olivia imagined a father would give his daughter. 'Thank you,' she whispered.

Olivia waited until she was in the elevator before she pulled out her copy of *Beloved* and wrote *Jack—Jubilee Station* inside the cover. It wasn't much, but it was something to go on. She'd make it up to William somehow.

CHAPTER 32

Rosemary
May 1964

Jack's father's sixtieth was shaping up to be the social event of the year. When Rosemary and Jack arrived late in the afternoon, preparations were in full swing. They found Gwen, Jack's mother, talking to a group of women who were hanging decorations and dressing the tables in the barn. She rushed over.

'Well, hello there.' Gwen hugged Jack and then pulled away. 'You've put on a bit of weight.'

'Hello, Mother, you're looking as wonderful as ever.' Jack gave her a kiss on the cheek and then grabbed Rosemary's hand. 'This is Rosemary.'

'Ah, the new girl.'

Jack smirked. 'You make me sound like some lecherous fiend with a string of conquests.'

Rosemary watched them carefully. Jack had a confident way with her, but it was clear that Gwen was in control. Not like her own mother, who allowed her sons to tell her what they wanted and what she needed.

'You're as beautiful as your reputation suggested,' Gwen said, assessing her, a seemingly rehearsed smile on her face.

'Thank you. It is very nice to be here.' Rosemary held out her hand. Gwen shifted slightly, then returned the handshake, locking her cool grey eyes onto Rosemary. This woman was not one to be easily won over. Rosemary couldn't tell if she was just being overprotective or if she didn't like her.

'So, you're Italian.'

And there it was. A statement rather than curiosity. The emphasis on the *I*. Gwen wasn't sure about her son dating an immigrant.

Rosemary felt her shoulders broaden and her feet pushing into the ground, ready to attack. She clenched her teeth and started counting to ten, as Marie had advised.

'Just a little trick to keep that fiery temper of yours under wraps,' Marie had said with a slight grin. 'You're going into enemy territory. Those folks aren't as accepting as we are here in Sydney. They hear all these ridiculous rumours about the dangers of migrants.'

'So, I should not say I will eat their children.'

Marie laughed. 'Yeh, I think you better take a break from that one.'

Rosemary kept her eyes on Gwen and smiled. 'Yes, from Sicily.'

'Family?'

'No. All lost in the war.' No matter how many times Rosemary told the lie, it always made her heart lurch. Though at this point, for all she knew, they could actually be dead. She would never know. She shook away that devastating thought.

Another woman rushed over, breaking the tension. 'Hello, Jack!'

'Aunt Vera!' Jack embraced the woman with affection—much differently from the way he'd greeted his mother.

Vera turned to face Rosemary and grabbed her hands. 'Now, who is this divine creature?' She looked Rosemary up and down with friendly eyes. 'I'm Vera. Jack's aunty and the black sheep of this family.' She winked at Jack. 'I taught Jack everything I know about how to break the rules.'

Rosemary caught the dark look that briefly shifted across Gwen's face.

'Well, hello, everyone!'

They turned towards the sing-song voice. Lacey looked sensational in her riding wear, and her flushed cheeks only accentuated her beauty. She glided over to Gwen, who kissed her cheek while giving Rosemary a sharp gaze.

A vice squeezed Rosemary's heart, and her confidence wobbled. Lacey owned the moment, and her poise cemented in Rosemary's mind the fact that she tightly held Jack's world. Rosemary wasn't interested in entering some catty competition, but given the way Lacey glared at her, she knew she'd already been snared and pulled in.

'Ah, Lacey,' said Gwen. 'How was your ride?'

'Fabulous. Frank's just finishing up with the horses.' She turned to Rosemary and gave her a bright, forced smile. Her teeth were perfect. 'Hello again. Or should I say, *Buon pomeriggio, come va?*'

Rosemary also forced a smile and felt the tension increase again. '*Sto molto bene. Grazie.*' For the benefit of all, she added, 'I am very well, thank you.' Seemingly sensing the tension as well, Jack moved in close behind Rosemary and placed both hands on her shoulders.

'Whereabouts in Italy are you from, Rosemary?' Gwen asked, her nose in the air.

'Genoa,' she replied, feeling guilty for lying again, although it was partly true, and nervous about being questioned further.

'Ah, our Lacey spent two years in Genoa studying after high school. You two might have a lot to chat about.'

'Of course.' Lacey let out a soft laugh and looked directly at Rosemary. 'Plenty of time.' She looked around the barn and continued before Rosemary could respond. 'Has anyone offered Jack and Rosemary drinks?'

Jack smiled politely. 'We'll go up to the house.' Unease worked its way through Rosemary. Something wasn't quite right between Jack and Lacey. 'We've just got in, and I think Rosemary would like to freshen up first.' Jack nodded at her.

'Yes, that would be nice,' said Rosemary.

'Of course, let me come with you,' Lacey purred. 'I can help Rosemary get settled in.'

On one of their dates, Jack had told Rosemary they were like cousins. Their families' cattle properties were next to each other and had been for generations.

'She's just protective. She's the same with her horses,' he'd said with a laugh.

But Rosemary could already see the truth. Lacey didn't see Jack like a cousin. And she was protecting Jack—from other women.

FINALLY ALONE, Rosemary pressed herself against the closed bedroom door, having convinced Lacey that she didn't need help.

She needed some fresh air.

She walked to the window, opened the curtain and lifted all the sash windows. A cool breeze pushed past her. Jubilee Station ran all the way to the horizon. The house was surrounded by lush, mani-cured gardens. Green popped against the golden fields beyond, and roses and gardenias offered a sense of romance.

If only the family were as inviting.

A soft knock on the door pulled Rosemary away from the view. She took another deep breath and plastered a smile on her face. Already this was a big mistake.

Her instincts had warned her.

She tensed, ready for Lacey to intrude again, but when she opened the door, she found Vera standing there holding two martini glasses.

'I thought you might need one,' Vera said, handing her a glass.

'My sister-in-law tends to make people drink. A lot.' She laughed. The sound rang out loud and happy. Before Rosemary could utter a response, Vera shut the door and put her fingers to her lips as she locked it.

'To stop sticky beaks.' She walked over to the sofa and patted the cushion next to her. 'Please join me.'

Rosemary did so and took a sip of the martini. The alcohol settled her a little.

Vera turned to face her straight on. 'You really are the most beautiful woman. I can see why Jack is so besotted.'

The words came out hot before Rosemary could stop them. 'You think Jack is only interested because of the way I look? I have a mind too.' She placed the martini glass down on the coffee table. 'I am not just an empty vessel.'

Vera immediately grabbed the glass and handed it back to her. 'I don't doubt that at all. I can see how much he admires you.' She chuckled. 'Has he seen this fieriness?'

Rosemary went quiet. She'd forgotten to count to ten. 'Yes.'

'Well, my dear, I'm quite certain that Jack is aware of your mind. You're miles ahead of the vacuous women he usually escorts to events.' She leant in close. 'And you've majestically rattled both Lacey and Gwen.' She plucked an olive off the toothpick and popped it into her mouth. 'I love it. It's about time. Those two have been scheming about a marriage since Lacey was waddling around with a diapered backside.'

Rosemary sighed. This wasn't what she wanted. To fight for Jack's affection. To seek approval. She'd left all of this behind. 'We are just friends.'

Vera waved the comment away. 'I can tell that you're in love with him and vice versa. I'm afraid that horse has bolted.'

'Why do you care so much about Jack and me?' She studied Vera.

'Because I'm a romantic, and I love my nephew. He's always had big shoes to fill. His father's and his older brother's. Like I said, we're both black sheep. He wanted to be a journalist and turned his back on the station. And I refused to marry for anything less than the greatest love.'

'There is no great love in your life?'

'Was. Killed in the war. You only have that kind of love once in your life.' She got up and left the room with a smile.

Rosemary sat, perplexed. Was Jack really in love with her? And if he was, she shouldn't let it go.

AFTER ROSEMARY BATHED AND DRESSED, she strolled along the large hallway at the top of the main staircase. Portraits on the walls showcased the family's history—generations of men, women and children.

'There you are!' Jack bounded up the stairs, pulled her in and kissed her passionately. She felt his body tighten as he wrapped her in his warmth. 'You look wonderful. I'd hoped the dress would suit. I wasn't sure about black, but you make it look sensational.'

Rosemary smoothed the thick taffeta skirt. He had impeccable taste. 'Thank you, Jack. But you must stop buying me these dresses.'

'I don't buy them for you. I buy them for me.' He winked. 'I'm the lucky bloke who gets the best view.'

Rosemary pulled away and smiled. He looked so handsome in his tuxedo. His hair was combed, and his shave was fresh. 'You look handsome, and you smell nice too.' Like sandalwood and spice.

He leant in and gave her a less-fervent kiss. 'I was wondering where you got to?'

'I was looking at your family on the walls. Impressive.' She leant over the banister. 'This is a beautiful home. Very grand.'

'It's one of the oldest in the district. Built in the mid-1800s.'

Rosemary smiled. Australia was a new country.

He threw his head back and chuckled, seemingly reading her thoughts. 'You must laugh at us when we say things are old when they're only a hundred or so. In Italy, it's more like thousands of years.'

'History has to start somewhere,' Rosemary said, smiling at him.

'Yes, it does.' Jack lifted Rosemary's hand, kissed her palm and placed it next to his heart. 'Come with me.' He guided her down the stairs and out a set of double doors into a large sitting room. French windows lined one side, and they opened onto a wide verandah. Lit lamps sat on small tables and sideboards, coating the room in a warm amber glow.

'Sit with me.' Jack placed his hand on the small of her back and led her to a peacock-blue velvet chaise lounge.

'The French make love on sofas like this. Are you going to seduce me?' She leant back. 'I do not think your mother would approve.' She gave Jack a playful smile.

'I have something more romantic.' He reached into his jacket and pulled out a small black box.

Rosemary caught the Fairfax & Roberts logo stamped across the lid. Her heart stopped, and the world slowed as Jack opened the box to reveal a diamond necklace.

'Jack,' she whispered. 'I cannot accept this.'

He lifted the necklace out and placed it around her neck. After ensuring the clasp was in place, he leant in and kissed the side of her neck. 'I've fallen in love with you, Rosemary Benito,' he whispered in her ear. 'I want to love you for the rest of my life.' He leant back to look at her. 'I hope you feel the same.'

Rosemary nodded and kissed him, long and slow, her unease scattering like autumn leaves. Sweet love swirled up from the pit of her stomach. She felt connected with him.

Maybe she could really do this. Maybe, like a kite, she could be free in a sense but also tethered to him.

'There you both are.' Vera flounced into the room. 'Your mother is wondering why you haven't made an appearance. You've been summoned.'

Rosemary got to her feet.

Vera's eyes glowed. 'I see Jack's given you his gift.' She nodded at the necklace. 'It looks divine on you.'

Rosemary placed her fingers on the diamonds and squinted at Jack accusingly.

Vera walked over and linked her arm with Rosemary's. 'It's okay —he needed a woman's opinion. But he chose this one himself.' She winked at Jack. 'Not just a pretty face, my nephew.'

'Aunt Vera says it as she sees it. Or thinks it. Lucky you're my favourite aunt.'

'I'm your only aunt.' She laughed. 'But I'll take the compliment just the same.'

As they walked out, Vera leant in close to Rosemary and whispered, 'This is just a start. He was looking at diamond rings, too.'

As they walked towards the lights and the music and the cheerful chatter, a knot grew inside Rosemary's chest. Was this all happening? Was she ready?

CHAPTER 33

The party was in full swing.

Jack was off with some friends, and Rosemary's head was spinning as she tried to remember all the people she'd been introduced to. Some were friendly, some curious, and others, like Gwen, weren't sure about her. For many, she was the first migrant they'd ever been introduced to. Her accent stood out among the broad Australian voices filling the room.

She stepped outside for some air. The sky was a carpet of stars. It didn't look like this in Sydney, but it reminded her of the sky back home. A twinge of homesickness squeezed her chest.

Rosemary touched the necklace nestled into the groove of her neck. Tonight, Jack had told her he loved her for the first time, that he wanted to be with her.

He was thinking of marriage. She felt her heart could burst with happiness, yet she couldn't shake the terror of what marriage could mean for her life. For her freedom.

She'd spent the evening watching the couples at the party—the men in groups talking business and sports and the women fussing over them, serving them and looking after the children. They had safe lives. They were protected and had secure homes doing what was expected of them. Rosemary wished she could also happily accept this path. It would make things easier. She just couldn't shake the yearning inside. It glowed and pulsated with possibility.

She was tethered to this force as much as she was to Jack.

Hearing voices nearby, she moved around a corner and into the shadows. She needed a break from all the questions and curiosity.

'She's certainly exquisite,' said a woman. 'I can see why Jack's smitten.'

Rosemary peeked around the corner and saw two women Jack had introduced her to. Coral had told her she looked like a movie star. Edith had been aloof and, with her chin stretched up, announced that she was Lacey's best friend.

'That's why he's infatuated, Coral. What breathing man wouldn't be?'

Edith lit a cigarette and offered it to Coral.

Coral took a long drag and exhaled. 'I don't know. Have you seen them? It doesn't matter where he found her. You can just tell. This is more than just some crush. Besides, I don't believe that he's one of those men.'

'All men of Jack's social standing and family background are "one of those men",' said Edith. 'They marry the right girl. It's what their families expect. It's what this family expects of Jack, and he knows it.'

Rosemary held her breath.

'Besides'—Edith took a drag—'the Emersons, especially Gwen, would never accept an Italian migrant as part of the family, let alone one who has no family. God knows where she's come from. Anyway, it doesn't matter. It's already been decided.'

'People change their minds,' said Coral.

'Not these people. Come on, I'm parched.'

Rosemary remained in the shadows. Heat stormed through her body as a sticky web of prejudice and deceit consumed her. Who did these people think they were? Deciding who married whom—

She stopped, the wind knocked out of her. It was no different from her own arranged marriage. The stark reality sent a shiver down her spine. How much stock did Jack put in his family's expectations? And what had been decided? Was it about his career? Jack had told her that his family wanted him back on the farm. They'd said it was time he finished up in the city and returned home to take up the family legacy.

Sadness yanked at her heart. She knew that if he returned, he'd fade into the land and she'd lose him. This place was his home. But it could not be hers. This town would be just the same as her village back home. People knew too much about each other. They lived on gossip like oxygen.

Inside the barn, a piano began playing, and guests started singing. But Rosemary didn't want to go back in. Instead, she walked through the garden, running her hands along the hedges clipped into sharp edges. The scents of roses and gardenias filled the evening air. She moved in and out of the shadows that the light from the barn created. As she moved further down the gravelled path, something shifted behind her.

She gasped.

'Shouldn't you be inside?'

Rosemary spun towards the voice. Frank was leaning against a small tree. In the moonlight, its white trunk glowed, ghostlike. He wore only a shirt, no jacket, and his tie hung limp around the collar, like cold linguine. She wasn't surprised. At the ball, he'd appeared uncomfortable in his tux. A solid body caged inside formal wear.

The image discombobulated her, and she reached up to touch the gold cross she usually wore. Instead, she found the diamond necklace. She flushed with heat.

Tonight, she'd watched Lacey and him interact. When he spoke with her, he dropped his broody aura. They appeared very close. Rosemary didn't trust either of them.

'I wanted to get some fresh air,' Rosemary said, keeping her distance. She shivered against the cool breeze. 'The sky is lovely here. Clean and crisp.'

'Yeh, she's a beauty.' He took out a silver flask, undid the lid and took a sip. He offered it to her.

'No, thank you.'

'How are you finding it?' He placed the flask in his back pocket. 'Jack's family can be quite intense. One reason he prefers to live in the city. The gossip out here is class A.' He stepped up close to Rosemary. This was the most he'd ever spoken to her. 'You know, you're the main subject of the talk tonight.'

'Me?' She plucked a gardenia from the bush next to her and took in its scent, trying to ease her nerves. 'I'm sure Jack has brought many girls home before me.'

'Nope. You're the only one. He's really putting the cat among the pigeons.' He looked her up and down, stopping for a moment at her cleavage. 'You being an Italian. And an immigrant.'

Rosemary wanted to tell him that the two things meant the same thing but kept quiet. Her intuition was telling her not to rile him.

Frank moved closer, and Rosemary's skin prickled. She could see his face clearly now, and he was gazing at her the same way Paolo did that fateful night in Genoa. The hairs on her arms stiffened. She moved back and hit a hedge.

'They're all saying how beautiful you are. That you could be one of those Hollywood starlets.' Frank closed the distance between them, trapping her. She could smell the tobacco and whiskey on his breath. Adrenaline coursed through her body as it prepared to flee or fight, and her breath quickened.

She knew what drunk men were capable of. Alcohol had turned her father into a cruel man, and she could see the coldness in Frank's dark eyes.

Rosemary stayed still, keeping her gaze on Frank.

He took out a cigarette packet and offered it to her. She shook her head.

'You too good to have a drink or a smoke with me?' he snarled, revealing polished teeth. 'Not handsome enough for you?'

Rosemary remained silent. Frank's black eyes bored into her. What had happened to him to make him so hostile?

He shook the packet at her.

'I do not really like to smoke.'

'Go on. One won't kill ya.'

She could take one. To settle him. But she didn't want to show him he scared her. She straightened her shoulders and returned a defiant gaze. Just then, a rustle under the gardenia bush startled them both, and Rosemary took the opportunity to slip away.

The firm hand on her forearm made her freeze. Frank pulled her close, and she could feel the hardness of his chest against her. She felt him nestle his face into her neck.

'I know.' The words came out harsh and quiet.

Rosemary wrenched herself away from him, but Frank's grip strengthened. He yanked her in so her face was inches from his. A sneer dripped from his lips.

'You know nothing about me,' she said. The anger searing her veins chased away the fear for a moment.

'You're married.'

The panic returned like a sledgehammer to her heart. 'I do not know what you are talking about.'

'Jack's mother asked me to use my political connections. It took a bit of digging. Maybe you should've changed your surname, too, Rosamaria Benito.'

Rosemary struggled to inhale. If they found out the papers were fake, she'd be deported. Everything would be for nothing. The tears threatened to spill, and she stamped her feet to stop them.

'Let me go,' she hissed. 'You do not care about anyone. Not even Jack. You think you can stand there and scare me? How I came here is none of your business. What happened to my marriage is none of your business, either. How dare you pry into my personal life!' She sucked in a deep gulp of cold air. 'I cannot believe a mother does not care about her son's happiness. You cannot make people love each other. I know this.'

Frank squeezed her wrist. 'Don't worry about hurting Jack's feelings. You were just his expensive plaything before his marriage to Lacey.'

Rosemary pulled her arm away with force. Frank's nails left behind scratches on her skin. 'You lie. Jack would tell me.'

'Why? Why would he? Come on, haven't you noticed how Lacey is always around?'

'This is not true. No woman would let her fiancé see another woman.'

'Lacey's smart,' he said with a smirk. 'Practical. Lets him have his fun so he'll be all hers when the time comes. She wants him to get it out of his system and screw around with loose women first, then commit to her.'

Rosemary's fingers flew to the diamond necklace.

Frank glanced at it. 'That is just a gift to give you false hope. It is not a ring. There is already a ring.' He stepped close again. 'That ring is not for you.'

Her hand moved into action before her mind could register what she was doing. Frank didn't flinch under the hard slap. He simply touched his face and wiped away the blood from the cut her nails had caused. Then he smiled, lit another cigarette and walked away, the cigarette bobbing like a lone firefly lost in the woods.

THE DANCE FLOOR swelled with gelato-coloured taffeta dresses and black suits. Next to the barn door, where Rosemary stood, scanning the room for Jack, a group of men were camped around buckets of beer. The empties lay scattered at their feet.

Through the staggering, laughing guests, who were competing to be heard over the band, which was now playing a cover of Johnny Mathis's 'Chances Are', Rosemary spotted him on the dance floor.

With Lacey. She moved towards their table, fighting the violent urge to throw glasses on the floor or burst out crying. At the table, Vera was talking to another woman about the birth of Princess Margaret's daughter.

Vera turned towards her. 'Hello, dear. You're quite pale. Are you okay?'

'Yes, I am a little cold. I am going to go get my wrap from the house and freshen up.' Rosemary picked up her purse and glanced at Jack, who was saying something to Lacey as he held her close and swept her across the makeshift dance floor. Rosemary's heart splintered and shredded her insides.

Stupida.

She rubbed the heel of her hand across her eyes, not caring what effect it would have on her mascara and eyeliner. She pushed back through the crowd, ignoring the whistles and comments from the group of men at the door, and headed straight to the house.

In the large hallway, she slipped off her satin heels just as the enormous grandfather clock chimed midnight. She stood and stared at the clock face, willing her mind to decide what to do.

Inside her bedroom, she paced and vowed never to see Jack again. Knowing her temper was fired up, she took deep breaths to calm herself. She needed to think. No wonder Gwen and Lacey had been so smug. Jack had made a fool of her, and she'd allowed it, blindly letting herself fall in love with him. A man whose life she could never be a part of. She stopped and closed her eyes tight.

How could she have let this occur? She'd let her guard down and let the unthinkable happen. She'd become a conquest. The gifts, the attention, the affection—all part of a trick.

She opened the French doors, and the cool breeze rushed in, carrying the sounds of the party with it. Nausea pooled at the base of her throat. Jack would marry Lacey.

She needed to get out of here.

She'd take the train back to Sydney. Jack had mentioned that Jubilee Station was about twelve miles from Manilla. She could walk that distance. She'd walked longer distances in Sicily. They already thought she was some peasant girl. She'd give them more gossip.

Once she was dressed in her powder-blue capri pants and lemon-yellow shirt, she sat on the bed, her suitcase and beauty case on the floor next to her. She lifted her foot and studied her new court shoes. Their beauty reminded her of her own inner strength.

'Let us see if you will be practical and beautiful.'

CHAPTER 34

Olivia

May 1989

Bertie stood in front of the butcher-papered wall. 'So, your mum was in love with Jack Emerson?'

'Yeh.'

'What happened?' Bertie prodded with care.

'They broke up. Then she finds out she's pregnant and runs. I get the impression Mum was good at running away.'

'Did Marie say why she ran?'

'No. I gather it was because she was pregnant and—'

'Unmarried,' Bertie interjected.

'The thing is, I've just discovered that she was married.' Olivia passed the marriage certificate to Bertie.

'It's in Italian.'

'I know. I've now got more questions than answers. What happened? Where do I fit in all of this? Do I even.'

'It's an Italian marriage certificate. Maybe he died. Or they got a divorce?'

'In Sicily. In the 1950s. Not likely.' Olivia took back the certificate. 'Catholics don't divorce. Especially provincial Italian ones.'

'Marie didn't tell you anything else.'

'Only stories about Mum's time in Sydney. She told me they had a huge fight when I was about two years old. They stopped talking to each other. Completely. Marie was devastated when I told her Mum had passed. So many secrets.' Olivia shook her head.

Bertie put her cup down on the coffee table. 'Olivia, people usually keep secrets out of shame, fear or both. I know. I have a few of my own.'

She moved next to Olivia and took her hand. The warmth made Olivia feel safe.

'I also found myself unmarried and pregnant. My baby boy was forcefully taken from me.' She paused. Tears glistened in her eyes. 'They came in while I was still recovering from the brutal birth. It had been exhausting, and all I wanted to do was sleep. They told me adoption was the best option for my baby. I'd been thinking about it when I went into labour, but after giving birth, I changed my mind. The social workers were relentless, coming with forms and telling me that if I signed, he'd have a better life. That being a good mother was about making sacrifices for your child. That, as his mother, this was the greatest gift I could give him—the best decision I could make.' A small smile tugged at the sides of her deep rose lips.

Olivia squeezed her hand. Her heart sat heavy knowing that even the effervescent Bertie carried her own wounds. Reaching out slowly, she placed her hand on Bertie's forearm. 'You don't have to tell me.'

'No, I want to. One thing about secrets is they eat you up. Sometimes, saying them out loud gives the heart a reprieve.'

Olivia swallowed the lump lodged in her throat. Here it was. The perfect opportunity to confide in Bertie about her drinking. She would understand. She knew about pain and loss. And Bertie was right—the secret drinking took a piece from her each time. It numbed her pain but demanded a darkness that it fed off afterwards.

She opened her mouth. Her mind conjured up words, but none emerged.

Shame silenced her.

Bertie patted Olivia's hand. 'One day, they came to me with more papers, saying they were official documents to help with welfare. I was so tired.' She hung her head. 'I didn't realise I'd signed away my rights to be my son's mother. When I woke in the morning, feeling stronger and clearer, knowing I could raise him, they told me he was gone.'

'Which hospital?' Olivia whispered in disbelief.

'St Elizabeth's.'

Olivia blinked. 'That's where Mum worked and where Marie was a nurse. A midwife.'

'Then your mother and her friend would've known what was going on. I don't blame her for running. Your mother was how old?'

'Twenty-three.'

'One year younger than I was.' Bertie took a sip of tea and sighed. 'I never saw my son again. I tried, but those files are closed.'

The sadness felt suddenly overwhelming. 'I'm sorry,' Olivia said, her voice cracking. 'It's all just so much. All this pain. I don't under-stand why life has to be so hard.' Bertie collected Olivia in a hug. 'Especially for women.' Olivia sniffed.

'I know all these secrets are upsetting. And maybe you're resentful at your mum. But as a young woman, she lived in a different time than you do. And she was an immigrant, surviving alone, with no family to look out for her. I can tell you right now, Australians weren't always gracious to migrants. Still aren't always.'

Olivia grabbed some tissues and blew her nose. 'What about this Jack Emerson, who might be my dad? Did he know about me? And if so, why didn't he fight to see me?'

'Jack came from a very wealthy family. His family ran a lucrative cattle farm. One of the oldest ones in New South Wales. He was also the black sheep—pardon the pun.' She nudged Olivia, easing some of the melancholy. 'He also ran away from his family's expectations. Your mother and Jack had a lot in common.'

'People did a lot of running back then.'

'Well, it was the sixties. We were running away from it all—the traditions, the establishment, the war.'

Olivia peered up at Bertie. 'I did something terrible.'

'My perfect, sweet Olivia did something wrong? Do tell.'

'Bertie, do you know what the property was called? The one Jack's family had.'

'No. Why?'

'I went to see this solicitor today. Mr Templeton. William. He met my mother when he was in Italy on his honeymoon back in 1960.'

'Goodness, this is a small world.'

'I know, right? He looked after Mum's and Shirley's affairs, and his law firm also organised my school fees. He told me he couldn't tell me anything. Client confidentiality.' Olivia stopped. A flush of heat moved up her face. 'He got a call, and I—'

'Go on,' said Bertie.

'I snuck a peek at the file.' Olivia rushed on. 'There was a note with a Jubilee Station logo. I went to the library afterwards and found that there's a Jubilee Station registered in Manilla, New South Wales.'

'Manilla?'

'Yep, it's north, near Armidale. Bertie, do you think this is Jack's family's property?'

'I believe it was up north. It could be. Like my dad used to say, you never know your luck in the big city.'

Olivia's skin tingled. Sebastian had said the same thing.

'Or, in this case, on the farm.' Bertie continued and offered Olivia an astute look. 'There's only one way to find out. Go and see them.'

She laughed without humour. 'I can't. What, just turn up and say, "Hi. My name is Olivia. Is Jack here? I think he may be my dad." That's ludicrous. And embarrassing.'

'From what I can see, you have two choices. Find out or don't. Either way, you'll have to live with the consequences.'

Olivia sighed. Bertie was right. So, what did she truly want?

CHAPTER 35

Rosemary
May 1964

Rosemary woke with a start. Her heart settled when she heard the girls laughing downstairs and realised she was safe at home.

After Rosemary had left the property, a waitress from the party pulled over and offered her a lift to town.

'Would you like a ciggie?' the young woman asked as Rosemary watched dark shadows roll past outside the car window.

Rosemary shook her head.

The woman extended one hand, keeping the other on the steering wheel. 'Beatrice. But everyone calls me Trixie.'

'Rosemary.' She returned the handshake.

'I saw you at the party.'

Trixie braked suddenly, sending Rosemary forward. The beauty case on her lap acted as a buffer.

'Struth. Bloody roos.' Exhaling, Rosemary watched the kangaroo bound into the scrub at the side of the road. 'Sometimes they cause more harm to the car than themselves.' Trixie accelerated. 'Are you okay? You look so pale.'

'I am just tired.'

'Were you walking into town?'

'Yes.'

Trixie glanced at Rosemary and then back at the road. 'I don't blame you.'

Rosemary sat silent.

Trixie continued. 'I saw how he danced with her. I would've walked up and socked him in the nose before I left. What a bastard!' She took a drag on her cigarette. 'You're better off without that one. That whole family is trouble. Up there in their mansion, lording over the rest of us.' She squeezed Rosemary's hand, which was gripping the handle of her beauty case. 'You're better off without him, love.'

Trixie dropped her at the station and wished her luck. 'You sure you're gonna be alright? Trevor doesn't open the ticket office until seven.'

'Thank you. I will be fine.'

'Well, if you get spooked, the cops are just next door.' She gestured to the police station over her shoulder. 'And Denise opens the diner at six.'

Rosemary settled herself inside the small waiting room and took out her copy of *Pride and Prejudice*. She always drew strength from Elizabeth. She focused on her book and avoided all thoughts of Jack, Lacey and Jubilee Station.

It was late afternoon when she snuck back into the house. Only Eleanor was at home, sunning herself in the backyard. Rosemary hurried upstairs, wanting to avoid any questions about why she was back two days early.

The train trip to Sydney had given her too much time to think about what Frank told her. Her anger increased with each country town the train stopped at. By the time she got off the train at Central Station, she'd vowed never to speak to or see Jack again.

The late morning light streamed into her room. Rosemary lay in bed, willing herself to get up. *Fermare l'autocommiserazione*, she chastised herself. Stop the self-pity. The phone downstairs trilled. She wondered if it was Jack again. Yesterday, after she'd bathed and locked herself in her room, the phone had rung, and she'd cracked open her door to listen.

'She's asleep,' Nora told the person on the other end. 'I think it's best to let her be for a few days.'

Nora wasn't stupid. Rosemary's locking herself in her room and not coming down for tea would be evidence enough that something had happened.

The phone rang all day yesterday, stirring her from her sleep.

She knew she'd probably bruised Jack's ego by running away. She imagined him getting in the car and driving to town. Going to the train station master and asking if Trevor had seen her and being told that, yes, a young woman had bought a ticket to Sydney early in the morning. That she'd boarded the 7:35 am train. Jack would know she'd gone home. Would he realise why? What would Frank say to him if he asked? Would he admit to revealing Jack's planned engagement?

Rosemary turned and pushed her face into the pillow, trying to forget the look on Frank's face when he told her about Jack and Lacey's arrangement. She cringed, knowing that he knew the news had toppled her despite her best efforts to hide her emotion. His premeditated cruelty stabbed at her heart over and over.

There was a soft knock on the door. Nora's voice floated behind it. 'Rosemary.'

Silence.

'Jack's on the phone.'

Rosemary sat up. She wanted to scream at Nora 'Tell him to never call again!' Just the sound of his name stirred up her embarrassment and anger. She stared out the window. It promised to be a grey, rainy day. The perfect backdrop to how she felt. The light caught her interest, though. She'd neglected her photography lately. Maybe looking at the world through the camera's lens would ease the pain.

'Is she okay?' Eleanor's voice joined Nora's.

'Still asleep. I don't know what's happened, but that's the third time Jack's called today. Not counting all the calls yesterday. If he's done anything to hurt her, I'll skin him myself.'

Nora's concern tugged at Rosemary's heart.

The conference outside her bedroom door grew. She heard Pamela's voice. 'She'll let us know if she needs us. She knows how to look after herself. We've all been hard done by when it comes to men. Even if you look like a movie star with a figure that could stop a charging army, you're never protected from heartache.'

Rosemary smiled. Pamela was always the wise, uncomplicated one. No wonder she excelled at her job.

Rosemary threw off the covers, walked to the door and slowly opened it. Peeking out, she saw the three women in a huddle. 'Please. Do not worry about me. I am okay.'

Eleanor pushed open the door and gave Rosemary a hug. 'Are you sure? You don't have to be brave for us.'

Rosemary relished the embrace. 'I am alright. But I do not want to speak to Jack. Tell him I have gone away to visit a friend.'

She sensed her friends' curiosity. She didn't want their pity, but she was surprised to find that she did want to talk about what had happened. Maybe sharing would make it feel less embarrassing. Help take the edge off her simmering anger. She leant against the door-jamb. 'Jack is promised to Lacey.'

'What do you mean?' Eleanor's blue eyes grew wide. 'Like engaged?'

'Not yet, but it is all planned. He will be engaged to Lacey. I was only a plaything. This is why men are no good.' She felt her anger melt into tears, which pooled inside her.

'What a bastard,' Pamela said.

'Are you sure?' Nora asked. 'He seemed so genuine, and you don't see a man look at you like Jack did.'

'I am certain.' Rosemary wiped away her tears.

CHAPTER 36

Olivia

May 1989

'Okay, I've got Snakes lollies, chips and ice cream. The good kind.' Demi held up the two videos. 'You choose which one you want to watch first. *Big* or *Beaches*. Happy or sad?'

'You choose. I'll get the popcorn.'

Olivia had told Demi all about the trip to Marie's house and how she'd kissed Sebastian many times because, thankfully, Clare was gay!

But Olivia was still brooding over something.

'What's up your bum?'

'Nothing. I'm just tired.'

'I know you, Olivia Bennet. Something is not okay. And as I'm the bright star in your universe, you must tell me everything.' Demi winked.

'Can we just watch a movie?' Olivia placed the popcorn on the coffee table and sat cross-legged on the couch. Gin jumped up into the diamond gap. 'See, even Gin's waiting.'

Demi sighed. 'Okay. This is my plan. *Beaches* first. My cousin says it's great but sad. Then *Big*. To make us laugh. It's the yin and yang of movie experience.'

Olivia smiled. Demi always got her sayings mixed up. She didn't have the heart to say that yin and yang complemented each other. Maybe sadness and happiness did too. Maybe all this stuff about her mum was about learning *everything*—the good, the bad, the sad and the happy. Maybe it was about balance. Right now, she didn't have the energy to think about any of it.

'Ready?' Demi prodded her with her toe.

'Sure.' Olivia shoved a handful of popcorn into her mouth. All she really wanted was to escape.

As the end credits rolled, Demi sobbed. 'That was just too sad.'

Olivia wept too. It had been every bit the heart-wrenching movie Demi's cousin had warned her it was.

Demi stood. 'I need a drink. Have you got any wine?'

'In the kitchen.' She thought of the empty bottle of vodka in her cupboard, waiting to be thrown out when she was alone.

Demi handed her a glass of wine. 'I need to laugh now. Ready to watch *Big*?'

'I need to tell you something. Ask you a favour.' She looked at her friend.

'Okay ...'

'When I went up the coast with Sebastian and discovered that Marie is my godmother and—'

'Oh my God! Is Marie your mum?'

'What?' Olivia gaped. 'No. Why would you even say that?'

'Because you've been really sad and preoccupied.'

Olivia sighed. 'Because I'm so confused.'

'About The Quest Wall?'

'Yes. And ...'

'What, Livvie?'

'I think I know where Jack Emerson is.'

'What? How?' Demi yanked the bag from her. 'This can wait.'

'I went and saw the solicitor from the receipts. He called me because ... Oh, Demi. There are more secrets. Mum was married.'

'Wait! One thing at a time.'

Demi picked up a marker out of the dish on the credenza and wrote *Married?* on The Quest Wall. She turned around. 'Where? When?'

'March 1960. Messina. In Sicily.'

'Wow!' She wrote the details, followed by two exclamation marks.

'This is all so intriguing.' Demi flopped back on the couch. 'What happened?'

'I don't know. More secrets Mum never shared with me.' Olivia sat beside Demi. 'Nothing's easy.' She released an exasperated hiss of air. 'Mr Templeton couldn't tell me anything about the receipts either. Client privilege and all that.'

'So how do you know where Jack Emerson is?'

Olivia flushed and relayed what she had done.

'Way to go, Olivia!' Demi high-fived her.

'I'm not exactly proud of it.'

'Olivia, you have a right to know. It's not like you're deranged. An information thief, but not a psycho.'

'Hilarious.' Olivia grabbed a cushion and hugged it. 'I want to go and see Jack. But I don't want to go on my own.'

'I'll go with you.'

'What about work?'

'I'll ask one of my cousins. They all owe me for the mixtapes I make them.'

Olivia dared to get her hopes up. 'Will your parents let you?'

'Don't you worry about that. Yiayia loves you. She'll convince them. She always gets so sad thinking about you on your own.'

Demi popped her legs onto the coffee table. 'So, where are we going?'

'Manilla. Northern New South Wales. We can catch a train to

Tamworth, then change to go straight to Manilla. I rang the New South Wales tourist centre.'

'How long is that going to take?'

'Seven, nearly eight hours.'

Demi whistled. 'That's a whole day.' She went out to the verandah and lit a cigarette. Olivia came up beside her. Demi snapped around. 'I'll ask my cousin Stefanos. He's always got some car he's fixed up. But he might want a kiss from you. As payment.'

'What! No.'

'Settle down. Only joking.' Demi threw her a mischievous grin. 'Seriously, he'll be happy to help. I sometimes give him some of my weed when I have to hide it.' She threw Olivia a thoughtful look. 'Will you be okay in the car? I mean, you should be. That beast of Stefanos's is impenetrable steel. The Hulk couldn't do any damage to it. Plus, the colour will scare all the other cars away.' Demi snorted out a laugh.

Feeling a rush of gratitude, Olivia threw her arms around Demi and took in the comforting scent of tobacco and vanilla musk. 'You're a good friend. Even if you smell like an ashtray.'

Demi laughed. 'You're stuck with me, Olivia Bennet.'

CHAPTER 37

Rosemary
May 1964

She stared out of the window. The sunny day beckoned. It was too beautiful to stay inside and wallow. No, she would not let a man, even one who'd made a fool of her, take away her *dolce vita*, her good life. She had shamed herself once by giving in to a man. She would never do it again.

A date with her camera and Sydney was just what she needed.

As she sipped a coffee, she mapped out her day. She'd take a bus to Coogee and pick up the walk to Bondi. Jack wouldn't return until that evening. He wouldn't want to disappoint his family, so there was no way she would bump into him. Just thinking about Lacey and Jack spending time together refuelled her anger. She spouted Italian expletives under her breath as she got dressed and prepared her camera. A long walk and lunch in Bondi would quell her fury.

On the midmorning bus to Coogee, Rosemary hid behind her dark glasses and a scarf, drawing second glances. Marie believed that when Rosemary dressed incognito, she carried an air of intrigue and mystery. Today, Rosemary wanted to be in disguise. She wanted to hide away with her shame. But as the bus meandered along the Sydney streets, her thoughts returned to Jack and Frank.

Regret pierced through. Maybe this was her fault. She'd kept so much of her life from Jack, but she had to. He'd tried to find out more about her, and all she'd offered were inconsequential details. Enough to satisfy him but nothing too personal. She was good at turning the conversation back to him. She'd ask him questions about Australia, the news, the arts, people, history. Anything to keep the focus off her past.

The only subject Rosemary was happy talking about was her future. Jack was supportive of her photography and love of reading. He'd even introduced her to new authors: Steinbeck, Salinger and Alexandre Dumas. The more she thought about how generous he'd been, the more ludicrous his deceit seemed.

Could Frank have been wrong?

The bus lurched to a stop, and the driver announced they were at Coogee. Rosemary got off and walked down to the main beach. As the fresh, salty air washed over her, she felt serenity flow through her. She watched the waves roll in and pound the shoreline. The breeze whipped her cotton dress around her long legs.

Clarity entered her thoughts.

She needed to be brave and confront Jack. She was sick of running away.

THE PHONE RANG ONLY ONCE before Jack picked it up. Rosemary could feel her energy tighten around her like steel armour, creating a barrier, making her voice sound cool and neutral.

But her heart burnt with heat at the sound of his voice. She missed him.

'Rosemary. I've been so worried.'

His concern nearly broke her resolve. She wanted to forgive him, but she also wanted to hate him.

'Rosemary?'

She gripped the phone, staying silent. Outside, bats screeched, and people chatted. The living room was cool. Shadows filled the room. The lamp next to the phone offered the only source of light. She sat on the worn velvet seat attached to the telephone table and peered out the window at the stars in the inky sky. She imagined herself standing on the windowsill, face towards the moon, ready to fly. She wanted to fly away and keep flying forever. But she'd already done this. She'd already run.

'I am here,' she whispered.

'I've missed you. It's been nearly a week. What happened? You just disappeared. You won't return my calls.'

Rosemary fell silent again, content to hear his voice.

'Talk to me, Rosemary.'

She surprised herself by weeping. 'I am sorry. I need more time.'

'No. Rosemary. Wait. Please don't hang up. Are you at home?'

'Please do not come to see me,' she whispered and hung up.

She grabbed her jacket and wrapped a scarf around her head. She was grateful the evening would hide her tearful eyes. Lastly, she picked up her camera and purse. She needed a purpose: the hospital. The maternity ward. A place of love and hope. She'd take photos of the babies if Matron would allow it. If she didn't, she'd sneak in from the kitchen.

Her time on the wards with the new mothers always made Rosemary feel a sense of hope. If there was anything a maternity ward taught you, it was that life goes on.

When she arrived, one of the ward nurses snuck her into the nursery, and she was able to take some beautiful photos of babies sleeping and being bathed and held. Her favourite photos were those of the babies being cuddled and nursed by their mothers. The most poignant photos were those she took in the unmarried mother's ward, where heartache, fear and shame filled the rooms. This overwhelmed Rosemary with sadness.

She took some time to sit with the mothers and let them talk about how they were feeling. Some were angry, others distraught.

THE NEXT DAY, Rosemary sat on a wooden bench and watched the waves at Bondi. Every so often she turned towards Jack's apartment, looking for some sign. She'd decided the night before while photographing the babies, photographing hope, to go see him and explain. She imagined Jack running out, crossing the road, causing the cars to stop, then lifting her in his arms. But the apartment stood silent.

Late morning surfers caught waves, landed on the sand and then paddled out to do it all over again. Would she ever learn how to surf? The beach was dotted with people wanting to salvage their summer tans. The sun's rays were warm, but the breeze coming off the ocean reminded everyone that winter was around the corner.

Would he even be home? Jack had no idea she was here.

She wished she could sever the source of her love for him.

The past few months had been wonderful—exactly what she'd imagined living in a big city would be like. Though Sydney was smaller than the cities she'd seen in the movies, like London, New York and Paris, it was still a place where she could be herself. Independent. No longer under her father's strict control. Yet her heart ached for her family. She missed them, and it only got worse the longer she stayed away. The more she allowed herself to remember her past life, the sadder she got.

Rosemary stood and adjusted her coat, preparing to go home. She turned away from the beach and saw Jack standing on the curb.

Surprise rushed through her, followed by unchecked affection. How long had he been standing there? Rosemary walked towards him slowly. Her heart pounded, and she endeavoured to push down her emotions. He looked even more handsome than the last time she'd seen him, but there was a pained look on his face.

'Hello, Jack.'

Rosemary stood a few feet away. She didn't trust herself not to rush into his arms and kiss him.

'Rosemary.' He stepped towards her.

She held up her hand. 'No, Jack. Stop.'

'Why?'

'Why?' Rosemary whispered. Tears immediately burnt her eyes. She swallowed hard to stop them. 'You deceived me.'

'Deceived you?' His face contorted with confusion. 'Tell me what happened. One moment you're at the party, and the next, I'm told you've left. Then you won't return my calls.'

What? How could he stand there and pretend nothing had happened? '*Bastardo!* You led me on for months! The whole time there is an engagement planned. This makes me the wicked woman. I am not a sinful woman.'

He blinked. 'Engagement? To who?'

'Lacey.'

'Who told you this?'

'Frank told me.' She couldn't hold back the tears. 'You made a fool of me.'

A few people stopped to see what was going on, and a surfer in his fifties, his skin tanned and leathery from years of sun and salt water, approached.

'You alright, love?' he asked Rosemary.

'She's fine.' Jack stepped closer to her, and she flinched. She could smell his cologne, and it took all her resolve not to press her lips to his. Instead, she watched the exchange, worried for Jack but also glad he was being challenged.

'Doesn't look like it to me.' The surfer propped up his board and looked at Rosemary. 'My car's up the road. I can take you home.'

She looked at Jack.

'Rosemary, please. Can we just talk?'

She smiled at the man. 'Thank you. I will be fine. I will stay.'

'Fair enough.' He looked at Jack. 'If you do anything, I'll come back and knock ya block off.'

'I'm sure you will.' Jack held up his hands. 'She'll be safe. I'll be the perfect gentleman.' Jack looked at Rosemary and offered his handkerchief. 'Although I don't think I'm safe.'

'This you are right about.' She took the handkerchief and wiped her tears.

They both watched as the surfer slouched up Campbell Parade towards his car and strapped his board onto the roof. He took one more look at Rosemary. She waved an assurance, and he got in the car and drove off.

She turned back to Jack. 'Okay. I will talk to you.'

'I have some fresh coffee. Will you join me?'

Rosemary adjusted her headscarf. 'One coffee.'

THE MOMENT they stepped into Jack's apartment, Rosemary, fuelled by anger and hot shame, unleashed everything she'd been holding back for the last week.

'Why, Jack? Why do this to me and Lacey? I have seen the way she looks at you! And you are so friendly with her!'

Jack wrapped his arms around her. She tried to push him away, but he held her tighter and made shushing noises into her hair. Emotionally exhausted, Rosemary relented and dropped her head onto his chest, allowing his warmth and beating heart to soothe her.

Jack lifted her face and wiped the tears away from her eyes. She peered up, and he met her gaze with a look full of concern.

Without thinking, she kissed him. She just wanted him. To be loved.

In that moment, she felt all the pain dissolve. Pushing away all the warnings clanging in her head, she moved closer.

Jack pressed himself against her. 'I love you,' he whispered in her ear. His breath was soft and warm. 'Let me in. Please.'

In response, she reached down, took his hand and led him to his bedroom. Nerves danced inside her chest.

In the bedroom, they stood facing each other. Jack reached down and stroked Rosemary's cheek. She took his hand and kissed his palm.

He walked over to close the blinds.

'No. Leave them open. It is a beautiful day. This is a beautiful moment.' She glanced down. 'This is my first time,' she lied. 'I want to remember all of it,' she said, slamming a lid against the dark memories of Genoa that seeped into her mind.

He looked at her with concern again. 'Rosemary? You've never?'

She shook her head, and her cheeks flamed. The deceit pounced in and seared her hidden shame. Her guilt clawed at her heart. In retaliation, anger ricocheted out. 'Why? Is this not good for you?'

Jack chuckled. 'No.' He held up his hands in surrender. 'I know this isn't something you just give away. I want you to be sure.'

She should've counted to ten. 'I am sorry I—'

She didn't finish. Jack strode to her, grabbed her around the waist and kissed her. Rosemary stepped back slightly, her chest heaving.

'Rosemary.' Her name fell from his lips like a prayer. He brushed his fingertips down her cheek and gently along her lips. The blue in his eyes smouldered and darkened as his lips briefly touched hers. Full and sweet like honey. Shivers ran down her body, and the anticipation simmered all the way to the most intimate part of her. She breathed out his name, and all warnings burnt up and floated away like ash. *This was how your first time was meant to feel.*

Jack gently unzipped her dress and slipped it off her shoulders. As it fell to the floor, he leant down and kissed her shoulder, moving across the dip where her neck met her chest all the way to the other side, followed by kisses up her neck.

Rosemary moaned. Her body filled with desire, and she grabbed his hair. He moved his mouth back to hers, and she accepted his tongue, relishing his slow and unhurried attention.

Jack stopped kissing her to unbutton his shirt. Rosemary placed her hands over his and took over. She opened his shirt and then ran her hands over his chest. She loved the feel of the soft hair that spread across the toned muscles, which tensed under her touch. She followed the trail of hair downwards, and when she got to the top of his pants, she ran her finger inside the band and pulled Jack into her for another kiss. She wanted to slow the moment down even more.

Jack moaned into her, clearly wanting more. She could feel her arousal building and worked hard to control herself. She knew where they were going. They would get there. Eventually.

'Rosemary—'

She put her finger on his lips. 'Shhh. *La pazienza è una virtù*, my love.' She cupped his face. His blue eyes blazed with desire as he held her gaze and unbuttoned his trousers. He moved the zip down, and his pants dropped. He stepped out of them and knelt in front of Rosemary, placing his hand on the skin above her stocking. Rosemary gasped as he stroked the soft curve at the top of her thigh.

The touch tickled her and she giggled, which brought a smile to Jack's face. He leant in and kissed the skin at the uppermost part of her leg, then unclipped her stocking. He rolled it down before moving up her other leg with more kisses and rolling the second stocking down.

They stood in front of each other. Rosemary's breathing slowed, and goosebumps erupted all over her body as she caught sight of his white briefs straining. Her shyness returned as Jack slipped off his socks and shoes and then slid down his underpants.

He stood there. Naked. A magnificent man, the years of surfing having sculpted a hard body. A light tan, a remnant of summer, remained on his skin.

Rosemary froze. It had felt easy up to this point. Now she was nervous again.

He gave her a light kiss. 'Are you okay?'

Rosemary nodded.

He moved behind her and kissed the tops of her shoulders. With his broad hands, he unclipped her bra and then draped it over a nearby chair. He remained behind her, brought his arms around her and trailed kisses down her back. 'Beautiful,' he whispered. He tucked his fingers into her underwear and slid the garment down her long legs. She felt him stand up behind her before he swung her around to face him. She loved the feeling of their naked bodies together, and her nerves melted away. Once again, he explored her mouth with passion, and she returned her tongue with hunger.

Without warning, Jack lifted her and laid her on his bed. She giggled with shock, and he kissed her again before moving his lips down her body. He spent time with her breasts, and she wanted to cry out when his mouth encased her nipples. When he rolled his tongue around them, she gripped the sheets and squeezed. He looked up at her and smiled, then continued making his way down her body. A rippling wave of sensual delight washed through her. He stopped to kiss and caress the curve at the top of her inner leg. He looked up again and gave her his cheekiest smile. Rosemary bit her lip and braced herself. She'd heard about this from Pamela.

It was everything she'd imagined.

More than she'd imagined.

She climaxed, and after she regained her breathing, she reached down and tugged his hair to bring him up. Their connection was beautiful, and she wanted all that it could entail.

All his love.

WHEN ROSEMARY WOKE UP, a different light was filtering into the room. The day had moved into late afternoon. She looked at Jack, asleep beside her, and stroked his chest with her fingertips. A tenderness swirled in her chest. She shifted closer to him, and a warm contentment filled her body. She was happy, falling deeply in love with him. He stirred, and a smile moved across his face. He grabbed her and pulled her in.

'Hmmm. Aren't you a gift for a bloke to wake up to.'

She chuckled. 'It is late. And I am hungry.'

'Well, we can't have you withering away. Why don't I go get some things and we can have a very late lunch?'

'This is a good plan.' Rosemary gave Jack a soft kiss on his cheek and got out of bed, still naked. She grabbed the sheet to cover herself, but Jack caught her hand and pulled her back into bed.

'Nope. Not yet. I'm not finished with you.' He tickled her and showered her with kisses.

Rosemary squealed.

Suddenly, the bedroom door slammed open, and Jack shot up next to her.

'Lacey! What the heck? he fired at her

'Impressive.' Lacey smirked as she looked hard at Rosemary.

Rosemary glanced down at her exposed breasts, then quickly wrapped herself up. In doing so, she exposed Jack's nakedness.

'Well, well, what have you two been up to?' She lit a cigarette.

'Lacey, do you mind?'

'Anything you say. Anyway, I need to talk to you.' She turned and sauntered out, leaving the door wide open.

Rosemary watched, fuming, as Lacey positioned herself on the couch, her long legs crossed, and looked out the window, smugness stamped all over her face. Like a cunning cat. *Il gatto che ha ingoiato l'uccello.* Rosemary was the bird Lacey had swallowed with her poise and confidence.

Jack got out of bed and threw on a bathrobe, then rushed out of the bedroom, closing the door behind him.

Rosemary heard him talking, but there was no anger in his voice. Why was he not angry? This made no sense. Lacey had intruded as if it were something she did all the time. *And she has a key*, Rosemary suddenly realised.

Her thoughts flew back to what Frank had said. Had she just let Jack take advantage of her? One last fling? She got out of bed, and her hands shook as she forced the zip up her dress. She picked up her stockings and slammed them into her purse. She was a fool. *Uno stupido sciocco.*

She stormed out of the bedroom, then stopped abruptly. Jack and Lacey stood in the kitchen, their faces turned away. He held her hand, and they were whispering. Then Lacey lifted Jack's face. The gesture contained a familiar tenderness.

A sudden wave of nausea pushed itself up Rosemary's throat. How could she have been so blind? She grabbed her coat and rushed out of the apartment, slamming the door behind her. When she got outside, she took off her shoes and ran to the tram station as if her life depended on it. The tears ran hot down her face.

Relief flooded her when the tram pulled in. She raced on board and moved to the back corner. As the tram moved away from the platform, she saw Jack, dressed in beach shorts and an unbuttoned cotton shirt, his chest exposed, breathing heavily and scanning the area. Rosemary put on her dark glasses. The vehicle was crammed with people heading back to the city after a day at the beach. She quietened her breathing and closed her eyes, willing her heart to still. In her mind, she saw herself push past everyone, lean out the window and scream 'Bastardo!'

CHAPTER 38

Olivia

June 1989

The car Demi had borrowed from her cousin Stefanos screamed Greek hoodlum. The bright-orange Chrysler Valiant Charger bore a detailed black bonnet and stripes at the sides. Stefanos had also added a second muffler, which rumbled as Demi and Olivia drove through Manilla. Olivia hated the attention, but Demi loved it.

Fifteen minutes later, they pulled up to a huge wrought-iron arch —Jubilee Station floated on it in cursive lettering.

'Do we just drive through?' Olivia asked. Her stomach punished her with somersaults.

'Well, there's no gate.' Demi looked around. 'Look, we can always say we got lost.'

Olivia nodded, then winced when the muffler roared back to life. They drove up a straight driveway before turning at a bend. A huge sandstone house came into view.

Demi whistled. 'What a mansion.'

The double-storey home stood on a rise with two turrets at

each end. A white wrought-iron balustrade ran across the entire top floor and contrasted against the golden paddocks and cerulean sky.

'Looks Edwardian,' Olivia said, marvelling.

'How do you know, you big nerd?'

'It's like the mansions in Glebe.' Olivia took in the slated, tiled roof, wooden French doors and bay windows. She counted three chimneys.

Demi drove around the semicircular driveway, past the enormous front door, and parked facing the road they'd come from.

'In case we need to make a fast getaway.' She grinned.

'What?' Olivia heard the worry in her voice.

'Only joking.' Demi squeezed Olivia's hand. 'It'll be fine.'

Olivia stepped out of the car and walked with Demi up the front steps. When she got to the front door, she hesitated. Her lips dried, and she pressed them together to bridle the chaos that stampeded through her mind. Goosebumps raced up her arms, and she shivered. This was it. Her father could be behind that door. She looked at her friend.

Demi nodded. 'Go on.'

Olivia took a deep breath. 'Here goes nothing.'

'That's the spirit.' Demi squeezed her hand.

Olivia reached up, waited a moment, then rang the doorbell.

Nothing happened.

They looked at each other. Demi placed her ear against the closed door. 'Someone's coming,' she whispered and stepped back as the door opened.

'Olivia! What are you doing here?'

―――

The housekeeper poured coffee for Demi, Olivia and the woman who'd opened the door—Everly.

'I can't believe you're here.' Everly lit a cigarette and offered one to Demi, who accepted, eyeing Olivia. Olivia had mentioned Everly only a few times to Demi.

A large grey cable-knit jumper hid her old acquaintance's thin frame. Deep, dark bags hung under her pale blue eyes. At school, Everly had always been slender, a great equestrian. Now, her gauntness worried Olivia. A tiredness sat upon her body as if life had pressed down on her and left a permanent mark.

'I'm just as surprised,' Olivia said.

Demi coughed.

'Oh, gosh. This is Demi. My friend from Sydney.'

'It's nice to know Olivia has friends,' said Everly, looking at Demi. 'She was always so quiet at school.'

'She still is.' Demi smiled at Olivia. 'But I'm trying to get her out of her shell. One layer at a time.'

'What have you been up to?' Olivia asked. What she really wanted to ask was: Why are you here and how are you connected to Jubilee Station?

'I'm a freelance photojournalist,' said Everly.

'That sounds exciting. You always did like taking photos at boarding school.'

'Yeh, I kind of fell into it. I got a cadetship with the *Sydney Morning Herald*. My uncle pulled some strings, and I got to take photos for stories. Not the exciting stuff I wanted to do, though. I got bored. So, I packed up and went to London. I found work with magazines, taking photos. Until the boredom returned. Turns out staying in one spot didn't sit well with me.' She took a drag and followed it with a sip of black coffee. 'I travelled around the Continent working as a freelance photographer.' She leant forward. 'How about you?'

'I work in a bookstore in Annandale.'

'Why am I not surprised?' Everly studied the burning end of her cigarette. 'I really should slow down on these.' She looked at Demi again. 'Olivia always had her head in a book at school.' She sat back and crossed her lean legs. 'I always thought you'd become this brilliant writer.'

'There's still time,' Demi said, winking at Olivia. 'So what made you come back to Australia? Here.' Demi swept her hand to take in the land in front of the terrace.

'I'm not well.' She cleared her throat. 'Just out of rehab, actually. Why I'm sucking on these cancer sticks like they're lollies.' Everly turned to Olivia. 'Drugs and alcohol.' She shrugged. 'We have a love-hate relationship.'

Olivia placed her hand on top of Everly's. Her throat constricted, and she forced herself to maintain steady, even breaths. Everly looked at her, and for a moment, Olivia felt as if she were looking in a mirror. This could be her future if she continued her dysfunctional relationship with vodka.

'How did you do it?' Everly asked.

'What?'

'You lost your mum, and you were all alone, and you turned out fine.'

She tried to swallow. 'I'm not fine. I hide away from everyone. Escape into my books. I'd still be a hermit if it weren't for Demi here.'

'Well, us Greeks, we like to put our big noses in other people's business.'

Everly laughed.

'We all carry some pain around with us,' Olivia said. 'I'm realising that. Sometimes, you just have to take a huge breath and try to face it head-on.' *Where had that come from?*

'Or find the answers,' Demi interjected, giving Olivia a pointed look.

'What answers are you trying to find?' Everly asked. 'Is this why you're here?'

'I don't know.' Olivia looked at Demi.

'Tell her.'

Olivia rubbed her fingers together and then closed her hands tight. She latched on to the small ribbon of quietude and stilled the thumping in her chest. 'I've always wanted to know who my dad is.'

Everly tilted her head. 'You said your dad died.'

'I was ashamed to admit the truth. Everyone at school was so posh, and I felt like the barefooted orphan in rags.'

'But people's parents die all the time. My dad did. That's why I've always called Jubilee Station home.'

Her jaw dropped slightly. She'd had no idea. Everly had always radiated a happiness that lifted the spirits of everyone who entered her orbit.

We all have baggage, she thought. *We just carry it differently.*

Hot tears drummed behind Olivia's eyes. She looked down at her scuffed ballet flats. 'I caused the accident that killed my mum.' The words came out like a soft breeze. Everly looked at her. Concern filled her face. 'I used to badger her to tell me who my dad was, but she never would. In the end, my stubborn persistence killed her. All I wanted was any piece of information, however small, about my dad. If I'd had something, I would've ... could've started searching for him. Instead, I had nothing.' Olivia closed her eyes tight and whispered, 'I had nothing.'

'Let's go for a walk,' Everly offered gently. 'We can talk more, and I'll show you my horse, Xander. He's a beauty. Some fresh air will do us all good.'

Demi fell in love with the horses. 'I wish I could ride,' she said to Everly as they strolled back to the house.

'Come back and I'll teach you. The distraction will help me.'

'Everly, why did you get involved in drugs?' Olivia asked. 'You seemed to have everything going for you. And you were so generous with your time when I was at boarding school.'

'Partly because I never wanted for anything, and I was spoilt.' She stopped and lifted her face to the sun. 'I didn't know how lucky I was.' She smiled at Olivia. 'And I am lucky. My aunt and uncle took me in, warts and all, after my dad died in a farming accident. Mum never got over it. She lives in Queensland on the Sunshine Coast. I came straight back here after my stint in rehab. I didn't want to see Mum until I was, well, you know … "better".' Everly made air quotes. 'I think my wild ways crushed her already broken heart.'

When they reached the house, a tall, elegant woman stood on the terrace.

'Who are your friends, Everly?'

'Olivia, Demi. This is my Aunt Lacey.' Everly looked at her aunt. 'I hope you don't mind—I invited them for lunch.'

'I thought you might. Welcome,' she said to Olivia and Demi. 'I've already instructed Carla to set two extra places. She makes the best lemonade. I know it sounds cliché, but she does.'

Olivia couldn't help staring at the woman. There was something familiar about her. She was crease-proof. Her white shirt, crisp and bright, accentuated her lean frame, and her burgundy trousers, with a single pleat down each leg, made her legs look even longer than they were. Silver strands glistened in her blonde hair, curled into a chignon.

Olivia sat next to Demi, and on the other side of the table, Everly relaxed next to her aunt, who patted her hand. They had a closeness —more like mother and daughter than aunt and niece.

'It was very nice of you to visit Everly,' Lacey said, pouring a glass of lemonade for Olivia.

'Well, they didn't come looking for me, actually.' Everly lit a cigarette and flapped the smoke away. 'It was a real surprise to see her on the doorstep. But a great one.' Everly grinned. 'Olivia used to board with me. We were on the same floor, and I was her buddy when she first arrived.'

'That was lovely of you, Everly.' Lacey studied Olivia. 'Who were your parents? My husband, late husband, Jack, used to be on the board at Our Lady of Peace. A fine school. If we'd been blessed with a daughter, I certainly would've sent her there.'

'Your husband was called Jack.' Olivia worked at keeping her voice calm and neutral.

'Yes. Jack Emerson.'

Olivia felt the world turn as the realisation slammed into her. Lacey was the woman in the articles in her mother's trunk. She'd been so nervous that she missed the connection. Olivia was certain it was her. She was still beautiful.

She caught the glance Demi threw her. Had Demi realised the same thing?

'Mrs Emerson—'

'Please. Call me Lacey.'

'Lacey, did your husband ever live in Sydney?'

'Yes. Before he came back to help his father with the property. After my brother-in-law, Everly's father, died in a tragic accident, he moved back in 1965. Six months later, we were married.' She looked directly at Olivia. Her blue eyes had darkened. 'Why do you ask?'

She took a deep breath. 'My mother passed away when I was thirteen, and some items that belonged to her recently arrived in a steamer trunk. Items I'd never seen or heard about. I never knew my father. Mum refused to discuss it with me. I've always wondered who he was. And now there are these items that don't fit the person my mother was or how she lived her life.'

Lacey took a sip of her lemonade. Her face was a blank canvas. 'And you think there's a connection to my husband?'

'Maybe.' Olivia reached into her bag and pulled out a photo. 'There are several photos of my mum with this man.' She handed it to Lacey.

Lacey glanced at the photos and abruptly got up and walked to the edge of the terrace.

'Aunt Lacey, are you okay?'

When there was no response, Everly shrugged at Olivia. In the distance, cattle lowed.

Lacey turned around and then looked down at the photo again. 'This woman. She's your mother.'

'Yes,' Olivia replied.

'She was stunning.' She walked over and handed the photo back. 'The man in the photo is Jack Emerson, my late husband.' She sat back down next to Lacey. 'He always loved beautiful things.' Lacey directed her gaze at Olivia, and for a moment, Olivia saw resentment in her eyes.

'Did Jack have an affair with my mother?' The words floated out like fragile bubbles. She braced herself.

'Not an affair.' Lacey pulled out a gold cigarette case from her pocket, withdrew a long white cigarette, and, leaning back, lit it and took a deep, slow drag. She looked like a Parisian model. All that was needed was the Eiffel Tower in the background.

'Before we married, in September 1965, he was free to do as he pleased.' Lacey crossed her legs gracefully. 'Men need to sow their wild oats before they settle down.' She straightened and crossed her legs. 'Our marriage had been planned, expected, for years. We both wanted it.'

The defensiveness in Lacey's voice unsettled Olivia. It didn't match the woman's demeanour.

'Did you ever meet her? My mother?'

'No. Why would I? I don't mean to be impertinent, but women like your mother were Jack's playthings.'

Demi grabbed Olivia's hand and glared at Lacey. 'Mrs Emerson. I never knew her mother, but she doesn't sound like someone who was reckless with her affection. She was a single woman, a migrant, away from her own family. People usually don't keep secrets unless they need to. Unless something forces them to.'

'It's okay, Demi,' Olivia said.

'No. It's not. *Káti myrízei.* I need a cigarette.' She stood, and Everly threw her the packet. Demi yanked one out, lit it and paced. Then stopped. 'By the way, that's Greek for "something stinks".'

Lacey waved for Carla's attention. 'More lemonade, please.' She glanced at Olivia. 'I'd offer you something stronger, but that's not possible.'

'It's okay,' Everly said. 'They know about my addiction.'

Olivia squirmed. What she needed more than anything was the warm comfort of vodka.

'I'm sorry,' Demi said. 'I know this is all very English. Australian. Whatever. But all this fake politeness is driving me nuts.' Demi turned to Olivia. 'Just ask her or I will.'

Olivia swallowed. The question was primed and ready, but she couldn't find the strength to speak the words.

Everly gave Lacey a pointed look. 'My aunt will be gracious. I know she will. She's the queen of graciousness. Aren't you, Auntie Lacey?'

'Of course.' She offered Olivia a thin smile. 'What is it you want to know, exactly?'

Demi sat on the other side of Olivia. A brutal energy vibrated off her, shrouding Olivia with security. She took another deep breath.

'My mother lived in a boarding house in Surry Hills. I've spoken to the woman who rented rooms to her, and I've also talked to my mum's best friend. They both knew of Jack Emerson and said he wanted to marry her. That he loved her. Then something happened, and he was erased from my mother's life.' She gathered speed as she spoke, just wanting to get it all out. 'My mother finds herself pregnant, changes her name, moves to the Central Coast and six months later, I'm born. You tell me that my mother was just a plaything, but from what I've found in the trunk, their relationship seemed to be more than that. He showered her with very expensive gifts—haute couture gowns, shoes and a diamond necklace. Who does that if they're not emotionally invested? Or in love?'

A darkness filled Lacey's face. 'I heard Jack had become infatuated with some European woman. But she was not as wholesome as you made out.'

'Is this really necessary?' Everly said.

'Olivia here wants the truth, so I'll give it to her,' she said coolly. 'My mother-in-law did some digging. She was concerned with the ... now, how did she put it?' Lacey feigned deep thought. Her lips curled up at the edges. 'Yes, I remember. Salami strumpet.'

'Aunt Lacey! Really.'

Lacey held up her hand towards Everly, keeping her gaze on

Olivia. 'Your mother was married. She came here as a proxy bride. I think you're looking for the wrong man.'

Bile forced itself into Olivia's mouth, and she coughed. 'How do you know that?' She needed to defend her mum, regardless of what she had done, for whatever reason. 'But anything could've happened to her husband or the marriage—'

Demi pushed down on Olivia's arm and shook her head. 'No. Not here.' The warning shone brightly in her eyes. Olivia clamped her mouth shut. Tight.

Lacey stood. 'I think there's been enough secret sharing today. Everly will show you out.'

Olivia could barely breathe. She should've left it hidden. Like her mother had done.

Lacey stopped at the open French doors. 'Regarding Jack being your father, well, that's not possible. We tried to have children but were never blessed. Jack was sterile.' A darkness flashed in Lacey's eyes before she turned and left them all reeling.

CHAPTER 39

Rosemary

May 1964

At work and home, Rosemary avoided everyone. She was grateful Pamela was on an extended layover in London and Eleanor had been working late because of a big account her boss was involved in.

Nora was the only one around, but she let Rosemary be.

Rosemary was grateful. She didn't have the strength to face the girls. She was too ashamed and angry. Taken by Jack not once, but twice.

She went over it all again and again in slow motion. Every time, the pain gutted her. The gentle way Jack walked out of the bedroom after Lacey's intrusion. Their closeness in the kitchen.

She was a nonentity compared to Lacey. Unsophisticated. No social standing. An immigrant with no family, no wealth, and a past she'd buried. Jack had called several times, but she'd ignored him. The last time he'd called, he'd insisted Nora take a message.

Rosemary stood on the landing and listened.

'I'm sorry, Jack. It's not my place to pry. I don't know what's happened, but I think it's best that you don't call her again.' There was a pause. 'Jack, if you turn up here, you will not be invited in. These are Rosemary's wishes, and, as the closest thing to a mother she has, I also forbid it. Goodbye, Jack.'

Nora hung up and looked at Rosemary. 'I'm here if you need me.'

'Grazie,' she'd said to Nora and moved back into her room. A coldness had run through her bones. All men wanted was control, and they behaved like dogs in heat, seizing what they wanted when the urge took them. She no longer wanted to be a part of it. She would be independent.

AT THE HOSPITAL, all the nurses were run off their feet. The past week had seen another bumper number of births.

Rosemary finally caught up with Marie when she popped down to the hospital kitchen for a cup of tea. 'Let's sit outside and catch some late afternoon sun. It will bring some warmth to our tired bones.'

They settled down on the old, splintered bench and sipped their tea, enjoying the fresh breeze.

'I always count back to figure out what was going on nine months ago,' Marie said, taking off her shoes and rubbing her stocking feet. 'All I can work out is that spring makes people horny. Or it's warm enough to shag in cars.' She laughed.

Rosemary smiled. Her mind tiptoed back to her sexual awakening, only to see the memory ripped to shreds by Lacey's arrival.

They sat in silence, watching pigeons pecking at crumbs, until Marie lifted the watch on her uniform. 'I better get back.' She looked at Rosemary. 'I won't ask what's happened, but I've got my suspicions. And he's not worth it.' She stubbed out the cigarette and flicked it into the garden. 'Are you going to be okay?'

Rosemary hugged her. 'I am good.' She kissed Marie on the cheek. 'We must have bad times to appreciate the good. I have come here alone, and I have survived. When it is the right time, I will talk about it.'

'Ok.' Marie gave her a weak smile. 'You're my best friend, Hollywood.'

'*Anche tu sei la mia migliore ragazza*. The best girlfriend I have ever had.'

After Rosemary's shift, Matron Florence Jackson and Gladys came into the staffroom as she was tidying herself up for the bus trip home.

'Sorry to do this on your way out, but Matron wants to speak to you,' Gladys said and walked out.

'Hello, Matron.' Rosemary scoured her thoughts for anything she might have done during her shift. She'd spent some time talking to one of the new mothers; she was always getting pulled up for spending too much time delivering the food trays.

'Rosemary, I've received your application to study as a nurse at St Elizabeth's.'

The hairs on Rosemary's arms stood on end. She'd forgotten about the application. Her preoccupation with Jack had taken up all her energy and focus. She braced herself for the rejection.

'Yes.'

'We have looked over all the applications. There were quite a number, which is why it's taken so long to get back to you.'

'I understand. Thank you for your consideration.'

'Rosemary, we'd like to offer you a place here at St Elizabeth's. You will start your training in September. Congratulations.'

Rosemary stood there. Speechless. She blinked.

'Rosemary? This *is* good news?'

'Si, yes, sorry, grazie, thank you. I am very excited. I am ... my words are lost. Sorry. This is wonderful news. I will work very hard.'

'I know you will, Rosemary. And your Italian will help us with the Italian mothers who come in. You don't happen to know how to speak Greek or Maltese?'

'No. But I can pick up languages quickly.'

'Well then, you're more of a find than we realised. Come up to my office this week so we can complete all the paperwork.'

Rosemary waited until Matron left before squealing. She couldn't believe it. She was going to train to be a nurse. Then, she would be a doctor. Her dream was coming true. She wished she could write to the contessa and Viviana to tell them the good news.

'What did cranky pants want?' Gladys said, stepping back into the staffroom. Rosemary wanted to tell Gladys that her comment was like the kettle calling the pot black. One of her favourite English phrases.

'I have been accepted to be a nurse.'

'I gather by the grin on your face this is good news.'

'Very good news.'

'Well, I'll miss ya. You're me best worker.'

Rosemary's smile grew wider. Gladys had taken a chance on her when she turned up with Father Silvio Paoletti for the job. 'I cannot thank you enough. You have been kind to me. And good.'

With that, Gladys walked over to Rosemary and hugged her. Hard. Moved, Rosemary returned the hug. Gladys never showed any affection.

She knew that her—what was it they said here?—*la corteccia era peggio del suo morso.* Her bark was worse than her bite.

Gladys pulled away and wiped her tears with her apron. 'Well, I better pull meself together. We don't want the other girls thinking I've gone soft.'

'No.' Rosemary took her hand and squeezed it.

She was going to be okay. When she'd come to Australia, she'd had no friends, no job and no place to live. A lump jostled inside her throat, and emotions rushed in. She now had all three and much more.

She picked up her belongings and left the staffroom. It didn't matter about Jack. She was going to be a nurse. She was going to be independent, look after herself and have a profession. Nobody could stop her now.

CHAPTER 40

Olivia

June 1989

A siren outside woke Olivia. The sound was followed by the bells of St Brendan's calling people to Mass. Olivia glanced at the empty bottle of vodka on her bedside table and cringed before pushing herself deeper under the covers. She didn't want to face the world. As much as she'd tried not to, she'd pinned her hopes on Jack Emerson being her father. Even if he had been, he'd passed away. In all the shock and emotional upheaval, she hadn't asked how or when.

This was turning out to be a big bowl of *skatà*, as Demi put it. She wished she'd just left it. Every bit of it. If she'd let it go all those years ago, her mother would still be here.

Sleep was teasing her when the buzzer rang.

Go away!

She looked up at the pressed-metal ceiling, following the burnished floral vine that crept along it.

The buzzer sounded again, followed by a loud pounding.

Crap.

Olivia got out of bed, grabbed the empty bottle and shoved it into the bin in her bathroom. On her way to the door, she tripped over the phone, which was hanging off the hook, and kicked it out of the way. *One problem solved.*

The banging started up again, followed by the buzzer's trilling. Olivia winced as it reverberated through her pulsating head. Whoever it was wasn't giving up. She padded downstairs and smoothed down her hair. She'd tell whoever was at the front door that she was sick. Then she could go back to the business of disappearing. She flung open the door.

Her heart dropped to her ankles.

'Demi called me.' Sebastian lifted a bakery box. 'Croissants that need some coffee. Can I come in?'

She smiled and felt guilty for not calling him when they got back from Jubilee Station. They went upstairs, and Olivia collapsed onto the sofa and told Sebastian all about the trip and how she was so tired of everything. Tired of her life, of who she was. Olivia lifted the throw over her head. She didn't want to cry in front of Sebastian yet again. The tears came anyway.

She felt his arms wrap around her and tried to shove him off, but he held her tighter.

'Go away, please,' she sobbed inside her makeshift tent.

He lifted the wrap off her and rubbed her back. She cried into his warm chest, his arms a safe haven against the disappointment flicking at her heart.

When she finished, she kept herself buried in his body. His gentle scent, citrus and woody, always made her feel secure. Olivia felt Sebastian take a deep breath. His hand stroked her ponytail. The meditative action comforted her.

Olivia lifted her face. 'I think I've made a mess of your shirt.'

Sebastian pulled his shirt away and inspected it. 'Just tears. Better than mascara smudges.' He winked at her.

She smiled weakly. 'Is that a regular issue for you?'

'Not unless fifth graders wear mascara. You're my token grown-up this week.'

Sebastian leant in and gave her a sensual kiss, and all thoughts left her mind. When he pulled away, his eyes glowed. 'I wish you'd called when you got back from Manilla.'

'I'm sorry. It's just ...' She placed her hand on his cheek. 'Look at you. You could have your pick of any girl. Someone who wants to go out all the time. Who wears sexy dresses. Who doesn't look—' She placed her hand on her scar. 'I will never look like the other girls.'

'Thank goodness. I want you. There's something about you, Olivia Bennet. And I want to discover all of it.' He leant forward and kissed her on the cheek. 'All of it.'

She shifted and pressed her lips to his. A heaviness pushed against her most private place. She pulled away.

Sebastian stroked her scar. 'You don't have to do anything you don't want to. I'm not going anywhere.'

Olivia looked at him. She'd known him for months. All he'd ever wanted to do was help her, from that very first day in the bookshop. He never judged and was always there. Strong and calm.

Demi's voice popped into her mind. 'If you're going to pop your cherry, then Sebastian's your guy.'

Horrified, Olivia had swatted Demi's arm when she made the comment weeks ago. Now, it felt right.

She chewed her bottom lip. 'I need to tell you something.' Sebastian focused his blue eyes on her. A wash of heat floated up her back and across her chest. Soon her face would be glowing with embarrassment. 'I'm—' She swallowed. 'I've never ... I mean. Well, I've never done this. Been with a man. You know ...' She looked down at her bare feet.

Sebastian lifted her chin and stroked her cheek. 'Like I said, we don't have to do anything that you don't want to.'

She brushed her lips over his. 'I want to.'

Olivia sat back, keeping her eyes on Sebastian. She took off her dressing gown and folded it over the sofa's arm, then stood and undid the buttons that ran down the front of her pyjama top. Sebastian kept his eyes on her. She slid one of the sleeves down her arm.

He stood and took the other side. Standing in front of him in her plain cotton bra and undies, she shivered. Not from any chill but because Sebastian was looking at her with such intensity. Her shyness gave way to desire, and she followed Sebastian's large hands as he unbuttoned his shirt. He took it off and laid it on the sofa next to her dressing gown. She placed her hand on his broad and tanned chest, just underneath his throat, above his sternum. Sebastian inhaled sharply.

She pulled her hand away. 'Sorry.'

He grabbed it and placed it on his heart. 'Don't apologise.' He kissed her again, then whispered in her ear, 'Are you sure?'

'Yes,' she breathed back.

With that, he picked her up and carried her to the bed. Then stopped abruptly. Olivia followed his gaze, and her body froze. The chifforobe door was open, revealing a half-empty bottle of vodka. Sebastian placed Olivia back on her feet. He walked over and picked up the bottle.

'What's this?'

Olivia felt as if wet sand had been shoved down her throat. 'Sebastian' was all she could croak out.

'How long has this been going on?' His stony eyes glared at her.

'A while,' she whispered. Then, a little more loudly, 'It's only to dull the anxiety.' She felt her tears hot and ready to burst out. She bit down on her bottom lip, trying to stop it from quivering.

'This'—he shook the bottle at her—'will kill you! Damage your perception of the world. I know. My father drank too much and look where it got him. And my mum.' He slammed the bottle back in the cupboard before stalking towards her bedroom door.

Olivia raced after him. In the living room, he put on his shirt.

'Please.' The tears streamed down her face. 'Please.' She hiccupped and wiped her wet nose. 'People make mistakes. You did.'

'What do you mean?' He fixed the unfamiliar glare on her again. She felt as if she'd been punched in the belly.

'You got in a car, high on drugs and alcohol. At least I do it in private. I don't hurt anyone.' The words fired out of her. She rubbed her wet nose with the back of her hand. 'I only hurt myself.'

Sebastian glared back at her. Hurt riddled his face while anger flashed in his eyes. Her words stung back at her, and she desperately wanted to suck all the hurt back into her mouth. She stepped forward a little. Inching slowly towards him. 'I'm sorry.' She searched his face. 'I'm so, so sorry. I shouldn't have said that. That was so mean.' Her heart ripped open. How could she have said that to him? Olivia let her tears fall, wet and messy.

The stormy look evaporated from Sebastian's face, giving her the courage to keep going. 'You have your brother. Your nonna. Friends. I have no one. At least, I used to feel like I had no one. A long time ago, I discovered that vodka could dull the sharp edges of my life. I'm trying to stop. I really am.'

She dropped her head and wrapped her arms tight around her body, letting herself succumb to heart-wrenching sobs. Before she could drop to the floor, she felt his arms around her. Lifting her into his chest. She grabbed his arms and hung on for dear life.

Sebastian placed his lips on the top of her head and shushed her.

She let herself be held. She wanted to stay in his arms forever. Then, lifting her tear-stained face, she moved onto her tiptoes and kissed him. 'I'm sorry.' Her words brushed his warm lips. 'No one knows. Not even Demi.'

An impulse flowed through her veins, and she kissed him again. Slow and deep. 'Make love to me,' she whispered.

Without a word, she led him back into her bedroom.

This was what she wanted. This was what she needed.

CHAPTER 41

The next morning, Olivia woke to a grey sky, but she didn't care. Nothing was going to ruin her mood. She heard clattering in the kitchen and reached for her dressing gown.

'Good morning, sleepyhead.'

Olivia glanced at the kitchen clock. 'It's 7.30. I hardly slept in.'

'I know. I just wanted to say it. They say it in the movies all the time.'

'Mr Allessi, I do declare, you surprise me. First, you know who Jane Austen is, and then you deliver a line from a rom-com.'

'My secret's out. I enjoy reading Austen and watching chick flicks. Does this mean we're over?'

Olivia looked down at her bathrobe. 'If you can handle this robe, then we're even.'

'Deal.' He leant down and kissed her. 'I made you some breakfast.'

Only then did Olivia notice the spread on the table. He'd used a tablecloth, and there was a bundle of flowers from the garden in a glass.

'I have to scoot. I need to get home, shower and change. I can hear young Amy Shultz now, her hand raised, asking, "Mr Allessi, how come you're wearing the same clothes as yesterday?"'

Olivia laughed at his attempt at a ten-year-old girl's voice.

'They're very astute, these future women of the world,' he said.

'Well, we can't have that, can we?' Olivia kissed Sebastian again and felt as if she were floating on a cloud.

When he left, she sat down to have breakfast but had barely sugared her tea when the buzzer blared. She looked around, wondering what Sebastian might have forgotten. She ran down and opened the door. 'Miss me already?'

'I hope I'm not intruding.'

Olivia felt as if the wind had been knocked out of her. It wasn't Sebastian but Everly. It took her a moment to respond. 'No.'

'Can we talk?'

They headed up the stairs, and Everly waited until Olivia had stepped into the apartment before entering. She looked around. 'This is lovely. Exactly the type of place I imagined you'd live in.' She walked over to the bookshelf. 'I gather you've read these.'

Olivia couldn't help but smirk. 'Some more than once.'

'Let me guess. Austen, Brontë ...'

'And new writers I discovered at uni and working in the bookshop.'

'The one below? It looks all closed up.'

'It's just been renovated. I've had the past six weeks off. It's due to open next week, I hope.'

'Sorry I've come so early.' She nodded at the table. 'I don't sleep well. Still, I didn't plan to disturb you this early. When I got here, I sat at the bus stop waiting, but then I saw this gorgeous guy step out your front door onto the path. What a spunk!' She winked. 'So I took a chance, hoping you were up too.'

'I'm glad you did. It's nice to see you again.' Olivia meant it. Everly had always been so kind and friendly. She made her feel good about herself. 'Would you like some breakfast? There's plenty.'

'No thanks. Not a big fan of food before midday.' Everly smiled, then turned towards The Quest Wall. 'What's all this?'

Olivia stepped up next to her. 'It's all about the items in the steamer trunk.'

Everly took it in. 'This is pretty impressive. Looks like one of those boards on *The Bill*.'

Olivia chuckled. 'That's what Demi reckons too. Would you like a drink? Tea? Coffee?'

'Tea, thanks.' She perched herself on the stool. 'I'm sorry about my Aunt Lacey.'

'Is that why you're here? To apologise?'

'I know you're upset.'

Olivia leant across the counter and placed her hand on Everly's arm. 'Not at you. Not even at your aunt. I'm angry at myself.' Olivia glanced at The Quest Wall. 'I should've just let the past lie. That's what my mother wanted. I'm being punished for disturbing it.'

'Why did you? You know,' she said, taking another sip, 'want to know more?'

Olivia exhaled. 'Deep down, it's important to me to know who my dad was. Mum was so secretive about it—well, about everything in her life. You know she was Italian. A migrant. She came here on her own. Lacey was right, you know.'

'About what?' Everly gave her a quizzical look. 'Olivia, this is really hard for me to do.' Everly's eyes glistened, and she rubbed them.

'What is?'

Everly slid an envelope over to Olivia. 'After you left, Aunt Lacey locked herself in her room. She wouldn't come out or speak to me. When I asked what was going on, she freaked out and told me it was none of my business. She kinda went on a bender, drinking and losing it in her room. Which was weird because I'm normally the one to do that. Anyhow, later that night, I went in to find her passed out on the bed, with a box of her personal mementos strewn across the floor. I found this letter in it.'

CHAPTER 42

Rosemary

June 1964

As she was opening the lid of the biscuit tin, the doorbell rang. Her chest tightened. Jack. She didn't move. The doorbell rang again. She took off her shoes, tiptoed on stocking feet to the sitting room and peeked out the lace curtains.

Lacey?

She marched to the front door and flung it open. 'What do you want?'

'My. That's not how one greets a friend. May I come in?' Lacey adjusted her cashmere gloves. Always immaculate and poised. Only the subtle sneer revealed that she wasn't the polite, warm woman she pretended to be.

Rosemary gripped the edge of the door, ready to slam it in her face. But if she did, she'd only prove that she was the peasant girl Lacey believed she was. She stepped back and opened the door wider.

'Please,' said Rosemary. She looked straight at Lacey, making no attempt to hide the coolness she felt for her.

'Thank you. It's got chilly outside.' She took off her coat and slung it over her arm while glancing around. 'Pretty. Is there somewhere private we can talk?'

'We can talk in here.' Rosemary directed Lacey into the living room.

'Thank you. Do you live here alone?'

Rosemary knew Lacey would know she couldn't afford to rent a place on her own. Especially if Jack had told her she worked in the kitchens at St Elizabeth's. The woman was good—she'd perfected the refined skill of putting someone down, of making them feel small with subtle attacks.

'No. I board here with two other girls.'

'And you like that?'

'Yes, they are warm, kind and caring women.' Rosemary looked pointedly at Lacey, who held none of these qualities. 'We are family.'

'And where is your family, Rosemary? Jack never mentioned.'

The question stoked the anger inside her. How dare he talk to Lacey about her! She could feel her face flame and started counting to avoid slapping Lacey across her perfect porcelain-made-up face.

Before Rosemary could answer, Lacey continued.

'Actually, no need to tell me. I already know you are from Genoa, well let's just say, you were once in Genoa. I took the liberty of writing to an old friend of mine there. As it turns out, he was acquainted with a Paolo Orsini. He knows all about you. About what you did.' She held up a letter. 'It's all here.'

Rosemary recoiled with dread. A cold steel knife blade cut up her spine.

'You see, Rosemary, I don't mind Jack having a plaything before we marry, but that's over now. I have this letter with all the sordid details to confirm what I've always suspected. That you are a whore.' Lacey inched closer to her. 'Leave now and never see or speak to Jack again. Otherwise, I will have to tell Jack who you really are. That you are no better than a common prostitute.'

Rosemary's stomach dropped, and she wanted to vomit. A terror rendered her speechless. Lacey's serene demeanour ignited an inner rage. 'There is no Jack. I am finished with Jack. He is yours.' It took every ounce of her self-control not to fling herself onto Lacey and strangle her slender neck. Instead, she moved close enough to smell the expensive perfume she always wore.

'You are a wicked woman,' she said quietly.

'You know, Rosemary.' Lacey turned and faced her straight on. Her eyes darkened. 'You would never have fitted in Jack's life. This'— she tucked the letter back into her handbag—'is my insurance that you will *never* see *or* speak to Jack again.'

CHAPTER 43

Olivia
June 1989

The phone rang again.

Olivia sat up on the rug. The bottle of vodka rolled away from her. She picked up the receiver and heard Demi's desperate hello. She hung up and then shoved the phone off the table.

She willed herself to sleep forever. Willed herself to disappear from who she was.

CHAPTER 44

Olivia opened her eyes and stirred. Gin moved off her chest and snuggled into the crook of her knees. A knocking disturbed the dark tomb that was her bedroom.

She turned over and tried to ignore the sound that was making her head vibrate. The knocking continued. Stopped. Then started again with a little more force. She heard a voice.

'Olivia?'

She cocked her head. It wasn't Demi. She wouldn't be polite. She'd holler. Something about the voice reminded her of the way her mother used to say her name. The thought brought everything back to the surface. The conversation with Everly sat raw in her mind. Tears stung her eyes, and her heart ached for her mum. It was all too surreal. Had her mum used her body for money? The discovery pressed down hard onto her chest.

Maybe she had come to Australia to get away from living this kind of life. To start again. But this didn't explain the Italian marriage certificate William Templeton gave her. Olivia's mind battled with her heart. Desperately grasping at all the possibilities until one landed. Through research, she'd unearthed information about Italian bride ships. After World War II, Italian girls came to Australia as proxy brides. They married in Italy while their new Italian husbands were in Australia. The girl's brother, father or uncle stood in for the groom. One young girl got off the ship in Melbourne and disappeared. Another arrived to find her husband had died in a farming accident the week before her ship docked in Brisbane. There was also a kind of shame for not marrying for love. Did her mother also feel this shame? What happened to this man? Maybe he died? Why did her mother never say anything? She pushed her head back into the pillow. All these thoughts and questions made her head throb.

Olivia sat up. *Unless ... she had no choice but to survive in Australia, single and alone!* This hope dug deep into her heart, refusing to believe the letter that Everly showed her. Her mum was so ... pure, and she went to church. It didn't make any sense.

The banging knocked her out of her thoughts. Olivia pulled the quilt off the bed and wrapped it around herself. Maybe she was dead, and it really was her mum? She walked into the living room and glanced at the cuckoo clock. It was late afternoon. She stopped and wanted to feel her mum's arms around her, soothing her.

'Olivia?' the voice said again behind the door. 'Darling, are you in there?'

She placed her hand on the cool door with care. She imagined opening it to see her there. Then her mum would take her in her arms, kiss the top of her head and whisper sweet Italian words to her. Olivia placed her forehead on the door.

'I know you're in there,' the voice said. 'Everyone is worried about you. Bertie let me into the building. She's also been worried sick about you.' There was a pause. 'It will be okay.'

The voice was kind, but Olivia couldn't identify it. 'Who is it?' The words came out croaky. Drinking herself into a stupor had dehydrated her.

'Marie. Marie Middleton.'

Olivia cracked open the door, and she found herself in her godmother's arms, where she let herself sob. Marie held her and rubbed her back, shushing her in a quiet voice. When Olivia was spent, she pulled away and used a corner of the blanket to mop up the tears and her snotty nose.

'What are you doing here?'

'Can I come in? I'm dying for a cup of tea. It was a long drive down.'

Marie looked around the apartment. Olivia followed her eyes. It was a mess. Takeaway boxes with uneaten food still in them were scattered across the living room. Empty bottles of vodka. Flat Coke in bottles. Chocolate wrappers. Gin's food was scattered all over the kitchen floor, and the ants had found a feast.

All the windows and doors were pulled closed, and the curtains were drawn shut against the sunny day. The air was stale. Olivia was sure she stunk.

'Well, at least you're eating.' Marie held up a jumbo bag of salt and vinegar chips and threw Olivia a sympathetic smile. 'Have you eaten a decent meal?'

Olivia shook her head.

'And I suppose a shower hasn't been high on your agenda the past few days.'

'Do I smell that bad?'

'Yes. But I've had my fair share of heartache. I get it.' Marie started collecting the takeaway containers.

'Why are you here?' Olivia asked her.

'Sebastian called me. He's quite astute. He remembered I worked at Tamworth Hospital. Olivia, I need to tell you more about your mum.'

'MUM HAD NO CHOICE, DID SHE?' Olivia said. She unfolded Everly's letter. Everything Marie shared about her mother was in the letter, but the truth had been twisted into a distorted mass of deception.

'No, sweetheart, I don't think she did. Or that she felt she didn't. We'll never know what she went through. But I certainly don't judge her. When she told me what she did—the whole sordid ordeal to get her ticket and papers back—all I wanted to do was scream to the heavens. Instead, I did what she deserved. I supported her. With no judgement. I want you to do the same.'

'I do,' Olivia whispered. She picked up the photo of her mum. Ripples of air filled her lungs.

Olivia walked over to the credenza, picked up the envelope and slipped out the marriage certificate and a bundle of official papers which were yellow and brittle. Their secrets held together with a red ribbon. She handed the gold wedding band to Marie. 'Was she ever married?'

Marie's eyes widened.

'You know.' Olivia's words slipped out like a hushed prayer.

'Yes, but—'

'To who? Where is her husband?'

'It was all a ploy.' Marie grabbed her hands. 'Fake. To get her to Australia. It was the only way. Australian immigration rules allowed wives to join their husbands after they were married. It was known as—'

'Mum pretended to be a proxy bride!'

'You know about this?'

'I researched it. When I was trying to find out about Mum's life here in Sydney. In the '60s. As a migrant.' Impatience pinched at her chest. 'How?'

'Some woman Rosemary knew who had the connections and the means. She arranged it all.'

Olivia's head spun as some of the pieces of her mum's past began to crash together.

MARIE PLACED a mug of tea in her hands. Olivia took a sip. The warmth settled around her like a warm blanket.

Marie checked the time on the cuckoo clock. 'I'll whip something up for dinner.'

'Don't you need to get back home, to work?'

'Sweetie, I have no family. I work all the time. I have so much leave I can take a world trip. Twice.' She smiled. 'I told them my goddaughter needed me.'

'I like that.'

'What?'

'Being someone's goddaughter.'

Marie took Olivia's hand. 'I know I haven't been here for you. I mean, a godmother is supposed to step in. Something I didn't do because I didn't know ...' Marie stopped and shook her head, working at stopping the tears that welled up. 'Then you landed on my doorstep. I couldn't believe it.'

Olivia squeezed her hand. 'It's okay. One thing I'm learning is life is never easy.'

Marie let her tears fall and wiped them with the heel of her hand. 'You know I'm here for you.'

'I do.'

―――――――――

MARIE HAD STAYED for a few days, and they'd continued getting to know each other. Being able to share stories about her mum had brought some sunshine back into Olivia's life. The black mass of sadness didn't take up so much room inside her heart anymore.

Olivia confided in Marie about her drinking and admitted that she thought she should see someone. 'Like a psychologist.' The idea didn't frighten her as much now.

Marie left Sydney with a promise that they would write to each other and make plans for Christmas. Knowing she didn't have to worry about being alone for Christmas again filled Olivia with joy.

CHAPTER 45

As Olivia was locking up the shop at the end of the day, a loud wolf whistle startled her. Demi was walking up the street towards her with Sebastian at her side. He was shaking his head and pointing at Demi. Olivia laughed and waited.

'I ran into this crazy woman.' Sebastian leant down and gave her a kiss on the cheek.

'Man, call that a kiss?' Demi stepped forward and planted a kiss smack bang on Olivia's lips. 'Greek passion.' She winked at Sebastian.

'How does Theo put up with you?' Olivia asked.

'Oh, there're no complaints there.'

'I know passion.' Sebastian winked at Olivia.

'Oh, I bet you do.' Demi nudged him.

'I think we better get you inside before a war breaks out between the Greeks and the Italians,' Olivia said with a laugh.

When they entered Olivia's apartment, Demi gasped. 'It's gone.'

Sebastian followed her in and stood in front of the wall, now stripped of the butcher's paper. He wrapped his arms around Olivia. 'Are you okay?'

Olivia looked up at him to see his signature crease of concern between his blue eyes. 'It's fine. I'm okay. I promise I'll tell you everything. But first, I can smell moussaka, and after my first week back at work, I'm famished.'

Demi warmed the moussaka in the oven according to her grandmother's strict instructions while Sebastian made the salad—the way his nonna had instructed him to do. Olivia poured the wine and set the table. She had her first appointment with the psychologist next week and had promised herself, and Marie, that she would drink only in company and when she was happy.

Over dinner, they chatted about their weeks, and Olivia talked about how much she loved working in the fresh new bookstore.

'Any other news?' asked Demi.

Olivia got up and fetched the bundle of letters and a manila folder. 'Helena dropped the letters off with her translations at the bookstore before story time this morning.'

Both Demi and Sebastian leant forward.

'And ...' Demi's eyes widened. Sebastian sat quietly and offered her a smile.

'No mention of who my dad was and nothing about her time in Italy. Only bits about missing the sea. In the first letter, there's stuff about the boat trip to Australia. I now know who Viviana is. It's what I've always thought—she's mum's younger sister.'

'Nothing about who your dad might be?' Sebastian's face held a wash of concern.

Olivia smiled to reassure him. 'No, only that she had found love with Jack. She does write about her time in Sydney, though. I'm really pleased about that. At least I know more about her life before she had me. At this stage, I'll take what I can.' Olivia flicked through the letters and pulled out one. 'There's this one letter written before she left Sydney. It's the only one addressed to a Signora Castello.' Olivia flicked through the translations. 'Here.' She stabbed her finger onto the typed words.

Demi leant over. 'It's all typed. Jeez, Helena's perfection incarnate.'

Olivia laughed. 'She was meticulous. Anyway, I did some research and found that *Castello* is an old name in Sicily, around Messina. Nobility. In the letter, Mum mentions that she misses them.'

'Them?' Demi asked.

Olivia scanned down the page. 'Here. *Send my love to Lucia. I hope she is keeping up with her studies.* I think Lucia is Carmela's daughter. Maybe sister.'

Sebastian began clearing the dishes. 'Sounds like they were good friends.'

'For sure.' She flipped the page over. 'There's this one line ... here! *I cannot thank you enough for helping me and for securing my papers and the money.*'

'The papers?' Demi said.

'Proxy papers. Marie told me that Mum was a proxy bride.' Olivia's heart started to pound. 'Oh! It gets better. The papers are fake. It was a way to get Mum to Australia. There were so many young women travelling to Australia as proxy brides at the time. She would've blended in.' She rushed back over to the credenza and fished around. 'I found this photo at the state library. This ship was full of proxy brides.'

She handed them a photocopy of the image—a large group of young women gathered on the deck of a ship.

'Pretty ingenious.' Sebastian lifted his glass.

Olivia nodded. 'She was so brave. Imagine coming here alone.'

CHAPTER 46

Rosemary
September 1964

Shirley O'Connor invited Rosemary Bennet into her home with open arms. Changing her surname had been bittersweet. To be more Australian and to disappear as Rosemary Benito, furthering her escape from her life in Sydney. Plus, she didn't want Jack or anyone else finding her.

Rosemary immediately felt Shirley's maternal warmth. Fresh scones were piled high on a table dressed with fancy dishes.

'I'm overjoyed about you moving in, Rosemary,' Shirley said when Rosemary had inspected her new room.

A soft, briny breeze washed over her as she sat on the verandah. The seagulls breaking the silence. Shirley offered Rosemary a scone. 'So, you're from Italy. Very glamorous. I've never been anywhere but Sydney, and even that's too busy for me. I like the quiet community here in Killcare.'

'Yes, I'm from a little town too, in Sicily—' Rosemary stopped. Could she trust Shirley?

Shirley placed her hand over Rosemary's. Her soft brown eyes were reassuring. 'You told me the basic details, that's all I need to know if that's the way you want it. But you can trust me.'

Rosemary had already told Shirley that she was pregnant and was a proxy bride, but that it didn't work out. Shirley sensed there was a lot more to the story but didn't want to push it.

'Thank you.' Overwhelmed by Shirley's kindness, she swallowed the lump in her throat but couldn't push back the tears. Water marks rippled out onto Shirley's linen tablecloth.

'Oh dear.' Shirley moved her chair over and hugged Rosemary. 'You're safe here. Your little baby will be safe, too. You can have a new life here.'

Shirley grabbed both of her hands and looked directly at Rosemary. 'I've missed the sounds and busyness a child creates. This house has been too quiet for too long.'

Rosemary nodded. She gazed out over the rolling waves. The cottage sat on the edge of sand dunes that framed the beach. Seeing the ocean reminded her of Patti. It would be a pretty place to raise a child. She placed her hand on her belly. What do you think, my sweet little *bambina*? Or will you be a little *bambino*?

Her thoughts went to the items she'd carefully packed away in the trunk. The symbolism tugged at her heart. The trunk carried her few possessions from Italy. A life now abandoned. She hoped there would always be a piece of it that lived inside her forever.

It had taken her many sleepless nights to decide what to do with the items Jack had gifted her. Every time she imagined seeing him, to return them, bitterness filled her mouth. She couldn't see him again. It was dangerous. Whenever her mind wandered to their lovemaking, a sharp pain slashed her heart.

No! It was over.

She would allow herself one privilege—she'd tuck her precious memories of Jack, her first true love, in her heart and would keep the gifts as a reminder of that love. To help her bury all her memories of Jack and her life in Sydney, she placed all the photos she took, along with her passion for photography, the dresses and shoes from Jack, the necklace, everything into the trunk.

The trunk would remain in storage, and when she graduated with her medical degree, she'd share its contents with her child, as an offering to Heaven. She hoped there would come a time when she could share her story without her heart being ripped into pieces. If she was to do this, she had to share it all. The good and the bad. Of her sacrifices for a new life. Of fleeing Sicily and the treacherous man she had been promised to, of sacrificing her virginity for her ticket to Australia, albeit against her will, and of her love for Jack.

CHAPTER 47

Olivia
June 1989

Olivia wrapped the towel tight around her head and tightened her bathrobe around her. A muted doorbell trilled as she stepped out of the steamy bathroom. The late afternoon had swept away a glorious winter's day, bringing a chill into her bedroom. Her heart fluttered as two incompatible emotions hurdled each other. Marie had left, needing to get back to Woolbrook, but Sebastian had stayed.

'Did I hear the buzzer—' She stopped as she entered her living room. 'Everly!' She stood next to Sebastian—with another woman.

'I thought it was Demi?' Sebastian threw her an apologetic look.

Everly stepped over to Olivia. 'I hope you don't mind. This is my Great-aunt Vera. I think you need to hear what she has to say.'

'No. I mean yes. Let me get dressed.' She grabbed the collar of her robe and raced back into the bedroom. *Oh God! Oh God!*

She flung on a pair of track pants and her Sydney Uni jersey. Ripped a comb through her hair and pulled it tight into a ponytail. She stopped at her bedroom door and pressed her palm to quieten her hammering heart. Composing herself, she stepped back into the living room. 'Can I offer you something to drink?'

'Tea?' Everly looked over at Vera, who nodded.

'I'll do it.' Sebastian jumped up. As he passed Olivia, he grabbed her hand and squeezed.

'Thanks.' She offered him a small smile, then indicated the sofa to Everly and Vera. 'Please.' Working at keeping a serene face as her stomach clenched, she sat in the wing chair opposite.

Everly jumped in. 'I went to stay at Aunt Vera's. I hope you don't mind, but I told her about everything. I felt so bad about how it all ended last time I was here.'

'It's okay. I shouldn't have shot the messenger. You were only trying to help.' Olivia shrugged.

Vera accepted the tea from Sebastian and gave him a warm smile. Something about her made Olivia feel safe. She didn't have that harsh look Lacey did. Her eyes held a gentle warmth.

Vera took a sip. 'Lovely.' She placed the cup down on the coffee table and turned to Olivia. 'You were not told the complete truth. Jack was not sterile. That was a cruel lie. It was Lacey who was unable to have children. That's all she ever wanted. To marry Jack and be a society mother. As it turned out, one cannot have all they want.'

Olivia nodded. One thing she knew all too well.

Vera continued. 'As the years went on, their marriage became a bitter one. Lacey blamed Jack for not falling pregnant. As it turned out, she had become quite at ease at withholding the truth.'

'Are you saying that Jack might've been Livvie's dad?' Sebastian moved over and perched onto the wing chair's arm and grabbed her hand.

'Not might. Was.'

'How do you know?' The hairs on Olivia's arms quivered. She calmed her breath.

Vera picked up her cup and took a slow sip. 'Jack had gone up to

Gosford for some meeting. Later that night, in his hotel room, he got sick. He fronted up at Gosford Hospital—'

'Where Mum worked.'

'Yes. They reconnected. Your mother told him about you, and eventually, he told her about his cancer diagnosis. Quite advanced.' Vera's voice caught, and a misty sheen filled her eyes. It was evident the memory still hurt.

'Mum must've been devastated.'

'She was. Terribly. As it turned out, it all ended up being a tragically sad meeting for both of them. He told me everything. Making me promise that you were to be looked after and sent to a good school. He knew how bright you were. Your mum was very proud of you. They both were.'

'But why didn't Mum tell me ... about any of this?' Olivia felt a thousand feet stamp on top of her chest.

'They both knew how much losing each other hurt, even after all those years apart. This unrequited love.' Vera slowly shook her head. 'They both didn't want to put that sadness, that devastation, possibly regret, onto you as well. Easier you just never knew.'

'When did Jack die?' A cold numbness flooded her cheeks.

'1976. A year after he was diagnosed.'

A memory surfaced in Olivia's mind. 'Oh my God! I remember when I was around ten, we were at the beach, and afterwards, this man came up. He bought me an ice cream.' Olivia looked at Sebastian. 'That was Jack!'

'Possibly.' Vera nodded. 'He told me you were at Our Lady Queen of Peace. I knew people who taught there. Mrs Crawford was one of them.'

Olivia's eyebrows rose. 'You knew Mrs Crawford?'

'I was also a student there. It's where all Sydney society sends their daughters.'

Olivia shook her head. The connections had been all around her, and she'd been unaware. 'Mrs Crawford was my favourite person there. She was such a kind principal. I think she looked out for me a little more, you know, because of my mum.'

'She was pretty special. I think she's just retired,' Vera added. 'Anyway, I went and saw her once I knew you were there. I wanted to know how you were going and if there was anything I could do for you. She said you were an excellent student and had plans to go to university. The Artemis Scholarship, the one you got when you finished year twelve, was bequeathed by my family's estate. Although Lacey never knew about it. Still doesn't.' Vera threw her a conspiratorial wink.

Olivia felt as if the wind had been knocked out of her. 'So, my scholarship really was charity after all.'

'No,' Vera said firmly. 'No. Mrs Crawford had already gone to the board to create another scholarship for a student who wasn't the dux but had finished in the top five. You were already the one she'd decided on.'

Olivia nodded, feeling relief seep in.

'All I did was bequeath the funds,' Vera continued. 'Which I have done ever since on Jack's behalf. This year, the scholarship will be given to a seventh young woman. Six years after you were our first.'

Suddenly overcome with gratitude, she stood to hug Vera, who gladly accepted. There were more people who cared about her than she ever could have imagined. Life was a mixed bag of heartache, joy and wonder.

They spent the rest of the afternoon chatting about Jack until it was time for Vera and Everly to leave.

'I would love to keep in contact,' Vera said. 'I know your dad would like that.'

'I'd like that too.' Bliss settled like a warm quilt around Olivia.

Later that night, after Olivia discussed the day's events with Sebastian, she glanced at him and smiled to herself.

He was the biggest silver lining of the ordeal. He'd helped her overcome so many fears and had helped her see what she was capable of.

Another plan formed. She was going to Italy.

CHAPTER 48

March 1990

The melodic sounds of the Sicilian dialect drifting under her balcony filled Olivia with joy. She looked out across the iridescent Tyrrhenian Sea. The spring morning was warming up.

She placed her hands on her stomach. The butterflies were constant.

Olivia had been constantly reminding herself that the decision to find her mother's sister, her Aunt Viviana, had been hers. Sebastian and Demi had offered to travel with her, and at one point, she'd nearly relented, but this was something she wanted—needed—to do on her own. She'd hidden away from adventure for too long. Her fear had been suffocating her ability to grow, to become wiser through lived experiences. Working with the psychologist helped. The affirmations she'd tucked away in her journal reminded her to focus on the destination instead. Plus, finding the courage to tell the flight crew. They constantly checked in with her. She even got the good headphones!

She also wanted to connect to her mum on a spiritual level. She wanted to immerse herself in the culture her mum had lived in as a young woman.

She'd arrived in Patti two days ago and had spent most of her time using her mum's camera to take photos of the town in which her mother had grown up.

A scooter beeped, and a barrage of angry words spilled into her room. Olivia smiled. She loved the vibrant energy of this little town.

She moved to the bed and took out the wallet she kept her travel documents in. She slid out the letters her mum had planned to send to her sister, as well as one to Carmela Castello. Her chest tightened, and she swallowed the lump in her throat. Today was the day.

Olivia tucked the letters in her backpack and headed downstairs. The aroma of coffee enticed her to the dining room, and she sat at a small table next to an open window. The smell of wild fennel mixed in with the briny scent of the sea below the town.

'*Buongiorno*,' Franca greeted her. '*Hai dormito bene?*'

'Si. I slept well. Grazie.'

'*Va bene*. Coffee. Something to eat.'

'Thank you.' Olivia opened her map and studied it. Franca soon returned with an espresso. 'You are meeting someone? Yes?'

'They don't know I'm coming. I think my aunty, *zia*, lives here.' Olivia pointed to the map.

A frown crossed Franca's face and she went over to her daughter, Teresa, who sat heavily pregnant on a stool behind reception. Olivia didn't understand any of their strong Sicilian dialect, but Franca spoke fast, with passion, and Teresa glanced at Olivia with a look of pity. She replied to her mother with just as much passion and then shoved her back over to Olivia.

Franca sat down next to Olivia. 'I am sorry. No one lives at this house.'

'Oh.' She took a deep breath and tried hard to hide her disappointment. She had come all this way.

Franca leant in close to Olivia. 'Why do you want to find these people?'

'My mother was from Italy. She migrated to Australia when she was nineteen. Her surname was Fazo. She wrote a letter to a Viviana.' Olivia took out the letter and gave it to Franca.

Franca stared at the letter and made the sign of the cross. '*Dio mio*. You are Rosamaria's daughter?'

Olivia's hope returned. 'Yes,' she said eagerly. 'But she changed her name to Rosemary.'

Franca turned to her daughter and spoke Sicilian again.

Recognition lit Teresa's face, and she waddled over. 'We all knew we would come to know what happened to Rosamaria.' She also made the sign of the cross and then kissed the gold crucifix that hung on her pendant. 'One day, before she was to be married, Rosamaria ran away. I do not blame her. The man her father chose was old. Much older than Rosamaria. And he was not a good man. I would do the same.'

'Teresa!' Franca shook her hands at her daughter.

'Si, Mamma. I would.' Teresa turned to Olivia again. 'Salvatore, Signore Fazo, was a hard man. We know he beat his wife, Orazia.' At the mention of her name, the two women made the sign of the cross and kissed their gold crosses.

Olivia knew this meant she'd passed away. 'When did Orazia die?'

'Last winter,' Teresa said. 'It was a broken family. The two older boys moved to Canada, I think a few years after Rosamaria left. She brought shame on the family by running away.'

'But she was being forced to marry a man she didn't love.' Olivia heard the anger in her voice.

'Italy was, maybe still is ... how do you say it ... from behind—' Teresa sighed.

'Backward?' offered Olivia.

'Si.'

'How about my mum's dad?' Olivia couldn't bring herself to say *grandfather*.

'He drank himself to death years ago. With the older boys gone, the farm went to ruins. He could not make his payment. We do not know why. But Carmela Castello, she owned the land. She is a contessa, a countess, and she let the Fazos stay in the house. She is gone too. But her daughter, Lucia, now runs the villa as a day spa for rich tourists.'

The other letter.

Franca squeezed Teresa's arm. 'Tell her.'

Teresa rubbed her swollen belly. 'Everyone thinks that Signora Castello helped Rosamaria to go away.'

Excitement bubbled inside her. This was all in her mother's letters. She wished Demi and Sebastian could hear this. Her phone call home tonight would cost a fortune.

'Because Rosamaria gave ... what do you say ... instruction to her Lucia.'

'She was her tutor?'

'Si. Your mother was very smart. My teacher told me she wanted to be a doctor. She spent a lot of time at the villa. A week after her family discovered Rosamaria was gone, a local farmer walking to the village saw the contessa's car heading towards Messina. He said there were three people in the car.'

'Did anyone talk to the contessa?' Olivia asked.

'No,' Franca interjected. 'No one must go against Carmela Castello.'

'Mamma is correct. There was nothing Salvatore Fazo could do.'

'Is Rosamaria good?' Franca asked.

'I'm sorry.' Olivia bit her bottom lip. 'Mum died when I was thirteen.'

Franca and Teresa each made the sign of the cross.

'Mamma mia.' Franca reached over and gave Olivia a big hug. She smelt of honey and lemons.

'I am sorry,' Teresa said. 'There is too much death in our lives.'

Olivia couldn't agree more. She picked up the letter. 'Do you know where Viviana is?'

Franca and Teresa both shook their heads. 'No,' Teresa said. 'But I know who will. Lucia.'

Franca smiled at Olivia. 'Yes.'

Teresa stood up and rubbed her back. 'Come, I will drive you there.'

Olivia swept a glance over her very pregnant belly. 'Are you sure?'

Teresa looked down and laughed. 'This is nothing. Number four. I am like a cow. I can give birth, then get back to work.'

'I really appreciate this,' Olivia said, collecting her things. 'Thank you for talking to me.'

'*Mia cara.*' Franca kissed Olivia on both cheeks. 'I knew you belonged to Rosamaria. You are like your mother. Very beautiful. Except your hair. It is like *autuno.* Autumn.'

Whatever happened from here, Olivia knew coming had been the best decision. People still cared about her mum.

TERESA PULLED up to Villa Castello in a battered yellow Fiat and beeped the horn yet again. Villa Castello sat on top of a hill, its majestic facade facing the sea. Cream rendered walls sparkled under the Sicilian sun. Stone cherubs on the roof heralded the Fiat's arrival. Two staircases swept up from the sides of the circular carriageway, now used for cars, to a large arched set of double doors. Above, stained glass glistened like jewels.

'*Una villa maestosa.* A grand villa, yes?'

'It is. It looks like a Cinderella palace.'

Teresa laughed. 'Yes, but this one does not have a handsome prince. Lucia Castello never married. The contessa liked no man for her.'

Olivia snorted. 'This marriage thing doesn't seem to be positive in Sicily.'

'It can be.' Teresa rubbed her belly again. '*Mio marito,* Paulo, my husband, we love each other very much. Sometimes he makes me *pazza*.' Teresa circled her finger at the side of her head. 'But then, all Italians are. But Sicilians are the worst. *Andiamo*. Come. Let's visit Lucia. She would be happy for the company.'

As they walked across the gravelled path, Olivia imagined ornate coaches driving up for a ball or an imperial visit. She wished her mother had felt safe enough to tell her stories about the place where she'd grown up. It would've been exciting to hear about her tutoring in this villa.

Teresa rang an enormous brass bell with a large lion's head on top. A maid answered the door, and Teresa spoke to her in Sicilian. From their tones and facial expressions, Olivia could tell they knew each other.

The maid turned to Olivia. 'Welcome. Please come inside. I will see if Signorina Castello can see you.'

They stepped inside. The walls, covered in a rose marble, matched the tessellated tile floor that ran across the expansive entrance. Wide gilded French doors sat on either side. A large stair-case curved upwards. Stone busts lined one side of the foyer on stone ledges that jutted out from the wall.

'Come.' Teresa directed Olivia's attention to the sculptures. 'These are the ancestors.' Olivia followed her and looked at all the busts. Striking and noble people stared back, their existence perma-nently preserved. The bust at the end was whiter than the others.

'That one is my mother. Contessa Carmela Castello,' said a voice in English with a soft Italian accent.

Olivia turned. A poised, confident-looking woman stood on the staircase. Dressed in jeans and a white shirt, the only evidence that she'd had maids help her dress was her black hair, which was pulled into an elegant chignon.

'You must be Olivia.' She walked down the stairs, and Olivia went to curtsy. She'd never met a countess before.

'No, no, no.' Lucia waved. 'We do not do this. It is 1990, not 1790. Please, call me Lucia.' She gave Olivia a warm smile. 'In Italy, we greet each other like this.' She gave Olivia a kiss on each cheek. Her perfume was divine.

She stood a little shorter than Olivia. In fact, Olivia was on the taller side of most of the women she'd seen in Sicily.

'Come into the parlour.'

Lucia slid open one of the French doors and escorted them inside. Olivia gave a little gasp. The walls were covered in paintings. Cream silk-covered chairs with ornately carved arms sat on either side of a large sofa in a contrasting gold and soft blue floral fabric. Above an enormous marble fireplace was a gilded gold mirror, and in the middle of the room, a decadent crystal chandelier loomed and sparkled. The ceiling was divided into panels with filigree patterns spilling over each border, similar in design to her pressed-metal roof at home. The room was bewildering and beautiful. Olivia wondered if her mother had felt the same way about it. Had the opulence become 'normal' as she spent more time here? Had she sat in this room? There was still so much she wanted to know.

Lucia pulled a large gold cord. Olivia had seen people summon servants this way in movies, but never in her life had she thought she'd see it in action. The door opened, and an elderly maid entered. She stopped and looked at Olivia.

'Angela has been with us for many years,' Lucia said. 'She also knew your mother.'

Angela smiled at Olivia. 'Your mother was a kind and beautiful woman.'

'Thank you.' Knowing her mum was well regarded sent warmth across her chest.

'Would you like tea? Coffee? Wine?' Angela asked.

'A coffee would be nice,' said Olivia.

'*Prendo un bicchiere d'acqua, grazie.*' Teresa rubbed her belly.

'Teresa just asked for some water. I am sorry, I think it's better not to speak Italian when not everyone understands.' Lucia gave Teresa a pointed look, and Teresa shrugged sheepishly.

'I understand a little,' said Olivia. 'But the Sicilian dialect is very different.'

'Yes, the dialects change a lot the further north or south you move from Rome.'

'I didn't know this before I came here,' said Olivia.

'Well, it is good you have learnt something new. Yes?'

Olivia smiled.

The door opened, and a different maid arrived with the refreshments. She poured coffee into a fine china cup, placed a cube of sugar on the saucer and passed it to Olivia. Lucia sat poised until everyone had received a drink, then waited until the maid left the parlour. A ribbon of pride wrapped around Olivia's heart knowing her mother had once tutored this graceful and articulate woman.

Lucia placed her coffee on a side table. 'Your mother. She was Rosamaria Fazo.'

'Yes.'

'I can see her in you. You are beautiful, just as she was.'

'I seem to be getting that a lot lately.' Olivia placed her hand on her scar and shrugged, glancing down.

'You think that this scar on your face changes this? No.' Lucia patted her chest and looked at Olivia intently but kindly. 'Beauty comes from here. I can tell you are a kind person. Just like Rosamaria was.'

A blush warmed Olivia's cheeks. She didn't know what to do with a sincere compliment in general, let alone one from nobility. She liked Lucia very much.

'In Australia, my mother called herself Rosemary. Before I was born, she changed her surname to Bennet. But before that, it was Benito. My mother never spoke of Italy or her life before I was born. She used to always say that the past is gone, we cannot change it, and that we must live in the present.' Olivia stopped to recall the Italian words. '*Ill passato é andato. Dobbiamo vivere oggi.*'

Teresa smiled and took a sip of her water. 'My mother says the same.'

Lucia laughed. 'I think all Sicilian mothers say the same. Sicilians live in the moment. They have to. Life has not been easy for a lot of the people. Feudal system, poverty, the wars—it has made life hard.' Lucia gazed at Olivia with warmth. 'I know Rosamaria has passed away. Please accept my condolences. You must miss her a great deal.'

'I do. I miss her every day. But how did you know? I only just told Franca and Teresa this morning.'

'In this village, everyone knows everything. This is why the telephone is like gold in the homes.' She grinned. 'Franca called me just now and told me that Rosamaria's daughter was coming and that Rosamaria had passed.' Lucia got up, sat next to Olivia and took her hand. 'You are here to find answers. Yes?'

Olivia nodded.

'What do you want to know?'

Lucia shared with Olivia about Rosamaria's life before she fled Sicily. Across the hour, Olivia learnt even more about her mum. If anything, she gained a reverent understanding of all the choices Rosamaria made.

'I've been told that no one from my mum's family is left in Patti. Do you know where Viviana might be?' she asked hopefully.

Lucia handed the letters to Viviana back to Olivia, looking thoughtful. 'She lives in another village. She married a local boy, for love. If it had not been for your mother leaving, she too would have had to marry someone she hated. But when Rosamaria left, your nonna, Orazia, stood up to Salvatore. Viviana married the boy she loved.'

Olivia smiled at this thought. So, her mum's actions had helped her little sister to have a better life. Rosemary would be so happy to know this. Pride filled Olivia's heart and then excitement.

'Is it far?'

OLIVIA SHIELDED her eyes against the late afternoon sun shining through the car window.

'She is home.' Lucia indicated towards a balcony. The French doors were wide open, and white sheer curtains skipped in the breeze. She gave Olivia an encouraging smile.

'Thank you. *Grazie,*' Olivia said nervously.

She walked up to the bright blue timber door while a flock of butterflies flittered inside her belly. To stop her hands from shaking, she tucked them into a ball.

She took a deep breath and knocked. She listened, and her heart buzzed when she heard movement inside.

The door opened.

A woman with short auburn hair stood in front of her. She had the same high cheekbones as her mum, only hers had a smattering of freckles. She also had the same cupid's bow.

'Viviana?'

'Si.'

Olivia handed her a photo of her mum and her just before the car accident.

'*Mi chiamo* Olivia Elizabeth Bennet. I'm Rosamaria Fazo's *figlia.* Her daughter. I'm your niece.'

Viviana blinked as her hand flew to her mouth.

Olivia remained still and took in a gentle breath. Waiting.

Joy radiated from the centre of her chest when a wide smile beamed across Viviana's face, making her freckles dance.

Olivia found herself in the warm embrace of her aunt. Tranquillity flowed through her, and she felt her mother's presence.

She pulled away. 'About Mum.' She faltered and stopped.

Viviana placed her hand on Olivia's now-wet cheek. 'I understand. I always knew it in my heart that Rosamaria had gone from us for good. You carry this sadness in your eyes.' Viviana placed her hand on her chest. 'I have always carried my sister here.' She picked up Olivia's hand and placed it onto her own heart. 'And you carry her too. She will always be a part of you.' Her eyes glistened with love. '*Vieni dentro*. Come inside and tell me all about Rosamaria and the wonderful life she had.'

CHAPTER 49

Back at the pensione, which hummed with tourists checking in, Olivia asked Franca if she could use the phone.

Olivia headed to the little room adjacent to the dining room. The size of a large closet, it was where the only phone in the pensione was housed. A comfortable chair in a faded floral pattern and a matching footstool sat next to a small table with the telephone on top. Olivia took out the codes she needed. Before she dialled, she pulled out the *Daily Mirror* and glanced at the advertisement that she now knew by heart. Anticipation and apprehension braided together. What would Sebastian think—say?

Although this had been the biggest adventure of her life, she was missing him. Over the past year, she had come to know the honest, kind and gentle man he was. He had infiltrated her heart and her mind in a way that nobody else ever had. A spark of confidence ignited. He would be pleased, but ... She stopped. She wouldn't go there. Not yet.

She picked up the receiver.

'Hello.'

Hearing his voice, she grinned. 'It's me, Olivia. Oh my goodness, Sebastian. I've got so much to tell you.'

'How are you going? I miss you. We miss you.'

Olivia's heart flipped. 'I miss you too.'

'Is anything wrong?'

'No, not at all. I'm loving Patti. Everyone is so friendly.'

'Have you found Viviana?'

'Yes.' Through all the joy and a little weeping, she told him all about her time with Lucia and then meeting her aunt. 'It's been so surreal.'

Olivia exhaled. The trip had also shown her she could try new things, experience new adventures and even travel. That she was braver than she ever had imagined she could be.

Her finger traced the circle she made around the advertisement. Her heart hammered in her chest. 'Sebastian, I've come to another decision.' She squeezed the phone tight.

'I want to apply for a curator's position in London.'

There was silence on the other end.

'Sebastian?'

'I think that's a great idea, Liv.'

'You do?'

'For sure.' He went quiet again, then asked, 'So, you would be leaving Sydney, I guess?'

'Yes, I think the commute each day would be a little too long.' She let out a small laugh, then reached inside herself and grabbed some newfound courage. 'And I want you to come with me ... if you want to.' There was silence on the other end again.

Sebastian cleared his throat. 'That would make me so happy, Olivia! I would follow you anywhere, especially now that I know how it feels to be so far away from you. I'm dying over here! It's like my lifeblood has been drained.' He laughed.

A deep warmth spread through Olivia. Not only had she found out who her father was, discovered more about her mother and the amazing person she was, found her aunty in Sicily and released herself from the guilt of her mother's death, but she had also found the love of her life.

'There's something about you, Olivia Bennet.' Sebastian chuckled.

Olivia smiled.

BOOKS FEATURED IN THE STORY

In order of appearance

Forrest Gump (Winston Groom)
Hattie and the Fox (Mem Fox)
Twelfth Night (William Shakespeare)
Patriot Games (Tom Clancy)
Jane Eyre (Charlotte Brontë)
The House of the Spirits (Isabel Allende)
Love poems (Pablo Neruda)
Secret Diary of Adrian Mole (Sue Townsend)
Breakfast at Tiffany's (Truman Capote)
Mrs Dalloway (Virginia Woolf)
Rebecca (Rebecca du Maurier)
My Cousin Rachel (Rebecca du Maurier)
Emma (Jane Austen)
Sense and Sensibility (Jane Austen)
Tess of the d'Urbervilles (Thomas Hardy)
A Room with a View (E.M. Forster)

The Graduate (Charles Webb)
Beloved (Toni Morrison)
Pride and Prejudice (Jane Austen)

DEAR READER

Dear Reader,

I hope you enjoyed ***There's Something About You, Olivia Bennet***!

After years of writing stories and then tucking them away in the 'bottomless drawer' or that mysterious folder on my desktop, I finally decided to set them free! And guess what? You're the one who inspired me to do it! It's because of you that I reached deep into my writer's soul, found a bit of courage (and maybe some caffeine), and brought my very first novel out into the world. Thank you for taking this journey with me—I hope you enjoyed the ride!

I'd love to hear from you! What parts made you smile, laugh, or swoon? What did you love the most, and what moments are still dancing around in your mind? If there's something you're burning to share, whether it's your favourite scene, a character you connected with, or anything else, I'm all ears. Your feedback means the world to me, so don't be shy—let's chat! You can write to me at contact@valeriegmiller.com and visit me on my website at www.valeriegmiller.com.

If you enjoyed the book, I'd be incredibly grateful if you could take a moment to leave a review. Reviews are like little beacons that help other readers discover new authors like me. Your thoughts and insights could make all the difference in helping someone else find their next favourite read. Thank you so much for your support! If you have time, please leave a review on Amazon and/or Goodreads, or other preferred online book stores.

If you'd like to stay connected and hear all about my writing adventures and life as an author, I'd love for you to subscribe to my newsletter. As a thank you, you'll get exclusive access to the epilogue of this story—just for my readers. Can't wait to share more with you! Here's the link: valeriegmiller.com/epilogue

Thank you from the bottom of my heart for reading this story and spending time with my characters and me. It means the world to have shared this journey with you. Until next time, happy reading!

With endless gratitude,

Valerie G Miller

DO YOU WANT TO KNOW MORE ABOUT OLIVIA AND SEBASTIAN?

Do you want to know more about Olivia and Sebastian?

Thank you so much for reading *There's Something About You, Olivia Bennet*! If you'd like to stay connected and never miss an update on my upcoming books, writing tips, and exclusive content, be sure to subscribe to my email list. As a special thank you, you'll receive an exclusive epilogue that takes Olivia and her story one step further—just for you! Sign up today at valeriegmiller.com/epilogue and let's continue this journey together!

ACKNOWLEDGEMENTS

Where do I even begin? Writing this book has been like unlocking a secret trunk of time—each chapter, each scene, each sentence a hidden treasure waiting to be revealed. Much like my character, Olivia Bennet.

I couldn't have done it without the amazing people who held my hands and heart (and sometimes my sanity) along the way. Who listened to my ideas and discoveries. Who supported me and gave me valuable advice.

First and foremost, a gigantic *thank you* to my characters who whispered their stories to me in the middle of the night when I really should have been sleeping. You've made me laugh, cry, and occasionally question my grip on reality—this book wouldn't exist without your insistence that your tales be told!

A huge, heartfelt thank you to my two wonderful editors. To Rachel Small who took my first draft and made it sing through her structural and copy edits. Her talent helped me to develop my writing craft to a new level I couldn't do on my own. Rachel helped me to find the inner voices and emotions of all my characters. To my proofread editor, Jo Speirs—your fine eye for detail polished this story until it shone brightly. Your meticulous editing made me see I am truly the Queen of Commas—a reign I needed to tone down! You are both the unsung heroes of this journey, who skilfully refined my words until they shimmered like a dazzling Sicilian summer sky. Your sharp eyes, brilliant insights, and endless patience turned my ideas into something articulate and beautiful. You found the heart of this story and helped it beat stronger—I'm forever grateful for your guidance and expertise.

To my wonderful beta readers, Danielle Toffoli, Seodin Hevey, and Josie Norton, your insights, feedback, and encouragement were invaluable. You walked through this story with fresh eyes, catching the little details and asking the tough questions that made it stronger. Your enthusiasm kept me going, and your suggestions helped shape the story in ways I couldn't have done alone. Thank you for investing your time and energy into this journey—I'm so appreciative of your support and belief in this story.

I owe a tremendous debt of gratitude to my agent, Fiona Smith (Beyond Words Literary Agency), whose wisdom and guidance were instrumental in shaping this story into its final version. Her keen understanding of both the market and the heart of the narrative helped me refine and elevate the manuscript far beyond what I had imagined. She believed in this story from the start, championing it with passion and dedication, and for that I am endlessly thankful.

A huge thank you to my stepsister, Cathy, who is also one of my biggest fans and a superstar at combing through my manuscript with an eagle eye for any typos. My aim is always to deliver a story that's my very best, but if any pesky errors have slipped through, I sincerely apologise.

Throughout this journey, my family and friends have been my rock, listening to countless ideas, concerns, and every twist and turn along the way. Your unwavering love, patience, and belief in me as a writer have meant the world to me. You've celebrated my highs, supported me through the lows, and never stopped believing that this story would come to life. I am deeply grateful for your constant encouragement and for standing by me every step of the way. A special mention to my husband, Tim, who always makes dinner and washes up, gifting me with valuable time at the end of each school day so I could work on this novel. You are my hero.

A special shout-out to my writing tribe, The Paper Dolls, my fellow book-loving companions and sisters-in-arms, who cheered me on with a confetti cannon of enthusiasm at every milestone (even the small ones). You turned this solitary journey into a party, and for that I'm forever grateful.

And last but definitely not least, to you, dear reader—thank you for picking up this book and travelling through time with me. I hope you found a piece of your heart nestled within its pages, just as I did while writing it. Here's to many more adventures together!

With all my love and a sprinkle of historical magic,
Valerie G Miller

ABOUT THE AUTHOR

After relocating from Sydney, Valerie G Miller now lives in Brisbane, Australia, with her husband and daughter. In 2021, she completed a Master of Letters in Creative Writing at Central Queensland University.

She writes historical fiction with dual timelines. Knowing how our past informs our present—how history defines our place in the world—excites her as an author. Her stories always have romantic elements because love truly does make the world go round. Valerie is currently dabbling in writing magical realism, and she also loves reading and writing short stories.

As a young girl from an Italian family, she discovered the magic of words. How putting different words together could conjure up an image, a moment, an emotion.

You will always find a novel and a notebook filled with ideas and observations tucked away in her handbag. She believes stories are medicine for the soul and that books make the world a happier place.

CONNECT WITH VALERIE

Visit her at www.valeriegmiller.com

f facebook.com/valeriegmiller

⊙ instagram.com/valerieg.writer

@ threads.net/valeriegwriter

Printed in Great Britain
by Amazon

57279412R00219